DATE D''

MERLIN'S
BLADE

MERLIN'S BLADE

ROBERT TRESKILLARD

ZONDERVAN®

ZONDERVAN.com/
AUTHORTRACKER
follow your favorite authors

We want to hear from you. Please send your comments about this book to us in care of zreview@zondervan.com. Thank you.

ZONDERVAN

Merlin's Blade
Copyright © 2013 by Robert Treskillard

This title is also available as a Zondervan ebook.
Visit www.zondervan.com/ebooks.

Requests for information should be addressed to:

Zondervan, *Grand Rapids, Michigan 49530*

ISBN 978-0-310-73507-6

All Scripture paraphrased by the author to approximate a fifth-century cultural context.

The characters and events depicted in this book are fictional, and any resemblance to actual persons real or imagined is coincidental.

Any Internet addresses (websites, blogs, etc.) and telephone numbers in this book are offered as a resource. They are not intended in any way to be or imply an endorsement by Zondervan, nor does Zondervan vouch for the content of these sites and numbers for the life of this book.

Cover design: brandnavigation.com
Cover photography: Alamy, Shutterstock, Dreamstime
Interior design: Ben Fetterley and Greg Johnson/Textbook Perfect

Printed in the United States of America

13 14 15 16 17 18 19 /DCI/ 20 19 18 17 16 15 14 13 12 11 10 9 8 7 6 5 4 3 2 1

† *In loving memory of my mother,*
with thanksgiving for her life and love. †

Psalm 65

PROLOGUE

THE DRAGON STAR

BOSVENNA MOOR
IN THE YEAR OF OUR LORD 407

The pine trees mocked his youth, their thin, green fingers fretting in the wind. If he didn't move fast, they would betray him — he just knew it — and the deer would get away ... again. Arvel wiped his brow, stole across an expanse of dead pine needles, and crouched behind a bush strangled by bindweed and its poisonous red berries.

Holding his breath, he nocked an arrow.

The three deer chewed and sniffed.

Arvel's throat tingled and his body tensed. He parted the leaves at the side of the bush with his arrow as shadows danced on its pewter tip.

The deer twitched their ears and turned their heads in unison.

Arvel drew back the bowstring — and winced as the wood creaked.

Instantly, hoofs jerked and legs tensed.

He sped the arrow toward its mark, and it pierced the buck deeply. Even as the does vanished into the forest, the antlered one fell.

Arvel whooped, and the sound echoed across the rock-strewn hills and faded into the deep forest. He stretched his shoulders to ease the tension as he inspected his prize. The meat would feed his family for many days. At only fourteen winters, he had downed his first deer.

A spring gurgled only a stone's throw away, and he longed to drink the pure water. But did he dare leave his kill? In answer, the wind sighed and clattered a branch behind him. He pulled out his knife as he turned to study the bushes. Thieves hid nearby, he was certain, ready to creep out and steal his meat.

With wary eyes he cleaned and skinned the buck, daring to imagine the celebration his family would hold that night. His little sister would prance and play, and his mother would stir the stew pot and praise his skill with the bow. He grinned at the thought. Ah, and they would have smoked meat all through the winter if his hunting went like this, enough to share and hopefully boast about. After all, wouldn't he be the best hunter on the moor — just like his father?

His grin faded. His father had been taken as a slave by raiding warriors. Arvel drove the knife deep into the buck's haunch and waited for his vision to clear. When he finished cutting up the meat, he placed it inside the folded deer hide. Then, just as his father had taught him, he knifed holes along the edge of the pelt. Through these holes he threaded twigs to seal the meat well enough for the hike back to his borrowed boat and the long row home.

The sun reddened as Arvel axed down two saplings and roped the hide-bound bundle to them for a makeshift sled. The job done, he hefted the poles and made his way through the trees with some difficulty. Finally out on the open moor, he spied his boat — a large coracle — in the distance, tied up along the shoreline of the marsh.

He crossed the moor, struggling due to the weight of the sled, and finally reached the marsh's edge. Panting, he loaded his meat into the boat's hull, then took his seat. The wood groaned under the pull of the oars, and the boat rocked as he glided away from the shore. Arvel's stomach soured. He trusted his own booted feet more than a jumble such as this. Glancing back at his precious venison, he wondered why he had borrowed *this* boat.

From the branch of an alder that stood among the sedge grasses, a red-legged raven swooped down and snatched up a frog. The bird flew to the prow, looked at him with menacing eyes, and then ripped the frog to pieces, gulping down its wriggling legs.

"Get away, you!" Arvel swung an oar at the bird, and it flapped away.

Twilight descended as he rowed. The stars appeared, but they refused to reflect off the turgid water. The moon raised its leprous head through the trees, casting anxious shadows on the reeds that rattled against the boat.

Lifting, dropping, and pulling the oars, Arvel felt as if someone was watching him. Closing his eyes, he listened but heard nothing except the clicking jaws of insects ... the croaks of frogs ... the calls of a few birds ... and the greasy splash of the water. The impulse to turn around pressed upon him. Did someone lurk in another boat or on an island?

Ah, foolishness — not at this time of night. But the desire to look grew stronger. Hairs rose on Arvel's neck, and a chill slid down his tunic like a cold snake. Someone *was* watching him.

He turned, surprised to see he'd made so much progress. On his right stood the tip of Inis Avallow, the largest island in the marsh, and far down its length he spied the old, crumbling tower. As he rowed, the shadowy ruins and scattered descendants of an ancient apple orchard slid past him. But he felt no malice there.

He turned the other way and scrutinized the waters along the shore. The dark mass of a mountain, the Meneth Gellik, rose to his left. Soon he'd be at Bosventor's familiar docks and the safety of home. No need to worry.

Then he beheld the Dragon Star.

Arvel stared in awe. Across the southwestern sky floated a ball of blue flame with two tails, one straight and the other curving upward. Though these tails had inspired the star's draconian name, Arvel liked to think of the shape as an arrowhead. The star had appeared near the end of summer, and, fixed there in the sky each night, the mysterious blaze slowly moved westward toward the setting sun as the season changed.

He shook his head. It couldn't be. And yet the instant he looked away and back again, he knew the Dragon Star watched him like some bulbous blue eye. Was he going mad, like his grandfather?

Still, he couldn't shake the feeling. His throat closed up, and he wanted to leap out of the boat and swim for shore. But he forced himself to sit still, because a hunter mustn't give in to such panic. Certainly not the best hunter on the moor.

As he'd trained himself to do when hunting the tusk-boar with his father, he bent his fear and strung tight his courage. Picking up his bow, Arvel slowly readied an arrow. When he could wait no longer, he aimed right at the Dragon Star and let the arrow fly with a satisfying zip.

As the arrow splashed into a distant part of the marsh, Arvel smiled in triumph and turned away from the star to grip the oars.

But when his gaze met the horizon, he saw something unexpected.

The marsh lit up as if the full moon had burst into flame. Bright and brighter, an orange light flickered along the boat's rim.

A tremendous roaring filled the air, and a ferocious mass of living fire shot over his head. It descended with deadly power just beyond the marsh and struck a low hill. Chunks of earth and a white-hot blaze exploded outward.

He shrieked as his hair ignited and his eyebrows singed away. His clothing and skin smoldered, and within moments the boat's wood and leather caught fire like kindling.

The marsh and open water churned in liquid convulsion. The

boat spun and was thrown into the air, just as a crushing wind shattered all the trees and sucked Arvel's lungs empty. The aged boat ruptured beneath him, and he fell into the watery chaos.

His hands flailed at the venison as the waves roared over his head. He saw the beloved face of his mother and the face of his missing father.

But they faded, and a shadowed vision arose in their place.

Arvel beheld the clans and peoples of Britain gathered together. And each one — young and old, farmer, craftsman, warrior, chieftain, and king alike — worshiped the Dragon Star. Yet even as the people bowed, the Dragon Star betrayed them and blazed forth blue flames of destruction. All through the land it raged, along with swarming invaders who slaughtered, enslaved, and pillaged.

Death. Death and destruction.

The souls of many wept, and above all a woman's voice called:

Woe! Woe to Britain!
For the Dragon Star has come,
and who will save us?

PART ONE

GUILE'S DUST

Birthed as flame, the Dragon Star falling;
Wrapped in water, the deaf one calling;
Circled in shadow, the bound one weeping;
Maliced evil the banks entombing;
Hidden on hill, there the deep lake lies.

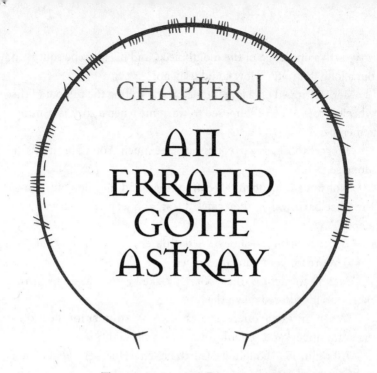

CHAPTER I

AN ERRAND GONE ASTRAY

THE VILLAGE OF BOSVENTOR
SPRING, IN THE YEAR OF OUR LORD 477

Merlin frowned. He didn't know what he wanted more: to talk with Natalenya or to hide. After all, how many young men walked past the house of the girl they admired while pushing an overstuffed wheelbarrow? And how many were accompanied by a boy wearing a too-big monk's robe who insisted on playing bagpipe?

Wasn't the rope, wooden tub, bundle of herbs, and sack of oats quite enough to fill the barrow? Did Garth really have to add a squawking hen and a young goat too?

Merlin turned his half-blind gaze to the bobbing boy with red hair. "You told me, 'Not another thing to deliver,' and now look what we've got."

Garth's lips let go of the mouthpiece, and his bagpipe squeaked out a long last note. "How could I say no?"

Merlin tripped on a large stone, nearly rolling the tub out of the wheelbarrow. "You're supposed to warn me when a rock is coming, remember?"

"I forget those eyes o' yours can't see much. You've been gettin' along so well."

"Not since you added *two* extra things, and they don't just lie in the wheelbarrow. No, they cluck, bleat, and leap out every twenty steps."

"But they're for the abbey. We'll drop 'em off on the way and — "

"They're for your Sabbath supper."

"Hadn't thought o' that." Garth kicked a rock away from the path, and it skittered down the hill.

"When they were offered, you said, 'A nice dinner for the brothers at the abbey' and 'Thank you very much.' Hah!"

"All right, so I thought it." Garth halted. "Ho, there, wait a bit. I saw somethin' move."

Merlin stopped pushing the wheelbarrow. "What now?"

Garth knelt down and advanced into the bushes on all fours.

Merlin could see only a smudge of Garth sticking out from beneath the green leaves, and then a colorful blotch flew out above the boy's head.

"I found me a tuck snack!" Garth bounced up and placed a warm egg in Merlin's palm.

Merlin judged the egg's size to be about half of a chicken's.

"Three of 'em!" Garth said. "Oh, but how can I carry 'em? The goat'll eat 'em in the barrow, and I can't hold 'em and play me bagpipe too."

Merlin reached out, felt for Garth's hood, and dropped his egg to the bottom. "How's that?"

"Perfect. Yer clever at times, you are."

Merlin held out his hand for the other two eggs and set them beside the first.

Fuffing up his bagpipe with air, Garth resumed playing as he marched down the hill.

Merlin followed, and as the hill leveled out, he was better able to keep the barrow steady. But that was when his heart started wobbling, because he knew by the big blur of a rock coming up that they were about to walk by —

"Look at that house," Garth said, stopping to take a breath. "A big house ... behind those trees. Didn't notice it on the way up."

In vain, Merlin shook the black hair away from his eyes. He wished he could see if Natalenya was home. "You've only been here a month ... but you've heard of the magister, haven't you?"

"Sure. The brothers at the abbey pay taxes to the ol' miser."

"He's not old, and his name's Tregeagle. "He and his wife have two sons and a daughter."

"Those the boys that called you 'Cut-face'?"

"Yeah." Merlin scowled at the memory. The hurled insults had been followed by a goodly sized rock, which had only narrowly missed his head.

But Natalenya was different. She never mentioned Merlin's scars. During worship at the chapel, she was always polite and asked him questions now and then, almost like a friend. So when Merlin's father had asked him and Garth to get charcoal with the wheelbarrow, Merlin suggested that Garth get a tour of the fortress too. The fact that they'd pass Natalenya's house twice was a small coincidence, of course, even if it was out of their way.

The problem was that an empty wheelbarrow was just too inviting, and practically everyone had given them things to deliver. And now they had the goat and chicken as well. Out of embarrassment, Merlin almost wished Natalenya wouldn't be home.

"What does the house look like?" he asked. "Tell me what I'm seeing."

"Ornate kind of ... Bigger than the mill, I'd say, an' made o' fancy stone. The roof's got lapped bark with a real stone chimney, not jus' a hole for smoke." Garth paused. "Why does the magister's door have a bronze bird on it?"

"It's the ensign of a Roman legion. An eagle, or an *aquila*, to be precise. His family's descended from soldiers on the coast."

"Huh. Why'd the Romans come here? Nothin' here but hills, woods, an' a bit o' water."

"For the tin and copper. A little silver," Merlin said. "None of the brothers explained that?"

"Haven't had time for history, what with fishin', seein' you, workin', and eatin' o' course."

"Do you see anyone at the Magister's house? Maybe a daughter?"

"Nah ... no girl. Nothin' but a little smoke."

The sound of horses' hooves clattered toward them from farther down the hill. Merlin had just turned in the direction of the sound when Garth shoved his shoulder.

"A wagon!" Garth cried. "Out o' the road!"

The driver shouted as Merlin scrambled to push the wheelbarrow off to the side.

"Make way for the magister," the man shouted. "Make way!"

A whip snapped and the air cracked above Merlin's head.

The wheelbarrow hit a rock, and Merlin felt it tilt out of his control just as Garth ran into his back, causing him to fall, with a chicken flapping against his face. Merlin removed the feathered mass in time to see the blur of the goat leap over the tub and everything else tumble out of the barrow.

The wagon rumbled by and came to an abrupt stop in front of the magister's house.

Merlin sat up and rubbed his knees. He felt around for the bag of oats and found it spilled on the ground — a feast for the chicken and goat. At least it would keep them nearby.

The passengers climbed out of the wagon, and amid the general din of everyone walking toward the house, Merlin heard a soft, lovely voice and a gentle strumming. "Garth, is that a harp?"

"A small one, sure. A lady is holdin' it." Garth rose and brushed off his knees. "The magister ignored us, him in his fancy white robe. But did you see those boys? They'd liked to have kicked us."

Merlin pushed the goat away from the oats and knelt to scoop what grain he could find back into the bag. "How old?"

"Oh, the bigger one weren't more'n yer age, an' the other's about fourteen, I'd say."

"That's do-nothing Rondroc and Dyslan. I meant the one with the harp. Was that the mother?"

"Oh, no," Garth said. "Must be the daughter ... but a lot older'n your sister. She held herself straight and ladylike. Does she come to chapel?"

"Natalenya and her mother came two weeks ago. Tregeagle doesn't let them come every week." Merlin had never heard the magister's daughter sing so sweetly before.

Garth tapped him. "Hey, look at those horses!"

Merlin rubbed his chin and closed his eyes. "Pretty?"

"Very! That yellin' wagon driver tied 'em to a post an' — "

"Must be Erbin." Merlin chuckled and swatted Garth. "But I'm talking about Natalenya. I don't remember what *she* looks like. Is she pretty?"

"Blurs don't count for seein', huh? I guess *you'd* think she's pretty. Long brown hair and green dress, but *I* don't go for that. The horses look fine, though. White, with such shiny coats — an' so tall they match that fancy wagon. Me father's old wagon just brought fish to market. Sure woulda helped us gettin' the charcoal if I still had it."

Garth paused for a moment, and Merlin remembered that the boy's father had drowned in a storm not six months before while fishing on the Kembry sea. Twelve winters old, and Garth had already lost both of his parents.

After clearing his throat, Garth continued, "But *this* wagon's a real beauty, with a wide seat up front. The back box is fine for sittin' too, though you *could* just haul with it." The chicken jumped on Merlin's shoulder, and Garth swatted it away. "Get off, you!"

Merlin stood. "Better deliver these things and get the charcoal."

He righted the barrow, and they refilled it. He could still hear Natalenya's voice filtering from her home, and he wished he had something for her.

"Psst," Garth said. "Those nasty boys are comin' over."

Merlin turned toward the approaching footsteps and extended his hands in greeting, only to have them ignored.

"What are you doing here? Spying?" Rondroc said as he stepped up to Merlin. The older of Tregeagle's sons, Rondroc stood slightly taller than Merlin. His dark clothing lay on him like a shadow, and from his side protruded a short black scabbard.

Dyslan, the younger brother, wore reds and blues, with what looked to be a shining golden belt. He yanked on Garth's voluminous robe. "What's this for? Monks are getting smaller all the time."

"It keeps me warm," Garth said, his voice tight.

"It's kind of like a dress," Dyslan mocked. "If you had darker hair and acted kind of weird, I might have thought you were Merlin's sister."

"Leave Ganieda out of this," Merlin said, feeling his pulse speed up.

Rondroc pointed to the wheelbarrow. "What do you have a goat for? Taking your whole flock to pasture?" He and Dyslan laughed.

Merlin gripped the handles tighter. "We just had a look at the fortress."

"You?" Dyslan said. "Had a look? Ha!"

"Let's go, Garth." Merlin lifted the wheelbarrow, rolled it forward, and accidentally bumped into Rondroc's leg.

Rondroc grabbed the front edge of the barrow, stopping it. "You did that on purpose." His words were slow and dark. "No one uses *our road* without permission, so now you'll be paying our tax."

"Tax?" Merlin said. "My father pays every harvest."

"I've heard that your father's *behind* on his taxes."

"Liar. Our smithy does a good business, so the taxes are never late. And there's no tax for just walking."

"There is now." Rondroc rummaged through the barrow. His smirking voice made Merlin glad he couldn't clearly see Rondroc's face.

"None o' that is ours to give," Garth said.

"Hmm ... a tasty goat feast would pay your fee." The goat bleated as Rondroc picked it up.

"Stop ri — " Garth began, but there was a thump, and his voice choked as he fell to the dirt. Dyslan stood behind him laughing.

"We'll roast it on the fire tonight."

"Leave it alone," Merlin said as calmly as he could. He slipped his staff from the barrow, and the wood felt cold in his hands.

Rondroc set the goat down and swaggered over to Merlin. "Gonna make me?"

"Maybe," Merlin said, offering up a silent prayer. With his staff he tried to push Rondroc away, but the dark form disappeared. Someone kicked Merlin in the back, and he fell, banging his arm on the side of the wheelbarrow.

Rondroc laughed.

In the distance, a harp strummed faintly.

Merlin scrambled up and turned to face his mocker.

"Look out for Dysla — " Garth's voice rang out.

Too late. Rondroc shoved Merlin in the chest, and he fell back over Dyslan, who was crouching behind him.

A sharp pain shot through Merlin's skull as he bashed his head on a rock. Laughter swirled around him like thick fog, and for a moment Merlin lay still as his mind groped for its bearings.

"Stop it," Garth said. "Leave him alone!"

The voices intensified and faded as Merlin sat up. Time slowed. Someone yelled in pain at his left. Using the barrow, Merlin pulled himself up to a standing position and winced at the throbbing in his head. "Garth?"

The horses whinnied, and Merlin didn't hear the harp anymore.

"Want me to knock you down again? Or maybe a little poke this time, huh?" The sound of Rondroc's knife leaving its sheath roused Merlin from his stupor.

"I'm warning you, Rondroc." His hand shook as it strayed to his own dirk, a foot-long, tapered blade. But he realized how foolish that would be. Taking up his staff again, he tried to remember how tall Rondroc was.

"This time you'll stay down. Dirty villager. Not paying my tax."

Loud grunts and bangs sounded from near Tregeagle's wagon.

"Ronno, help! I'm stuck," came Dyslan's voice from the left.

Rondroc took a step toward the wagon and shouted in a higher pitch, "You ... little monk! Stop!"

Merlin's heart raced as his chance came. Leaping toward the voice, he held his staff back and spun around.

The staff whirled forward in a whistling arc. *Keep your head up, Rondroc.*

Crack! Natalenya's brother slumped to the ground.

For a moment Merlin stood still as a wave of emotions — from exhilaration to panic — flooded him. Panic won out. *What have I done?*

He heard thumping sounds, the neighing of horses, the jangling of tack, and hoofs clopping toward him.

"You can't *do* that!" Dyslan shouted.

"Merlin, over here," Garth called. "Get in!"

Merlin rubbed his head. "What?"

"In! I've got the wagon." A hand grabbed his arm from above. "The wagon?"

Garth pulled on his arm. "Hurry!"

CHAPTER 2

A PATH FOR WOLVES

Merlin found a step for his foot, climbed up, and fell into the back box of the wagon as it clipped down the hill. "What are you doing?"

Behind him, the chicken squawked.

"Borrowin' the wagon."

Merlin pulled himself into the front seat, bumping the bagpipe that rested between him and Garth. "You've got to stop ... It's not ours!"

"Don't call me a thief," Garth said, snapping the reins. "It was that girl ... She told me I could take it."

Merlin sat up. "Really? You mean Natalenya?"

"Natalenya, that's her ... The girl who sang."

"She gave permission?"

Garth turned and spoke right into Merlin's ear. "She said to take it. Said we can have it all afternoon. An' how's yer head? That was a chunk o' granite you hit."

"Hurts." Merlin shut his eyes and gingerly felt the back of his head. Bloody dirt and some small pebbles were stuck in his hair.

"She said it was to help us get away from her brothers."

"Huh." Merlin smiled.

"I threw almost everything in. Even the chicken. An' that rope's a beauty — woven just right! I tied it around the goat before I popped 'im over the side."

"Almost everything?"

"Not the barrow. I know it's yer father's, but it was too heavy. We'll swap for it when we're done."

The wagon hit a bump and jolted them both.

"Didn't Dyslan try and stop you or attempt to talk Natalenya out of it?"

"Oh, him." Garth yawned. "Nothin' but a slinky fish. Knocked the wind out o' him with me head an' pushed 'im into the hay trough."

"You didn't!"

"Did so. Workin' boys are stouter'n those, those — "

"Fly catchers?"

"That's it."

Merlin sat back, thinking about what had just happened. He reached out his hand and felt the softness of the stuffed leather seat and the smoothness of the wooden rails. Something seemed odd about Garth's account, but he couldn't think of a reason to doubt Garth, and he wasn't going back to check. Though why would Natalenya help them? He had just hit her brother on the head.

Another thought entered his mind. Would Rondroc report him to Tregeagle now? The magister was also the judge for the eastern side of the moor.

Maybe Natalenya would straighten things out. Or maybe not.

"Garth, promise me you're telling the truth."

"I *promise*."

Merlin let himself relax. "It certainly makes our job easier. We can get the charcoal in one trip."

"An' yer father'll make the braces faster for the abbey. This morning Kifferow told me to hurry up 'cause he's runnin' out o' nails too."

"Does he have the roof up?"

"He's workin' on it, but it looked kind o' wobbly to me."

"Too bad about our horse ... If his hoof pad wasn't swollen, my father wouldn't have run out of coal."

"Merlin?" Garth asked.

"Yes."

"I'm glad we are."

"What?"

"Gettin' coal. Together," Garth said. "Gettin' to know you this past month's been fun."

Merlin tousled Garth's hair.

They descended a hill and soon arrived in the valley, where the rushing of the Fowaven grew louder, swollen as it was by the spring rains. The wooden bridge echoed the clopping of the horses' hooves, and it groaned under their weight. The wagon slowed as the horses trod up the opposite hillside, so Garth kept the reins cracking while they wound back and forth up the incline.

At the crest, the trees thickened, the shade grew dense, and the coolness felt refreshing on Merlin's face. A bird chirped as it flew across the path, darting from tree to tree. The scent of moss and mushrooms filled his senses, along with dewy flowers and ever-fragrant pines.

"Didn't know it was so nice up here," Garth said.

"I wish we had a forest over the whole mountain. Can you smell it?"

Garth sniffed the air. "Mmm ... Sure, but I smell somethin' *different*!" He took a deeper whiff. "Someone's roastin' meat!"

Merlin raised his nose and inhaled again. "Now I smell it."

"The juice must be jus' drippin' off the spit."

"That's funny," Merlin said. "No one lives around here. Where's it coming from?"

"A bit o' smoke's floatin' from the trees to the left ... somewhere in the woods. Must be lots o' meat roastin'."

"The only thing off that direction, I think, is the old circle of stones. But no one goes there anymore."

"I'd take a big hunk right now if I could — "

"No. We *need* to get the charcoal."

The woods thickened even more, and ancient oaks cast shadows across the path. Garth's stomach gurgled so loudly that Merlin could tell the boy was still thinking about the roasting meat.

"Be on the lookout," Merlin said. "It's a trail off to the right. My father and I come here often, so I know the route, but I'd probably never find it on my own."

Soon they arrived at the track, and Garth steered the horses down the ruts. After a little while they rolled into the large clearing where the char-man kept hills of buried, smoldering wood. The transaction was short: three screpallow coins bought them a full load of cooled charcoal for the wagon box, which they had to load themselves using wooden shovels. Their stack of items to deliver, along with the goat and chicken, had to be moved up front.

When they'd finished the task, Garth turned the wagon around, and it bumped back up the hill.

"Hey ... the goat's eating my tunic!" Merlin yelled. He tried to push its head away, but it kept shaking free and nipping more of the linen into its mouth. The chicken fussed at Merlin's feet and pecked at his boots. "Tell me again why we didn't drop them off on the way?"

"Here." Garth pulled the goat's head away with the rope. "I wish *I* could eat somethin'! I'm hungry as a sea bass."

"Eat your eggs."

"They're still too hot from sittin' in that char-man's fire while we loaded up. Besides, I've got to get the mud off 'em before I can eat 'em."

"Mud?"

"To keep 'em from explodin' while they cooked."

Garth turned back onto the main road and followed the ridge southward toward Bosventor. They went down one hill and climbed the next, Garth snapping the reins for speed. And he kept sniffing the air. "Once on top, I bet we'll smell that roastin' meat again!"

"So?"

"Hey, a puff o' smoke's crossin' the road ahead."

Merlin sighed.

"Ahh! Incredible!" Garth took four big whiffs. "That's the best smellin' meat in the world. Great gobs o' juicy chunks poppin' with fat." He took another deep whiff, pulled the horses to a stop, and handed the reins to Merlin. "Hang on to these."

Merlin let the reins out as the horses bent down to graze on the grass by the side of the road. "Something wrong?"

The boy jumped down. "Goin' to see what's cookin'."

"Garth, get back here!" Merlin yelled.

The boy shushed him from the edge of the road. "They'll hear you." The lower branches of the pines parted and closed to mark his passing.

"Come back!" Merlin called as the chicken flapped up and landed on his shoulder. The goat shifted and started eating his sleeve. *What's the boy doing?* Running off into the woods alone, where some strangers were cooking meat? For all Merlin knew, they were thieves — or worse.

He tied the goat's rope to the railing, then felt for his staff and found it in the foot box. Trusting that Tregeagle's well-trained horses would stay put, he noted the position of the sun and began tapping along the ground in the direction Garth had gone.

But the brush was thick, and Merlin had to force his way through. He wanted to call out the boy's name but feared giving away their presence, so he paused as often as he could to listen for the sound of Garth's eager footsteps. There was barely enough light falling through the trees for Merlin to navigate around their shadowy trunks, each of which he touched with his free hand as he passed. Branches barred his way, and he often had to duck to prevent his eyes from getting jabbed. The last thing he wanted was another injury to his already-scarred vision.

Above him, the calling, fluttering, and chittering of the birds ceased, the rustle of the squirrels halted, and all the woods became quiet as if to hide some secret from Merlin. Now he heard Garth ahead — not far off — but nature's silence unnerved him. His own heart thumped in his ears as he struggled through the increasingly thick thornbushes that grasped at him like small, sharp knives.

More than once Merlin thought he heard something behind him. A ravenous wolf hunting for prey, drawn to the smell of the meat? Ready to lunge at his throat? The boy knew Merlin's history with wolves. Why would he run off like that? Merlin checked his dirk and tried to ignore the trembling in his shoulders.

And Garth, that hungry sneak, was getting harder to track. He seemed to be crouching behind trees and waiting until he knew the coast was clear before skulking toward the source of the smoke. So whenever Merlin lost him, he had only the aroma to follow in the hope of hearing Garth again.

In this way Merlin found himself on a sort of beaten path — thin, secret, and snakelike — that meandered toward the delicious aroma. *Could it be a trail for deer ... Or wolves?* Either way, Merlin finally closed in on his friend.

Garth, plainly exasperated at being followed, turned on him to whisper, "Shah, Merlin. Yer lumbering is givin' me away! Go back an' watch the horses!"

Merlin ignored this rebuke, stepped toward the boy — a shadow against a pine tree — and grabbed the front of his woolen monk's robe. "We're going *together.*"

Unmatched in height and strength, Merlin began dragging Garth backward down the path as his friend dug in his heels and struggled to get free.

"Leave me be," Garth pleaded, "an' I promise I'll be quick!"

Merlin was preparing to retort that he wasn't about to trust Garth's stomach when he heard branches breaking ... and footfalls on the trail. He pulled Garth behind a bush, and they both dropped to their knees.

"Get that stick o' yers down, or we'll be seen," Garth hissed.

Merlin crouched lower, laid his staff on the ground, and peered through the leaves. Irritated at his blindness, he tried instead to focus on the noise creeping closer, a muffled mixture of heavy breathing and scraping steps. It sounded to Merlin like a great beast crawling toward them with scaled claws, sniffing and huffing for their scent.

"What am I seeing?" Merlin asked.

"Can't tell."

Legs passed into Merlin's view, mere blurs among the shadows. Then the legs paused.

"May we rest for a bit, O Father?" The voice reminded Merlin of a slow, scornful weasel. "Surely we have dragged this boon of yours for more than a league, and all uphill since we left the lakeside."

"Not now. Not now," a second voice answered, breathless. "We are almost to the gorseth, I say, and I will not stop until I have fulfilled the dictates of my vision." There was a slight Eirish lilt to both voices that reminded Merlin of his stepmother's, but this one had a darker timbre. Its richness made Merlin's ears long to hear more.

"Yes ... your vision," came the first voice, with the slightest hint of a scoff. "But what is this burden? Will you not tell me your secrets?"

Merlin squinted with his better eye. There, between the two men, lay a large object suspended inside a brown cloth, possibly made of leather. He nudged Garth and whispered as quietly as he could, "Who are they? What are they carrying?" His words were hardly more than an exhale, but the two men on the other side of the bush fell silent, listening.

Garth gulped and his stomach growled.

Neither of the strangers moved, yet a blue light began to glow from the object between them.

The scornful man on the left jumped back. "What is happening to it?" he cried, yanking off the covering.

Blue flames leaped from the object's surface, lighting up the woods and blinding Merlin completely for a moment. His face and hands turned hot, as if a fire raged just beyond the bush. Then he felt cold, as if winter had filled the land with snow and ice. After that the heat rushed back, followed by the cold. Merlin regarded the strange object with awe. What could it be?

"Beware, it tells us!... Beware!" the second voice said, now changing to a whisper. "Enemies are present."

Both men drew knives, the metal reflecting the strange light.

Garth yelped and darted away.

Merlin chased after him, ignoring the shouts from behind. Ducking his head and covering his face with his free arm to avoid unseen branches, he ran headlong through the forest. Branches scraped and scratched him all the way. Twice he tripped. Once he ran into a tree. And all the time he listened desperately for Garth.

But the boy ran too fast, and each turn Merlin made to avoid a tree found him more turned around. He stopped to orient himself by the sun, but his half blindness and the thick-leafed canopy prevented him.

In the distance, the horses whinnied in fright. He ran toward the sound, which grew louder by the step. Finally, his lip bleeding, his tunic torn, and his arms covered in cuts, he burst out onto the main track not four paces from the wagon.

The horses reared up in terror.

"Get in!" Garth shouted.

Merlin gave the frightened horses a wide berth, grabbed on to the wagon, which rolled back and forth, and pulled himself up to the box.

As Garth yanked on the reins in an attempt to control the horses, Merlin tried to see what was frightening them, though his scarred eyes prevented him. When the wagon jerked backward, Merlin grabbed on to the front rail and accidentally snagged one of the reins. Distant voices called from the woods.

The horses reared up again.

"Give 'em back!" Garth yelled, disentangling the leather straps from Merlin's fingers. The boy snapped the reins down as hard as he could, and the wagon shot forward. "Are they followin' us?"

"You don't know? Can't you look?"

"Why'd you talk? Why'd you let 'em know we were hidin'?"

"It was *your* stomach that growled."

They hit a bump, and the wagon rocked sideways. The goat tried to jump up onto the seat, his sharp hooves scraping across Merlin's leggings. Merlin pushed him down. "I was just asking who they were."

"I don't know who they were."

"Then why are we going so fast? Slow down."

"'Cause the horses are scared."

Yet Merlin heard the reins snap every few moments. "You should've eaten your roasted eggs."

"I woulda had a leg o' lamb if it wasn't for you." The wagon picked up speed as the road bent downhill, but Garth still kept at the reins. "What was that thing we saw?"

"You tell me."

Garth didn't answer as they careened down the hillside, slowing only enough to take the switchback corners. Merlin saw the ruddy blur of Garth's head turning, presumably to steal a glance behind them.

"Are they chasing us?" Merlin asked.

Garth scanned the hillside again. "Y-yes … *no!*"

The hollow thump of the Fowaven bridge sounded under the wheels as the wagon burst across. After they climbed up the hill beyond the bridge, Garth cracked the reins faster and faster. Mud flicked onto Merlin's face.

"Slow down, I said! This isn't our wagon, remember?"

"I know, I know … but that man wanted us to take it."

"You told me it was Natalenya. Have you been telling the truth?"

"Yer always thinkin' about her, aren't you?"

Merlin's face felt hot. "You better not have stolen this wagon, you hear? My father and I caught a thief yesterday and sent him to Tregeagle."

Garth hesitated before answering. "Sure … sure. I promise!"

The wagon raced by the large stone cross on the right side of the road that marked the entrance of the abbey grounds.

"Slow down!" Merlin shouted, for the horses had been worked into a lather of frenzied speed. He reached out, found Garth's jerking arms, and pulled on the reins. "Stop! Slow down!"

Confused, the horses careened to the right, off the road.

The wagon slammed over a bump, and Merlin bit his tongue.

The two jolted side to side as the beasts raced downhill. Merlin heard the sound of hammering in the distance.

Garth yanked the reins free from Merlin. "We're gonna hit the new buildin' — "

The wagon tilted on the hillside, and Merlin rammed into Garth.

"Look out!" Garth screamed.

"What?"

The shadow of a building loomed up on his right. People shouted and dove away from the thundering horses. Garth turned them aside just in time to avoid hitting the structure.

But not entirely. The back right wheel of the wagon caught a post. The wagon slammed to a stop, and the horses fell in a tangled heap.

A huge crack came from the roof, and Merlin turned his head just in time to see a support breaking away.

The whole structure trembled, then tipped and fell. It smashed into the back corner of the wagon and flipped it on its side, sending Merlin, Garth, and the livestock to the ground in a heap of limbs, hooves, and feathers. Charcoal flew everywhere, with most of it heaped in a big, dusty mound. As the soot settled, the workers and monks gathered to investigate. Abbot Prontwon found the pair and pulled them safely from the wreckage.

Merlin stood blinking at the scene around him. He could hear Garth peeling the shell off a roasted egg.

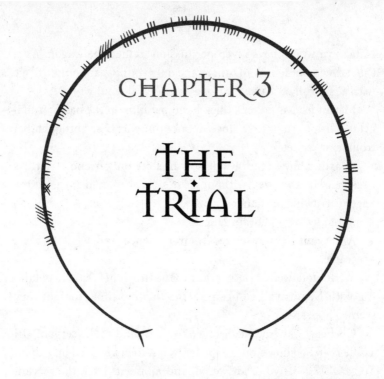

CHAPTER 3

THE TRIAL

Merlin's hand paused on the latch of the magister's front door. "Open it," his father, Owain, said. "You've got to face up to what's happened."

Merlin swallowed and pushed the door open, feeling upon it the bronze Roman eagle. Was it this very morning he'd had such high hopes of talking to Natalenya? And now here he was, about to stand trial before her father, Tregeagle, because Garth *had* stolen the wagon and lied about it.

How could the boy have been so thoughtless?

Merlin's father led him into the great hall. Pine logs blazed on the open hearth, scenting the air. Despite the warmth of the room, Merlin shivered, and it wasn't from the lingering chill of their evening walk. Judgment waited for him in the next room.

Merlin felt such shame for trusting Garth's lies … hah! As if

Natalenya would have given permission to take the wagon. As if she'd ever want to talk to him ... the only young man in the village with a face full of scars.

Merlin felt his father's thick hand pat him on the back. "You'll get to tell your story first, since Abbot Prontwon hasn't brought that troublemaker yet."

"Garth is my friend. Right now he's my only friend." Merlin's back tensed, and even without clear sight, he could imagine the anger furrowing his father's brow.

"Not anymore," Owain said.

A servant acknowledged their presence and went to alert Tregeagle.

Merlin followed his father over to the fire. If his chances of talking with Natalenya had been remote this morning, tonight they seemed hopeless.

His heart like lead, he listened to the sound of the servant girl as she marched down one of the hallways, then knocked on a door. Tregeagle's gruff voice answered, and moments later, the servant returned to them, her footfalls across the stone floor sounding to Merlin like a drum announcing his doom.

"The master is ready to see you."

Merlin tucked his hands under his legs and felt the hard edge of the seat. Never had he been interrogated like this. If only Tregeagle's words were as pleasant as the smell of coriander and honey that filled the magister's room.

"My sons tell a different tale. Why should I believe you?"

Merlin's father — his tas, as all fathers were called in Kernow — coughed nearby, and his presence brought Merlin a small measure of comfort. He sat up a little straighter and placed his hands in his lap. "Because, sir — "

"Because you stole my property?" Tregeagle interrupted his pacing and rapped his knuckles on the wooden table between them. "Because you marred the fine coats of my horses?"

"Because sir, if —"

"Because you knocked my son down and kicked him?"

Actually, Rondroc had knocked Merlin down first, but Merlin had already established that Tregeagle didn't want to hear anything of that sort. Maybe if he apologized for the wagon. "I'm sorry for —"

"So you admit it!" Tregeagle resumed his pacing, his tunic a white blur wrapped with a shining golden belt.

"Be fair, Tregeagle," Merlin's father said, his deep voice echoing in the room. "He said nothing of the kind."

Tregeagle raised his hand. "If you insist on speaking, Owain, tell me why your filthy charcoal filled the leather seats of my painted coach? Was this *your* clever idea?"

Merlin's father sighed. "You know it wasn't, magister. Our horse is lame, and my char-pile got low at the smithy. So the abbey sent Garth to help guide Merlin to fetch charcoal with my wheelbarrow —"

"For the record, what is this new boy's proper name?" Tregeagle sat down, slid a parchment onto the table, and scratched ink across the page with his quill.

Merlin spoke up. "His name is Garthwys, sir."

"Which would that be in Latin, Garthius or Garthwysus?"

"Either, I guess. He got impatient and thought —"

Tregeagle coughed. "He *thought*? Obviously there has been precious little of that from either of you. Three wheels broken, the sides damaged, and one of the axles bent. Is this friend of yours incompetent?"

Far from it, Merlin thought. Garth was good at most things. He could play his bagpipe. He could fish, as that had been his father's trade before Garth was orphaned. And Merlin knew he could drive horses well enough, at least when he wanted to.

Tregeagle stood again, shoving his chair into the wall with a bang, and leaned over the table. "Use your tongue, boy, or I shall call my lictor in to cut it from your mouth."

"Garth knows how to drive a wagon, sir."

"Then why did the fool crash it at the abbey?"

Merlin fidgeted in his seat. "Something scared us, sir. We were bringing the coal back when we smelled roasting meat. Garth was hungry — well, he's always hungry — and he ran off into the woods and left me holding the reins."

Tregeagle retrieved his chair and sat down again, the wood creaking loudly. "So who was roasting meat in the woods? Some vagrant?"

"I don't know, sir. I followed Garth, and we must have been near the old stone circle — "

Tregeagle clicked his teeth together. "The stone circle? It's been a long time since any of the *druidow*" — his voice betrayed a sneer — "dared show their faces around Kernow. So you held the reins. Did *you* try to drive the horses?"

Merlin clenched his fists under the table. "I'm half blind, but not half stupid. There were two men, and they had something strange with them, something heavy and dark. There were flames ... blue flames. And the men drew blades on us. Garth and I ran back to the wagon all spooked. He drove the horses hard till we neared the abbey."

What appeared to be a knife flashed before Merlin, and Tregeagle's deft hands played with it. "Scared of a blade, you say? Tell me what happened at the abbey. Any monks involved? Did anyone damage the wagon on purpose?"

Merlin swallowed, for the blade gleamed in the evening light that slanted through the shutters. "Nothing of the kind, sir. I thought we would crash, so I tried to get Garth to stop the horses. Only we left the road and — "

"How did the *dear* abbot react?" Tregeagle sharpened the knife, sliding and scraping it against a rock.

"Prontwon was irate, but Dybris calmed him down — "

Tregeagle slammed the rock on the table. "And who is this Dybris who ignores my loss? His name is not on the tax register."

"He's a priest who has been at the abbey only a month, sir. He brought Garth along with him."

Tregeagle sat for a while, drumming his fingers pensively on the table. "In my opinion, what you have told me is a preposterous lie." He bit off some cake and leaned forward, fresh honey on his breath. "Tell me. What *really* scared Garth?"

"I've already told you, sir."

Tregeagle raised his hand as if to strike.

Merlin flinched as the shadow drew close.

His father stood. "Leave my son alone. He's told you what he knows. Get your answers from Garth."

Tregeagle pulled his hand away. When he spoke again, something in his voice made Merlin's stomach clench with fear for his friend. "Since both of you are of no further use, I plan to do exactly that. Send the urchin in, and expect my judgment soon."

⚔

Merlin sighed as his father guided him down the hallway to the great hall. The voice of Abbot Prontwon echoed from the room ahead. "When it's our turn — Garth, listen up — what will you say?"

Garth mumbled something, but Merlin couldn't make it out.

"Are you ready to confess what you have done?"

"Must we put him through this again?" Dybris interrupted.

"Yes, we must. The falsehoods shall stop."

A harp sounded from some other room, and both monks quieted.

Merlin stopped walking, his heart thumping. Natalenya played the harp, but it was possible her mother, Trevenna, played as well.

"That," Prontwon said, "is the sound of heaven, which I want Garth to hear one day in our Father's feasting hall."

"He has told the truth. What more can we ask?"

"We love and forgive. But the magister renders justice."

Owain prompted Merlin forward once more, and he entered the hall just as Prontwon, moving more nimbly than his bulk seemed to allow, slipped out of his chair and fell on his knees before Garth.

"Garth, hear me." Prontwon's voice almost broke. "We will uphold you, but you must love the truth no matter the price!"

Merlin's father coughed loudly, and at the same time the harp music quieted. Merlin turned his head, trying to discover where it had come from.

Prontwon and Dybris stood. "How did it go?" the abbot asked.

In turn, Merlin took hold of their hands and gave a quick kiss to the back of each one. Then he shook his head.

"Tregeagle's in a foul mood," Merlin's father grumbled.

Prontwon placed a hand on Merlin's shoulder. "I guessed as much. We are all sorry for the difficulty this has caused." He turned to Garth. "Come on, boy. It is time."

Dybris pulled the boy's arm until he stood. Garth's feet scraped down the hall as he followed the two monks.

CHAPTER 4

THE JUDGMENT

Merlin's father led him to the open hearth in the center of the great hall. "Sit here. I'm stepping outside for some fresh air. Call me when Tregeagle's ready to give his judgment."

Owain's footsteps echoed across the tile, the door opened and shut, and Merlin stood alone with the fire sparking its pine aroma into the air. He closed his eyes and prayed that Christ would uphold Garth.

A harp tune echoed through the hall again.

Merlin lifted his head and listened carefully.

The beautiful notes originated to his right, from some other room. He tapped his staff across the floor until he found a wall; then he followed it with his hand. Sensing light and a draft of pleasant air, he halted before he stepped in front of the open doorway, hoping he couldn't be seen. The music lifted his spirits, and he wondered if his own mother had ever played an instrument.

The harpist sang ... with Natalenya's voice, high and sweet like a bird after a rain shower as it fluttered about the bushes near the smithy.

The wind did take my love away,
Over the seas and far away.
He's blown to south and blown to north;
He's blown so far from my own hearth.
Come home my love, come home today.
Over the seas and hills to stay.
Ne'er blown to east nor blown to west;
Ne'er blown to make my love a jest.
In deepest winter I am numb;
In spring I wait for him to come.
The summer dove doth always wait
For autumn rains to come so late.
The wind did take my love away,
Over the seas and far away.
He's blown from me and blown so far;
He's gone an' died in Gaulish war.

Natalenya ceased her singing. "Dyslan, stop spying. Go away!"

Merlin froze. Did she mean him? Or was Natalenya's younger brother nearby?

He heard shuffling, the echo of the harp being set down. And footsteps.

Merlin put his back against the cold wall.

The footsteps grew louder.

He wanted to hide but couldn't, considering his poor eyesight.

Natalenya walked around the corner. Her dark hair smelled of roses, and her green dress was a beautiful blur.

"Oh ... Merlin."

"I ..."

"Are you here to talk with Father about the accident?" she asked.

"Yes, I ..."

"Your foot was sticking through the doorway. Come in and sit down." She took his arm and guided him through the room to a chair, where he sat stiffly.

"I practice here in my father's library. Do you like harp music?"

"Yes, I …" He trailed off, at a loss for words now that she was speaking to him.

"My grandmother taught me that song. Grandfather died in Gaul fighting with Constantine's army. It makes me think of him."

Swallowing hard, Merlin asked, "Would you play more?"

"Any song in particular?"

"Uh … anything you'd like to play."

She picked up her harp and set it on her lap. "Maybe something brighter." Her fingers struck the bronze strings, and they hummed to life.

Merlin's breathing rose and fell with the melody, but after a few lines Natalenya stopped in midsong.

"Have you ever played?" she asked.

"No, I can't say that I — "

She slid her chair next to his.

Merlin's throat closed up.

He dropped his staff on the floor as she placed the harp on his lap. He held its smooth wood, amazed at how little it weighed.

"This is how you play." Her warm hand touched his and angled it toward the strings.

Merlin plucked them roughly. "Not as pretty as your playing."

"You don't have my fingernails, either." Her laughter filled the room, and the sound felt to him like a refreshing drink from the spring after working in the heat of the blacksmith shop.

Merlin ran his fingertips across the strings and experimented with the notes. The whole harp vibrated into his chest. It would take a lot of work to play a real song.

"You've got natural talent," she said.

"I do?"

She turned her head to listen. "Sure. What song is that?"

41

"I'm trying to remember ... I heard it many years ago."

"Let me give you my practice harp. It has only ten strings, but you could learn on it."

Learn the harp? He'd never thought about music. What if he damaged it? "I'd better not. I'm already in trouble with your father —"

"I saw what happened."

"The wagon's badly broken, isn't it?"

"I don't mean that. I witnessed what my brother Rondroc did to you. I had come to the doorway when I heard shouting. Father won't listen to me, and ... I've learned not to cross him."

"We say in the blacksmith shop, once burned, always careful. I have a few scars to prove it." He held up his right forearm for her to see.

She hesitated, then reached out ... but her soft fingertips touched the scars on his right cheek instead.

He tightened his lips and tried not to pull away.

She traced the long gouges that disfigured his eyelids and ran across his right temple and forehead. "I see you in chapel, but I've never asked what happened to your eyes. People talk, of course, but you never know whom to believe."

"Seven years ago. The memories are painful ..."

"They're faded now."

"No, I'll always remember." He turned away slightly, hoping the subject would change.

"I ... I meant the scars have faded. And your long hair covers many of them." She ran her fingers through his black curls. "You have an honest face, with a handsome nose. When we moved to the village a few years ago, your scars still looked red, but they aren't anymore."

He wanted to walk out. He didn't want to talk with her about this.

"How could Rondroc be so cruel," she said, her voice trembling, "as to knock you over? Let me look at your scalp." She walked behind him and gently leaned his head forward, probing the area where he'd hit the rock.

"Just because I'm mostly blind doesn't mean I can't take care of myself."

"It's a mess ... All crusted over. You should get it washed."

He turned his head away from her. "Is your brother all right? I hope I didn't hurt him."

"I saw him pull the knife on you; he deserved the thump." Natalenya moved across the room. "And your little monk friend was funny!"

"You mean Garth?"

"I laughed when he dumped Dyslan into the hay trough."

Merlin suppressed his own laugh. "I didn't know whether to believe Garth, especially after he lied and told me he had permission to borrow the wagon."

But Merlin couldn't bring himself to tell her that Garth had said *she* had given permission. And Merlin had believed it. What a daft slow wit he was. "I should have gone back to verify his story. I really should have."

Returning to him, Natalenya removed the harp from Merlin's lap and laid in his hands what seemed to be a flat, lightweight piece of wood.

"Here's my practice harp. I don't use it anymore, so please take it."

He felt two carved posts bending out from the top of the sound box. Shaped like a lyre, the harp had bronze strings stretched over an angled bridge. It was much smaller than Natalenya's lap harp. "I can't. Your father ..."

"I bought it with my own *denarii*. It's not up to him."

"I just can't. I'm sorry." He held it out to her, but she didn't take it. A loud voice bellowed from the corridor.

"That's Father," Natalenya said. "He's angry, as always."

"I need to go." Merlin found his staff on the floor, stood up, and set the practice harp on the chair.

Natalenya began to say something but stopped.

"What?" Merlin asked.

"Never mind." She walked with him toward the door. "I'm sorry for all this. I'll be praying for you."

Tregeagle's voice called out, "Lictor Erbin!"

The rough, familiar hand of Merlin's father guided Merlin to a chair in the great hall where everyone had gathered.

"Where'd you go?" his father whispered.

"Talking. With Natalenya."

"Garth must have had a hard time."

Merlin took hold of his father's arm. "What am I seeing?"

"Tregeagle's at a table, and there are now three soldiers with him from the fortress. Erbin just entered. He's kind of short but strong, with black hair and beard. Got a leather jerkin. And a long whip."

Tregeagle pounded the table. "Hear my verdict."

Everyone went silent.

"I find Merlin guilty of lying and of assaulting my sons. However, Merlin is found not guilty of stealing the horses and wagon due to the clear confession of Garthwysus ... and the meddling of monks."

Tregeagle scratched a stylus on a parchment as he recorded the decision.

"I find Garthwysus guilty of lying and of assaulting my sons. I also find him guilty of having stolen and damaged my property."

"I didn't steal the wagon!" Garth said. "I told you I was just borrowin' it!"

Tregeagle ignored the outburst and continued writing on the parchment. "And now for restitution. I charge you, Owain, as the blacksmith of the village, with fixing the wagon, along with the aid of your son. The bent axle will need straightening, and much of the wood will need to be replaced. You will procure other craftsmen for their services as required."

Merlin's father stood up, an edge in his voice. "Magister, who pays? My son is not responsible."

Tregeagle stopped scribing. "I said nothing about Merlin's innocence regarding *damaging* the wagon. Did not your son ride in it and interfere with the reins prior to the crash? Your son holds partial responsibility, and it is clear why I put you in charge."

"What of payment? My work is free, but I cannot pay others."

"The monks must compensate you for some costs. Is there anything Garthwysus owns?"

Abbot Prontwon spoke up. "He owns nothing, Magister, except an old bagpipe passed down from his father."

"Then it is forfeit."

"Nooo!" Garth sobbed. "I did nothin' wrong!"

Merlin reached out and found Garth's hand. It was sweaty, and the boy gripped Merlin's hand firmly.

"The abbey is required to sell it and give the money to Owain."

"You can't do that. You can't sell me pipes!"

"Costs beyond that, the abbey must find a way to pay," Tregeagle continued.

Garth let go of Merlin's hand and lunged at Tregeagle. Owain and Dybris grabbed Garth's arms and pulled him back to his chair.

"Now his punishment for stealing the wagon — "

Prontwon stood. "Is it not enough for him to be parted from his sole inheritance and the only remaining memory of his dead father?"

"No, it is not." Tregeagle clapped, and the thunder of it echoed in the great hall. "Repair doesn't pay for thievery. Erbin, what judgment had I decided for the imprisoned Connek?"

Erbin paused. "You know, Magister, that your judgment does not vary for thievery."

"For the sake of our guests, what is my unwavering judgment?"

"Flogging," Erbin said smugly.

The hall fell silent.

"In this case, Lictor Erbin, I no longer consider the testimony true regarding Connek's attempted theft."

Merlin stood. This was too much. That foul-smelling thief had tried to steal their lamb yesterday, but Merlin and his father had caught him. "Connek *is* a thief. Everyone in town — "

Tregeagle raised his voice. "Silence!"

Merlin sat down, his lips burning to say more.

"The nerve of you, Owain, tying Connek up and sending him here for my judgment. I now deem that Connek has done no wrong. He is to be released."

Erbin stepped forward. "I shouldn't flog him?"

"No. Instead, you will whip the young monk."

Merlin closed his eyes. This was *his* fault. He should never have cajoled Garth into walking up the hill past Tregeagle's house. Garth hadn't wanted to go that way — he'd been frustrated that the longer path would prolong their coal-gathering task. If Merlin hadn't convinced him, none of these horrors would have occurred.

Garth blubbered. Prontwon bent over and put his arm around the boy.

Tregeagle continued. "Not the full nineteen lashes, considering his age. Nine should be sufficient to teach a lesson. Guard, go and free the prisoner."

"Yes, sir." One of the guards left the room.

Merlin couldn't believe Connek would be set free.

Prontwon bowed before Tregeagle. "Is there some other punishment you would accept?"

"Gold. It has been the lifeblood of the empire, and I will accept it instead of the boy's blood. Three gold coins I ask. One for every three lashes, and I will halt the judgment."

Prontwon sputtered. "Magister, we — "

"Gold!" Tregeagle thundered. "Surely you monks have some squirreled away. Gold!"

"We are a poor abbey. We have not even one gold coin."

"Then my judgment stands."

"I beg you, allow me to take this punishment on his behalf."

Tregeagle pulled Prontwon up while laughing in his face. "You fool. You think I will have it said that I flogged the abbot of Bosvenna? An absurd request, Prontus!"

Guilt and remorse battled a rising anger in Merlin's heart as he listened to the exchange. Garth had done wrong, but nine lashes? He was just a child.

Abbot Prontwon tried again, "Mercy, Magister — "

"Mercy?" Tregeagle shouted. "The only one whom I would allow to take his place would be *him*."

Merlin's father leaned over and whispered through his teeth, "He's pointing at you."

The room spun. Merlin gripped his father's hand. The thick metal armband his father always wore reflected dizzily before Merlin's eyes.

Walking forward, Tregeagle mocked, "Have mercy, Merlin. Have mercy on the thief!"

"Sir, I — "

"Yes, have mercy. You who dare hurt *my* son!" Tregeagle slipped his knife from its sheath and waved it in front of Merlin's eyes. "Take his place so we can see mercy."

Silence filled the room, except for the sound of Tregeagle's clacking heels as he returned to the front.

"I ... I accept," Merlin said.

Garth caught his breath and stopped crying.

Tregeagle turned. "You *what*?"

"I accept!" Merlin's voice echoed through the room.

Tregeagle rapped on his table. "So be it. You shall — "

A stifled sob went up from somewhere behind Merlin. A girl's voice.

Tregeagle hesitated.

Merlin turned his head but could only guess who it was.

His father hissed in his ear, "You cannot. Are you a fool? Garth's done nothing but make trouble for you."

"I can't let him be whipped."

"Yes, you can. Wash your hands of this rascal!"

Merlin tightened his shoulders. "I'm responsible too, and I won't abandon him."

"You'll be scarred for life. Everyone who sees your back will think you're a criminal or a runaway slave. It will take weeks to heal."

Turning to his father, Merlin tilted his head until the light from the open window fell upon his face. "I'm already scarred. It doesn't matter anymore."

His father moaned.

"Lictor Erbin, we have a change." Tregeagle's voice betrayed no emotion. "Merlin is to be flogged in the boy's place. Guards, take Merlin outside to the post."

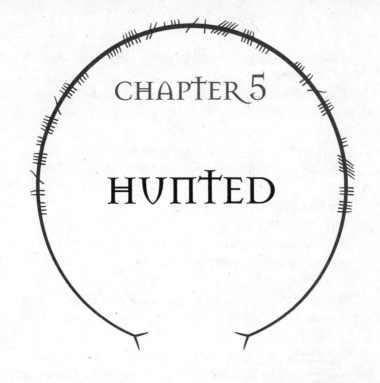

CHAPTER 5

HUNTED

Merlin stood, handed his staff and dirk to his father, and stepped forward. The guards grabbed him by the arms and thrust him across the great hall toward the light of the open front door. As he was pushed outside, a few raindrops fell on his cheeks. Dark clouds had thickened over the moor, and a shadow soon covered the mountainside.

Behind him, Prontwon's footsteps caught up to his father's. "This is not necessary—"

Merlin's father spat. "My son can make his own daft decisions."

Years of working the bellows in the blacksmith shop had added strength to Merlin's frame, and he could break free from the grip of the guards if he wanted to. He could tell Tregeagle he'd changed his mind. But he forced himself to remember Garth's plight and his own stupidity, and so he submitted as they led him away from the house.

Garth hung on to Merlin until someone dragged him away. "You needn't do it. Run!"

The guards roped Merlin's hands to a six-foot post and tore off his tunic to expose his back. His muscles tensed as he waited in the coolness of the evening breeze.

Merlin set his jaw and tried to brace his body.

Behind him, Erbin test-snapped the whip as he chatted with Tregeagle.

Dear God, help me, Merlin prayed.

Crack!

Merlin let out a painful cry, then shut his mouth. A great welt burned from his left shoulder blade down to the middle of his back.

Crack!

Merlin lurched but held his tongue as the gash crisscrossed the previous one.

Ca-chack!

Merlin let out a ragged breath. Another blazing welt, this time lower down. He imagined Erbin leering as he swished the whip around.

Crack!

The whip opened up a long cut straight down the middle of his back, and Merlin's body recoiled, his legs trembling. All of the other welts opened, and blood wept down his back.

"Lord Jesu … help," he whispered.

Crack!

Ca-tchow!

Crack!

The strikes felt like hot knives slicing open his flesh, and his knees buckled. Blood flowed down his breeches, and he cried out in great gasps.

Through the haze of a light rain, he heard Prontwon call on God's mercy.

He could hear his father yelling for Tregeagle to stop.

Tregeagle's cold voice answered, "You think I am harsh? Count him lucky. The tally will be nine. Do not tempt me to raise it."

His father said no more.

Merlin shook his head to clear it and pulled himself up. The rain slicked the rope, and he gripped it tighter for the final two strikes. "Father in heaven," he called, but he kept imagining an adder behind him ready to strike.

Crack!

Ca-wrack!

He dropped to his knees, all his muscles in a spasm. Vaguely, he heard the sobbing of a girl.

Dybris rushed to untie him. "So sorry ..."

Merlin fell to his side, and his father wiped the blood that leaked from his wounds. Merlin felt his head lifted from the ground, and Garth was there.

Tregeagle's voice echoed through the air. "Get your rabbling son out of here. My coach must be fixed and in perfect condition before it is returned to me. You have two weeks."

Merlin fought to sit up, the world shifting and swirling around him.

His father's voice faded until just a sigh remained, flitting away on the wind. His blurred sight exploded with light and colors, all hurtling toward him and pouring into his head. There was green and darker green and blue above that. His vision sharpened until he could see everything perfectly.

Strangely, his back didn't hurt, and the whipping post had disappeared.

He gaped in shock at the clear sight of tall weeds growing among grayish-red cabbages, whose pungence filled his senses. Sharply defined bees floated on thrumming wings, and a delicately feathered robin chirruped as she paraded through ... garden paths? Merlin's trousers were rolled up, and his knees were pressed into the coolness of the soil.

This was his family's garden. He had sat here for hours on end throughout the last many years, weeding by touch. The smithy stood to his left, and oaken roof timbers jutted out from its conical thatched roof. The granite rock wall was lichened green. Beyond the smithy squatted his family's house, smaller, with its low door closed and silent.

Where had everyone gone? How had he come to be here?

The sun rolled across the sky and fled away. Stars appeared, so bright that Merlin gazed upward in wonder. And he could focus on them.

But how can I see?

Then clouds rolled in, hiding the stars. Searing light flashed before his startled eyes. Deafening thunder struck at his ears.

Wolves howled in the distance, and Merlin jerked his head to look at the dark woods across the road — but no creature could be seen through the trees. He put a hand on his dirk and prepared to get up and run.

Then he smelled smoke. Hearing a crackling roar, he turned to see flames leaping from the roof of the smithy. Heat rolled over him and stung his face and arms. He started to rise, pushing off the ground with his hands, but his knees and fingers pressed into a sticky, dark liquid, which clung to him along with clods of dirt. He tried rubbing it off, but he could see now that it was blood.

The twisted body of a man lay facedown before Merlin. He wore a green robe, and a deep wound had been sliced between his neck and shoulder. The man's blood still seeped from the gash and into the soil around the now-crushed cabbages.

Merlin stiffened. He tried to shout but barely managed to rasp.

The sky lit up. Between him and the corpse, another man appeared, this one dressed in cloth that shimmered like pearl. His hair lay bright as silvered frost, and his eyes smoldered like melted bronze.

The man opened his mouth, and his voice rang in Merlin's head. "Servant who has suffered, the Lord greets you!"

Merlin tried to stand but fell back, dazed.

The man raised his hand, and a fountain of sweet-scented water flowed from his palm. "The Glorified One has ordained that a prophecy concerning your homeland would be fulfilled over ten weeks of years. For eight sevens, the power of dark fire has slept, clad in deathless cold, and for two sevens, it has grown under the mortal sky. This day it has awakened and is revealed in woe to the inhabitants of the earth."

"W-who are you?" Merlin stammered.

"I am a servant of the Most High. Fear not, for His mighty hand has chosen you."

Merlin felt his teeth begin to chatter. "I-I don't understand."

"FEAR NOT, MERLIN! The Lord has sent me to warn you. This day a man has come who has found and awakened Death and Hell. Beware him. BEWARE WHAT HE REVEALS. But fear not. Trust in God!"

The angel disappeared in a folding, collapsing cloud. And with him faded the vision.

Merlin's eyesight blurred even as the flesh on his back screamed in pain again. He cried out. The pale form of the whipping post appeared once more, and he leaned upon it.

An hour later, after a painful journey back to his straw bed in the smithy, Merlin shifted onto his other side and tried to keep his food down. His face felt hot, and his back throbbed as if thousands of wasps continuously stung him. A few embers in the forge cast their light to the roof thatch, but everything else lay in shadow as the last light of the setting sun blinked and died through the shuttered window.

He remembered again the vision he had seen and wondered what it meant. He rubbed his hands to make sure the bloody soil was gone. Then his hands shot to his cheeks and eyelids, confirming the old scars still marred his features. Opening his eyes again, he saw the familiar smears marring his sight.

How had he been able to see clearly — even for that brief moment? The smell of fresh straw filled his senses. The smithy certainly *wasn't* on fire, and therefore a dead man wearing a green robe *wasn't* lying in their garden. He wondered if it had just been a strange dream.

His father banged open the double doors at the front of the smithy and brought a sloshing bucket in. He filled a ceramic jar and set it on a small table next to Merlin's bed. "I'm glad we got you home."

Merlin drank, but his throat still felt dry.

Sitting in a nearby chair, his father folded his arms and said nothing for a while. When he spoke, anger tinted his voice. "You're going to take a long time to heal. How am I supposed to get my work done without you pumping the bellows? I'll have to run back and forth."

"Is that all you care about?"

"If I don't fix the wagon —"

"Let Tregeagle flog the anvil next."

His father pushed his stool back. "I told you not to do it."

Merlin sat up, and the pain made him regret it. "You think I deserved nothing?"

"Seizing Garth's bagpipe was unfair. Whipping you was worse."

"So save the bagpipe but flog Garth?" His father was full of nonsense.

His father stood. "When I was young, my father gave me a bow and quiver. One day I practiced with a friend, and he shot one of my father's hounds."

"On purpose?" Merlin touched one of the stinging welts, amazed at how much it had swollen.

"I don't know. But the dog died with the arrow lodged in its side."

"Did your friend get in trouble?"

"Yes, but I did too," his father said. "Both his bow *and* mine were taken from us, and I'll never forget the injustice of that day."

Merlin said nothing, waiting for his father to continue.

"Garth's only token of his dead father is his bagpipe, and it's cruel to take it away." Merlin's father raised his voice. "But you shouldn't have been whipped. You never would've taken Tregeagle's horses and —"

Merlin turned away and said in a soft voice, "You mean I'm not capable."

"I did my best when the wolves came —"

"You saved me —"

"Not enough!" His father's words were muffled by his hands as his voice broke. "You were so young ..."

Merlin lay down on his side again. "This has nothing to do with my blindness."

"You don't know what it's like for a father. I lived it all over again ... Watching you get whipped brought back the memory of how the wolves scratched your face. It was too much."

"I didn't think about that. I —"

"There you stood, your flesh being torn, and again I couldn't help. Again."

"I didn't want to be helped." Merlin reached out painfully and clutched his father's shoulder. Sliding his hand down, he brushed against the cold metal of the marriage-covenant band on his father's arm.

Owain patted him on the head. "You're braver than is good for a blind lad."

"Tas ... Father ... I know I've asked before, but when I'm better, would you please come to chapel?"

Even as Merlin asked the question, the armband grew warm. And then hot.

His father jerked away and stood. "Had enough of monks. The troubles they cause."

The gem on the armband gleamed red in the smithy flames. It reminded Merlin of the glowing eyes of the wolves from his nightmares, and he turned away.

Why did his father never want to go to chapel? Ever since Merlin started visiting four years earlier, his father had never approved. Sure, he'd blacksmith tools for the monks, but always grudgingly. And Mônda, Merlin's stepmother, treated the monks with open derision. She would yell at Merlin in Eirish if he even mentioned them.

His father filled in the silence by changing the subject. "How's your back? Your tunic's bloody, and you're sweating." He wiped Merlin's forehead with a dank-smelling cloth.

In truth, Merlin felt tired and weak. The darkness had crept into the smithy, and he yawned, hoping for sleep and the chance to forget his father's stubbornness, as well as his own painful welts.

"You get some sleep, and we'll talk more in the morning." His father slipped out the back door, and the iron latch clicked shut.

Merlin lay awake long into the night, unable to sleep, hot and in pain. Wondering if he had a fever, he felt his own forehead with little result. He tried to doze but couldn't get comfortable.

Outside, a wolf howled.

Then another. And close to the smithy. Too close. Were they after the goats? He lay perfectly still, straining his ears for any additional hints of the wolves' location. One breath became twenty, then thirty. Nothing. As he began to relax, he heard it: low growling, just outside the smithy's walls. A wolf began tearing at the slats of the window near the bellows, claws and teeth raking through the old wood.

They weren't after the goats.

"It can't be," he whispered. After seven years, they were hunting him again.

His trembling fingers traced the scars running from his eyelids as he forced himself to sit up on the bed. Finding the tin box of char, he slid off the lid, blew on the coals until they glowed, and finally held the tip of the rush lamp to it. The oil-soaked reed began to smoke but didn't light.

The wolf snarled now, and chunks of wood splintered and fell to the ground.

The wick flared, lighting the room with a pale shimmer. Barely enough for his feeble vision to guide him.

More wood cracked away as the wolf ripped at the shutter.

Why hadn't his father mounted an iron grate in the window?

Merlin fumbled next to his pallet and found his dirk. At least his father had made this for him.

Other wolves scratched at the double doors facing the road, and the hinges groaned.

Merlin's eyes searched for details, fear making his hands numb. Had he fastened the bar before bed? Leaping from his pallet, ignoring the pain, he ran barefoot across the blacksmith shop. The rush lamp gave enough light for Merlin to avoid the blur of workbenches between him and the doors.

The wolves clawed at the heavy doors and pushed them open a crack.

Merlin slammed his body into the oak timbers, sending pain shooting through the wounds on his back. Grimacing, he lifted the bar from the floor and banged it into place. He slumped down and sucked in a mouthful of air.

Beyond the bellows, the wolf at the window grunted as it scrambled through.

Merlin's heart pounded as he found his footing and ran toward the wolf. But he tumbled over a stool and sent his knife skittering into the darkness.

Weaponless, he jumped at the workbench, hoping to find his father's latest sword, but instead his panicked hands found hammers ... rasps ... chisels ... and scrap iron. *Where's the sword?* If only his eyes could show him. His mind sped over the previous day. Maybe his father had left it on the forge.

He turned. The wolf's dark shadow tracked nearer, now blocking his path. Its eyes lit up in the rush light: bright blurs of hunger, malice, and death.

Oh, God, please, he prayed. It was going to happen a second time. He hefted a hammer and threw it at the wolf, which yelped in anger. Merlin's escape lay over the workbench. He planted both hands and vaulted up, but — still stiff from his flogging — his foot caught one of his father's smaller anvils. He flipped to the ground, falling on his side. His wounds screamed, and pain ripped across his back.

Sucking air through his teeth, he reached to the top of the forge and groped for the sword.

The stink of rotting flesh sickened the air as the wolf rounded the corner. It snapped its teeth and lunged at him.

In one swift motion, Merlin found the sword's makeshift wooden handle and leveled the blade's point at the wolf. With a force that knocked the breath from Merlin's lungs, the creature impaled itself on the blade, yet it still tore at Merlin's forearm, snarling and thrashing as it died.

A moment later someone pounded on the double doors. "Open up!"

Merlin heaved the dead wolf away, slid the blade from its body, and limped over to the doors. Shaking, his back in agony, he unbarred the entrance.

His father burst into the room, the bright smear of a torch in his left hand and a spear in his right. "Wolves outside. Scared them off, and the goats are fine. What's — " His father stopped speaking and surveyed the smithy. "By the High King's justice, what happened?"

"A wolf ... the window," Merlin said. The bloody sword trembled in his hand.

Small footsteps interrupted his father's stunned silence as Merlin's nine-year-old half sister, Ganieda, padded into the smithy with a dark shawl over her head. She flew around the workbench and knelt before the great wolf's body.

She stroked its head. "Poor wolf."

Merlin touched the deep scars that emanated from his eyes and flinched as he remembered the wolves of seven years ago. "Get away from there, Ganieda!"

"She's my friend, and you murdered her." She began to sob.

Her wolf? Merlin knew the girl had an imagination, but this?

His father examined the wolf's body and whistled. "You killed it with one blow, and with my new blade, I see."

"I lost my dirk."

"You almost lost your life. Look at its teeth."

"She was just defending herself," Ganieda said between sobs.

These words stung Merlin worse than his wounds. Had his sister ever shed a tear over his scars, or the loss of his eyesight? Never. Had she expressed her thanks to him for saving her? Not that he could remember. And with each of her sniffles and cries for the wolf, the bile rose higher in his throat. Angry words were on the tip of his tongue when his father interrupted.

"You're a foolish girl. Now get up and wash your brother's arm while I put some planks in the window."

Merlin sat down on his bed, his head a little dizzy, and the slashes on his back beginning to burn.

Ganieda brought a wet rag from the washbucket and quietly began washing the blood from Merlin's forearm. "I'm sorry," she finally said. "I didn't know she bit you."

The rag dabbed lightly across his wounds, and he winced as the cold water stung.

"I forgive you," he said, but his heart wasn't in it. Did she really care for him? He didn't know.

"You didn't have to kill her."

"I don't want to talk about it."

Across the smithy, his father finished sawing a plank and began pounding it in place using an iron peg.

Ganieda wrung out the rag, the water dripping and splashing into the bowl, and then ran over to their father. "Can I help?" she asked, and he directed her to hold the planks in place.

When the window was boarded up, he asked Ganieda to hold a torch while he dragged the wolf's body outside.

"Are you going to build a cairn over her?"

"It's a dead animal, Ganieda."

"I know what you're going to do," she said, her voice rising in timbre. "You're going to throw her in the ditch!"

"Merlin, I know you're not feeling well, but I need you to hold the torch."

Ganieda ran shrieking from the smithy.

Merlin rose, ignoring the pain, and held the torch while his father dragged the wolf's body out past their stacked stone wall, through their iron gate, and to a ditch at the edge of their land.

"I know I've blocked up the window, but I wouldn't blame you for joining us in the house tonight."

"I'm fine."

"Have it your way."

Despite the attack, the smithy was Merlin's place, and he wouldn't leave it. From the fresh smell of his straw bed tucked against the eastern wall to the well-worn handles of the bellows near the forge — this was his home, his life. Here he could find comfort in the feel of his father's tools. The shape and coolness of the great anvil. The spinning sound of the grinding wheel. Even the acrid reek of the quench barrel.

His father left to go back to bed, and for the rest of the night, Merlin had terrible dreams about wolves. They surrounded his bed, and their claws ripped at his bloodied back. They scratched at his face, destroying the remnant of his sight. And no matter how many wolves he killed, they kept climbing through the window, each with sharper teeth and more evil eyes than the last.

Even the dawn and the rhythmic clanging of Merlin's father at the anvil didn't remove the specter. Each blur and shadow resembled a wolf.

Near midmorning, Owain completed the installation of iron bars in the window and went back to the house, leaving the smithy quiet.

Merlin hoped to get some proper sleep and was just dozing off when a knock came at the front door, which his father had left propped open.

"Excuse me ... young man?" The deep, lilting voice had a slight Eirish accent.

Merlin lifted his head. "I'm here. May I help you?"

"I assume this is the smithy?"

"The shop's here. I'll get my tas to assist you. Do you need something forged?"

"No, no ... thank you, but no. I am not here for the services of the notorious blacksmith." His voice was like cream, but there was something sour hiding in it. "We are here to receive, shall we say, a visit with our kin."

The man's voice was strangely familiar to Merlin, but he couldn't remember from where. As far back as he remembered, not a single relative had ever visited them. Certainly none from Erin, though surely he must be a relation of his stepmother, Mônda.

Yet why did Merlin recognize the voice?

The man stepped inside the smithy and walked over to him. Behind, another man followed. "Allow me to introduce myself. I am Mórganthu mab Mórfryn, and this is my son, Anviv. You must be ... Merlin?" He bent down and waved his fingers in front of Merlin's eyes.

Suppressing a spark of annoyance, Merlin ignored the fingers, sat up painfully, and placed the back of his hand to his forehead in a show of respect. "My father and I live here. Are you related to Mônda and my sister?"

"I am Môndargana's father. I have been away for a long time, but now I have been called here once more ... I should say ... to *this* somnolent village, specifically."

Again, the voice was familiar to Merlin.

The man waved his fingers for a second time in front of Merlin, and they smelled moldy, as if he'd been digging at the rotten innards of some tree. Merlin wanted to swat them away. He turned instead to greet the son by reaching out both hands. "Anviv ... Then you're sort of an uncle."

Anviv let his hands be shaken for a moment, and they were like two marsh eels after their heads had been hit on a stone.

Merlin wiped his palms on his tunic. Still needing to greet the agitating old man, Merlin reached out toward the dark form. "Welcome, Mórganthu. Our home is yours."

Mórganthu grasped Merlin's hands but quickly tried to pull away. Merlin decided to test the man's character and held on. Mórganthu's fingers were thick and strong, but why didn't they have calluses? Even the monks had coarse hands from labor. *Who is this man?*

Mórganthu grunted, but still Merlin wouldn't let go.

Finally, Mórganthu twisted a jagged fingernail into each of Merlin's palms.

Merlin jerked his hands away.

"Enough impudence," Mórganthu said darkly. "Enough. We will take our —"

"Excuse me if I continue resting." Merlin lay down again. Somehow his bed felt colder than before. "I'm sure Mônda will be happy to greet you after so long. The house is that way." He pointed and hoped they'd go away.

Their feet crept toward the back door, which Merlin's father had also left open. Merlin lay quietly, hoping to catch the conversation.

Mórganthu rapped on the door to their house, just a few yards away.

Merlin heard footsteps and metal clicking and scraping. Then the door creaked open. "May I help you?" Mônda said. "Do you need something smithed?"

A short moment later, she screeched in joy.

"Yes, yes, it is I. And here is your brother grown into a man. Do not hold me thus, my daughter. I am not a mound spirit that will disappear with the mist."

Merlin had never heard Mônda so giddy. "Come in ... please! We'll have food ready soon, and you must join us." The three entered, and the heavy oak door shut.

The sounds muffled, and Merlin wished he'd followed to learn more about these strange relatives.

But in a moment it didn't matter, for the voices changed to shouting. The door opened again, and someone ran from the house, presumably Anviv, since his strange father's low voice yelled as he came, cursing and struggling. "Owain! Owain, let go, you insolent son of a devil ..."

Ignoring the pain as best he could, Merlin stood and hobbled outside, where he could hear better and maybe see a little.

"Eat dirt for your meal," Merlin's father yelled.

Mórganthu crashed to the ground and shouted as Owain kicked him.

Merlin was in awe. Nearly every day his father's simmering anger boiled over, but this kind of rage was unusual. To get away from the quarrel, Merlin backed up until his feet hit one of the cabbages at the edge of the garden.

Merlin's father pushed a sobbing Mônda back into the house, where her weeping was muffled.

"Get up, druid."

Mórganthu unbent himself and stood.

"Never enter my house again," Owain said. "Never step on my land. You lost your welcome ten years ago, so stay out!"

Mórganthu's hand struck quickly toward the low thatch of the roof and seized what appeared to be an unwary red squirrel. It chattered frantically but could not escape. With a deliberate motion, Mórganthu drew a knife that flashed golden in the sunlight. "Heed. Take heed, Owain An Gof. If you ever lay hands on me or my kin in the future ... I promise to slit you like a rodent!"

He held up the squirrel, which squealed as he plunged in the knife. Mórganthu flung the carcass away. With a sickening sound, it landed next to Merlin, and its red blood spilled and seeped into the garden.

And that was when Merlin remembered where he had heard the man's voice. It had been in the woods with Garth. These two were the men who had been carrying that strange, dark object that burned with a blue fire.

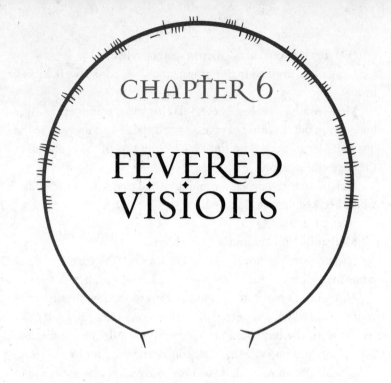

CHAPTER 6

FEVERED VISIONS

Dybris arrived after the noon meal and brought a healing ointment of thyme for Merlin's back.

Merlin's father harrumphed. "Will it push the bellows for me too? I've lost my helper, yet I'm expected to fix Tregeagle's wagon along with all my other work."

Dybris considered this. "I could seek permission from Prontwon to take his place. Merlin's healing shouldn't take much more than a week."

Owain banged his hammer on the anvil, loudly. "Nah. I don't want any jabberin' monk slowing me down. Best for me to handle the bellows —"

"Blowing hot air seems to be your specialty of late."

Merlin hoped his father wouldn't throw the monk out before the ointment was applied. Thankfully he merely banged the iron more loudly on the anvil. Merlin slid off his tunic so Dybris could rub the healing salve into the wounds. It stung badly, and he had to stop Dybris three times because of the pain.

After the monk left, Merlin's father pulled up a stool, leaned close, and said in a low voice, "I've been thinking..."

Merlin wanted to sit up, but the burning ointment kept him in place.

His father groaned. "How do I say this?... The truth is that I don't want you to go to chapel anymore."

"What?" Surely Merlin had misheard.

"No more chapel. These monks are causing too much trouble."

"Look, Dybris didn't mean to get you angry — "

"That's not it."

"Then what? Did Mônda tell you to say that?" Merlin hit the wall with his fist, but agony from the welt on his shoulder made him regret it. "She never wants me to go to chapel. Just last week she tried to kick me — "

"Leave your mother out of this."

Merlin wanted to roll his eyes. "She's not my mother. Why don't you ever talk about my real mother?"

"Why do you keep asking, eh?" His father slid his shining armband farther up.

Merlin scowled. Mônda gave the armband to his father when they were wed, shortly after Merlin's mother drowned.

"Mônda's your mother now. It's time to accept it."

"My mother died. You can't make me forget her."

His father stood and paced the floor, raking a hand through his thinning black hair. "I failed her too, you know. I've made a mess of my life."

"I didn't say that."

"Say it, then. 'Owain An Gof couldn't save his first wife from the water, couldn't save his ungrateful, foolish son from wolves or whips ... has a difficult second wife and an unloving daughter ... and he spends his time bending worthless iron."

He clasped his hammer and struck it sideways upon the anvil.

"I should've done something different. Maybe earned a chieftain's torc. Mônda says —"

Merlin stopped listening because his father was speaking nonsense again. "Tas, you're one of the most respected men on the moor. Everyone depends on you —"

"Fie! You know the old saying:

Unless one of six things you bear,
folk will not hear nor follow you:
A harp whose notes hang in the air,
or druid-coppered scars of blue.
Fine parchment of a monk in prayer,
or steaming food by wife who's true.
Sharp knife held at a back made bare,
else torc of gold or silver hue."

"So? You're a master swordsmith. All the warriors —"

"Hah! You think that loafer who ordered your wolf-killing sword will even pay for it? My work is nothing but a bucket of ashes, and you make it twice as hard. Stay away from that chapel. Do you hear?"

He strode out of the smithy and slammed the back door.

The day stretched on interminably, but Merlin's father didn't return to the forge. Though a cool breeze would slip in through the open front doors now and then, it brought Merlin little relief. By late afternoon, sweat slicked his hair, and it felt as if fire seared his back. He tried to rest, but he grew more and more agitated. His head felt heavy, and at one point the room flipped upside down. He closed his eyes. When he opened them again, a shadow stood over him with a whip. Merlin held out his hands and wanted to yell, but the man disappeared.

Soon the shadows convulsed again until the shape of a wolf formed between the workbenches. The light of its eyes filled the room, and it snapped and licked its teeth.

Merlin sat up in a panic. He had to get to his father. Get out of the smithy. Get away from the wolf. His blanket turned into cobwebs as he shoved it aside and stood. The room spun, and he waited for it to right itself. He tried to walk to the door but veered left and banged his knee into the forge, which he clutched to steady himself.

His hand rested upon the edge of the new sword — the one he'd killed the wolf with. He clutched the temporary handle, lifted the blade, and turned upon the shadows.

"Leave me alone!" he called. "I've got the blade. I'll kill you again."

The wolf's maw blazed out dizzying flames.

Merlin brought the blade up and sliced it through the air. The beast backed up. Its teeth glowed, and noxious vapors hissed from its nostrils.

Merlin's face burned. Why was he so hot? Sweat dripped down his forehead and across his scars, stinging his eyes. Once again, he raised his weapon at the creature, just as the jaws parted and it lunged at him with a howling cry.

Merlin jumped back as sparks burst from its mouth, burning his skin. He thrust the sword straight into the fiery throat. The creature's body turned into smoke and disappeared.

It was finally dead.

The weight of the blade pulled Merlin forward, and the room tilted. He fell with a black crash, and he could no longer breathe. He was floating. Sinking.

Merlin's heart and lungs threatened to burst before he felt himself begin to rise. Liquid flowed oddly against his skin. He struggled upward through the water, frantic for air, his lungs searing. He broke the surface, coughed, and sucked in the life-giving sweetness again and again.

Dark-green water surrounded him, and thunderclouds rolled above as rain poured from the sky. He wiped his face while kicking to keep afloat. He didn't know where he swam, but as in his previous vision, he could see clearly.

The world darkened again, and a burst of light jabbed into his eyes like nails. Thunder split the heavens, and voices floated to him. Faint at first but growing stronger.

"I've nothing to bail with ..." said a woman's voice.

"Keep trying," said a man. "I'm rowing, but we've sprung a leak. The shore's not far."

Merlin kicked his legs to spin toward the sound. A small dinghy rocked toward him. He called to it as the boat rowed nigh, but no one answered. When he reached up to grab hold of its railing, his hand touched nothing. Just air above and water below. He sank headlong, off-balance and confused.

Thrashing back up to the surface, Merlin sputtered. He glimpsed the occupants, and his heart leaped into his throat. The man was his father, though he looked younger. Was the woman Mônda?

No.

Drenched red hair lay upon her shoulders. Not his stepmother but his *mother*. Gwevian, dead now fourteen years.

Merlin called again, but the occupants didn't hear him, and the phantom boat swirled by through the swelling waves. By some miracle, some curse, he was witnessing the past.

Water lashed his face as he swam after them.

A bolt of lightning arced from the depths of the water and shot up to the sky. The entire lake lit up deathly white. Another of the fiery tongues shot up from the center of the lake and hit the boat, scorching and rending it in half. The two occupants fell into the water, stunned.

Darkness. Thunder. Merlin yelled again and swam toward the wreckage. "Father! Mother!" Water rushed into his open mouth.

Bubbles rose. His father's hand grasped a board, and he pulled himself up. Merlin tried to help, but his hand passed through his father's shoulder.

"Gwev — Gwevian!" His father hunted frantically among the flotsam, not finding her. "Gwevian!" He dove. Thrice he sought her below, each time surfacing more exhausted. Finally, his strength nearly gone, he kicked to shore, only ten yards away.

Merlin swam after him, tears streaming into the lake that had become his mother's grave.

His father collapsed on the shore, wailing in great gasps. His whole body shivered, and his mud-stained feet lay in the water.

Merlin pulled himself next to his father, tired and his limbs aching.

The moans of his father faded, and Merlin knew no more.

✝

Garth slipped away from the planting easily enough. That lazy monk Herrik, who was supposed to be working beside him, always snuck a nap during the hottest part of the day. *What a dodger!* When he sent Garth and his wooden hoe off to the eastern slope so he himself could "get some hard work done without interruption," Garth took his chance.

His stomach growled as he crossed the expanse of barren field between him and the Fowaven River. Abbot Prontwon had cut his tucker down to oatmeal and water for the week as punishment for crashing the magister's wagon — but they were fussing over nothing. He'd just borrowed it and planned on returning it after dropping off the charcoal.

As for the crashing, well, if that was anyone's fault, it was Merlin's. Sure, Garth had driven the horses a mite fast, but if he-who-wanted-to-slow-down-now hadn't grabbed the reins, Garth would have handled those beautiful, white, high-stepping horses just fine.

He felt a twinge of guilt over the flogging, but Merlin should never have asked to take his punishment. What a useless thing! Didn't Merlin know that he'd never have let himself be flogged? He was getting ready to bolt out the magister's front door — and he would have, too. He had run away from his father many a time to avoid a chastisement, and he wasn't about to take one from sour face.

And those monks! How could they side with the magister? He'd never forgive them for planning to sell his bagpipe. They couldn't do it, and Garth wouldn't let them. They'd have to rip it from his bloody fingers. If they found it, of course. And to make sure they didn't, he had hidden it in the bottom of Dybris's barrel of belongings. They'd never think of looking there, the big brutes.

Oh, the thrill of freedom as Garth hitched up his robe to wade across the fast-moving Fowaven. After reaching the opposite shore, he climbed the hillside into the trees and marched as quietly as he could through the dense forest. When he made it to the road, he slunk along, on the lookout for any strangers, until a distinctive fragrance halted him in his tracks. *Mmm.* Someone was roasting meat nearby.

He turned in a slow circle, trying to determine which direction the smell came from. His stomach hurt something awful, and he craved some of that meat. But *this* time he wouldn't get scared away before completing the job.

He shook his head at the memory. There had been nothing to fear. Just two tall men dragging a stone through the woods. And he had just been on the verge of finding the meat and gigging a large, juicy hunk ... *Better not think about food till I get some.*

What was it about that stone? He sure wanted to peek at it again. No men around, mind. Even through the bush where he and Merlin had hidden, he'd seen its dark surface glimmer as if silver was embedded in the rock. That was, of course, before those blue flames shot up from its surface. Now *that* was strange.

Another breath of the succulent aroma drove thoughts of the stone from his mind. Ah, the best smellin' tuck in the world. Great hunks of tasty meat roasting and dripping with fat!

He sucked in four more big whiffs and then hid himself behind a tree. Practicing stealth, Garth crept through the forest glade toward the delectable smell. Whenever a twig cracked, he crouched and froze for a bit. Finally arriving at the source of the aroma, he spied the spitted meat roasting over three fires. Sneaking behind a humungous twisted oak, he peeked around the trunk until he saw a woman in a green shawl and brown bonnet plucking a chicken.

She turned her head with a wary eye toward the tree.

Garth yanked his head back just in time.

Oh, if she'd just go away. One hunk of meat — just one! He sniffed the air and could hardly stop himself from running out to grab what he could. He closed his eyes and breathed in large whiffs of meat, his mouth watering. *Come on, woman, leave!*

Beyond the fires, a girl called loudly.

The woman tending the meat set her chicken down and shouted back, "She has, has she? Give me a bit o' time! Can't run in me old age." She walked off in the other direction.

Garth snuck over to the nearest fire and tried to pull off a chunk of beef, but he found the meat too hot to touch with his bare hands. He should have brought a knife. Lacking one, he went to one of the poor, lonely chickens, and the largest leg practically fell off in his hand. *There's a beauty.* Neither the chicken nor Garth would be lonely now. Oh, it felt as if he were floating in heaven!

Sneaking back to the twisted tree, he stopped at a large root and turned around just in time to see the woman striding back.

In his panic, Garth tripped and dropped the chicken leg as he fled to the other side of the tree. He froze a moment before hazarding a look.

The green-shawled woman stepped up to the fires, and seeing the roasted leg missing, she screwed up her face and looked around.

Garth hit his knuckles together until they hurt. *Oh, why did I drop it?* Just like when he let that big sea bass slip out of the net and his father yelled at him.

His mouth watered again, yet all he could do was take nibbles of the unsatisfying smoke. *Oh, please, woman, go away again! Jus' for a while, please?*

Another shout reached his ears. The green-shawled woman stood and stamped her foot. "Broke wha'? Oh, the love o' fire peat! How many times must I bandage that grandson o' mine?" She glanced back at the woods, blinked, nodded, then off she went.

Garth waited twenty heartbeats and then ducked around the tree to scoop up the dropped chicken leg.

But it wasn't there.

It just had to be. He searched all the grass in the immediate area.

Not taking chances, he ran over to the tripod again and sloughed off another juicy leg. He started to run while biting off a chunk — and smacked into someone.

Garth fell down on his backside.

"Hello, hello. And who might you be?" the man said in a deep, rich voice.

Bare feet were planted before Garth, dark and calloused with the dirt of many travels. Long toes sank into the soil like thirsty oak roots, ending with jagged nails. Above the feet a pair of stained woolen breeches rose up until hidden by a tattered sea-green tunic tied with a braided leather belt.

The man leaned over with a piercing stare, and from his chin hung a long black beard streaked with gray and white. At his neck rested a silver torc in the shape of a snake, with blue stones for eyes. His hand gripped a large walking staff carved with images of unknown beasts. At the top sat a small white stone in a silver setting.

Garth flinched when he spotted a slightly curved brass blade tucked into the man's belt. Dried blood stained the tip.

Garth was struck with the feeling he'd seen this man before, but where?

"Do you have a voice, boy? I asked your name."

"Sir, I'm ... I'm named ... Garthwys mab Gorgyr."

"Are you from Bosventor? Your accent is slightly wrong for these parts."

"No, sir! I come from Porthloc."

"I see. And what is this meat in your hand? From the looks of it, you are, perhaps, some sort of cook-in-training for the local abbey?"

"Oh no, sir. I can cook fish an' oysters ... but not chicken. I was just ... borrowin' this." Heat rose to Garth's cheeks.

The tall man bent his long legs and sat down next to Garth. In his left hand he held a chicken leg ... the one Garth had dropped, apparently.

Another man, whom Garth hadn't noticed at first, stepped back and busied himself studying the flowers on a nearby bush. This man was much younger than the first and wore a red-and-amber cloak that didn't quite hide his copper torc.

The older man beside him spoke. "So now, look at you ... You are not quite skin and bones, but you are hungry, yes? May I get more meat for you? Perhaps the whole chicken?"

"Yes, sir. I mean, no, sir ... if'n I can just have this one piece, I'll be right glad." Garth held up his chicken leg. "May I, sir?"

"Not yet." The man reached down for a strange stick hanging off his belt, unclasped it, and held it up.

Tied to the end were many strings of small seashells. Down the length of its handle had been cut a collection of lines. They almost looked to Garth like letters, but he couldn't make them out. They certainly weren't Latin.

"What are those lines, sir? On your stick, I mean? I've never seen words like those afore now."

"You ask a lot of questions, don't you, boy? They are *Ogham*, an ancient writing. Yes, yes."

The man waved the musically clinking shell wand over the chicken leg in many circles as he uttered some words in a strange tongue. While he did this, one of his sleeves slipped back on his arm, revealing that it was covered in blue lines of scarred tattoos.

That's funny, Garth thought. *Why's he have those marks on his arm? Is he a Pict?*

"There, there, all ready for you to eat. And if you want more, you are welcome to it."

Garth was amazed. Who was this man to be so generous? Much nicer than those stingy monks! And the chicken smelled so good. "Thank you, sir!" He took a big bite, chewed, and swallowed.

"Oh, the pleasure is all mine."

Garth reached out to touch the shells hanging from the wand.

But as fast as a shark to bloody bait, the man's hand clamped onto Garth's wrist. "Very interesting, yes? But do not touch, I say, do not touch."

Garth's breath caught in his throat.

The man let go, and Garth's wrist hurt. "May I ask you, sir — beggin' yer pardon — where did you get those seashells on yer what's-it stick?"

"Another question, I see. I found them over in the land of the Eirish. I have just come back from there after many long years."

Come to think of it, the man himself had a bit of Eirish accent. "You came over the sea?" Garth said. "You mean you sailed?"

"Yes, yes. How else would I get here? I have sailed all over. Across the southern sea to Gaul and Brythanvy. I have even been among the Kallicians. Do you like sailing?"

"Oh yes, sir!"

"Maybe we could go sailing sometime. Would you like that?"

Garth was nearly speechless. "Do you mean that, sir?"

"Surely, surely."

"That'd be just wonderful! Do you mind me askin', sir, what yer name is?"

"Oh, yes. Sorry to have forgotten those pleasantries. I am given the name of Mórganthu, and this is my son, Anviv."

Garth looked to Anviv, who was breaking off all the heads of the flowers and dropping them to the ground in an absentminded way.

Mórganthu coughed. "I am about to address the order of our brotherhood. Would you like to hear what I have to say? I have been waiting all my life to share such as this, and the stars will be in a highly propitious alignment tonight."

Taking another bite from his chicken leg, Garth suddenly remembered the silvery-dark stone, and realized why the two men were familiar. Would he get to see the stone again if he followed Mórganthu? These were strange goings-on, and if Garth stuck around long enough to eat his chicken leg, maybe he could get another. Maybe even a third.

He followed Mórganthu through a thick stand of pines stepped into a clearing, and realized he'd come to the old circle of stones Merlin had told him about. Stretching over a hundred feet from one end of the field to the other, the circle was made up of twenty-eight majestic rocks, each evenly spaced at twelve-foot intervals. The stones stood between ten and fifteen feet tall, and Garth felt very small next to them. The builders had cut smooth the side facing the center, while the outer faces had been left rough. Lichen covered their north faces, and rain, wind, and sun had weathered them for too many generations to count.

Inside the circle of stones sat what appeared to be more than one hundred men. Each one had blue scars on his arms like Mórganthu, and some had the marks on their faces.

"Sir," Garth asked, "are you a druid? Is this one o' yer gatherins?"

Mórganthu smiled. "Yes, yes, I am. And not since the bloody swords of the Romans drove us from the island of Inis Môn has our order of druidow met in such numbers."

Garth caught his breath as every one of the assembled men turned and saw him standing next to Mórganthu. Their stares made Garth want to hide behind his companion, especially when the nearest man's hand went to his blade.

"I have brought a guest, as you can see," Mórganthu announced. "And I declare him, by my right as the arch druid, my guest to witness our proceedings."

The men began to grumble.

"Do not gainsay me. By his actions I have deemed the lad worthy and not one who is persuaded against us. For shall not all witness the great change that will come upon Britain? Perhaps he will be an important part of that change." Mórganthu placed his right hand on Garth's head and held his staff up for all to see.

The druidow appeared to relax, though many still eyed Garth suspiciously.

He hid himself just outside the circle next to one of the stones as Mórganthu and his son walked down an aisle toward the center. As they passed, the crowd began to murmur.

"What has he brought?"

"The tarp ..."

"There is power ..."

"Why secret?"

Mórganthu stepped to the center of the circle. He stood next to a four-foot-wide patchwork leather tarp, which covered a circle of seven long wooden stakes driven into the ground, creating a small tent.

Mórganthu motioned for silence and handed his staff and chicken leg to Anviv.

Garth took a bite of his chicken leg but wished he had both.

"Brothers of our order! Blessed druidow, knowledgeable filidow, and greatly esteemed brihemow! You have been called here ... Yes, you have been called here to witness the rebirth and restoration of our order."

He paused.

The men shouted their acclamation. Staffs were raised all around, druid sticks shook, and small bells rang.

"What can give us back our power?" a tall man in red bellowed from the right.

Mórganthu pointed his finger at the man. "Do you think the gods weak? I tell you they have revealed a power to me! It is here in our possession."

He walked slowly southeastward and began a circuit around the low tarp covering.

"Revealed? How?" a balding man with a stout crutch shouted from the left.

The sun broke from the damp clouds and shone upon Mórganthu.

"Tell us. Why believe you?" another demanded.

"Believe ... believe," Mórganthu said as he turned to him. "This was revealed to me in a dream." Circling left-wise around the small tent, he retrieved his staff, and its white gem dazzled Garth's eyes. "A blessed dream."

"What did the gods say?" a short man in a pointed fur hat questioned from the right. Other voices seconded.

"Time. In due time. First, know that I have been chosen to reveal what has lain hidden for my entire lifetime." He untied the ropes so that the leather tarp quivered in the breeze.

The gathering became silent.

Mórganthu grasped the covering and pulled it away with a flourish.

"Behold!"

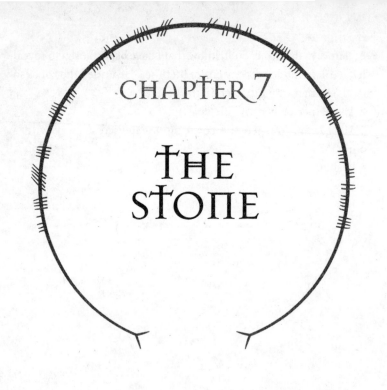

CHAPTER 7

THE STONE

A fly buzzed in Merlin's left ear, and he swatted the insect away. He shook his head and gradually realized he was sitting up. Birds called, and a light wind swept through his hair.

Opening his eyes, he found he could still see clearly, and his back didn't hurt.

He sat at the edge of a lake with lush grasses growing on the slanted shores. A dark line of trees swayed gently at the opposite bank, and beyond them stretched a ridge of hills. In the distance to his right rose a mountain covered in brown rocks and boulders. No, this was *their* mountain. The fortress stood on a flattened portion of the hill on the right side, but the cone of the mountain rose farther up on the left. His village lay on the other side of the mountain, and he —

The previous vision flooded back, and Merlin lurched to his feet. His mother! Heart pounding, he turned to his father, but Owain was gone. Only faint impressions in the mud remained as proof that his father had lain beside him on the bank.

A cry went up from the lake.

Two boats drifted near each other with a long, thin timber stretched from one to the other, the ends held by a man inside each boat. Between the boats, the timber hung over the water, and two strong saplings had been sinewed perpendicularly to it, left to drag in the water. Other men, four per boat, held oars while they looked intently into the water between the vessels. In the back of the boat on the left, one man stood, and he too peered into the water.

A man's gray hair broke the surface with a loud splash, and he sucked in mouthfuls of air. A chorus of shouts greeted him as he sputtered, sucked in more air, and was pulled into the boat on the right side.

The man who was standing, apparently their leader, flicked some lakeweed at him. "Why so long? A fool thing, Gavar, keepin' us scared like you'd been eaten."

"I was lookin' fer ... poor Gwevian," Gavar said, "but it was'na her body down there ... rather a great rock. Oddlike."

Before he could continue, the crew gave sighs of relief and catcalls.

But Gavar shook his head. "I'm goin' down again to get it. It's a different kind o' stone, and I plan to get it to shore fer a look."

One of the crew jeered. "Got a rock, you say? We're supposed to be after Gwevian. How'n a mollusk do you think we've time for nonsense? What would poor Owain say to yer foolishness?"

"Hey," another called, "maybe we should crack the rock on yer head, you lugger."

Old Gavar shook his head, spraying water in all directions. "No breaking it ... You can have a peek, sure, but nothin' more!"

The leader raised his hands. "Stop yer fightin'! We've work to do. The stone's yers, Gavar. But no time now. We're supposed to be dredgin' for An Gof's missus."

"No, I'm gettin' it now." And he dove into the water again, despite the protests of the men.

Soon his head appeared above the water — close to the shore where Merlin sat. Gavar stood up with a groan, and in his arms he cradled a large stone. "This … be … it."

"That be too big fer you to hold, Gavar!"

"How'd you pick that up?"

"Must be lighter than it looks."

Merlin's eyes opened wide as he beheld the stone.

It was about two feet broad and half that in thickness. Despite the algae and weed stuck to it, the mottled and craggy surface was unlike any stone Merlin had ever heard of or seen. Though rocklike, its metallic wetness shone with the reflected light of the dying day.

Something about it made Merlin shudder.

From deep within the stone, a faint blue light shone and then faded away.

Gavar carried the stone toward the shore with his wiry arms, and as he lifted it out of the water, his face grew red and his breath came in gasps. At one point he slumped down, but with a grunt he hefted the stone higher and made a final push for shore.

Finally, he threw the boulder just beyond the water's edge and collapsed next to it, crying out and clawing at his chest. His body stiffened, jerked, and his face went white. Coughing and choking, he reached out his hand, caressed the stone, and fell still.

The men in the boats blinked. Some dropped their oars; most turned pale. All spoke in whispers.

"What's happened?"

"Unnatural."

The leader directed the boats forward, and he and three others stepped ashore. By the time they got to Gavar, the man had slipped a little into the water, so they pulled him up onshore. One of the men knelt beside him and placed a hand on Gavar's chest.

"His stone did kill him," he said. "His heart's not boppin' anymore."

"What'll Owain say?" another asked.

The third man stepped back from the water. "This lake is bewitched!"

The leader, silent during this spectacle, now spoke. "Mum, all o' you. The thing was jus' too heavy fer his old drummer, so let's not be tellin' fancy tales. Remember his age an' how grand an effort it was."

Furtive glances answered him.

The leader spoke again, this time louder. "So now ... let's finish the dredgin' job we promised Owain. An' fer you who think different, know fer sure there's nothin' to fear as long as you stay in the boats, hear? Not more'n two parts to search, an' we can get away. We'll build a cairn for Gavar in the mornin'. I'll take his place at the oar."

The men climbed warily back into the boats, back-oared, and turned. They dredged the rest of the lake grudging and murmuring.

Merlin tried to take note of the men in the two boats and realized that every last one of them had died in the fourteen years since his mother had drowned. Not even one survived to testify about the events Merlin now witnessed.

Merlin knelt down near the stone and examined poor Gavar's face.

The head was cocked and the eyes rolled back. His arm still extended, and the lifeless, muddy fingers still touched the stone.

Darkness rolled across the lake even as a mist rose, sending a paralyzing chill deep into Merlin's bones.

Gavar's face turned green. His cheeks sank, and worms poured from his nose and eyes above his frozen smile.

Merlin turned away and retched.

―✝―

Garth stepped out to get a look as Mórganthu threw the tarp aside. There, in the center, lay the stone Garth had seen in the woods, nearly as dark as the night sky. Almost three feet long and half that high, its deeply pocked surface had an odd silvery sheen, neither stone nor metal.

Everyone whispered as Mórganthu tossed away the tent stakes.

Garth closed one eye and studied the stone. It wasn't huge, yet as he thought back over his short life, no boulder, ore, or rock that he'd ever seen looked like this. *Sure is pretty, though.*

An old man stood up on Garth's right and hobbled toward the stone, leaning on his staff. He wore a drab tunic, greasy breeches, and a shabby traveling cloak. Around his neck rested a torc of twisted bronze. The two ends of the torc had been hammered into the shape of large oak leaves and inlaid with amber.

When he finally reached the center of the circle, he pushed the white hair away from his eyes, wheezed, and spoke. "We've waited days for you ... to reveal this to us, and what is it? Just a — "

Mórganthu raised his hand. "A stone, yes, Trothek, but a stone with power to restore our order."

A man on the other side of the circle stepped forward. "What power?" He had a northern accent and wore a simple belted plaid.

Mórganthu answered, "*Power?* Why the power of this Stone can — "

"Fill a hole?" the kilted man interrupted. Laughter roared from those gathered.

"Let Mórganthu speak," Trothek called. Turning to Mórganthu, he touched the back of his hand to his forehead in respect. "Tell us ... of your dream."

Mórganthu held up his hands and motioned them to silence. "Last winter, during the twilight of the dark solstice, I dreamt!"

He began walking around the Stone.

"In my dream I beheld mighty Belornos surrounded by the fires of the blessed underworld. Without words, he bade me rise from my pallet and approach him upon a craggy path between two blazing pits. The heat burned my rags to ashes, and so I fell at his feet, though unscathed, with nothing on my back."

Mórganthu knelt before Trothek, acting it out.

"And there I found that he had dressed me in robes of argent and azure. With his mighty arm he bid me rise and pointed to the very Stone you see before you."

Mórganthu stood and scanned his audience as they pondered his words. "Then he prophesied that through this Druid Stone we will take back our riches ... and our reign over all the Britons!"

The men cheered, and Garth let out a cry as well.

"Then Belornos waved his hand, and I envisioned the location of the Stone, along with my task to fulfill the commands. I found it just as Belornos had foretold, a few days ago at the lapping edge of Lake Dosmurtanlin, north of the mountain."

Mórganthu paced in front of them.

"So now the druidow can rise up to take back the power we held from of old. And it begins in *this* village of Bosventor. Here we will draw the people back to the old ways, and our power will spread. The prophecy says the sacred groves on Inis Môn will be regrown, and within fourteen years we will again rule all of the Britons. From the fens in the east to my western land of Lyhonesse, we will be revered, and from the northern island brochs down to the southern sea, we will reign."

Everyone started talking at once, and a few arguments broke out.

A broad-shouldered druid in a gray, woolen robe stepped forward and scoffed. "Hah! How can a rock do all that? A stone cannot push this Christus back."

Many voices murmured agreement.

"Be ... quiet," Trothek said in a wheezy rasp.

The broad-shouldered druid faced Mórganthu and crossed his massive arms. "I will not be quiet! You've brought us across land and sea to show us a rock? Pah. We can perform all our rituals with the old central stone. Where is it?"

Mórganthu stared darkly at the man. "I have thrown it in the eastern wood. If you like, remove the new and put back the old."

The druid examined the new Stone, clearly suspecting some trap.

Mórganthu arched an eyebrow. "You are strong. Throw the new Stone away. If you dare."

"I will." He strode forward, and with his scar-tattooed arms, he seized one end of the dark Stone. "Curse you and your stupid Stone."

He pushed it up, planted a hand on the other side . . . and howled as a blue fire simmered from the surface of the Stone.

The Stone fell back into place with a thud.

He held up his hands, and the palms were red, possibly blistered, but Garth couldn't tell at his distance.

"Water! Water on 'em," the man yelled.

Trothek fumbled for a water skin at his belt and poured the liquid onto the man's hands. They were shaking so badly that most of the water fell to the ground, useless. So Trothek steadied them with his free hand, and as he touched the man's fingers, he exclaimed, "Your hands are cold. How is it they're . . . burned?"

Others brought water as well, and the man bit his lip until a red line of blood poured down his chin.

"Who now dares move the Stone?" Mórganthu shouted. "Who dares question its power? Let him step forward."

No one stirred.

Garth studied the rock. What secrets did it hide? Soon he couldn't look away, nor did he *want* to. As he gazed, a new and delightful feeling welled up within him. A vision filled his eyes — of himself, older and stronger, dancing in celebration with thousands of revelers before Mórganthu, who sat on a golden throne. Tables and tables of smoked and roasted meats lay piled up on all sides, and Garth ate until his stomach was near to bursting.

Glory!

The pain in his stomach completely eased at last.

He longed to bow down and worship the Stone.

In his glee, Garth forgot to breathe, and dizziness made him lurch. He grabbed the side of the standing stone beside him and closed his eyes. The ache in his stomach returned, and he realized he was neglecting Mórganthu's speech.

". . . and so, as instructed by our great god Belornos," Mórganthu continued, "we will celebrate Bel's High Day of Fire in less than two weeks. For with fire is life and death, protection and power. Then our complete authority on the moor will be sealed as we make a sacrifice in the old way."

Whispers of discontent rippled through the crowd. Garth didn't understand what they grumbled about, but many of the druidow seemed to have a complaint against these last words.

Mórganthu strutted around the Stone, ignoring them. "On Beltayne night we will see who pleases Belornos to be his servant in the underworld."

Trothek limped forward and faced Mórganthu. "S-stop! I have supported you ... my arch druid, but now ... you go too far. Would you strip away all our ... laws of the last two hundred years?"

"What? What is this?" Mórganthu asked, his neck snaking around to peer at Trothek.

"I said ... stop." Trothek pointed his staff at Mórganthu, but his speech grew even more breathless. "Our law no longer allows ... the old way of sacrificing ... and ... we will not ... do it."

"You question the power of the Stone?"

Trothek glanced at the powerful rock, a blue fire emanating from inside. "Not the Stone ... rather your authority, your power ... to command such a rite." He spoke louder. "You lead the ... druidow. But we filidow will not sacrifice ... as of old." Now he coughed violently, and a younger druid with a braided blond beard stood and supported him.

Mórganthu bent his head near Trothek's and squinted at him. "Do not oppose me, I say." Mórganthu's voice sizzled. "Arch fili though you be, I will throw you out!"

Trothek cleared his throat and looked Mórganthu in the eyes with a steady gaze. "Only by lawful vote ... of the six brihemow judges ... could you ... do such."

"Yes, yes. Do not insult me. I know our laws," Mórganthu said. "But you have lost your head, for your friend the arch brihem died last week at the chief gorseth of Boscawen and is not present."

Trothek closed his mouth.

"I was *with him* when he died," Mórganthu said. "Go ahead — try to oppose me!"

Trothek started to speak, but just a wheeze escaped.

The druid with the blond beard spoke up. "Shall I call the filidow to council?"

Trothek nodded. "Yes ... young Caygek ... do so."

Caygek stood as tall as he could, still a head shorter than Mórganthu, and lifted his voice. "Filidow and all who would join. Hear me. The arch fili has called a council to weigh the matters before us. Convene in the pines on the eastern side of the circle!"

The news spread like fire, but hardly any from the crowd walked past Garth to join the council.

As Trothek began to limp off, Mórganthu bared his teeth and grabbed the old man's arm.

With great difficulty Trothek ripped free and limped toward Garth. As he passed, Garth noted a large black mole on the man's cheek, just above his beard.

Mórganthu took a few deep breaths and raised his voice. "Brothers, we shall ignore this filidow foolishness, for now is our time to worship this Stone that has been given to us for our power and freedom!"

The druidow each got on their knees and held out their hands to the Stone. A chant arose in a foreign tongue, and the men fanned their arms up and down as the song floated on. A drum beat in time to the swaying.

At first Garth saw nothing different about the Stone. But he felt his head sway with the slow rhythm of the hands. His fingers twitched to the beating of the drum. He tried to look away from the Stone to glance at Mórganthu but couldn't.

The Stone grew larger in his vision until every detail of it gleamed. He wished to touch it, and he almost let go of the chicken leg as he lifted his hands in hopes of feeling such a delightful rock. When he found it too far away, he wanted to run to it.

The Stone emanated power.

It pulsed with the people.

Vibrated with their voices.

His heart beat to its rhythm.

Strength coursed in his blood.

He wanted to serve the Stone.

To belong to these people.

Wasn't that odd? He'd never seen anything so beautiful.

A hand clamped over Garth's eyes and pulled him backward. A man's voice echoed as if from a cave, "Don't look at the Stone ... *Stone*. You must leave this place. Bad things are planned here ... *here*."

Garth pulled the hand away and blinked. He felt dizzy. The man had a blond beard, and Garth realized it was Caygek. Behind him stood Trothek.

Caygek's brows knotted and his lips quivered.

Something dangled from Garth's hand ... a chicken leg? He became aware of the strange people around him, and a great fear clutched at his heart.

Garth slowly moved away from the circle, then taking a bite of chicken, he bolted through the woods, back the way he had come.

When Merlin next opened his eyes, everything was blurry again. The straw of his bed prickled his burning back, and he felt a wet rag hanging across his forehead. As his mind cleared, the familiar sounds of the smithy filled his ears.

He moaned, and his father stepped over from the anvil to feel his forehead. "Hopefully your fever's gone for good."

Merlin shook his head as his mind reeled with the things he had seen: his mother's death and the discovery of the strange stone in the lake — the very stone Mórganthu and Anviv carried in the woods days ago. Were they visions or delirium? His throat felt as if wool had been stuffed down it, and he drank some water. "What hour is it?"

"You've been asleep for nearly a day. I found you on the floor yesterday afternoon, and you've had me worried ever since."

"I'm feeling a bit better," he said, and it was true.

His father slicked the hair away from Merlin's eyes and went back to stoke the forge. Moments later someone rapped at the open door, a large shadow framed by the morning sun.

Merlin hoped it wasn't Mórganthu.

"Owain, my good, good friend!" the man's voice boomed.

Merlin's father set his poker down. "Come in, Kiff."

Kifferow stepped into the smoky room. "Heard Merlin was whipped. The news is everywhere."

"Just what I wanted to hear." Owain sighed.

Kifferow went straight to the mead bucket, just as he always did, glugged some, and belched. "D'I interrupt sumtin'?"

"Just your drinking, eh?"

Kifferow took another swig. "First drop today."

Merlin's father walked over, yanked the pail from the big man, and whacked him in his bulging belly. "And the last from my bucket."

"I'm not fat ... Merlin, am I fat?" Kifferow stretched taller but not any thinner.

Merlin laughed. He remembered the last time he'd shaken Kifferow's hands. Besides smelling of sawdust, the man's fingers had been as thick as oat bannocks and his hands slippery with sweat, the right hand more calloused than the other. But Kiff's round silhouette told all. "Let's just say you swallowed the bucket too."

Kifferow burped again. "Ahh, you can't see me through them scratches."

"My eyes see better'n a drunkard's, Kiff. And well enough to know you're the biggest blur in Bosventor."

Why did Kifferow and so many others act as if Merlin couldn't see at all? Sure, everything looked like colored smudges and shadows, but he could get around. Take care of himself. Even —

"Hey, Kiff," his father said, "did you hear Merlin killed a wolf two nights ago?"

"A wolf? Really? Sure it wasn't Muscarvel dressed up in a rug? Yesterday I heard he crept near the fortress and threatened 'em with a rotten eel."

"Yes, Kiff, a wolf. Right here in the smithy. Broke through that window."

"Musta wanted a drop o' your good mead, then."

Merlin's father pulled some iron from the forge and hammered it into shape on the anvil. "Well, then, take a lesson, Kiff, since the wolf swallowed Merlin's blade for it."

Kifferow picked up a heavy pouch and shook it. Recently forged nails clinked inside. "Enough here to begin fixin' the roof for them monks. Got any more braces?"

Owain pulled a set of iron braces from a barrel and handed them over. "Five. But I've got to work on the wagon. You need more?"

Kifferow grunted as he tested the strength of one of the braces. "I'll need three more by tomorrow. Double the nails too. Hey, you got plenty o' coal now, I hear, thanks to that wagon thief."

Merlin took his boot and threw it at Kifferow. "He's my friend, Kiff." The room spun, and pain exploded through Merlin's head, making him regret his outburst.

His father spoke up. "Leave him alone, Kiff. Just take your stuff and go, all right?"

Kifferow dragged his feet toward the door. "I'll stop by tomorrow. Keep yer mead bucket full, Owain." And with a somber whistle, he walked out.

Owain set his hammer down and walked over to Merlin.

"By the way, I've got something for you." He placed a leather-wrapped bundle in Merlin's hands. The seams had been stitched tightly, and the parcel had a long carrying strap. At one end Merlin's fingers found a buckle, clasped with a wooden peg.

"Where'd this come from? What is it?" he asked.

"You were sleeping when a certain someone dropped it off." He lightly punched Merlin's arm with the side of his fist.

Merlin winced and hoped his father didn't notice.

"I almost sent her away before I understood. She said you can keep it. Anyway, there it is. And now I gotta get to work on that axle."

Merlin sat in silence as his father pressed the bellows, pumping the coals into a hot orange glow. Could it have been Natalenya? After a moment Merlin found the wooden peg, loosened the buckle, and reached his hand inside the bundle. It was her practice harp.

He drew out the beautiful instrument and admired its workmanship. His fingers explored every nook and cranny, and when he touched the strings, they fairly sang on their own.

A rush of gladness swept over Merlin. Suddenly he looked forward to the hours of recovery stretching before him. He would learn to play.

Thank you, Natalenya.

CHAPTER 8

ΠΟΤΗΙΠG ΤΟ HOLD OΠ ΤΟ

I t's been a week and a half since the trial, and you say Garth is *still* sulking?" Prontwon set his bone-handled quill down on the table and slid some smooth rocks around to hold the parchment flat. "How can we help him?"

Dybris sat on a bench nearby. "I don't know. Garth hardly speaks to me."

"Has he told you anything more about the crash? What scared him? Why'd he drive the horses so fast?"

"He's refused to say, and I didn't want to bother Merlin until he's on his feet again."

"You saw him this morning, yes? How does his back fare?"

"It's healing well now. There's been no more sign of infection after that first scare. Ten days of rest has done him a lot of good."

Prontwon shook his ink pot and removed the stopper. "Good.

91

I shall speak with him soon. As for Garth, well ... I have my own suspicions as to what happened with him."

"Anything you can share?" The whole matter had puzzled Dybris. The tales he'd heard over the last month gave him great pause. When Prontwon had asked him to join the abbey, Dybris hadn't expected the area to be so wild and strange. Whatever had appeared in the woods, it had caused the boy to drive the magister's wagon like a crazed fiend.

"The time may come for telling, but not yet." Dipping his quill in the ink pot, Prontwon began copying a portion of Scripture.

"You don't think it has anything to do with the legends about Lake Dosmurtanlin?"

"No ... Garth and Merlin were up by the old stone circle when the boy got scared, not down by the lake. How many years has our good God given you, Dybris?"

"Thirty winters. Why?"

"Well, you seem too mature to be listening to Bosventor's old wives' tales. I never guessed you had such a fanciful imagination."

"You don't believe them? Isn't it true about all of the drownings? What about Merlin's mother?" Dybris studied Prontwon's expression carefully. Did he imagine it, or did a flicker of tension touch Prontwon's eyes?

"People drown all the time. That was an unfortunate accident."

"But I'm told their bodies were never found." Dybris paused, then decided he might as well ask what had been bothering him. "Are you sure there's not some creature in the lake?" He leaned over, setting his elbows on the table.

"Ach, now look. You've made my quill slip."

"Sorry, Abbot." But the table hadn't moved.

Prontwon fetched some light-brown pigment from a shelf and covered over the mistake with a brush. "People drown in the marsh too, but no one says that some dark creature lives *there*. And crazy Muscarvel doesn't count."

Dybris glanced at Prontwon. "Who's Muscarvel?"

"An old man who lives in the marsh in some God-hidden hut. Oh yes, I've seen him and his rusty sword, and he is definitely no spook." Prontwon sighed. "Anything else wrong with Garth?"

Dybris said nothing for a short time. A hundred more questions burned to be asked, but he swallowed them. "He's still not eating much even though he's no longer served oatmeal at every meal as punishment. Just plays with his dinner and doesn't ask for more."

Prontwon stopped copying and stared at Dybris. "That bad?"

Dybris nodded.

"If it is as you say, then the remedy is in his repentance."

"Yet the bagpipe ... Can we buy it back?"

Prontwon scratched his quill carefully across the page again. "It is impossible to know where the merchant went."

Dybris rubbed his temples and then covered his eyes. "I haven't told Garth yet that I found it hidden in my barrel — or that we sold it."

"For God's love, Dybris — "

"He still thinks it's there ... I didn't want to make matters worse. His nose twitches every time I go near the barrel."

Prontwon slapped the table. "But the boy needed to know. It was sold last week!"

Dybris sat in silence.

Prontwon bowed his head, and his lips moved in whispered prayer.

After some time, Dybris finally spoke. "I'm sorry, Abbot, for my delay. I'll go and tell him now." He rose to leave, but Prontwon put a hand on his arm.

"One other thought. Garth might need a break from the abbey. Get away for a while and come back with fresher thoughts."

"Who would take an orphan?"

"Troslam and Safrowana have a girl Garth's age, and the Lord has given them wide and loving hearts. Garth could even earn his keep by helping with the weaving. Shall I talk with them?"

Dybris nodded, his heart lifting somewhat. "A change would

certainly do him some good. But please pray while I let Garth know about the bagpipe. And forgive me, again, Abbot."

He ducked out the door of the round house they used as a scriptorium and walked along the path to the fields, dreading what he had to tell Garth. The sun had begun to sink, and soon the small abbey bell would ring, calling the brothers in for their evening meal.

There in the distance, Offyd worked near Garth, and beyond them Brother Neot instructed a group of other monks.

Offyd was breaking up the earth, and his wooden mattock sent up sprays of dirt, while Garth's hoe barely dented the soil.

"God's blessing, Offyd," Dybris called. "How is the planting today?"

"Fine ... if you count blows to the ground." He glanced at Garth. "Poor ... if you count the earth we've broken up."

Garth glared at Offyd but said nothing.

Dybris sat down on a hump of earth about ten yards from them and called out, "Garth, come sit with me a bit."

Garth dropped his hoe and approached Dybris, a downcast scowl on his face.

"Might as well give him the rest of the evening off," Offyd called.

"Peace," Dybris said, "this won't take long."

Garth sat, clamped his jaw, and squirmed his shoulders to keep Dybris's arm off.

Withdrawing his arm, Dybris selected a stalk of grass and began breaking it into tiny pieces. He didn't look at Garth. "I came to speak to you about your bagpipe."

"Do you have to sell it?"

Dybris closed his eyes for a moment. "You know why."

The boy picked up a clod of dirt and flung it far out into the field. "All I know is I hate you an' I hate Tregeagle. Get yer gold another way."

"From where?" Dybris asked. "This abbey isn't rich. If we have another bad harvest, we'll barely make it through the winter. I checked our stores in the cave just yesterday, and there's almost nothing left."

"You can't have me bagpipe!" Garth raised his fists and threatened to pound Dybris's shoulder.

Dybris covered each of Garth's fists with a hand and gently pushed them down. "It's already gone."

"G-gone? You f-found it?"

"Sold. A week ago. A traveling merchant bought it."

Garth's shoulders slumped, and his voice cracked. "Got nothin' now."

"I know it seems hard, but God can see you through."

"Me father's buried in the sea, and now his bagpipe's gone too. Got *nothin'*." He scrambled to his feet and stood with his back to Dybris.

Dybris rose as well. "I'm sorry."

"It was my only anchor! An' now I got nothin' to hold on to." Garth stuck his hand into a bag hanging from his belt and fumbled inside. "Almost nothin'," he mumbled.

"You still have your memories of your father. And when you're older, I'll help you buy another bagpipe."

Garth turned and yelled at him, "Not the same! ... Sellin' me as a galley slave would o' been better!"

"Garth — " Dybris began, but the sound of feet thumping in the distance interrupted him. They both turned. Dybris's stomach tightened. A great mob of men — maybe a hundred or more — marched up the hill from the river valley.

With a racing heart, Dybris stepped forward, looking for weapons, but spotted just a few knives and small hatchets hanging from their belts. Most of the men carried dried wood, as if they planned to make a bonfire somewhere.

If they weren't a war band, then who were they?

One man set the pace, and behind him seven men in green robes advanced in a circular formation. Each carried a short pole looped through the edge of a stitched leather tarp, which bore something large hanging in the middle.

The bearded leader of the group strode forward on long legs, his black and gray hair blowing in the wind. He wore a green linen robe that matched the others', yet with dark leather cuffs and a blue-lined hood. He carried an etched staff with a flashing gem on top.

The other monks gathered behind Dybris and Garth as the group marched closer. When the leader passed, he no more than glanced at most of the monks, yet when his gaze landed on Garth, it seemed to linger. Had Dybris imagined it, or had he seen a glint of recognition?

Dybris looked down in time to see the boy pull from his bag a small, shiny black crystal of tin ore — the kind they mined in the area, and then crushed and smelted. Garth held tightly to this, but his gaze brought Dybris's attention back to the strange men. Many of their knives were made of brass and curved slightly, the leader's the largest. *Sickle knives.* He examined the men closely. Their arms and legs had been scarred with blue tattoos. The word was on his tongue when he heard it murmured by the monks behind him.

"Druidow."

"Explains the smoke across the valley ..."

"Headed toward the village ..."

"So many ..."

"Jesu, help us ..."

Once the last straggler had passed and the road lay clear, Dybris took Garth's arm and walked with the other monks to the scriptorium as fast as he could without appearing panicked.

Bursting into the room, Dybris and the others related to Prontwon what they'd seen. The abbot listened to the report with a grave expression on his face, then dispatched a messenger to retrieve Migal and Loyt, who had been preparing the evening meal. Only when all twelve monks, along with Garth, had crowded into the room did Prontwon stand in their midst and address them.

"Hear me! What I have feared and, I am ashamed to say, tried to ignore for the past week has just been confirmed. The old stone circle on the other side of the valley has recently become the home of druidow once more, and from the count you have given, possibly their entire number in the land of the Britons."

No one moved or made a sound.

"From what you have said, they are headed to the village with some pagan intent. We must follow to know their plans. Brother Migal has brought us bread and a pitcher of water that we may not faint after our labors. However, considering what we may face, I suggest fasting for those who are able."

Some took bread while others refrained, but all refreshed themselves with the water.

"As the evening closes and we enter the presence of the sworn enemies of our God, let us pray our evening prayer of protection."

Dybris gave Garth a chunk of crusty bread as the brothers joined voices in song.

And then, with Garth lagging in the back, they set out for the village of Bosventor, following the path of the druidow.

As darkness descended on the smithy, Merlin lay on his straw bed practicing the harp. Over the past ten days, he'd learned to tune it and play a few songs, but his progress was slow. He'd rested under his father's orders, but now that the burning of his wounds had faded and his fever was but a memory, he yearned to be active again.

The door creaked open, but in the twilight Merlin couldn't see anyone. "Who's that?"

"Me." It was a small voice. "Your sister."

Just as he thought. "Bar the door behind you."

"Why?"

"Don't ask. Where's Tas? I've been expecting him." He reached for the mug of water next to his bed.

"I'll get it," Ganieda said.

She picked up the clay mug, but it slipped from her hands. The vessel shattered and the water spilled.

"I'll help." Merlin tried to find the pieces but touched his sister's trembling hands instead. "What's wrong?"

"Tas and Mammu left! They told me to stay with you. Let you sleep. But the fire's dying, and it got dark."

"Where'd they go?" He found the pitcher next to the broken mug and poured water into his mouth.

Ganieda climbed onto the pallet and sat beside him. "The miller brought a bag of barley after supper. And news. There's a problem down by the meeting house. The whole village is going to be there."

"The meeting house? Is someone to be judged?"

It was curious to have a meeting at night. Normally, the village elders met during the day inside the common house, which had been built next to the spring. The only time everyone showed up was to condemn a criminal to death — a rarity that had occurred only once in Merlin's lifetime. The magister, in consultation with the elders of the village, would make the pronouncement while sitting on what was known as the Rock of Judgment — really just a slab of natural granite that lay on the earth near the meeting house.

Ganieda began to cry. "I don't know. Tas wanted me to stay, and Mammu wanted me along — and they fought."

"How long ago?" He reached out and felt her soft hair.

She sniffed. "The sun was on the hearth when they left."

"Did they say for me to stay?" With his wounds nearly healed, he was looking for any excuse to be up and about.

"No ... they didn't say."

"Well, then, I'm going." Merlin found his stiff boots, pulled them on, and tied them. They felt good on his feet after so long.

"You can't leave," Ganieda said. "It's dark!"

"You think that matters to me?" *As long as there aren't any wolves along the path, that is.*

And just in case, he snatched up his dirk, slid the scabbard onto his belt, and tied it around his waist. Fear churned in his stomach like the tidewaters on the craggy Kernow coast.

"I mean me ... you can't leave *me*."

"Come along if you have to. Tas wanted you with me, and since I'm going, you come too … And you can help me get there faster." He stood up and found his staff next to the wall.

"You sure?"

"Stay close and don't wander off."

Outside, the last smear of the orange sun fell beneath the hill that stood between their land and the marsh. A chill wind blew as they set off down the path, Merlin tapping out ahead with his staff. He wrapped his cloak tighter, but could do little else as the gusts whistled through his hair and sent shivers down his back.

Ganieda hummed a slow tune he'd often heard Mônda sing. She slipped her small hand into his as they turned east onto the main road of the village and continued on toward the meeting house.

Merlin felt every sense crackle as they passed Allun's mill and entered a stretch of road flanked by heavy underbrush. Off to their right, he heard movements in the bushes.

A snarl.

Merlin kept walking, but his grip on his sister's hand tightened.

"Keep going," he whispered.

Deep growling now. Behind and in front.

Fear crawled up from the pit of his stomach and grabbed the inside of his throat. How many? Dogs or wolves? "Stay close," he said as he drew his dirk and whipped his staff around low to the ground.

"Don't hurt them!"

Her words barely registered as Merlin's mind flooded with memories of the attack seven years before. That time it had been the same: He and Ganieda had been alone on the path outside their house. Howling wolves had surrounded them. She'd been hardly two years old. Defenseless. He'd been eleven and had tried to save her by keeping the wolves back.

But they had attacked him — and she had never been touched. They knocked him to the ground and mauled him, scratching and biting his face. By the time his screams had reached his father, it was too late. His eyes had been ruined and his face marred forever.

"No, Merlin!" Ganieda pulled at his arm. "It's my wolf, Tellyk, and his friends. They want to see me."

Merlin snapped back to the present. For a moment he tried to comprehend his sister, then another snarl jerked his attention to the bushes. "Get behind me, Gana!"

CHAPTER 9

THE NIGHT OF DECISIONS

One of the wolves lunged, snarling, at Merlin's ankle. Panicked, Merlin jabbed his staff toward the sound and bashed the wolf on the side of the nose. With his other hand, he tried to stab it with his dirk, but the creature jumped back with a whimper.

Ganieda called out, "Go away ... Away, Tellyk!" She waved her hands toward the bushes. Swiftly the wolves slunk through trees and brambles, downhill and away from the village.

"Th-they're gone?" Merlin asked, still whipping his staff around.

"That's what I've been trying to tell you. They're my friends. Especially Tellyk."

He wished he could see her face to judge whether she was telling the truth. "When did you make friends with them? Why do they obey you?" Merlin took her hand again. This time it was his that trembled.

"A long time. I don't remember when."

As he struggled to grasp the implications of this revelation, Merlin noticed a smudge of light blazing farther down the road. "We'll talk about this later." He pointed at the light. "What's that?"

"A bonfire in the village pasture."

"Anything else? Do they have the gallows up?"

"I can't tell. There are lots of people ... shadows. The whole village must be gathered for the fire." Her voice turned petulant. "Why didn't Tas and Mammu want us to come?"

"Let's hurry." A blazing fire meant no wolves.

They approached the village green and entered through the main gate, which creaked in the wind. So why had everyone gathered? Merlin held Ganieda's hand as they walked toward the crowd. Soon he picked out amid the general noise a voice, strong and deep, speaking to the people. He'd heard that voice before.

"... to call you back to the old way. To call you as lost children back to the only way your ancestors knew — they who claimed this wooded land as their own and coaxed forth crops from the soil, who mined the streams for tin, who built your homes."

Merlin searched his memory, and a sickening feeling settled in his stomach.

"Your ancestors call you back to worship the old gods — the guides, the healers, those who bless your fields and cattle, who protect you from witchcraft and guard your children against the wailing *sidhe* ... the gods who are furious at your obstinacy."

Mórganthu!

"You have spit in their bright faces. They who have been faithful to you. Turn ... turn back!"

Brunyek, the oat farmer, shouted from the crowd. "Eaah! If they've been so faithful, why'd my two sheep get killed by wolves last week?"

"If *you* had been faithful, son of the ancient woods, then the god Kernunnos would have tamed the wolves and made them your friends."

Merlin held tighter to Ganieda's hand.

Mórganthu turned and held his arms out to someone in the crowd. "Olva, if you and your husband yet choose the druidic way, then the god Grannos will take your son into his arms and heal him."

The couple whispered to each other excitedly.

It bothered Merlin to hear this. How did Mórganthu know Olva's name and that her son was sick?

"And Brioc! I see the fear on your face with another year of uncertainty, debt, and too few lambs born. I proclaim that your crops will flourish and your flocks will thrive if you return and worship Crom Cruach and the great god Taranis again."

Brioc grunted from Merlin's right.

"And not least, Stenno." Mórganthu extended his hands to a young tin miner, his voice growing almost tender. "Your father would not have died and left you destitute if he had worshiped Belornos, protector of all who hew the earth."

Merlin fumed. Why didn't anyone speak out against this? These were lies. "Ganieda, are the monks here? Do you see them?"

She grasped his sleeve for balance and stood on her tiptoes. "Can't see over the people."

Mórganthu spoke louder. "All who hear my voice, come. Come and seek the druid way. Seek the secret knowledge, wisdom beyond your ken!"

"Where's Tas? ... Do you see him?" Merlin asked his sister.

"No. Just those near the bonfire. It's too dark everywhere else."

Mórganthu strode back toward the bonfire. "This! ... This is the source of wisdom!" With a flourish, he bent down.

"He threw a leather skin to the side," Ganieda said. "I can't see what's under it, though."

Merlin knew what was under the tarp but hoped he was mistaken. All the people around him stepped back, and someone's heel crunched on Merlin's toes. He backed up as well, then hefted Ganieda up so she was positioned above the crowd. "Tell me what else you see."

"A rock of some kind, black ... no, silver. Oh!"

A blue light appeared, and now even Merlin knew where the Stone lay.

The bonfire seemed to dim. Mórganthu stepped next to the Stone and raised his voice to a crescendo. "This Stone has been given by the god Belornos. He who loves it will be blessed, but he who is found unworthy of it will be destroyed."

All around Merlin, people dropped to their knees.

"What's happening?" he asked his sister.

"Men are bowing ... They're all druidow! They're mixed in with the people." She shivered as if with excitement, and Merlin set her down with a prayer.

The men raised their hands in homage — he assumed to the Stone. *Where are the monks?* Merlin wondered. *Where's Prontwon?*

Mórganthu spoke again. "Who will be the first among you to join us?" His voice was soothing and inviting.

The druidow rose to their feet as a lone voice spoke up. "I will be first."

"Good, good. Step forward. Who are you?" Mórganthu asked.

As the man stepped through the crowd to enter the circle, he spoke again. "I will be first, but not to worship your blasphemous Stone. I have come to speak truth."

Abbot Prontwon!

Prontwon stood before Mórganthu, his voice steady and his stout frame firm.

Mórganthu stepped back and studied the newcomer.

"Yes, I will be the first," Prontwon called out. "The first to stand against this trickster."

Mórganthu stepped forward again, but Prontwon continued. "I will show this Stone an idol and this man a liar."

"You ... you call the wrath of the gods upon you!" Mórganthu screeched.

Prontwon turned and faced him. "Your gods are demons from the pit of hell."

"Do not, I say, do not speak ill of the ruler of the blessed under-world, for Belornos will repay you."

"There is but one Ruler — the Son of God, Jesu the Messiah — about whom God has sent Holy Scripture into the uttermost parts of the earth by the power of His Spirit and the blood of His saints."

Merlin felt a cheer rise in his heart at Prontwon's boldness, but it died on his lips as the crowd remained silent.

"And this," Mórganthu shot back, "is a lying spirit who bewitches you all. Break the spell that chokes your life! Throw off the puny god of these little monks and their cross."

"The cross is for the forgiveness of our sins."

Flourishing his staff, Mórganthu pointed at Prontwon. "And do you know, O people, what this sin of your abbot is?"

Prontwon stepped back, paused a moment, then replied, "Go ahead. Tell them. It matters not."

"Hah. It does matter." Marching over, Mórganthu grabbed Prontwon's right arm and ripped the sleeve all the way to the shoulder.

"Tattoos!" Ganieda said. "Drawn on his arm. There's a snake with the horns of a goat. The symbols of the druidow."

Merlin held his breath. Had he heard right?

Mórganthu lifted his voice in victory. "It matters, I say. For the *sin* your abbot committed is that he, yes he, was a druid!"

The druidow snickered as the villagers fell silent.

"It is true," Prontwon said. "I was young. And foolish."

"Wrong! Wise beyond your years. My brother taught you, and you ate each word as if you were a starving bird."

"And in my hunger, I did not see clearly."

"Then how can you be trusted now?" Mórganthu jabbed the bot-tom of his staff down.

The abbot cried out, wrenched his foot free, and then limped backward. "Jesu opened my eyes, and I saw for the first time my need."

Mórganthu shouted so that it echoed off the rock walls of the village green. "A fool and the follower of a fool. Leave this Jesu!"

Prontwon turned to the people and implored them with raised hands. "Do not deny Jesu your Lord. What benefit did we ever receive from following these gods?"

"Benefit indeed," Mórganthu mocked. "All they have received from Jesu is slavery to the churchmen from Erin, slavery to their worthless writings, and slavery to the Roman army."

Prontwon lifted his head and stood as tall as he could. "The Word of God is priceless—"

Mórganthu's form forced him backward. "The writings of these monks are from the dead lands of the East, foreign and not to be trusted." His voice boomed from deep in his chest. "British ways for the Britons!... Away with the foreigners!"

All the druidow shouted with Mórganthu, stomping their feet and banging together anything that would make noise.

"Look, the old monk is shouting too, but I can't hear him." Ganieda laughed. "The villagers look funny covering their ears."

"British ways for Britons. Away with foreigners!"

Ganieda's voice rose higher. "That geezer of an abbot's climbing on top of the druid's rock. He's cupping his hands around his mouth."

"People, hear me—"

But Mórganthu struck the side of the Stone with his staff, and blue fire burst forth.

"The monk's legs are on fire!" Ganieda said. "You should see his face—all red, and his eyes are bulging."

Prontwon crumpled forward and fell off the Stone.

Merlin's heart hammered in his chest. Prontwon was on his knees, the blue light of the Stone dancing upon him. Brown-robed monks ran forward and put their hands under and onto the abbot, appearing to whisper prayers as the noise subsided.

Mórganthu declared to the people, "You see! You see for yourselves that the judgment of Belornos is upon him. He dared desecrate the Stone and is now struck down!"

Merlin could stand no more. "Stay here," he told Ganieda. He shoved his way through the crowd and broke into the center of the circle. The shadow of a tall man stood in front of the dying light of the bonfire and the weird blue flames of the Stone.

"Now, I ask once again," Mórganthu called. "Who will be the first to join us?"

A voice, young but firm, answered from the crowd. "I'll join." Someone short, dressed in a brown robe, stepped into the ring. "If you'll have me."

It was Garth.

"No!" Merlin yelled as he sprang forward and swung his staff at the dark figure of Mórganthu.

PART TWO

SHACKLE'S
POWER

Swift as the moon the white stag running,
Fleet as the owl the hunter hunting,
Sharp as the claw the swift spear striking,
Red as the sun the fresh life flowing,
Leaved in green, there all Britain dies.

CHAPTER 10

STRANGE MEETINGS

Merlin opened his eyes to see deep forest.

As his sight adjusted, he could clearly make out the details of his surroundings. He broke off an oak leaf and studied it in the low light that filtered through the trees.

Was it morning or evening? A vision or a dream?

Far off in the distance echoed the sound of someone sobbing.

He stood up from the grassy bower and scanned the trees in the direction of the cries but spied nothing.

A man's voice cackled from behind. "You'll never find 'im!"

Merlin whipped around, suddenly conscious that he had neither staff nor knife.

On a boulder inside the mouth of a cave sat a man of grotesque proportions. Nearly twice the size of Merlin, he had muscled arms that bulged in comparison to his scrawny legs. In one hand he held a large knotted club that could crush Merlin's head with one blow.

The man's shirt and bright red pants were torn and stained. One of his legs was shrunken, and its foot stretched and bent. His back curved so much that upon reaching his neck it had bowed toward the ground again. To compensate, his skinny neck craned upward so his ponderous head appeared to float in front of him.

"Search as you like. Crom says you'll not find 'im. Hahaha!"

His tongue licked at a few remaining stumps of teeth in his rotting gums, and his bulbous nose jutted forth between tiny black eyes. From this monstrosity of a head hung great knots of moldy yellow hair, long enough to pass his knees, and maggots and flies crawled in and out of the thick strands.

Merlin stepped back. "Find whom?"

"You don't know? Well 'ee's mine, an' I won't let 'im go."

Without moving his body, Crom snapped his neck forward so his mouth slavered within a few feet of Merlin, who cringed at the smell of decay. "I'll et 'im up one day. Maybe tonight. But before then, Crom Cruach thinks he'll et you!"

His teeth clicked forward, and Merlin ducked. The club rose and whizzed down.

Leaping to the side just in time, Merlin again heard sobs coming from the wood behind him. He darted through the pines toward the sound, and Crom limped after, smashing down trees with his club. Merlin soon found he'd entered a steep-sided canyon through which the crying echoed down from above.

Crom roared with laughter just behind him.

Onward Merlin ran. His gaze raked the rock walls, searching for a way out, but there was none. Instead, the ravine narrowed.

Crom limped on behind, whacking the cliff so that chunks of rock cascaded from above.

In desperation, Merlin broke off the sharp end of a dead tree limb and tucked it into his belt. Coming to a young oak, he leaped up and grabbed a branch overhead, bending the entire tree with all his strength. He clutched the branch with both hands and crouched behind a nearby pine.

Keep coming, brute.

Crom stepped closer, his sneaky black eyes darting back and forth.

One more step . . .

Crom sniffed and shuffled forward. Merlin let go of the branch. The tree whipped upward, clouting the giant's face, and Crom roared in anguish.

Merlin made a run for it, but an impossibly skinny foot jerked forward and tripped him. Before he could right himself, Crom picked him up by the scruff of his shirt and dangled him over his putrid mouth.

"You'll not see 'im again. Say good-bye, little crunchkin!"

Crom brought Merlin closer to his drooling lips.

Pulling the stick from his belt, Merlin jabbed it straight into Crom's eye. "Let me go, beast!"

The monster shrieked. He flung Merlin down the valley, fell to his knees, and pulled the stick out of his bleeding eye.

Merlin hit the ground hard, which knocked the air from his lungs. By the time he struggled to his feet, Crom had risen as well. With spit flying, the creature declared, "Won't just et you. Crom'll rip your skin off while you scream to the bloody heavens!"

There was no way past him.

Merlin ran in the opposite direction and soon came to a small trickle of a stream. At the end of the ravine stood a rocky hillside from which the water dribbled down. The sobbing sounds floated down from above.

Up Merlin clambered. When he neared the top, Merlin turned back to see Crom scaling the cliff faster than seemed possible. The monster's eye streamed red into his yellow hair, and he bellowed hideous threats. With a final burst of effort, Merlin pulled and kicked himself up the last few difficult feet until he could see over the ledge.

Not ten feet away sat a boy. His back was turned, but Merlin could tell he had red hair and wore a stained tunic and leather trousers. As the boy cried, he turned his head to the side, and Merlin saw blood and tears smeared across his face, all but obscuring the spray of freckles on his nose.

Was he Garth? Merlin studied the boy's face, with pouting lips and faintly upturned nose. He couldn't be sure, having never seen Garth properly. He called out, but the sobbing boy didn't seem to hear as he stared at a bloodied bundle of cloths in his lap.

Merlin scrambled over the ledge as a flash of light filled the sky. All at once, between him and the boy stood the man dressed in white, the angel from his first vision. He spoke, and his voice shook the air like a thousand thunders.

"STAND STRONG, MERLIN!"

Crom roared from behind, too close. Panic welled up in Merlin, and he wanted to run, but he kept his gaze on the angelic figure before him.

"I tol' you, little crunchkin," Crom said, his breath like rancid fire wafting over Merlin, "that the boy is mine."

As Merln turned to face the monster, a club thudded him on the head, and Crom pulled him back down the rocky slope.

✝

Merlin yelled as he twisted away from the grip on his legs. He kicked violently, but they were held too tightly. He struggled to sit up, finally opening his eyes.

A vague blur moved toward him, and someone grabbed his shoulders. "Easy, boy. You'll wake the High King himself with your bellowing."

Merlin drew in a great shuddering breath. "Tas? Where am I?"

"In bed. The sun rises, and I just started my work, no thanks to you."

Merlin touched his head; his right temple throbbed. "Crom hit me on the head ..."

"What?" The blur he knew as his father's face drew in closer. "Don't you remember last night? Mórganthu, it was." His father stepped away for a moment, then pulled up a chair.

"I recall walking with Gana ... Oh ... now I remember."

His father slammed his hand on the table next to Merlin's bed. "You caused a riot."

"Me? And Mórganthu did nothing?"

"You swung first, rabbler."

"Only after Prontwon was hurt."

"Allun and Troslam helped me pull you —"

"I can handle myself!" Merlin sat up, but his head pulsed, and he almost fell over.

"Can you now?" Owain said. "After Mórganthu wrenched your staff away, he walloped you like hot barstock on the anvil. The druidow wanted to rip you to rags. We took you out."

"What happened to ... to ..."

His father itched his beard. "To your *friend*? Mórganthu ended the meeting and announced he'll speak again at noon today. Garth marched out with them like a dwarf legionnaire."

"And Prontwon? How is he —"

Owain snorted. "Don't know. I was worried about you. Carried you home. That Garth, he's caused enough trouble!"

"You care too. Remember the bagpipe?"

"Stop risking your life."

Merlin leaned back against the rock wall of the smithy. "And you've never risked yours? You've hinted of your past. Tell me, Tas."

There was a long pause, then Owain cleared his throat. "I can't."

"Did you ever care about something enough to risk your life for it?"

His father drank from the pitcher and wiped his mouth against his sleeve. "Just for my family. Family is all that matters."

Merlin felt a tightness in his chest, but he pressed further. "And the villagers have no families? Tell *them* what you know about Mórganthu."

"You want me to preach like Prontwon? You're more of a fool than I thought."

Merlin couldn't hide his excitement. "You're respected, Tas. They'd listen —"

"Did that staff completely addle your brains?"

"You threw Mórganthu out—"

His father put a hand on Merlin's mouth. "Why'd you bring Gana to the bonfire and leave her?"

"I—"

"Mônda and I came home—and I lugging you. But Ganieda was gone. Know where I found her?"

Merlin shook his head.

"At that Stone. Some of the druidow were guarding it, but a lot of villagers hovered around. Some were touching it."

"Who?" Merlin was shocked.

"Grevin. Stenno. Priwith. And Olva brought her sick child. Two of Tregeagle's men were there. I had to drag your sister home." And then his father's tone turned to a whisper. "Did you sense it? The Stone's power?"

"You mean the flames?"

"I've never seen anything like it. The longer I looked at the Stone ... It's hard to describe. It stirred something deep within me. I wanted to touch it, but I had to get Gana back."

Merlin thought about the Stone. It had hurt Prontwon and enchanted Garth. How did it have such power? If only he could see it clearly, maybe he'd understand. "Are you going at noon?" He reached in vain for his father, who had risen.

"Yes. But early. I want to see the Stone without Mórganthu present."

"I'm going too, then." Merlin stood. His head still hurt, but he wasn't about to let his tas go near that glowing rock alone.

"No more rabble-rousing?" His father's tone felt like ice pellets.

"No lashing out. Promise. I've had enough lumps for a while."

"Tregeagle might put you on a galley."

"I thought about that."

His father grasped Merlin's shoulders and shook him gently. "Not enough!"

"I need you, Tas—" Merlin reached out and hugged his father, who stiffened at first but slowly hugged back, gripping Merlin's head and hair in his calloused hands.

"Not enough, son. Not enough."

Merlin's first meal of the day was a poor one: the milk was sour, and there weren't enough oats for his liking. No one else complained, but he was glad when Mônda took the dishes away and his father asked him to go to the nearby smokehouse and buy fish for their evening meal.

And the best part was that his father considered him healed enough for such a job.

Merlin wrapped his harp in its leather bag, swung it over his shoulder, and grabbed his staff. As he had numerous times before, he went out behind the house, climbed the slope, swung over the wall, and carefully found the worn track leading to the docks and marsh beyond.

This was the perfect time to go, as the fishermen would be out on the marsh, and the docks would be clear. After buying the fish, he could sit and think for a bit. Maybe play the harp. He followed his nose to the satisfying smell of the smokehouse, which lay near the shore of the marsh, next to the docks. Here Megek, an elderly fisherman, dried and preserved the fish others brought in from the wetlands.

The smokehouse was an old stone building divided in two — one half for curing the fish that hung over smoldering wood, and the other for gutting and cleaning the fish. An iron-plated door separated the rooms.

Merlin knocked on the outside door and tried the latch, but he found it locked. He called, but no one answered. Odd; Megek was always there during the day. As Merlin walked away empty-handed, he heard a woman's voice from uphill.

A man answered her in a demanding tone. "Give me! Offered a pay ya for all o' yar *eiskes*. The ard dre said."

"You can't have them," the woman said. "These are for guests, I've told you already. Let go!"

By the sound of her voice, the woman was young and from the moor somewhere, but the man? Merlin thought he sounded Eirish.

"Stops askin'," said a man whose voice rattled, "an' sticks her wit' a blade —"

"Shame, McGoss! Ask, take, then pay. No hurtin'! So lass, *give*! The crennig man said ya'd just bought his last."

The woman screamed.

Merlin strode up the hill but marred his entrance by stumbling on a root. A mass of men in multicolored garb surrounded the woman. How many? Six? Merlin started to raise his staff ... then put it down. He prayed God would give him wisdom to help the woman, as well as protect himself.

"Is something wrong? May I help you, ma'am?"

"I ... ohh," she began but stopped short.

One of the men peered into Merlin's face. Somewhere metal slid against metal — maybe a sword from a sheath. "He's short o' sight. Look at his scars." It was McGoss, with the rumble in his voice.

"Are they stealing your fish?" Merlin asked the woman.

"No, no, it's all right. Really. I'm fine. Believe me." But he detected a shrillness in her voice that belied her words.

He struck his staff on the ground, gripping it to hide the tremor in his hands. "Leave her and her fish alone. And we say fish with a *p* here in Kernow. *Pyskes.*"

The men moved around, and Merlin couldn't keep track of them. Had someone gone behind him?

A hand grabbed the back of his tunic and jerked him up so the tips of his boots barely touched the ground. He felt empty air in all directions.

"Put me down." He wanted to lash out but prayed instead.

"Since 'ee's a lad o' the tongue," the giant of a man said from behind, "let's see if 'ee knows to say 'pummel' wit' a *p*."

"Let me stick 'im first" came McGoss's voice.

"McEwan, what's that on his back? Some sort o' bag?"

Merlin reached to snatch the strap but missed as they pulled it from his arm. The wooden peg clattered on a rock at Merlin's feet, and the foreigners hushed.

A new voice spoke. "McEwan, let 'im down. Yar roughin' a *shanachie*, an' here's 'is harp."

"Who cares?" McGoss said.

"I do," the voice spoke again. "An' while I lead, we'll nay break the laws o' our people."

McEwan, the big man, dropped Merlin, and he fell on his feet, struggling for balance. Strong hands steadied him. He spun to defend himself, but the man had disappeared like a ghost. A blur of yellow moved below him. Was the big man on his knees?

"Forgive me, bard, for layin' me hands on ya."

Was this a taunt? Merlin was about to explain that he wasn't a bard when another voice spoke.

"I'm O'Sloan, an' I lead this band. Forgive us for botherin' ya. An' lass, for the bard's sake, we bid ya well. Now out o' here, lads."

They placed the harp in Merlin's hands — case, wooden peg, and all — and the colorful forms of the men disappeared.

"Who were they?" Merlin asked, hoping the woman knew.

She stepped forward, and the smell of smoked fish filled the air. "The question is, who are you? Every time I see you, Merlin, you surprise me. First you teach my brother a lesson. Then you're whipped for Garth — "

"Natalenya?" Had he really just faced those men in her presence?

"And last night, other than Brother Prontwon, you alone stood up to that horrible druid — "

"You saw it?"

She placed her hand on his tunic, over his heart. "And now these warriors bow to you as a bard."

Merlin's face turned red. "It's *your* harp! If they'd asked me to play, they'd have beaten me with it *and* taken your fish."

"Well they didn't, thanks to Jesu."

Merlin nodded, his heart grateful. "Who are they?"

"Warriors. I've never seen their like — wild hair, armbands, jewelry, and beautifully embroidered jerkins over their tunics. The sides of their sleeves went down to their knees. Have you ever seen ..."

Her words trailed off, and Merlin felt her staring at him.

"You're so brave." She pushed away the curly black hair that partially hid his scars. "I saw you in chapel all those times, and I never knew you were so brave."

His hands began to shake worse than before, so he put them behind his back. "What are Eirish warriors doing here? Are they from Lyhonesse?"

She took a deep breath. "I don't know, but they all had swords, and the one that picked you up was like a monster. When I saw it was you, I planned to just give them the fish."

"But your father ..."

"If it meant keeping you from getting hurt, I'd have been glad to let my father's guests starve. I don't care if they are the High King's men."

Merlin almost jumped. "The High King's men?"

"Shh," Natalenya said, stepping closer. "I shouldn't have said anything. There's war on the eastern coast."

Merlin nodded. He had learned the news from an iron merchant who had come to their shop two weeks ago. "What have you heard?"

"A host of wild men have landed along the coast, pillaging whole towns. Rumor has it that even Lundnisow may be in danger before the year's out. High King Uther is coming through to raise troops from Gorlas."

"Your father would've been furious if you'd given up the fish." Her hair smelled like the heather that grew on the mountain near her home.

"I don't care. You've had enough happen to you lately."

"Why didn't Megek help?"

"When they threatened him, he barred the door. He's very old, so I don't blame him. How's your head?" She touched the bruise where

Mórganthu had hit him. "You seem to be getting knocked about up there of late."

"He hit me pretty hard, didn't he? Actually, I don't remember. Tas told me everything." Merlin moved backward a step.

"Mother and I saw it. We prayed for you."

"My tas is going to see the Stone at midday, and I have to keep an eye on him. But I want to sit on the dock and pray first. I like to listen to the birds." His voice quavered a little. "Would you care to join me?"

She nodded, and he hoped it was a smile he'd seen on her face.

As they walked, colorful blurs waved in the sunshine to their right. He reached out and picked one — a wildflower, orange — then gave it to Natalenya. She put it in her hair, and he smelled its sweet fragrance as she guided him over a muddy spot and onto the first plank of the dock.

They sat at the end of the dock, where birds twittered and chirped among the tall sedge grasses that seemed to grow out of the morning fog. A few boats tied nearby bumped each other on the dark water.

"Did you say your tas wants to see the Stone?" she asked, breaking the silence.

"Yes, but I need to somehow stop him from going, or else help him while he's there."

She was quiet for a while. "It made me want to look at it. There's something spiritual about that Stone. It grabs your heart and twists it."

"But I don't understand. How can it do that?" Merlin asked. His throat felt suddenly dry as he realized how near Natalenya sat to him.

Natalenya put a hand on his shoulder. "It's dangerous. Don't let your father or anyone you know get near it. Prontwon did and is deathly injured... I hope he recovers."

"As do I." Merlin splashed the water with his feet. "The Stone does seem to command attention. Last night after the druidow left, some villagers were touching it. Even two guards from the Tor were there. Hopefully your father wasn't angry."

"He will be if he hears that. He dreams of piles of gold and lots of men serving him. I ... I pray for him. He's changed since I was young."

"My tas and Kiff fixed the wagon, so hopefully he's happy with it."

The sound of soft, slow paddling floated to them across the marsh. They stopped talking and listened.

"Who's that?" Natalenya asked.

"A fisherman. Do you see him?"

"No. The fog hasn't fully lifted ... Wait ... I see a boat." She got up on her knees. "It's not like the others," she whispered. "It's like a floating island with grass and mushrooms. If it wasn't moving, I wouldn't know it was a boat at all."

Merlin stood, one hand on his dirk. "Who's in it?"

"A man. He's paddling toward us." She rose as well and stood close. "He's old ... and *wild*. Gray hair down to his waist, and he's in rags. Let's leave."

"Muscarvel. The wild man of the marsh," he whispered back. "Have you heard the tales?" Merlin bent down and put on his boots, but before they could leave, the boat gurgled past them toward shore. He felt Natalenya's hand take hold of his arm.

"Where's he going?" he asked. "Did he ignore us?"

"No, he's on the dock! He's holding a sword, and his eyes — "

Dripping footsteps creaked toward them, and the dock swayed beneath the man's feet.

They were trapped.

Merlin stepped forward to face the stranger.

CHAPTER II

A GIFT AND A PROPHECY

Dybris paused before opening the chapel door. Had he heard someone calling?

Brother Crogen puffed up the path behind him. "Hou, there!"

Dybris turned to greet the pear-shaped little man but could barely keep his eyes open.

Crogen stopped short and studied him up and down. "Before you go in, be aware our heavenly Father is very close to taking Abbot Prontwon home."

Dybris stepped away from the door. "What do you mean?"

"Look at you: dirty and soaked to the bone."

"You know where I've been." He couldn't keep the weariness from his voice. Where could that boy be?

Crogen plucked numerous pine needles from Dybris's hair. "Yes, and while you've been scouring the woods all night like you'd lost your best quill, Prontwon's near death."

"I knew he wasn't well, but — "

"Think he's illuminating a manuscript in there?" The man's eye's bulged out at Dybris.

"I — "

"Think he prefers to sleep here instead of at the abbey?"

"Of course not ..."

"Then what in the name of all that is holy *do* you think, Dybris?

"Everything I know is coming to an end." Dybris leaned on the chapel wall and covered his face.

Crogen patted him on the shoulder. "Well, then, go in and see if your prayers can do more than your muddy feet. I'm off to get some herbs to help him breathe."

Their eyes met, and Dybris saw compassion on Crogen's face. The man truly cared, and that gave Dybris strength.

After Crogen left, Dybris entered the chapel, closing the iron-banded door behind him. The darkness engulfed him, pricked only by the light from two small windows. A silver cross sat on a table, along with a candle that had sputtered to almost nothing.

Prontwon, sleeping, labored for breath.

"Oww — " Dybris muffled an outburst as his knee hit a bench.

Prontwon stirred, turned his head, and then closed his eyes again. "Crogen?"

Dybris sat beside the abbot and took his hand, clammy and limp.

Prontwon's chest rose and fell in small gasps, but it soon passed, and with renewed strength he squeezed Dybris's hand and peered at him out of the corner of his eye. "Ah ... it is you. Did you find Garth?"

"No."

The dark sleeve that Mórganthu had ripped lay open. Dybris cringed as he glimpsed the scarred and tattooed flesh underneath.

"You are wondering ... why I hadn't told you?" Prontwon asked.

"Yes."

"All the brothers know, but I needed to discern your spirit and was waiting for the right time."

"Tell me now."

"The youngest son of a farmer, I despised my father's simple ways. I ... wanted to see the world. How foolish." Prontwon studied the distant reaches of the thatched ceiling. "I met Mórganthu's older brother, Mogruith. He taught me, and I ... became a druid. Gave my all, I did."

"How old were you?"

Prontwon thought for a moment and then spoke with labored breath. "Seventeen winters. Mogruith in his late twenties. Missionaries came from Padraig and ... brought Christianity. I hated Jesu because ... the people turned away from us. They neither needed our protection from witches ... nor our gods and holy days. Christianity was too simple ... or so I thought. How could there be only ... one God? How could there be no more need for ... sacrifice? How could water wash away ... guilt?"

Dybris wiped sweat from Prontwon's forehead. "As many thought."

"Oh, but I was ... naive. Thought I held the secrets of the ages when I ... didn't even understand to ask the right questions." A tear streaked across his face. "Then my poor mother grew sick." He swallowed. "She was dying ... as I am now."

"No, you're not. Rest a few days."

Prontwon wiped his tears and shook his head. "I tried my druid arts to heal her ... but she only ailed the more. My father told me in his simple way ... I should call on the Christian God. Oh, I laughed in his face. But as my mother ... fell into death-sleep, I wept." He smiled now as the tears streamed down. "There, with Father's arm around me ... I prayed to Jesu, and told him I'd ... follow him if he would heal my mother."

"Was she healed?"

"No. She died that hour. But beforehand ... she opened her eyes, reached to the heavens, and — with the most pure joy on her face — called, 'Jesu, I come to you!' My father, he told me ... about the monk, Guron, who brought the true worship ... of the Lamb to the moor and founded our western abbey. After my time of … grieving, I went to Guron. Mogruith never saw me again."

Dybris studied the old man's eyes. "Why have you hidden the druid scars from me? From the people of the village?"

"Ashamed … of my past, mostly." Prontwon shook his head. "Even afraid … of leading astray. Were any more from the abbey deceived last night?"

Standing up, Dybris gave Prontwon as reassuring a look as he could. "None! None of the brothers followed Mórganthu. Just Garth."

"It is … sufficient, we will pray."

The door to the chapel opened, and Brother Offyd stepped in. "A word with you, Dybricius." His face was ashen.

Dybris tried to let go of Prontwon's hand, but the older man gripped his wrist. "Don't leave me … alone."

"Only for a moment. Brother Offyd needs to speak with me."

"Ahh …" Prontwon let go.

Dybris followed Offyd outside and closed the creaky door. "What is it? You look sick."

"It's Brother Herrik. Crogen had just arrived at the abbey when he found Brother Herrik in the scriptorium."

"And what? Doesn't Crogen want us working on the parchments?"

"That's just it. He wasn't copying Scripture. He was drawing a … a diagram of sorts."

"A diagram of what? Speak plainly."

"Of the Stone. The Druid Stone. He was drawing it."

Dybris shut his eyes tightly. "Dear God, give us strength."

Merlin heard the slashing of the sword as it whirled dangerously near. He pushed Natalenya behind him and faced the madman.

"What do you want of us?" Merlin demanded.

The man did not speak but swung his sword in another arc. This time it swept a rush of air past Merlin's cheek.

With a loud, vibrating jolt, the sword jammed into the wood between Merlin's feet.

"He's bowing," Natalenya whispered.

The man's damp hair smelled like wet peat. With his heart pounding, Merlin asked, "Are you Muscarvel of the marsh?"

"I am that I was. Thy glucking servant, scarred one. I am poor Musca, now old and frail, but this fish longs to bite the fetid trunks, does he not?"

"What would you have? Do you need food? Coins?" Merlin reached for his bag and pulled out a few brass ones. He held them out.

The man slapped Merlin's hand, and the coins plinked into the water.

"Need not the janglings of men!" Muscarvel shouted. "Marsh feeds poor Musca. I hunger and eat the flesh of evil birds, chew the foul frog from its hole. Thirst and drink water where the rooted rushes seize the clay. Suffer cold, and the banks of the sun-bit bog bring fire for my hearth. Poor Arvel needs naught but what Christ provides!"

Natalenya tapped Merlin's shoulder. "Let's leave."

"Wait," Merlin answered. Muscarvel had some reason for coming. "If you need nothing, Arvel, tell us why you're here."

"Poor Musca has naught but what my Father above has given. This I nurtured and shaped for you through long years of cold and heat, biting flies and sliming mud. This I give to you, great lord, that the weight of its angry darkness may be gone from my soul."

What had Muscarvel said? He *was* crazy to think that Merlin was a lord.

Muscarvel fell prostrate on the dock, reached between Merlin's feet, and grasped the blade of his own sword, stuck there in the wood. With halting words he shouted:

Seventy years — have flown and wore
Since Dragon Star — fell on the moor.
I saw this thing — come down and roar.
Then I was young — in days of yore.

I will not see — this strange tale spend,
Nor see it twist — waylay and wend.
But though you grieve — and cannot mend,
Yet you will see — the utter end.
The gory past — or so 'tis said,
Will cut afresh — and dagger bled.
Make victims drown — in their blood red,
And strike bright world — turn on its head.
The cock will crow — to moon and soar,
The mouse in greed — brings forth a roar,
The boar be caught — by apple core.
And hammer strike — the anvil tor.

He trembled as he raised his voice still louder:

The grave will gaze — from its pale bed,
As ash will birth — the dagger dread.
The wren so young — with darken'd head,
Will caw death chant — and evil wed.
Upon high hill — in fortress fast,
The hawk will fail — to heed the past.
Land of all night — hold on to mast,
For altar's foe — trust Christ at last.
The bear will charge — with steel claw free
'Gainst hoary swell — of peoples be.
All things will lose — and dead the tree,
Lest wisdom to — he bend the knee.
Hell dog will dark — the sun's bright face.
The beast will rise — from secret place.
All men will flee — to water trace,
Till sword and spear — with prayer grace.
The beast will bring — forth fetid birth,
And bear will scratch — and prove his worth.
But land will not — have new its mirth,
Till red-leg crow — be brought to earth.

The black tomb of — snake's winter sleep,
Bring forth the dead — from cavern deep.
Then evil foes — come out and creep,
Drive off the hawk — to danger keep.

Muscarvel clambered up with his rags flapping, and their green reek smote Merlin. The man grabbed Merlin's hands. He had the grip of a biting turtle, yet his fingers were so thin.

He shook as if an invisible creature tore his back. The final words came out in agony:

When hope is lost — and foes a throng,
When jaws be sharp — and claws are strong,
When thralled the men — and all is wrong,
Recall thy gift — to sing bard's song.
For three must seek — and prize the pure,
That has been lost — in bleak azure.
Go find and seek — but ware the lure.
Take narrow way — when none is sure.
And at the end — death's head will rise,
Kill, take, covet — fill ears with lies.
Pure love will doubt — take all as guise,
Ere noble one — gives up his prize.
Then red-leg crow — at last will kill,
To take and steal — and veil with skill.
And hence the tale — shall wait until
The chosen ones — their call fulfill.

Muscarvel's words fell away from him in the grief of tears. As he spoke again, a calmness, if not a saneness, returned to his voice. "Great lord, besides a few final tasks, I am now free. But you … you shall bear these words as a dark burden until your death. I merely carried them. You must live them."

A shiver ran through Merlin. The man was mad — but nonsense though his words sounded, he said them with such sincerity and conviction that they somehow rang true. Why had Muscarvel spoken these words to him?

Natalenya, now holding Merlin's arm, whispered in his ear. "He's crying as he pulls something from a moldy pouch. Oh, Merlin, it's beautiful."

Merlin could see the gleam of gold in the man's hands.

"Great lord, this also I have kept for the day of your rising. The Christ hid it in a bog, and I found it! A great chief of men died I know not when, and I wrenched it from his leathern neck."

Natalenya pulled Merlin closer. "It's a torc of fine workmanship. Made from thick braids of gold. On its ends are crafted what look like the heads of falcons."

Reaching up, Muscarvel placed the torc upon Merlin.

He felt the cold, heavy weight of it on his neck and collarbones, and he reached up to touch the ancient curves of the torc with his fingertips. *I don't deserve this. Who am I? No one. Just the blind son of a blacksmith. Why had Muscarvel done this? And who was he?*

Muscarvel plucked his sword from the plank and yelled, "I'm free!" He ran down the shaking dock and jumped into his boat. His paddle sloshed through the water swiftly, and his parting words called back to them through the mist.

"Lost the meat! I'll find it, Father. I'll find it yet!"

For a long moment Merlin and Natalenya stood side by side, speechless. When the sounds of Muscarvel faded, Merlin listened instead to Natalenya's breathing, so close beside him.

All at once, she turned toward him. "I should go. Here." She rummaged in her bundle, then pressed a smoked fish into his hands. "It's no golden torc, but it's the least I can do after you saved me from those men."

The scale-free fish felt soft against Merlin's fingers, and the mouth-watering aroma made his stomach growl. "Thank you."

She laughed. "Thank *you*, Merlin."

Her two soft hands grasped his free one for a moment, and then she was gone.

He picked up his staff, tapped his way back to the end of the dock, and sat down, alone with his thoughts once more. He laid his staff beside him, peeled off the fish's skin and chewed it, relishing the smoky flavor before swallowing. For a while he just sat and ate the rest, thinking of Natalenya ... of the warmth of her hands ... of the Eirish men who would steal fish from a woman but wouldn't touch a bard ... and of Muscarvel.

His good mood soured. Pulling the last of the flesh from the fish's bones, he held the bare spine in his hand. This was how he felt. Like a dead fish, blind and useless.

Father, what is my life? Do my efforts even matter? I bared my back to the whip, took a beating from Mórganthu, and what does Garth do? Off with the druidow.

And Mórganthu had shown the village what a fool Merlin was. He couldn't fight properly, and he wasn't respected enough in the village to speak. It was his father who needed to stand up and tell the people the truth about Mórganthu. *Why won't he do it?*

Maybe Prontwon would try again when he got better. Or Neot. Or perhaps Dybris, the new monk, could convince the people. Certainly blind Merlin could never sway their minds. What could *he* do? And what of this torc Muscarvel had given him? He reached up and felt the intricate lines of the ancient gift resting around his neck. He touched the gold falcon heads fashioned on the ends. What was he supposed to do with it? He hadn't earned such a thing. Everyone would laugh if they saw him wear it. Ha-ha! There goes the blind man who thinks he's a chieftain!

And all Muscarvel's other gibberish.

In anger Merlin spread the ends of the torc and pulled it from his neck. He loosed the ties of his bag and shoved the torc inside, where it clinked against his few coins. He rose and set off for home. Muscarvel was mad, plain and simple.

When Merlin arrived, he found the house quiet.

"Tas?"

He stepped into the room and listened. "I'm over here," his father said from a stool at the table. He sounded tired, and a little angry. "Waiting for you. Quite awhile to buy some fish."

"Where are Mônda and Gana?"

Owain rested his forehead on the table and then thumped his head on the wooden surface. "Oh ... I don't know exactly. I worked on the sword for an hour or so, and when I came in — "

"Mônda almost never leaves the house."

"I know. I'm afraid they've gone to her father."

"To Mórganthu?"

"Yes." His voice sounded empty. "Mônda and I have been arguing since last night. I wouldn't let her go. So now she's left."

"I hope you don't plan on following."

His father stood, and his words bit like a blade. "I've been wanting to, but *you* were gone. I don't want you getting in any more trouble. Like a cracked anvil, you are. What took so long?"

"Megek didn't have any fish — "

"And so it took *longer*?"

"Natalenya was there."

"Ahh."

"She'd bought all that was left. Tregeagle's hosting a feast tonight."

His father moved toward the door. "That still doesn't account for your time."

Merlin backed up, blocking his father's exit. "There were others. Eirish warriors."

"Eirish ... here? In Bosventor?" He clutched Merlin's shoulder.

"They tried to steal the fish."

"The people settled in Lyhonesse rarely come here ... much less Eirish raiders. How do you know?" his father asked. "How — "

"How can I know, because I'm blind?" Merlin tightened his jaw. Why did it always come to this? Didn't his own father think he was capable of anything? "Their speech gave them away, and Natalenya told me their clothing matched her father's stories. Apparently Tregeagle's fought them in the past."

His father turned away and whispered so quietly, Merlin barely heard it.

"As have I."

Merlin placed a hand on his father's shoulder and gently turned him so they were again face-to-face. "What did you say? You've fought in a battle?" Merlin wished he could see his father's features. Years ago he would have felt the whiskered cheeks, but now that he was older, it somehow didn't seem right.

"Long ago," his father said. "Before I met your mother."

"You never told me."

His father went to the wall and took down his sword, swung it, and put it back up again. "How many Eirish warriors were there?"

"Could have been six, maybe more."

"Sure it wasn't just one, and a wee one at that?"

"I'm not stupid." Merlin said.

"I'm teasing. Why didn't you ask Natalenya?"

Merlin tapped his staff. "I didn't think to."

"Maybe you had other things on your mind?"

Merlin blushed.

His father whistled. "That's what *really* took so long. Let's go find Mônda and your sister before Mórganthu does."

Merlin wanted to tell him not to go, to somehow prevent his father from going near the Stone. But how could he say no to bringing Mônda and his sister back home? He nodded, and his father took him by the arm.

Leaving the house, they made their way to the village pasture where Mórganthu had placed the Stone the night before.

"People are here, but I don't see Mônda ... or Gana," his father whispered. "Druidow are guarding the Stone, but their weapons are old and rusty, and their muscles are too little kindling to start a fire with anyone serious. Maybe that's why they're not stopping anyone from approaching the Stone."

"Who's here?" Merlin asked, offering up a silent prayer, for he could see now that a faint blur of blue flames radiated from the Stone.

"A crowd. Hen Crenlyn just walked by us. He's looking at the Stone like it was a stump. Olva's on the other side looking on. Brunyek's further off, but I can tell he's peeking at it. Stenno's here too."

"What's he doing?" Stenno wasn't much older than Merlin, though he streamed for tin to support his widowed mother.

"He's on his knees near the Stone, holding his hands in front of it like he's warming them."

"That's bad."

"It's really interesting ... I wish you could see the Stone. You'd understand."

Merlin didn't want to, and for once in his life, he was glad of his blindness. His father led him toward the Stone but then stopped.

"What's wrong?" Merlin asked.

"Kiff's here. I hadn't noticed him on the ground on the other side. He has one hand on the side of the Stone." Raising his voice, his father called out, "Kiff ... Hey, there!"

But Kifferow didn't answer.

They walked over to him. Bending down, Merlin's father spoke into the man's ear, "Kiff, it's me, Owain." He shook Kiff's shoulder. No response. Muttering, he braced himself and pushed the big man over onto his back.

Kifferow sneezed, shook his head, and sat up. "You ... You did that!"

"Sure, I pushed your pig belly over."

"You broke my dream." Kifferow rose to his feet with a grunt and belted Owain across the jaw, knocking him down. "You take that!" he shouted, raising his fist again.

"Kiff, stop!" Merlin stepped in between the men, but Kifferow slammed him in the shoulder, knocking him backward. The world turned sideways, and Merlin found himself lying across his father's legs with his face in the dirt.

Mônda appeared from the haze and called out loudly, "Leave him alone, Kiff. And Merlin, get off your father!" She wrapped her arms around her husband's shoulders and clung to him so fast that she gouged Merlin's elbow with her armband. The wound throbbed as Merlin rolled off Owain's legs.

Kifferow huffed but backed away as well.

"The Stone will help you understand," Mônda said. "Look at it. Look at the Stone." She reached out her hands and turned Owain's gaze to the blue flames.

Merlin's father shook her off. "Leave me alone, all of you."

The gem in Mônda's armband began to glow, and then his father's began to gleam as if in reply. Mônda mumbled some strange words, and Owain's head snapped up and turned toward the Stone.

Merlin pulled himself to a sitting position just as his father crawled toward the Druid Stone.

"That'll teach him," Kifferow said. "Now he won't interrupt me!"

Desperate, Merlin grabbed his father's foot to stop him, but the action barely impeded Owain's progress as he dragged Merlin closer to the Stone.

"Tas. *Tas!* What are you doing? Kiff, help me!"

The big man stepped closer, but instead of helping, he snatched Merlin's arms and dragged him away. "Be quiet and let him take a good long drink. He'll never forget the sweetness."

Merlin struggled, but the carpenter's grip was too strong. "Let go," he yelled, thinking of Natalenya's warning.

Kifferow laughed, and his breath smelled like ale. "He's smiling. Feel the Stone, Owain. Touch it!"

Owain reached out a wavering hand to touch the glowing surface of the Druid Stone.

"Merlin, it's magnificent."

CHAPTER 12

TOUCHING FIRE

"No!" Merlin yelled as he kicked Kifferow and twisted out of the big man's grasp. He flung himself forward and rammed his father in the side, knocking him away from the Stone.

Owain yelled and turned back with a ferocity that astonished Merlin. A fist hammered him in the gut.

Merlin fell back from his father's blow, and his right hand landed on the Druid Stone and stuck fast, as if it were covered in soft pine tar. The Stone felt warm to the touch, its surface partly rough, partly smooth. And it quivered like a wolf ready to pounce.

Merlin's body stiffened, and the ground tilted. He jerked his left hand up to prevent himself from falling over, and now both hands were stuck to the Stone.

The Stone grew larger and then melted away, his body seeming to plunge inside, as if the Stone had become a hole leading to a creature's lair. He fell into silent darkness, it seemed, for hours.

Without warning he felt cold flagstones under his fingers. His groans echoed off walls that appeared from nowhere, and the dense air smothered him like frozen spiderwebs. Where had his father, the grass, and the Stone gone? He looked around, and his blurred sight sharpened. Once again he could see clearly.

He lay in a chamber made of solid granite, with neither window nor door. A bluish light flickered from torches held by intricately forged iron holders. Cold smoke poured from the torches, filling the lower half of the room. Merlin coughed.

In the center a square stone pillar rose from the smoke. The top was draped with a blue cloth decorated with dizzying spirals and symbols. From where Merlin knelt, he could tell that something rested on top.

He wanted to see what was on the pillar, but his legs ached and he couldn't stand. The desire burned within, and in desperation he cried out, "Will anyone help me?"

A cold voice answered him: "Rise and see!"

Merlin's numb legs obeyed and lifted him up to see four drinking horns placed at the corners of the pillar. Each was fashioned from the long curving horn of a ram, spiraling inward and downward and held by an iron stand shaped like the cruel talons of some giant creature.

The first horn was red as blood, the second bright golden, the third sickly white, and the fourth pale silver. Each was filled with a different liquid.

The bodiless Voice called out again, "Take and drink!"

Merlin leaned forward to peek inside the dark-red horn. It held what appeared to be the purest of water, so clear and fresh he could see down into the depths of the horn. As he stared, the water flickered with visions of vile, base, and godless things. The images kept changing, and Merlin desired to take up the horn and fill his body, soul, and spirit with the wicked degradations.

He called out to God for help, and a revulsion of sufficient strength finally rose up that forced his eyes shut. The images fell away into darkness. The desire left him.

He pulled himself away from the horn and opened his eyes to see the golden horn before him. A bubbling, creamy brown liquid filled it, and he listened to its frothy sound. As each bubble burst, he heard soothing words issue forth. He strained his ears to hear, and every utterance called him to lie and deceive. Drums began to beat in his ears until the horn shook and he felt his head would burst with the vibration.

Stopping up his ears did nothing; the calling would not cease. The temptation grew to embrace the horn, let the deceits fill his soul, and make the raging words go away. He reached out his hands, hoping for relief.

Then a memory arose of his father. With downcast face, he spoke to Merlin, saddened because of a childhood lie Merlin had told. His father implored him to choose the right and turn from falsehoods. At first Merlin wanted his father to go away, and he swept his hands to dispel the image, but his father's face remained. Slowly, Merlin's heart broke. The desire to take up the drinking horn faded, and Merlin was free again.

The third, a whitish horn, now stood before him, but he distrusted it. This time he wouldn't look inside. Closing his eyes, he leaned forward to determine if he could smell it, and a sweet aroma drifted deep into his lungs.

He felt stronger, taller, and wiser, filled with his own greatness and ability to lead. Visions appeared of men bowing as his kingly torc was placed around his neck. It smelled so wonderful that he found himself staring at the liquid in the horn. It flowed green as the nectar of garden flowers, and with just a taste he could do any task, no matter how difficult. One sip from the horn, and he could have anything he wanted. He would be the supreme authority once this sweet liquid coursed down his throat.

In joy he grasped his own smiling face, and there he felt the scars. Deep and thickened. And he knew that few could love the gross disfigurement he'd been cursed to carry. His pride drained away, and he was once again the normal, scarred Merlin.

He approached the final corner of the stone pillar and the last drinking horn, which stood so tall he couldn't glance inside. Its silver glimmered in the light of the blue torches, and it was magnificent. Even a great king would be proud to drink of the heady ale lurking there. A longing to see what was inside overcame him.

He hefted himself up onto the pillar, now strangely widened into a table, and knelt in the middle. There he peered over the silver horn's filigreed edge. Inside lay a black liquid, thick and rich. His hands reached to the horn and stuck to its sides.

Small bolts of lightning shot through his arms and across his chest. There, in his pain, a terrible vision engulfed him.

He was the adviser to a king and led warriors beyond count across Britain. Each battle brought death. His warriors' limbs lay hacked at his feet. His enemies' heads lay piled as a mountain. No matter where he wandered, all had been slain. Death and ruin abounded. Merlin stood alone, a curse on mankind. His hands lifted the terrible horn with the slop of dark liquid toward his lips.

Closer it drew until Merlin cried out, "God, save me from this curse!"

His hands dropped the horn with a crash upon the table. Before the liquid slimed across the surface and touched him, he leaped to the ground.

And there, amid the hiss of the torches, the Voice himself rose from the ground. His robe enshrouded him in darkness, and his flaking claw held a sword as pale as dead flesh. He lifted it to strike the head from Merlin's body.

"Bow and worship!"

Defenseless and with nowhere to run, Merlin yet found strength welling up inside. He shouted, "I'll never worship you. Though you slay me, I will hold fast to Jesu!"

Malicious laughter echoed through the room.

"You *shall* worship me! This village shall worship me! This island shall worship me! All shall worship me!"

Merlin backed up against the wall. "Never!"

In a rage, the Voice sliced his sword at Merlin's neck, and all went black.

—╋—

With Offyd tending the sleeping Prontwon, Dybris closed the chapel door and walked down the path to the village pasture and the gathering of the druidow. As he passed the houses and gardens of the villagers, he wondered if Offyd was right. Had any of the brothers besides Herrik fallen victim to its temptation? They were often scattered in different fields, and it would be easy to succumb, to sneak away, maybe even to worship the Stone.

But the main thing was to find that rascal of an orphan.

Dybris himself had felt the tug on his own heart as he looked at the Druid Stone the evening before. Had felt the desire to touch its rough surface and see what secrets it contained.

His thoughts were cut short by footsteps hastening toward him from behind. It was Tregeagle's wife, Trevenna, and her daughter, Natalenya.

"Dybris!" Trevenna called. "Offyd told us you were on your way to the gathering."

Dybris hesitated. "I'm checking to see if any of the brothers are there."

"Will you stand up to Mórganthu as Prontwon did?"

He winced. "No, I was only going to — "

Trevenna grasped him by the elbow and faced him. "But it is needed."

Dybris did not know what to say. Trevenna looked at him with fearful eyes, her chin uplifted and her brown-gray hair tousled by the light wind. Here was the proud wife of the town magister and who was he to gainsay her?

"The people need you ... need someone!" Trevenna said. "With Prontwon ailing, they have no one to guide them. Who will tell them the truth?"

"Arguing with the druidow won't accomplish anything. Really now, I just want to find Garth."

Natalenya stepped forward. "What if the villagers leave the faith?"

All this talk made his head hurt. He desperately needed a little sleep. "I confess that I haven't given it much thought. I've been concerned about Garth and the other monks."

The women continued to plead with him as they walked down the hill toward the gathering on the village green. When they reached the gate, Dybris saw a thick crowd of people around the Stone. From their midst came shouts and the sounds of a scuffle.

"It's Merlin!" Natalenya cried out, and she ran ahead of them into the throng.

Through the cold fog, Merlin heard someone call faintly. Warmth shocked his face, and he sucked in the air.

"He's breathing," someone said from far away.

His shoulders warmed and his arms tingled.

"He's waking," said another.

Merlin opened his eyes. Light shone between two darkly smudged forms.

"Oh, God ... Oh, God!" someone cried nearby. Was it his father?

Merlin's legs tingled, and he tried to sit up.

"Help him," someone wailed. It was Natalenya's voice.

Hands supported him. He rubbed his face and rose up on an elbow. "Natalenya?"

Her voice trembled. "Oh, Mother, don't look — "

Merlin's father was crying.

"What's happening?" Merlin asked as a choking smell filled his lungs. "What's wrong?"

Natalenya spoke. "We pulled your hands off the Stone, and a big man yelled at us, and he ..."

Trevenna continued from his right, dignified in spite of the trembling in her voice. "We saw the struggle and how you accidentally touched the Stone. We pulled you free, but that man touched the Stone too. He said, 'This is how,' and then he caught fire and burned to death."

Owain's sobs grew louder. "Kifferow!"

Natalenya helped Merlin sit up. "It was terrible. He yelled but couldn't pull his hands away."

As Merlin crawled over to his father, the smell of burning flesh made him gag. He placed an arm around his father's back but found Mônda's hand already there.

She jerked her arm away and hissed at Merlin. "Leave him alone. Can't you see he's suffering?"

Merlin ignored her, holding tighter to his father, whose body heaved as he knelt before the smoking body of his friend. "Tas ... Tas, I'm sorry."

"Why'd you interfere?" his father snapped. "Kiff wouldn't be dead if you'd left us alone."

"What happened to Kiff was meant for me. The Stone tried to kill me."

"Then, then — "

"If you'd touched it, maybe you'd be lying in Kiff's place."

His father beat the ground as Merlin glanced at the shadowy forms of people gathered around them.

A deep voice spoke. "And so here are the mongrel and his whelp come to lick my feet!"

Mórganthu.

Owain stood. "Look what you did!"

"I? I did nothing," Mórganthu scoffed. "I was not even here. Are you sure *you* did not cause this amazing spectacle?"

Merlin's father stepped back and shook his head, his voice raspy. "Then why did this happen? Kifferow touched your Stone, and it killed him."

Mórganthu sniffed, but Merlin heard no sorrow in his voice. "A moment. In a moment I will answer your question. Everyone, back away from the Stone and sit."

The people moved away. Merlin rose and found himself in the

center of the widening circle, with his hand on his father's shoulder. He wondered where Natalenya had gone. Mórganthu stood nearby like a dark statue.

With his father guiding him, Merlin retreated to the inner edge of the circle, where they sat down next to Mônda and Ganieda.

Merlin placed his arm over his father's shuddering back. From the other side, Mônda's sharp nails pricked Merlin on the back of his hand. He yielded by moving his hand farther down and hung on to his father's thick leather belt.

In the center of the gathering, Mórganthu seemed to be biding his time.

"What's he waiting for?" Merlin muttered, turning toward his father.

Owain twisted around and appeared to survey the gathering. "He's a showman," he said, his voice tinged with anger and pain.

More and more villagers gathered, and by the sound of them, it seemed the entire village had come.

Just as Mórganthu cleared his throat to speak, Mônda dropped her hand down and gouged Merlin again. He jerked his hand away and nursed his wound. There was blood. Why was she doing that?

Mórganthu raised his voice. "I declare to you ... I declare that the Stone is angry with this village. The Stone has slain this man because he was found unworthy of it. All who fail to worship and truly love this Stone will be destroyed!"

Mórganthu struck the Stone with his staff, and blue flames erupted from its surface.

Merlin covered his eyes. "Don't look at it, Tas."

"Why not? It's amazing. If you could just see it properly."

"You're right," Mônda said. "And the Stone will make you a chieftain if you follow it. See the respect shown to my father?"

Merlin whispered in his father's ear. "Mórganthu is lying. Kiff worshiped it, and it killed him!"

Owain shook his head as if shooing away a buzzing gnat. "Yes, that's right, he was killed. I remember now." Yet he kept looking at the Stone.

"That's wrong," Mônda whispered. "The Stone tried to save Kiff. Don't meddle like Merlin did. The Stone is wonderful."

"It's wonderful to see," Owain said. "I've never felt like this."

"All ... All who desire peace need to worship the Stone," Mórganthu shouted. "The great god Belornos gives it to you as a gift. You need only fear if you fail him. This man" — he kicked Kifferow's charred leg — "was killed because not enough of you have chosen to turn back to the old ways."

"Psst! Tas," Merlin whispered. "Is Garth here? Do you see him?"

"Sure. Across the circle. That Dybris fellow's jabbering at him, but the boy just keeps shaking his head and turning away."

"Will you take me there?" Merlin asked. "I want to talk to him."

"No. Owain will stay here," Mônda said.

"I'm going to stay here, Merlin. He's surrounded by the druidow, and he looks fine."

Merlin felt helpless.

"Who will step forward?" Mórganthu asked. "And return to the old ways? The ways of Britons before this blight of monks."

"Tas — "

"Don't listen to him," Mônda interrupted.

"Don't bother me anymore, Merlin, I'm looking at the Stone. It's — "

Merlin shook his father's shoulder. "Are any other monks nearby? Any of the brothers?"

"You don't care," Mônda whispered to Owain.

Owain brushed Merlin's hand away. "Why should I even care? Why should you?"

Merlin became infuriated at Mônda's interference. "I need to know. Tell me, please! Look around."

"Just Dybris. Satisfied?"

"No, I'm not. You need to speak out against Mórganthu. Tell the people the truth."

Mônda kissed Owain loudly on the cheek. "My father is good. You like him, Owain, don't you?"

"He looks stronger today … and kind. He's not so bad."

What was going on in his father's heart? Was this his father talking?

"Surely," Mórganthu said, his words as slippery as a frog, "surely you all see the beauty of the Stone. All who desire it, come forward!"

The shuffling began. Merlin looked behind him and was amazed how many blurs of people moved toward the Stone.

"Tas, how many?" Merlin asked. "Who's going forward?"

His father didn't answer.

"Tas?" Merlin turned back, but his father was gone. Panic set in, and he patted all around for the familiar shape. He soon discovered Mônda and his sister were missing too.

Merlin's blood raced through his heart, and his legs tensed to spring forward and drag his father back. But it was too late. He felt the chains of his blindness and raged against his inability to stop what was happening.

"Tas, come back!"

The nightmare of the previous night was happening again. But at least Dybris stood nearby. Merlin waited for the monk to speak up, but he heard nothing as the flow of villagers walked to the front of the gathering. Why hadn't Dybris said something?

Merlin prayed for strength. His father and the villagers were in danger, and the evil spirit in his vision wanted all the Britons to worship the Stone. With his hands trembling and his knees shaking, Merlin stood amid the jostling crowd and raised his voice for all to hear.

CHAPTER 13

STANDING STRONG

G ood people of Bosventor, hear me!" Merlin called.

The forms moving around him paused, and he sensed them turning to face him.

"Brother Prontwon spoke the truth to you last night. He told of the deception of this Stone and the curse of the old ways."

No one responded.

"He told you not to give up on Jesu. He told you to — "

"Shut yer mouth, Merlin. We heard Prontwon last night. Nothin' new," someone bellowed.

"I'm not telling you anything new," Merlin answered. He wondered if the speaker had been Brunyek. How could *he* follow the Stone? He was a hardworking farmer, and Merlin knew that he faithfully attended chapel.

"I speak of something older even than these gods the druidow worship. I tell you of the Great Ith'esov, the I Am who makes a covenant of peace. I'm telling you about His Son, Jesu, who made all things new. This is the God that created the whole earth and — "

"Be quiet, Merlin," a voice shouted out.

"You be quiet," another shouted nearby.

"Stay out of this, Allun!" the first man said.

The two scuffled, and someone cried out as he was thrown to the ground.

The first man spoke again. "You, Merlin, don't tell us what to do. Let the heads of the families decide. Let Tregeagle decide, I say — "

The tall figure of Mórganthu stepped forward. "Steady, steady, my young man. This dispute is entirely between Merlin and the kind personage of myself."

The man backed off.

"Now then," Mórganthu said as he snaked his arm around Merlin's shoulder. "What is the trouble? Does your head hurt from last night? Terribly sorry. Civilized men like us should settle things properly. How may I help you?"

Merlin wanted to pull away from Mórganthu and clout *him* in the head. Send him crawling away from the village never to return. But Mórganthu waved something in front of Merlin's face that had a strong aroma, like pine mixed with bitter berry. After only a few whiffs, Merlin's anger faded, and he couldn't remember what he'd been about to say. He tried to speak, but only gibberish fell from his tongue.

"There, there," someone beside him said. "We all feel a bit confused now and then."

Merlin walked beside this kind stranger, who placed an arm over his shoulder. "Who are you?" Merlin asked.

"A friend" said the man with a gentle voice.

"Where are we going?"

"To the Stone, where you'll be happy."

The stone? The Druid Stone? That's what he was speaking against. And the voice belonged to Mórganthu. A surge of anger flowed through him. Yanking away from Mórganthu's arm, he turned and inhaled the fresh air.

Mórganthu pulled at his collar, but Merlin ducked and broke away. Now he could think straight, and he remembered his task. "Everyone, hear me! This man deceives you. Kifferow died *because* he worshiped the Stone. There is nothing but death where the druidow lead!"

Mórganthu snarled and threw Merlin onto a pile of musty leaves. The arch druid's voice roared, "Hear me! Hear, my people. Ignore this son of a braggart. He is no leader of men! He is but a boy who is blind, cursed by the gods."

Mórganthu pulled off his hood so the torc at his throat gleamed. He lifted his arms, allowing the sleeves to fall down and reveal the myriad of blue tattoos that Merlin knew to be there. Then Mórganthu shouted to the people, "Remember the song our ancient bards sang . . .

If ever one of six things you bear,
the folk will hear and follow you:
A harp whose notes hang in the air,
or druid-coppered scars of blue.
Fine cape and hood o'er brihem's hair,
or knowledge wise of fili true.
King's knife held at the back made bare,
else torc of woven metal hue.

"This boy," Mórganthu said, "this boy is no chieftain of men! He has no torc or office that you should follow him. Ignore his doggerel, and let us begin our worship of the Stone."

The villagers laughed as Mórganthu kicked Merlin.

"No torc! No voice. Get away from here," the people jeered, mimicking Mórganthu. Some even spit on him.

Merlin brushed the dirt off his face. No torc? He felt the hard curve of metal hidden in his pouch. With new confidence he stood again before the villagers. "Give room, good people." He swung his staff out in a gentle arc so everyone backed away. He untied his bag and reached in.

"All of you, listen to me! You have known me as Merlin, the blind son of your blacksmith, sport for your children, and one of no account. And so you ignore my words and follow this man, this liar —"

Mórganthu stepped up again and yelled "Silence!" but Merlin kept on speaking.

"Look and see what my God has given as a sign for you to follow me and turn away from this druid madness."

Merlin pulled the torc from his bag, and it flashed golden before their eyes. He bent the ends out and placed it around his neck. Taller he felt, and princelike before them. His blindness but a mystery, and his scars the marks of a true warrior.

Hushed murmurs weaved through the crowd as the villagers turned toward Merlin.

"All of you, come away to hear my words."

Merlin oriented himself by the position of the sun, walked a good distance from the Stone, tapped until he found the granite slab that was the Rock of Judgment, and climbed upon it. And to his utter amazement, the people followed. He had expected one or two, but so many? Even Merlin's father had come, his covenant armband flashing in the sun and his dark beard hanging down onto his chest. But was that Mônda pulling on his arm?

Mórganthu fumed as he, Anviv, Garth, and the druidow were left standing at the Stone. He turned to his son. "What is this? Where would Merlin get such a sign of power? Beyond the land of the Eirish, no torc has been made of that ilk since that cursed Agricola and his Romans stripped us of our treasures."

"My father," Anviv said, "may I go and *taunt* the blind one?"

"Ah, yes. I see, I see. Raise his bile. Let him make a fool of himself for wearing that torc?"

"Exactly."

"No ... this is a more serious puzzle than your renowned heckling can solve." Mórganthu closed his eyes for a moment.

"Then, my father, I think it is time to call your *friends* to come help us. Let the silly blind one, shall we say, be seen no more among the people."

Mórganthu sucked in air between his dry lips. "You are wise, O son! Our thoughts run in the same *river*." He walked south across the village pasture and stopped at the stone wall that encircled it. Then he whistled down into the small tree-filled valley where the village spring ran.

Six warriors burst up from the brush, hair hanging past their shoulders and distinctive clothing showing through their traveling cloaks, which had been thrown back in the sunshine. Their tunics had been cut with a long slit in front, the sleeves tight to the elbows but billowing downward. Over these they wore embroidered leather jerkins. Their belts held swords with curved jeweled handles, and stiff boots covered their laced leather leggings.

Mórganthu addressed one among them who had a long, gray-streaked beard and a slim silver torc at his throat. "Welcome officially to the first of many villages we will rule, O'Sloan, my war-band leader."

O'Sloan bowed.

Next, Mórganthu turned to a man at O'Sloan's right who stood a head and a half taller than the others. "And you, McEwan Mor. I have need of your swift Eirish club."

Another warrior, dark of hair as well as countenance, stepped forward and fell to his knees before Mórganthu. "Ard Dre," he said with rattling voice, "fer a bit o' gold, I'm willin' fer thy deed, nay matter the blood!"

O'Sloan pulled the man up and yanked him back. "McGoss, ya were nay called for'ard. We should hear the task afore we speak o' knifin'."

Mórganthu spoke low of his mission, and McEwan looked out toward the massed villagers. "Ya mean that'un there standin' on the slab? Ya wish us to knife that'un?"

"Yes, yes. He is the one."

A warrior in blue snorted. "Ken ya believe it, O'Sloan? 'Tis the bard 'imself."

"Och, man, we canna do it. 'Tis against our law!"

"What? He is no bard," Mórganthu said. "You are mistaken."

"Nah, I canna be. He has the torc o' a bard, an' the harp o' a bard, an' he is speakin' as a bard. In our view o' things, we dare nay chance it. Isn't that so, McEwan?"

The big warrior nodded. "We'll nay touch 'im, nay hurt 'im. If ya try, we'll oppose ya."

"What of McGoss?" Mórganthu asked. "Surely he will do it."

O'Sloan placed a hand on the hilt of his dagger. "We'll slit 'im first, we will. Such is our laws, an' ya well ken the curse that would visit us fer even thinkin' such a thing."

Mórganthu swore. "So you break your oaths so easily, O'Sloan?"

"We'll do as ya say in all else, but ya ken our ancient laws, and we daren't grieve a bard."

Mórganthu rubbed the bulging veins on his face. "I shall let this matter pass, but you *will* show your loyalty. Or else I shall send you back where you will eat the rags of your thievery at the hands of that two-faced Christian Eirish king!"

O'Sloan bowed before Mórganthu. "As sure as our lives depend on ya, we'll do yar biddin' in all else. Give name to the task."

"Go, all of you! Go back to camp and await my orders there."

O'Sloan's eyes lit up, then he seemed to hesitate. "We been sittin' by the stream all mornin', so we'll gladly go back to yar vats o' drink an' victuals, but ya'll have to promise us ya will nay hurt the bard."

"Yes, yes. I promise I will not hurt him." He waved them away. "Your copsed path is there."

O'Sloan and his warriors descended into the small valley again and headed eastward.

When they were out of earshot, Mórganthu walked back to Anviv. "I promised I would not hurt him, and I will not. But I swear I will cut off my own hand if this meddling son of Owain An Gof does not die before the Beltayne fires are lit tomorrow eve!"

"O Father," Anviv asked, "may *I* have this boon?"

"Not you. I cannot risk that. Cannot risk losing you. You must lead the druidow when my spirit departs to be renewed in the waters of the deep. Fetch our new friend Connek from where he loafs by the meeting house."

Anviv nodded and headed back toward the village, returning shortly with the thief beside him.

Mórganthu whispered a long time in Connek's ear. About halfway through, Connek grinned. Finally, Mórganthu held out three gold coins.

Connek groped for them, but Mórganthu knocked the thief's hand away. Connek's eyes followed the coins as each slid back into Mórganthu's bag.

First the largest coin ... *clink.*

Then a thick one with a horse pulling the sun across the sky ... *clank.*

And finally one stamped with the head of the dead usurper King Vitalinus Gloui ... *chlink.*

Connek licked his lips as he left Mórganthu, walking with determined steps to Merlin and the meeting of the villagers.

It appeared someone was arguing with the scarred fool.

"And why can't we worship this Stone *and* your Christian God at the same time? None of the other gods seem to mind." A low rumble — half laughter, half assent — went through the crowd.

"Priwith," Merlin said, "you yourself have sat under the monks' teaching. You know God commands us not to worship anyone or anything else."

"But it is the most striking thing I have ever seen."

"That may be true, but that doesn't mean we should worship what has been created. That's like confusing your goat and its milk, but the Druid Stone isn't even like that. Pledging yourself to it is joining yourself with evil."

"I sense nothing evil about it …"

"I understand you don't feel its presence, but evil lurks there nonetheless. Go and see Kifferow's body. Go ask the good abbot."

"Kiff was a drunkard," someone yelled from the crowd.

With wide eyes, Connek took note of Merlin's heavy golden torc. There was more gold on that soon-to-be-cut neck than Mórganthu had offered him. He slid his rusted knife out and tested its edge with a sweaty thumb. Surveying the large crowd, he shook his head in dismay.

Some bloke next to him had a coughing fit, and half the crowd turned. Connek's cheeks flushed red as he pushed his knife up his sleeve. He pretended to cough too and kept his hooded face down.

Soon the attention went back to Merlin, and Connek ever so slowly worked his way through the crowd until he stood just behind the inner row surrounding the Rock of Judgment. The gold torc peeked out from underneath Merlin's thick black hair and dazzled in the afternoon sun.

Connek imagined how it would feel to slip the heavy torc into his own bag.

The silly talk seemed to go on forever, but to his delight, it finally became a confrontation. And if it turned to blows, then in the confusion he could —

"All of you, hear me," Merlin called. "Don't give your lives into the hands of Mórganthu."

"We've heard *enough* of your monkish talk," a man to the left shouted. "I'm going to the Druid Stone to see it again."

The people murmured in assent and turned to walk back to Mórganthu. Only Tregeagle's wife and daughter and a monk in his ridiculous robe now stood between Connek's knife and Merlin, with that tempting prize. The monk had his eyes closed, foolishly praying to his god, and the women, conferring together, would never be able stop him.

Best of all, Merlin was blind as a worm and wouldn't even flinch. Connek's memory still burned with images of Merlin and his father wrestling him to the ground, trussing him, and sending him to Tregeagle for judgment. No more would he smell these spoiled rich people's food. No more would he go around in near rags or sleep in the cold with nothing but his cloak. Gold to finally live at ease!

Connek slipped his hand into his sleeve and gripped his trusty knife. Just last month it had helped him secretly kill and rob a man in the woods outside the village of Meneth Garrow. Oh, how it itched to be used again. Just two more steps and he'd plunge it into the braggart's chest, grab the torc, and run.

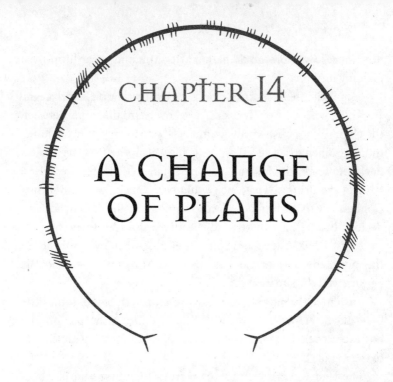

CHAPTER 14

A CHANGE OF PLANS

As Connek tensed his legs to lunge forward, the sound of horse's hooves pounded down the road. Up the main village track from the east galloped at least twenty horsemen. The ones in front wore ring-mail doublets, while the rest were clad in thick leather jerkins. Many had longswords at their belts, and all carried spears and shields. Their steeds glistened with sweat, and the riders looked grim with their long whiskers and polished helms.

Seeing the large crowd gathered in the western half of the village pasture, the warrior in front raised his arm and led his band to the open eastern side. Right up to Merlin and Connek.

Rat bones!

Connek's face grew hot with anger as he hid his knife once more. He shouldn't have waited. If he'd killed Merlin instead of daydreaming, he could have run to the safety of the nearby woods. But not now. These warriors would gallop after him and spear him like a jousting dummy.

Four men lifted ox horns and let out a blast that hurt Connek's ears.

The warrior in front had a dirty yellow beard that hung between the chains of a polished silver amulet — ripe for plucking, Connek thought. Then his gaze fell on the golden boar securing the leader's dark-red cloak, the insignia of a personal soldier of Uther, High King of the Britons. That, too, would be excellent loot … But then Connek saw the two-handed sword strapped to the man's back and decided that perhaps there were easier targets for his thievery.

Mórganthu, Anviv, and some attending druidow edged up to the mounted warriors. Connek could see Mórganthu's stiffness as he surveyed the situation.

Trevenna, the magister's wife, whispered in the ear of some little brat, maybe eight winters old, and handed him a cheap coin. The boy raced over the stone wall and disappeared up the path leading to the top of the hill.

The lead warrior swung down from his horse and laughed. "You're a peculiar village with such a young chieftain." He stepped up to Merlin, who had just descended from the Rock of Judgment along with the monk.

The monk whispered to Merlin, who thought for a moment and then shook his head. "I'm not a leader here."

"Should I believe this?" the warrior asked.

"These people follow their own hearts."

"Yet you bear a torc of such workmanship."

Oh, how Connek wished to rip the torc off that neck! *Soon, soon.*

"But for your age," the warrior continued, "I would swear that *you* feast our host this night. Where is your chieftain, then — Tregeagle — whom men here call Magister?"

"Tregeagle resides up the hill." Merlin held out his staff toward the Tor. "His wife and daughter are in your presence, and you are expected."

The man squinted. "You see well for being blind."

"God has made up for what I lack."

Trevenna introduced herself. "Are you his battle chieftain, the one called Vortigern?"

"I am that and more." He turned away from her and surveyed the field, the village's meeting house, and the spring beyond.

"As there is good pasture here," Trevenna said, "and very little on the Tor, my husband will come down to greet you. But what of ..." Her eyes searched among the men.

Vortigern cleared his throat. "The High King? Uther is coming ... and Queen Igerna ... along with their daughters and son."

"How soon?"

"Morning. Kyldentor hosts them tonight, and Uther is inspecting their fortifications. We will hold a court of fealty here tomorrow when the sun stands over the trees."

Mórganthu's eyes opened wide and then narrowed into tiny slits. He shot Connek such a glare that the thief stepped backward and tripped over the feet of some pesky villager, who snarled at him.

The High King was coming? Not Gorlas, the king of Kernow? Not the king of Difnonia or of Kembry? But the *High* King? Fear tightened like a noose around Connek's throat. To get the three gold coins, he must kill Merlin before the Beltayne fires next evening. Yet to commit murder while the High King's warriors were here? He'd have to choose his place and time *very* carefully.

Shock hummed through the crowd at the news, but Tregeagle's daughter appeared calm. Vortigern also noticed the girl, and his gaze lingered long. "Is this your daughter, Natalenya, whom I have the pleasure to meet?"

As Trevenna nodded, he yelled, "Vortipor! Get your mud muckers down from your horse and meet Tregeagle's daughter." He turned back to Trevenna. "Excuse my son while he finds his feet."

Soon a young man stepped through the ranks. He was tall and thinner than his father, with russet hair, a flat nose, and dark eyes. His beard was patchy and short, and he wore a reddish-brown cloak sewn with silver threads.

"Vortipor, this is the harpist we've heard about."

The young man bowed, took up Natalenya's hand, and kissed it. Connek almost laughed when her face turned white.

Trevenna quickly stepped between them. "My family and I are honored to have you and the High King as guests."

At that moment, Tregeagle, followed by Lictor Erbin, rode into the pasture on the family's white horses. They cantered around the group of warriors, rode up to Vortigern and Vortipor, and dismounted.

Connek cased Tregeagle's finely tailored saffron tunic, his white linen trousers, and his amazing belt made from Roman gold coins. Soon, Connek would have clothes like that. And if he wore Merlin's torc, then some other village far away might make *him* chieftain, which would mean that *he* could collect the taxes — *hah!* — and rob everyone legally!

Tregeagle grabbed the hands of each man in turn and greeted them with a grand smile. "Welcome to Bosventor. Come, shake off the dust of the road and let us fill the welcome bowl together."

"Villagers of Bosventor! Distinguished guests!" a voice called from behind. Along with the others, Connek turned toward the Druid Stone, where Mórganthu stood, feet planted, both hands on his staff. How had he slipped away without keen-eyed Connek noticing?

"You who know me as the arch druid," Mórganthu said, "and you who do not, I call you to come and see the Druid Stone."

He struck the Stone, and it glowed dimly blue.

Once Connek looked, he felt an invisible hand grab him by the scruff of his neck so that he couldn't turn away. Inside the Stone, a vision appeared of him smirking and wearing a golden torc while he stood over the mangled body of Merlin.

At the same time, one of the druidow beat on a drum. It pulsed *throom, throom* in his ears, and Connek found his feet moving forward against his will. By some unspoken accord, the villagers formed a wide circle around the Stone.

Connek could hear Tregeagle, that mealymouthed magistork, screeching at the villagers. He heard Vortigern's harrumphing laughter cut short.

Mórganthu, that benevolent leader of men, called out, "Tregeagle, Magister, we have not had the pleasure of your presence. Come forward and see what brings your people happiness."

Trevenna drew close to Tregeagle, but he ignored her and turned to his lictor, Erbin, who Connek thought was dressed like a clown in his Roman breastplate and red cape. Tregeagle, a frown on his chicken-thin lips, whispered to him with creased brow. But Erbin's eyes gazed at the Druid Stone. Tregeagle couldn't get his mighty lictor's attention though he waved and called.

It would have been a great time to steal from Erbin if not for the two Vorti-whoevers.

Connek laughed when Tregeagle snatched the *gladius* from his lictor's scabbard and marched up to Mórganthu. *Hah! Tregeagle's in for it now.* Connek had seen what Mórganthu had done to the druidow who opposed him. He'd seen their bodies in the woods.

Tregeagle shouted and swore at the druid. "Cease this enchantment!"

"Calm. Calm yourself, orphaned son of the Romans. In the Druid Stone you will fulfill your deepest desires."

"Stop your babbling. How do you know what I desire?"

"Magister," Mórganthu said, "what you desire is power. But even more you desire coins. Gold coins!" Mórganthu raised Tregeagle's belt and tapped a gold coin.

Tregeagle slapped Mórganthu's hand away. "And you'll give me gold? Hah. Take your rag-loving brigands and get out of my village."

Mórganthu peered long into Tregeagle's eyes. Then, glancing at the gathered warriors, he sighed. "A bargain. We will pack up and depart your village if I fail to make an iron coin turn to pure gold before your very eyes."

Tregeagle whistled and, without warning, grabbed Mórganthu by the tunic, holding the flat of the gladius to the druid's face with the blade edge up against his nose.

Mórganthu blinked.

Tregeagle smiled, his brows furrowed. "I accept. But know that I carve the noses off duplicitous imps." He let go of Mórganthu, who staggered before catching his fall.

"Give me a coin, then ... a *bysall.*"

Tregeagle drew forth a slightly bent iron coin. "Make it into gold!" he scoffed.

Mórganthu took the small coin and held it before the people. "Watch." He struck the Druid Stone with his staff, and it blazed up. Mumbling some indecipherable words, he threw the coin onto the black surface of the Stone.

Tregeagle puffed his cheeks out, for there lay the same bent coin, but it was now pure gold.

Connek's heart nearly stopped beating. It could make gold! He yelled and pounded his fist into the air.

All around him, the people shouted and stomped their feet.

Tregeagle fell to his knees. Not daring to touch the blue fire, he gripped his sword and flicked the glimmering coin off the Stone. He held it before his puzzled eyes, scratched the coin on the edge of the sword, and marveled at the gold shavings left in the palm of his hand.

"How did you do that?"

Mórganthu grinned. "Not I. It was the Stone. Try another coin. The Stone gives permission."

Tregeagle pulled from his bag a handful of silver, brass, and iron coins and threw them onto the Druid Stone, each one turning instantly to gold. The magister's hands shook as he swept the golden trinkets off the Stone with his blade. Gathering them up, he held them before his spinning eyes. And he laughed until all the villagers laughed too.

Connek didn't join them.

His reveling turned to anger as the coins fell into the grubby hands of Tregeagle. Connek walked forward, fell at Mórganthu's feet, and begged for coins to put on the Stone too.

Mórganthu bent down and whispered in Connek's ear, "Begone! You shall not get crumbs from my plate unless you do my bidding before tomorrow night." And Mórganthu kicked him.

In blistering rage, Connek retreated toward the outer circle of villagers, but three women almost ran him down. That too-good-for-you Trevenna was first, followed by the bizarre Mônda and her daughter, Ganieda.

Trevenna ran to her husband and knelt beside him. She pulled on his shoulders and spoke in his ear. Tregeagle ignored her and braved the blue fire, raking newly made gold coins off with his bare hands and showing them to her. She, unbelievably, spurned them.

In contrast, Mônda and her daughter gawked at the gold coins and hugged Mórganthu, who greeted his daughter and granddaughter with a broad smile. They danced around Mórganthu and the Stone to the beat of the still-throoming drummers.

Soon the villagers danced as well, and Connek found himself moving in rhythm with the drums.

Bag it, why couldn't he stop his feet? This hadn't happened *before* when he looked at the Stone. He concentrated but could barely slow his steps for a moment before his feet danced off again. He wondered if he wore bewitched boots, but they wouldn't hold still long enough for him to pull them off, curse them!

The warriors watched with fascination but did not dance. Once as Connek passed, he saw Vortigern's mouth hanging open in a grin as he looked at the Stone. Each time Connek rounded the circle, the battle chieftain was the same, his glassy gaze fixed on the strange, mesmerizing, and ever-burning surface of the Stone. What was Vortigern thinking? What did he see in the Stone that made him waver there like a stalk of grain caught in a spinning, shifting wind? Another time around, and Vortigern had pulled out his blade and thrust it at an invisible foe. What enemy did he see? The fool! If Connek could just control his own boots, he could slip over there and rob the warrior blind.

But time blurred, and soon Connek knew only the movement of his feet and the forever dazzling-blue flames of the Stone. After hours of this, it seemed to him, the ground was littered with huffing and retching villagers. The Stone dimmed, the throoming ceased, and Connek's legs collapsed beneath him.

Someone shrieked.

Mônda ran from the center looking everywhere among the people. "Owain!" she cried in vain.

If the blacksmith was gone, then where was his son with the pluckable torc?

The gate. They'd been over by the pasture gate! Alarmed, Connek tried to sit up but almost vomited. He lay down until the queasiness passed, then clawed to his knees and spied past the warriors to the gate.

Owain, the monk, and that wretched Merlin had disappeared.

Merlin feared for his father. He, Dybris, and Prontwon had all been talking with Owain in the chapel for half an hour, and his father still hadn't made full sense of the situation.

At first Merlin thought it was hunger, so Dybris brought fresh bread from the table, and they'd all eaten. But Merlin could detect no improvement in his father's condition. Even taking a cold, wet rag to his father's face had not removed the stupor.

"Owain," Prontwon rasped from where he lay, "when you were young, you claimed Christus ... as your own. Tell us about that."

"Told you before ... Can't you remember?"

Dybris paced back and forth. "*We* remember, but you — " He threw up his arms.

Owain stiffened under Merlin's hand. "Want to see it again. The Stone is calling ..."

"Tas," Merlin said, "remember Kifferow. Don't go back!"

Merlin's father shook his head. "Kiff ... That was a long time ago. Better now. Saw him just yesterday."

Dybris stopped pacing and whispered in Prontwon's ear, "Why are we wasting our — "

Prontwon shushed him. "Dybris, if we cannot defeat the power ... this Druid Stone has over Owain, how can we have ... hope for anyone else?"

"Why can't we Christianize it?" Dybris asked. "Like the standing stone by the abbey spring?"

"A pagan stone ... that the people formerly worshiped ... yes, and we carved upon it a cross to point them to Christ. But how do you ... propose to do that to this Druid Stone?"

"I've been thinking about it — "

"Some things cannot be changed," Prontwon said, his voice weakening. "Owain, you're a ... respected elder in the village."

"Respected?" Owain slurred. "Not the way *my* tas was. He saved the whole fortress once ... Snuck up on those filthy Prithager."

"Who is *your* enemy, father?" Merlin asked.

"Meddling monks. Mônda's telling me ... telling me to leave here! Where is she?"

Prontwon shook his head. "We need ... to pray. Let us anoint Owain with oil and lay our ... hands on him." He fumbled through a bag and handed his oil flask to Dybris.

Dybris held the tube upside down, and not even a drop was inside.

"It must have leaked ... Well, we can never run out of prayer, thank God."

They bowed their heads and laid hands on Merlin's father and prayed. After some time, Merlin thought he heard a noise beyond the closed chapel door. He turned his head to listen over the earnest words of the abbot but heard nothing more.

A moment later the chapel door creaked open a little.

Merlin concentrated on the sound. Something scraped.

"Come in," he called, interrupting Dybris.

Outside he heard the fading sound of footsteps running away.

CHAPTER 15

THE GALOW GOLM

For his evening meal, Garth sat with the druidow near the Stone and ate roasted grouse with a chunk of tangy goat cheese. The fili named Caygek sat next to him, but Mórganthu had cuffed and threatened this man once, so Garth tried his best to keep their interactions short.

"You're from the northern coast?" Caygek asked while he braided his long, curly blond beard.

Garth thought it'd be fun to grow a beard like that one day, only his would be red. He stuffed his mouth full of cheese and nodded.

Caygek pointed to Vortigern's camp near the village meeting house. "Seen warriors like those before?"

Garth went on admiring the horses, which grazed near the warriors. Fine, strong horses, those. He wished he could ride one.

"I live far from a village," Caygek said, "so I haven't seen fighting men in a few years. My father was a warrior, and I learned from him but haven't had much chance to use my skills. See my sword?"

The blade reflected the man's blue tunic. It was of fine workmanship, long and sharp. Much better than the other druidows' weapons but not as fine as Merlin's dirk, which Garth had held a few times. Now that was a real beauty, with razor-sharp edges and a surface like a fine mirror. Even the hilt of Merlin's dirk was amazing: the guard tipped with silver, the handle of black leather interspersed with silver rings, and a round pommel that held a small green jewel.

Garth bit off a hunk of greasy meat, tastier than the boiled mutton they'd had last night. The druidow had stolen the sheep from the monks, and it served those brown-robes right for selling his bagpipe. He hated them for it.

"Do you like it here with the druidow?" Caygek inquired.

Garth closed his eyes and swigged from his waterskin. Oh, how he liked it. No more tending the sheep. No hoeing or planting. No milking the goats. No sneaking tuck from the barrels in the cave. Now it was one adventure after another. And no more being teased for looking like a monk!

And the Stone made him feel strong and important. Why did he need parchment learning when he could see wonderful things in the Stone? And now he even dreamed about it during the day, which was kind of strange. Even stranger, he'd snuck a peek at Dybris earlier, but a floating image of the Stone blocked his vision.

Just as well ... He'd never forgive that man for stealing his bagpipe.

"So I hear your father was a fisherman," Caygek said. "Do you like the sea?"

Garth almost groaned. Would the man ever stop pestering him?

Thankfully someone ran up, calling for Mórganthu. *Connek*. Garth's lip curled. Why they allowed this thief with them, he didn't understand. Maybe the druidow, in their kindness, were helping him.

Connek, out of breath, ran to Mórganthu and Mônda and gave

them some news. Connek pointed up the mountain toward the east side of the village.

Mônda pleaded with Mórganthu, but he shook his head. She sobbed and grabbed his arm so tightly, Mórganthu couldn't pry her off. Finally she spoke in his ear, and Mórganthu blinked and smiled. Garth liked it when Mórganthu smiled. He wished he could hear what they were saying. Maybe if he snuck behind, he could —

"Gather!" Mórganthu commanded the druidow. "We will fight our enemies! They move against us, and so we will call on Lugh with the *Galow Golm*. With the power of the Stone, perhaps we may destroy them."

Most of the men rose.

Garth stood too, but Caygek whispered to him.

"Only druidow proper form the Knot of Calling. Filidow and brihemow aren't allowed. And you don't want to take part, trust me."

Garth searched the nearby bag for another fatty grouse leg, but finding none, he sat down with a small wing. He thought back to that first day when he had stolen the chicken leg and was thankful he didn't have to sneak anymore. But where did that Trothek fellow go? The one Caygek knew. It seemed like forever since the old man had stood up to Mórganthu.

A few druidow had been sent away, and they sat down near Garth. One of them spoke, a squat man with a cloak the color of lobsters. "When someone needs pushing, Podrith the novice always get pushed."

"What do you mean?" Garth asked, but Podrith just grunted and shuffled through the bag of meat.

Caygek squinted at the novice and whispered in Garth's ear, "If you're ever in trouble, come find me." He got up and slipped away.

Garth wondered what *that* was supposed to mean, but the activity around the Stone distracted him. The druidow formed two concentric rings. Then they interlocked hands in such a way that their arms crisscrossed the rings and formed a knot.

They all started walking in a jerky rhythm by ducking under

raised hands or stepping over lowered hands. The drummers started, and the druidow chanted in their foreign tongue.

Mórganthu stood in the center, shook his staff before the Stone, and looked to the sky, where a few wispy clouds swirled.

Garth wiped his mouth with his sleeve and turned to Podrith. "What's he doin'?"

The man stared back with bloodshot eyes. "Yer a fool jus' like them filidow. Watch and learn the power of the druidow."

The living druid knot pulsed to the beat of the drums. Garth rubbed his eyes, for the men seemed to fade. When he looked again, they had been replaced by the apparition of a monstrous white snake. The creature's rippling muscles propelled it through its own knotted coils. The shiny head passed in front of Garth, having swallowed its own tail. The fangs dribbled a track of blood on the pressed grass, and the eyes gazed at him with a pale blue light.

Garth's arms jerked to his sides and stuck there. His legs clamped together, and he fell over. He struggled to sit up but could only wriggle on the grass.

Mórganthu shouted, and the daylight disappeared as storm clouds blew in. Wind gusts sucked at Garth's hair. Branches ripped off, crashing from their ancient moorings. Garth wanted to grab hold of the grass, but his arms wouldn't obey him. Men shouted, women screamed, and horses whinnied.

Above the coiling snake, the shadowy figure of Mórganthu struck his staff into the blue fire of the Stone. Lightning burst upward from it, and Mórganthu fell back even as the apparition of the snake blew apart, and individual druidow arose where the chunks of flesh had been.

The lightning shot into the sky like an arrow and struck down on the east side of the village.

—————+—————

Merlin sat on the floor next to his father and held on to his sweaty hands. He could feel Prontwon's torn sleeve against his knee as the old man finished his breathless prayer.

At that moment the hairs on the back of Merlin's neck prickled. His scalp tingled, and even his hands felt strange. What was happening?

He looked up as an ear-splitting explosion sliced open the roof of the chapel, and a blazing arc of lightning struck Prontwon. The room exploded with blinding light. Merlin was knocked back, along with his father and Dybris.

Pulling himself up, Merlin saw the lightning split apart, surround Prontwon like a brood of parasitic worms, and sizzle into his chest. A fading wail escaped Prontwon's lips. The room darkened as thunder rumbled across the mountainside. "Where are the candles?" Dybris called as he fumbled around. Hail stung Merlin's face as it shot through the newly formed hole in the roof. He tried to cover Prontwon's head, but the hail ended as quickly as it had come. A smudge of daylight showed, allowing him to find the older man's trembling hands.

"I see oaks ... beautiful firs," Prontwon whispered.

"You're here, Abbot, in the chapel," Merlin said, his stomach sinking with dread.

"A mist is rising ... leaves ... trunks ... Why is it all gray?"

Dybris found a place next to Merlin. "We're beside you."

"The sun ... it is setting ..."

Merlin held Prontwon's hands tighter, shaking his head against the tears stinging his eyes. "No, the sun's come out again. Look at the light. Even I can see it!"

"So dark ..."

Dybris placed his hands on Prontwon's heart and bowed his head.

"I see two trees ... with a light shining between ..."

Merlin held Prontwon's right palm to his own cheek. *Please, God, don't let him die! We need him here ... You know we do.*

"I hear the voices ... of my mother and father calling ... calling me to come." Prontwon's voice grew fainter, but Merlin could hear his smile.

Dybris put an arm around Merlin.

"And there ... a cross. I see a cross."

Prontwon moved his hand to the top of Merlin's head as if in blessing and held up his other arm to heaven. With a final exhale of joy, he called, "Jesu, I come to you ..." And with that, his arms fell limp.

Tears coursed down Merlin's cheeks.

His father groaned from beyond the fallen benches.

"Go to him," Dybris said.

Merlin crawled away, searching for his father, and found him curled against the wall, shuddering.

"It hurts," Owain whispered.

"Where, Tas? Where did the lightning strike you?" Merlin's fingers brushed over his father's torso, seeking the wound. A tight fear clenched his heart. *How bad is it?*

"Ahh ... my armband. Why does it hurt?"

There was something strange about his father's band, and Merlin was more than glad to get rid of the druidic thing. "Here, let me take it off." He reached out and felt the icy metal of the covenant armband.

"Leave it alone!" Owain pushed Merlin in the face and scrambled to his feet, kicking him in the stomach in the process.

Doubled over on the floor, Merlin reached out toward the shadow that was his father. "Tas!"

But Owain didn't turn.

His father ran outside just as hail began pouring down once again.

Owain ran, not knowing where he went as the hail stung his flesh like a shower of sparks from the forge. Nowhere did he run, and yet everywhere, as his feet thrashed through the ice-pocked dirt of what seemed like all the tracks and paths of Bosventor. Nowhere did he find shelter, and yet all around, the fading hearth fires of his neighbors called to him.

As he ran, his fingers clawed at his armband and then caressed it. Though his path meandered, inevitably and without reason he found himself in the pasture of the Druid Stone once more.

And there stood his wife, Mônda, with her goodly father who smiled on Owain as a prodigal come home. All else blurred but their sweet faces as he fell sideways to the turf. "Take it off ... Take it off. In the name of mercy, take it off!" he called.

Mônda bent down and, with her long black hair covering his face, touched his covenant armband, whispering words that took away the pain.

Owain relaxed ... until his fingers curled against his will. His elbows jolted straight, his legs numbed, and his back went rigid. He wanted to scream, but his mouth wouldn't obey.

"My daughter," Mórganthu said, "your spell of binding has grown strong since the first days of your union. Here is one of my enemies, and what shall I do with him?"

Mônda looked at Owain in love, and this gave him hope. She would help him, she would —

"To the Stone. Take him to the Stone," she said. "Then he will *always* be mine."

CHAPTER 16

THINGS FORGOTTEN

Merlin sat on his hands, leaning against the wall where his tas had left him. "Go and tell the brothers about Prontwon. I'll stay and keep vigil."

"I'm sorry about your father, Merlin," Dybris said.

"Nothing can be done now. He's gone."

Dybris helped Merlin stand up and gave him back his staff. "Don't give up. You can pray. All of us can pray."

Merlin nodded.

"And don't forget Garth. Keep praying for Garth."

"I will."

After Dybris left, Merlin pulled up a bench so he could sit near Prontwon's body but decided to stand instead. He found the old man's hands and folded them upon his chest. How could he have died just when Merlin needed him most? When everyone needed him?

Then Merlin did something he'd never done in life. He reached out and felt the shape of Prontwon's face. He knew the man's voice. Knew the gruffness when the abbot coughed to rebuke an improper joke. Knew his earnestness when he corrected Merlin's thoughts about God or the Scriptures. Knew the abbot's kindness when he held Merlin's hands in greeting.

Yet Merlin couldn't remember the man's face, since his family had little to do with the monks before Merlin became interested in following Jesu.

Thus, he had never seen Prontwon smile or laugh, nor had he seen the twinkle that must have been in the old man's eyes when he teased.

Warm sunshine filtered through the hole in the roof, and there Merlin stood, feeling the old man's stubble and the shape of his nose. The forehead that held such intelligence, such wit, framed by his balding head and his surprisingly thick eyebrows.

Merlin held back a sob, for only in the coldness of death did he now understand Prontwon in a way God had intended him to be known and yet had always been hidden from Merlin. He patted Prontwon on the shoulder and sat down to pray for his own father, whose face he knew.

The room grew dark, and Merlin pulled his cloak about him, feeling suddenly chilled and alone. He tried to imagine the shape of his father's eyes, and he begged God to open them.

But the wind began to whip through the rasping chapel door. A small animal pawed through the crack and jumped onto an unsteady bench several feet in front of Merlin.

The creature began to purr.

Soon the cat fell silent, but Merlin felt it watching him. He held his staff between himself and the black shadow where the cat wisped its tail. He kept praying, but it was hard to keep his mind on the words.

More cats arrived. One by one, they crept hush-clawed into the chapel until Merlin was surrounded by a coven of silent felines.

Some on benches, some on the floor, and some on the table near the far wall.

Fear crawled into his heart, but he kept praying for his father despite the unnerving presence of the abbey's sudden guests.

They hissed. Then they began to yowl, and the din of it unnerved Merlin. If the cats attacked, what would he do? He wanted to make a mad dash for the door and slam it closed behind him. That would leave the animals locked inside with ... with ... Prontwon's body! The desire to defend the poor abbot and the desire to flee overwhelmed him. His stomach began to burn.

"God," he called amid the angry spitting of the cats. "Protect me now. Protect your servant." Even as the words died on his lips, a melody came to him, an old song Prontwon had written based upon a psalm.

Merlin hadn't tried to memorize it, but the monks had sung it many times. He slid his harp from its bag, and with shaky hands plucked out the melody. His voice rose above the vehemence of the cats.

Yet their hissing grew louder, and their paws crept closer.

Merlin imagined their angry claws digging into his flesh. He drew his harp tighter against his body and continued to play the notes. Flaming his courage with a spark of love for his father, he sang the song with a wavering voice.

A cat landed on each side of his bench, and Merlin flinched. They let forth a terrible screech so that he almost fled — only his commitment to the abbot kept him firm. His heart pounded as they scratched at the wood and splintered its surface like an old bone dug up from a grave.

Owain lay on the grass, rigid and unable to move. Two druidow grabbed his wrists and stretched his arms above his head. They pulled him onto his back and slowly dragged his heavy frame across the grass.

One of the druidow swore. "Why do we get all the lugging jobs? 'Take him to the Stone,' the arch druid says, and so we do, but why pick someone as thick-limbed as this lout?"

Owain's head slung backward, and he saw their heels kick, kick, kick. Finally a heel bashed him in the nose. The blood ran down his cheek and onto his ear. He blinked and through the haze saw the Druid Stone draw closer as they heaved his body forward.

Strangely, Owain felt relief that his struggle would soon be over. Twice before in his life he'd felt this way. The first time he was very young — the day after Whitsuntide when his family had been visiting relatives who lived in a *crennig* built out on a lake for the natural defense it offered. That day, while playing on the house's ledge, he'd tripped and sunk into the cold water. He had flailed and kicked, sure, but nothing brought him up to air. He gave up the struggle then too ... but why couldn't he recall the rest of the story anymore?

The druidow dragged him closer to the Stone, and, upside down, he saw another man kneeling with his hands on it. Brioc. Upon his head sat his tricornered leather hat.

As if reacting to Owain's presence, the Stone raged forth bright blue fire. Brioc yanked his hands away from the Stone and held them before his face.

Owain smelled burning flesh. He closed his eyes and wished his ears were covered too, as Brioc shrieked and ran away.

The druidow dropped Owain's leaden arms onto the grass. "Get a gander at the Stone," one said. "Mórganthu's right that a man should never anger it!"

"Stop gawkin', fool, and roll this 'un over. We've orders to lay *his* hands on the Stone."

Merlin's jaw trembled as the cats scratched closer, their shrieks so near that his arms felt the spit from their fangs.

But a memory flickered like a candle, brighter than his fear. It was his mother, visiting him where he lay in bed crying from his father's chastisement. Her oval face bent down to him, framed by her wavy red hair. She smiled and placed her warm hands on his cheeks. He could smell the sweetness of heather on her clothes.

"Merlin, sweet bairn, do ya ken how much Father loves ya? Gruff like a bear he is, but don't shut yer heart to him. He needs ya! And he desperately loves ya. Always love him."

Her face faded like a phantom, and in her memory he sang out the last verse of the abbot's hymn with all his strength. When the song was finished, Merlin called out before the evil assembly of felines, "Begone! In the name of the Lord God of Hosts. In the name of Jesu the Messiah. In the name of the Sanctifying Spirit. Leave this place!" He set down his harp and picked up his staff. Gripping it in the middle, he jerked it left and right to knock the cats off the bench.

But nothing was there.

The howling and manifest switching of their tails faded, and the room became silent. The cats had vanished. The sun shone again through the hole in the ceiling, lighting up Merlin where he'd fallen on his knees in sweet praise to God.

He pleaded again in earnest for his father.

⊢———

Someone shoved Owain facedown in the moist grass.

"Here, Podrith, pull him forward a bit more. Don't grab his sleeve; you're just tearin' it. C'mon, like this."

They grasped his hands, and Owain's mind flashed back to his near drowning. The water had filled his lungs, and the light above had faded. But someone grabbed his hand. His own father pulled him from the water to the bright day and the sweet air. His father had found him. There was life. And air!

Only because of his father's love did he survive to tell the tale to his own son. To Merlin.

Why had he forgotten his son?

Merlin's face appeared before his darkened eyes. He could see the handsome curly black hair, his grin, and the innocent mischievousness.

He could see the man Merlin was becoming. The strength in his back, legs, and arms. The self-assurance despite his limitations.

And Owain could see the scars — the scars that stabbed at his own heart every time he looked at them. *Failure. You failed him. You didn't protect him that day.* But oh how he loved his son. If he could just say it instead of hurting him. Instead of insulting Merlin's God.

God?

Was it God who gave Merlin the ability to resist? To keep struggling for air? To cling to life even when it beat him down? Owain had always puzzled over his son's inner strength. His own power was fueled by anger at the injustices he'd suffered, as well as the fear of failure. And his fear stoked the anger like fire heating iron until he was able to bend those emotions to his will. Able to survive the calamities of his life.

But what of the Christ — the Messiah — whom Merlin professed? When he was young, Owain had known Jesu. Or so he'd thought. Had he believed only because his father believed?

When the prayers of the monks failed, and he'd been forced to accept that his beloved Gwevian had drowned, he'd given up his own slim faith. Blamed God. Just forgotten. Why *had* he forgotten? Had not the Christ suffered for him? Had not the Christ —

The armband burned with renewed fire, and the Stone rose up before his darkened vision. His hands floated so close, he could feel its frozen heat sucking the life from his bones. Chilling his heart and suffocating him so he no longer felt the love of his friends, his family, his God.

His God!

It was as if something snapped, releasing his imprisoned body. Owain yelled, kicked, and fought once more. Just as in the water when his father had taken his hand and given him hope.

There was hope. There was always hope.

He fought like a man possessed, and the druidow let go. More of the beasts surrounded him and tried to hold him down, but he climbed onto his knees and burst up with strength forged from long hours pounding out iron. Lashing out, he struck down one druid with the side of his arm and smashed another with his elbow. Flailing his fists, Owain soon scattered them and, rising, sprinted away.

He had to get to the one place he thought safe: his smithy. But the covenant armband from Mônda burned hotter and hotter, and her voice and footsteps haunted him from behind.

CHAPTER 17

SHACKLED SECRETS

Stop pulling me, Mônda!" Owain swore as he used a poker to unbury the red coals from the ashes of the forge and layered some grass, twigs, and bark upon them. "Why did you follow me here?"

"Come back to the Stone." Her eyes pleaded with him, and his heart longed for her love. But what she wanted for him would destroy him. Didn't she know that? She took hold of his hand the way she had done the day they'd first met, and her tender touch sent shivers up his arm. He had fallen in love with her that day, hadn't he? She was still beautiful, wasn't she? But now she was asking him to gaze at the Stone.

To worship it.

To touch it.

To give himself completely to it.

To bind himself to her forever.

But Merlin's warning rang in his ears, and Kifferow's dead body floated before his eyes. A fear and revulsion awoke in him, and Owain shook her off.

He needed to work on something — anything — to force the image of the Stone from his mind. "I choose the Carpenter! Away."

Her expression changed, and she came at him again, this time with frantic clawing.

"By the holy name of Jesu, let me alone."

She let go and fell to her knees, her tears spattering the dirt and ashes.

Owain's voice turned gentler, and he set his poker down. "I relent. Stay here and choose Christ with me." He sat beside her. "Don't go back to your father and his curse of a Stone. You're my wife and I love you. Stay!"

In one swift shrieking motion, Mônda ripped the covenant band off her arm and hurled it into the now-burning forge.

Owain's eyes, heart, and hands went to where she threw it, and before he could turn back, she was gone, the door banging shut behind her.

Dust hung and swirled in the air like a phantom.

Owain staggered toward the ground.

Merlin was anxious by the time Dybris and the other monks prayerfully entered to take Prontwon's body and build a cairn over it on top of the mountain.

A mournful lament rose as Merlin stepped outside and began tapping his way to find his father. He'd normally take the downhill path to the main road, but he hesitated. That would take him past the druidow and the Stone. Was his father there? Even if he was, Merlin feared facing the druidow without anyone to help him. Instead, he directed his urgent footsteps across the high road of the village and hoped, beyond mercy, he'd find his father at home.

Using his staff to find the large stones set at the corner of each intersection, he eventually chose a downhill path to the main road, turned west, and left behind the village green and the distant chanting of the druidow. After he passed the miller's crennig, he sharpened his ears for any sound from his father's smithy, but he heard none. He did, however, smell the whiff of the forge. His father must have lit it at some point in the last hour, and in that he found hope.

Finding the large stone that lay outside the blacksmith shop, he stopped to listen but again heard nothing. And the smell of the forge had faded, which made no sense. Why would his father light the forge, let it die, and not work?

He pushed the door open and entered. The blacksmith shop was cold, and nothing glowed within. He shivered. All was silent except for a slight scraping of the wind on the boarded, iron-grated window.

"Tas?"

A gasp escaped from near the coal box.

Working his way to the sound, Merlin discovered his father curled on the floor.

He took one of his father's hands. The palm was hot, with wet pus oozing from some burns. His father moaned and fumbled with something in his other hand, a curved object, his covenant armband.

But no. Merlin grabbed his father's arm to pull him up, and his fingers touched the thick metal band still coiled around the arm. Two bands? Puzzled, Merlin reached for the other mysterious object. This one was smaller, which meant it must be his stepmother's matching armband.

A shuddering cry escaped his father's lips as Merlin hefted him into a sitting position.

Merlin unclasped his father's hand and took the object from him. What was it about these armbands?

Owain scratched at the dirt as if trying to find the band, moaning even louder.

Despite the coldness of the room, the bracelet was unusually warm. Merlin explored its shape, details, and gems. As his fingertips traced the hammered edge, the metal began to burn, singeing him. He dropped the bracelet. *What bewitchment resides here?*

Finding a thick leather rag on the tool table, he used it to pick up the bracelet and fling it in the quench barrel near the anvil.

A loud hissing escaped, and steam split the air. But the hissing didn't stop as it should have. The water boiled and churned, and a sickly sweet smell filled the room.

Merlin's limbs suddenly felt like slack ropes. He fumbled for the tongs to retrieve the bracelet, but they were nowhere to be found. Feeling lightheaded, he kicked over the barrel, sloshing water across the floor.

The air soon cleared, and Merlin felt his strength return. There was only one solution for these fetters that had chained his father's soul to Mônda for so long. He picked up the muddy jewelry with the leather rag and set it on the anvil. Then he slid the larger band from his father's arm using the same rag.

A withering howl escaped from Owain's lips.

Merlin felt the skin where it had rested and found thick scars from many burns. Why hadn't he known of his father's suffering before? *Dear God, help me destroy them!*

He set the second fetter on the anvil. After locating the hammer, he hit each piece with four merciless blows. The gems shattered, and the bracelets bent nearly flat.

Owain cried out, "No, no!" Lunging forward, he tried to snatch them, but Merlin pushed his father's hands back. The wind outside whistled, and evil voices floated on the air as Merlin felt along the table for one of the chisels. Grasping the largest, he placed it over the flattened armbands, and lifting high the hammer, he let forth blow after blow until the armbands spewed forth sparks of light and finally split.

Merlin heard a hissing and frying, and harsh smoke made him back away. The wind ceased, and the bedeviled voices faded.

His father whispered, "Jesu holds me up."

Working his way around the forge, Merlin knelt and planted his hand underneath his father's damp and chilled neck. He laid his ear against Owain's tunic and heard the steady rhythm of his father's heart.

"Tas, I'm here."

His father shook and said loudly, "I choose the Christ!"

Time passed while they held each other in a tight embrace, each warming and drawing strength from the other.

"Put some coals on the forge," his father finally said. "We need to finish the new sword."

"You have the strength?"

Owain tried to stand but fell back shakily. "It doesn't matter. I need to give it to the High King."

"But what of the man who asked for it?"

"He wagered away his money. I want to give it to Uther."

Merlin stood. "We only have until tomorrow."

"*We.* I like that word. Help me stand, son."

Never in her life had Natalenya seen men act so crudely in her family's hall. If her father stooped to host any of the locals, they dined in fear of his short temper.

But these brutes! As the High King's men, they thought themselves due every privilege, yet they declined every grace. And why did her father insist on serving a meal of this size in the Roman style? To make her, Dyslan, and the hired help dish it up was preposterous. *Pile high the meats in the center,* she thought, *and eat like proper Britons!*

She wanted to get away, walk out under the bright stars, sing her songs, and most importantly, pray. How could her father ignore the tragedy happening to the village and make her wait on tables? But no, the men's fat-smeared pewter trenchers emptied faster than she could load them, and the bones piled so high in the *culina* that their hounds could chew for a year and a day and not finish them off.

And she could barely stand to think about the drinking bowls.

Vortigern would burp louder than her disgusting brothers combined and bang his bowl on the table until she refilled it. And then he would sit there with such a saintly smile, she hardly noticed her father's watered-down mead dripping from his beard onto his jerkin.

Such a beast! And her father not only suffered Vortigern and his boorish son, Vortipor, he even seemed to enjoy their company.

Men never had any sense.

To be fair, though, Natalenya realized that Vortipor was the real source of her loathing. Most of the others treated her with aloofness befitting the daughter of the magister, but not him. The rest just wanted their trenchers filled, while *he* seemed to want to fill his eyes with her every chance he could get. He'd even grabbed her twice by the sleeve and wouldn't let go until she listened to his fermented utterances.

Her mother, the lonely female at the feast, sat at the head table next to Natalenya's father, with Vortigern and Vortipor on his other side. Once, after Vortipor had accosted Natalenya, her mother's eyes warned her to stay away. But her glory-fogged father would call her over to fill a bowl, clean a spill, or show off by answering a complicated question in Latin.

She found herself clenching her teeth so that a headache soon crept up her neck and settled behind her eyes. When would this night be over?

Then it got worse.

Vortigern rose unsteadily before the assembly. "Hear me! Warriors of Kembry, Kernow, Difnonia, and Gloui, warriors of Rheged, Elmekow, and Powys, and yes, even you softies of Lundnisow and Dubrae Cantii—"

Grunts of protest greeted this last barb, and Vortigern raised his voice to silence them. "Men of Britain, how do we show gratitude to our host, the good Tregeagle?"

All of them shouted, stomped their feet, or banged their bowls so loudly that Natalenya closed her throbbing eyes and covered her ears.

"And, good Tregeagle, I request of you a boon. We would like to hear your renowned daughter play her harp for us."

The men shouted, "A song ... Let's have a song!"

Natalenya felt dizzy and grabbed a nearby timber to steady herself.

Her mother stared at her.

Natalenya bit her lip and shook her head slightly. Trevenna turned to her smiling father, put a hand on his arm, and whispered in his ear, but the men shouted louder.

"A song ... a song!"

"A ballad. A tale of a battle!"

"A harp!"

"And she's better lookin' than that old bard Colvarth." The men laughed.

Her father brushed his wife away and stood next to Vortigern. In one hand he held his bowl of honey mead and in the other a leg of lamb. "I grant you this boon, and may you and your battle chieftain glory over the enemies of Britain!"

Her father nodded curtly to Natalenya and pointed with the leg of lamb to the sleeping quarters where Natalenya kept her harp.

She retreated to her chamber and picked up her instrument. She knew her father would sell it if she ignored him. He was a man of little mercy, and if he could put a few more coins in his bag — while ensuring future obedience at the same time — he was sure to do it. Hot tears blinded her eyes as she remembered the day he'd sold her box fiddle because she was too embarrassed to play for an official from Armorica.

Yet even as a few tears fell, a plan lit up the gloom of her situation. A song. One she had learned last year from a minstrel traveling from Kembry to Gaul. These guzzlers would be drunk before long, and this song would be *most* fitting.

But she paused. How would her father react? Flinging her serving smock aside, she wiped her tears and knew no other song would suffice.

Her headache felt better already.

After tuning the harp, she practiced the melody and then strode boldly into the hall. The rush lamps had dimmed, and the hearth fire had begun its slow descent into embers as the servants clanked most of the trenchers away. Taking a low stool, she set her harp on her lap with its sound box against her shoulder. The bronze strings glistened in the flickering light, and its beech wood warmed in her hands.

She struck the strings, smiled at the hushing men, and closed her eyes. A small portion of the power of the bards claimed her, and she sang.

They arose — skillful warriors,
From Kembry — Gwyneth Dyn of old.
The young chieftain, Red Brychaid's son,
With his steel blade, ready and bold.
They conferred — practiced warriors,
From Kembry — Gwyneth Dyn of old.
Young Chaliwyr, Red Brychaid's son,
With deeds to smite their foes untold.
They darted — expert warriors,
From Kembry — Gwyneth Dyn of old,
To battle their foes from the sea,
With gashing blades, their banners unfold.

All the High King's warriors sat enraptured, perhaps with prideful remembrance of their own battles. Here and there they raised bowls of mead to their lips. The strings hummed beneath the touch of her nails as the melody echoed and filled the room.

They routed — clever warriors,
From Kembry — Gwyneth Dyn of old.
Amongst the host of Chaliwyr
The men charged, their red spears to hold.
They feasted — eager warriors,

From Kembry — Gwyneth Dyn of old.
With meat, and banquet's meady drink,
They drank deep bowls of fiery gold.
They awoke — drowsy warriors
From Kembry — Gwyneth Dyn of old.
Chaliwyr shouts, Red Brychaid's son,
Their foes' bright lances to behold.

Seeing her father's pleased face, she paused and then, with a silent prayer, sang out again, this time with a feel of sadness to her voice.

They sallied — drunken warriors,
From Kembry — Gwyneth Dyn of old.
Short were their lives, long is our grief,
Though seven times more foes lay cold.
They scattered — ashen warriors,
From Kembry — Gwyneth Dyn of old.
I know no tale of slaughter which
Records such ruin and yet is told.
They perished — beloved warriors,
From Kembry — Gwyneth Dyn of old.
Their wives and mothers voiced a scream,
Eight-score men died, one slave was sold.

The warriors were silent and sober. With loud lament, she finished the song.

They rotted — plundered warriors,
From Kembry — Gwyneth Dyn of old.
Ravens hover, ascend the sky,
As heaped on mound, their bodies mould.
I fain to sing — I wail, lament,
From Kembry — Gwyneth Dyn of old.
I mourn the loss of Rhyvawn's son,
His gallant deeds the grave enfolds.
I tell the tale — I tell it true,

From Kembry — Gwyneth Dyn of old.
Would that they had not shed their lives,
For never will I be consoled.

Natalenya let her hands fall away from her harp, and the strings resonated their last dying notes through the room. The men looked at each other somberly, their bowls of mead forgotten. Some even pushed the sop away.

Vortigern, however, appeared to have ignored the words of the song, and joking with Vortipor, he doused his throat with a long draught.

Her mother's face was radiant, but her father's lips lay stiff upon his face. Natalenya stood, placed her harp on the stool, and announced, "Such is 'The Lament of Arllechweth.'"

At that point her brother, Dyslan, chose to finish returning a stack of empty trenchers to the culina. His fast steps sped him behind a warrior who stood and pushed his bench backward. Dyslan tripped and crashed to the mosaic floor, sending dishes flying through the air.

Guffaws spilled out, and men slapped each other as Dyslan stood with chicken bones sticking out of his hair. In the confusion and enjoyment of the moment, her father and Vortigern walked down the hall to her father's private quarters.

Her mother stepped over to Natalenya. "Your father requested I bring him and Vortigern a sample of his best wine ... but I need to help Dyslan. Would you serve your father?"

"Doesn't Father drink that *before* meals?"

"Too many guests." And then her mother raised an eyebrow and whispered, "Vortipor."

Over her mother's shoulder, Natalenya saw him stalking toward them. He'd taken off his cloak for the first time, and his gold-threaded tunic contrasted sharply with his unpleasant face.

"I'll delay him," her mother said. "Quickly now."

Natalenya cradled her harp and fled through the stone arch that led to their sleeping area. As she turned the corner, she spied her wise mother step into Vortipor's path and greet him.

Having set the harp in her room, Natalenya entered through the culina's side door to find her father's wines. Squeezing past the bustling servants, she went to the rear and pulled two baskets of grain from a stone slab. She brushed away loose kernels and slid the stone cover to the side, revealing her father's cache of imported wine. From them she selected her father's favorite, the deep red Mulsum, took the small terra-cotta amphora out of the reserve along with a small crock of honey, and slid the cover back.

Although her father had forbidden her from tasting it, on more than one occasion she had sniffed its rich cinnamon, thyme, and peppery bouquet.

She walked down the hall to her father's quarters with the amphora and honey. She was about to knock on the door when she heard a voice say, "... so your daughter is uncovenanted. What would make you consider a match with my son? He'll soon be battle chief. Maybe more."

Natalenya halted before the door, with the round wine jar cold against her frozen hand.

"Does Uther esteem him?" her father asked.

"Uther pays no mind. His attention is to his wife, his daughters" — Vortigern's voice turned scornful — "*his son*."

"You do not like this new son? Is he unruly and spoiled?"

Vortigern cursed. "Just a whelp, he is, but he'll be like his father."

"You speak against the High King?" Her father's voice had a hint of shrillness.

"I do not, no. But the blood of a High King flows in my veins as well. Why rejoice when Uther's line continues?"

Her father clicked his tongue. "But he is married to your sister. Your line and his have come together."

"It is not as my grandfather would have wished."

Natalenya could almost taste his bile.

"Surely Vitalinus would have been proud to have his grand-daughter's son wear the High King's torc?"

"You know nothing of what Vitalinus wished," Vortigern said, his words hissing as if through his teeth. "*I* sat in his feasting hall at Glevum. *I* saw his glory and the gold piled high. Your pottage from the Stone today was nothing compared to my grandfather's treasures!"

A fist clunked onto the table. "You think the Druid Stone a joke, do you?"

"Not a joke, no. It gave me *better* than coins."

"I saw your face. I tried to show you the gold, yet you stared at the Stone forever, it seemed, and ignored me." Her father's voice lowered to a whisper. "What did you see?"

Natalenya heard a chair creak and groan.

"Nothing! Nothing, I — "

"You smiled as if you could touch your grandfather's treasures again. I saw it on your face the whole time the Stone enchanted you. What would you do if his gold found you again?"

Vortigern hooted. "I? Reward my followers richly! Not like that tight-bagged Uther. Tell me, how much has he taxed out of you?"

"What does it matter how much I am taxed?"

"Seen any of it again? How much?"

"Two priceless gold coins for each year of his reign," her father said. "Thirty-two have I paid him, but not all from this dirty village."

"And has he ever sent you even a rusty *coynall* to keep up the fortress?"

"I'd keep the gold if I were Uther."

"Tregeagle, you have expressed it properly." Vortigern said, and his voice dropped to a whisper so that Natalenya barely made out what followed. "If *I* were Uther ... reward those who helped me. No taxes ... share my great wealth. We'd ... rich *together*. I'd even promote my supporters ... away from outposts ... this place ... forsaken by the gods."

"If *you* were Uther," her father whispered back, "then *I* would ... you. And ... son."

"*If* is the key word. *If* I were Uther. The men are loyal. If anyone, mind you, if ... even snorted about the ... like this, they'd ... an arrow in their chest faster than ..."

Silence.

Back around the bend of the hall — where the feast was finishing up — Natalenya heard voices. And footsteps.

CHAPTER 18

HIDDEN PLANS

The footsteps grew louder, and Natalenya almost dropped the amphora. Either she had to enter now or she'd be caught listening in on her father and Vortigern.

Putting on her cheeriest face, she knocked on the door with the hand holding the crock of honey.

A pause. "Come in," her father called.

She opened the door and found the two men staring at her.

"Well ... Natalenya," her father said. "I expected your mother."

"She had to help Dyslan with his mishap."

"I see you have brought the Mulsum. Here, let me get my celebratory goblets."

Her father went to a cabinet at the back of the room, unlocked it with a small key, and opened the left door. Reaching to the back, he pulled out two very small goblets of cast gold, each with intricate scenes of Roman battles. Her father always brought out this pair when serving company. Only when drinking alone would he take one of the larger goblets from the other side of the cabinet.

He locked the doors again and made sure they were secure. Satisfied, he turned and walked back, carrying the goblets. He smiled at her. "Did you know we were just talking about you?"

"Really? Whatever about?" She feigned a smile.

"Oh, your harp playing. You've become skillful in the past few years. Your selection of ballads could be improved, however."

Natalenya set down the honey and then bit her lip while she worked loose the stopper sealed with pine resin. Her hands trembled so much as she poured the wine that her father quickly steadied her.

"Let's not spill what I have paid good coinage for."

"I'm sorry, Father."

She finished, replaced the stopper, and then stepped back.

Her father stirred some of the thick honey into each glass and then held up one of the goblets. "My friend, you won't find anything even remotely like it casked here in Britain. One sip and you will feel ten years younger."

"Will there be anything else, Father?" Natalenya asked.

"All is well. Just make sure you return my costly cargo to its place of safety."

Natalenya nodded and left the room, closing the door behind her. She walked a few paces from the door, shuffling her feet a bit to create a ruse of steps; then, turning, she tiptoed back. For a while she heard nothing but silence. Then the two spoke again.

"Fantastic," Vortigern said, then belched. "Haven't tasted the like since campaigning on the continent seven years ago. Not so good as a Falernian, mind, but still excellent."

"Very astute. I had it shipped from southern Gaul. No one else in the house is allowed any. Not even my wife."

"You don't think your daughter sipped it on the way?"

"Natalenya wouldn't dare. She saw what I did to a servant who tasted it once. Caught him with the smell on his breath. He paid dearly for that drop."

"Then why was she nervous? Do you think she overheard us?"

"Oh, no. She's always like that when handling expensive things."

"Are you sure that's it?" Vortigern asked.

"It is just a sign that she knows the value of true luxuries and will manage her future household with care."

Silence followed, then Vortigern said, "About that household. Vortipor is smitten with her. In no time they will be in love."

Natalenya stiffened.

"I have thought long and hard about whom to promise her to, and when," her father said. "Certainly none of the oafs around here are proper suitors. Not that they haven't tried. I have to keep myself from laughing each time one makes an offer for her hand. They all smell like billy goats and have as much money to their names."

A chair creaked. "Vortipor will hold great power one day."

"You are sure he will succeed you?"

"He's already one of the war chieftains, and I will arrange things. I'm near forty winters, and the road is hard. Soon I will ... I will rest, yes. And if I rest, then my sister, Queen Igerna, will agree to Vortipor's advancement."

"Does Vortipor have an *annulus pronubus*?"

Vortigern coughed. "A troth ring? You want to do this Roman-like, eh? Why not a handfast? We could bind their hands — and lives — together tomorrow if we wished."

"It is my way. If you don't like Roman customs, we can call it off — "

"No, no. Your method just takes so long."

Her father's voice became demanding. "So ... you are saying he does not have a ring?"

"Ahh, he could come up with one."

"Do you require a dowry?"

Vortigern snorted. "From you? In exchange for your timely support, I require only the things to make a home proper for a woman. Of gold, nothing. Vortipor has won much spoil. He already owns a large house on the coast near Regnum."

"It is agreed, then," her father said, sending a shiver down Natalenya's spine. "A *sponsio* before you leave. How long will you stay?"

"A day, maybe two. But why have a formal betrothal ceremony? Just let him ride away with her!" He laughed.

Natalenya fumed at this. What a swine!

"That is not our way," Tregeagle said. "An agreement now and a proper ceremony later. The most propitious would be after Vestalia. Maybe the second half of Junius?"

"Come, Tregeagle ... it would save you the cost of a wedding."

"Her mother would not agree — "

"Who says she has to agree?"

Both men laughed.

Natalenya chose that moment to leave, her heart racing three times faster than her quiet feet could take her. Back down the hall she flew, past the bend, and to the culina, where she put the wine back and slid the stone slab over the enclosure.

Turning around, she nearly collided with Vortipor, who towered over her, his face in deep shadow. He raised his arm threateningly above her.

She flinched and tripped back, knocking over a basket of grain.

Dybris sighed as he placed his last rock on Abbot Prontwon's cairn, which stood on the very top of the mountain. If he'd thought that losing Garth's allegiance to the druidow had been hard, this was worse. How could Prontwon have died like this?

This worship of the Stone had to be stopped — changed. Somehow.

The sun set as Brother Crogen's soft voice chanted over the new mound, calling out for God to guard the dead abbot's body, soul, and spirit. The other monks echoed his words. At the base of the cairn, Brothers Nivet and Migal placed a stone marker carved with the cross of Christ.

Dybris gazed at the cross a long time, remembering how he'd met Prontwon when the old man had visited their abbey on the coast. Brushing a tear from his cheek, Dybris recalled the abbot's firm hand grasp and friendly smile. His call for Dybris to join them at the mission up on the woodland moor. His counsel. Laughter. Sternness. Teachings. Hard work. Care. Someone coughed, and his memories fled. The cairn stone with the carved cross came into focus again.

In that moment an idea sprouted: a way to defeat the druidow and bring the villagers back to Jesu. It was dangerous, and Dybris knew it might fail. He looked out to the bleeding sun sinking in the west — and smiled for the first time that day.

Yes ... he would dare it.

Merlin and his father smithed together for the first time since Merlin's flogging. While they worked, his father described to him how the blade's bevels became smooth and straight. How the tip formed a more graceful arc and the tang was lengthened.

During each heating, Merlin worked the bellows while his father tended the coals. The bellows were positioned near the window so they could suck in the extra fresh air and feed the fire. More than once Merlin reached out and touched the new iron bars his father had fit in the window. *No more wolves will get through there,* he thought contentedly.

The oversized forge required constant attention to spread the heat around the blade: cooler for the tip, hotter near the guard, and the tang out of the coals. His father had an expert eye to know when the blade's color meant it was ready for the hammer. And as this was best judged in the dark, his father preferred swordsmithing after sundown. Too hot and the metal would spark and ruin its strength. Too cold and his father would tire from excess hammering.

Merlin found peace in the rhythm of heating and hammering, heating and hammering. Some of his happiest times were working with his tas after dinner. No farmers impatient for a tool to be fixed. No horses to shoe. Just him, his father, and a blade.

Once the color was true, his father would clamp onto the handle a special pair of tongs he'd made that would allow Merlin to hold the sword without getting burned, as well as maneuver it without losing his grip. Timing was critical, and his father's forearm burns testified he didn't want the blade slipping in the tongs.

During each hammering on the anvil, Merlin held these tongs with both hands. Despite his blindness, he had learned from his father over the past five years to lift the sword slightly off the anvil between hammer blows. This was important to keep the heat from escaping into the anvil. By doing this the visits to the forge were reduced and each blow strengthened.

Now and then during the hammering, his father would call "Trelya," which meant that Merlin should flip the sword. This was tricky because Merlin had to lift the sword, flip it, and set it on the anvil at the correct angle in time for the next hammer blow.

In this way father and son worked together as one man: lifting, dropping, hammering, lifting, turning, dropping, and hammering. But the part Merlin liked best — when his father wasn't sullen or angry — was heating the blade, because there was time to talk while Merlin worked the bellows. Maybe tonight he could get more answers from his father than he had been privy to these many long years.

"Tas, how'd you decide to become a blacksmith?" Merlin asked.

"It's a long story."

"I'd like to hear it. We have time."

His father paused, and when he spoke again, it was so quiet Merlin barely caught his words. "The truth is that I stumbled into the craft. When your mother and I traveled to Kernow, I needed work, and a monk at Isca Difnonia told us this village's blacksmith needed a helper. So we came to Bosventor."

"Was that Elowek, who owned the smithy before us? I hardly remember him."

"That was he. I learned the trade without planning on it, sword-smithing and all. When he died I bought the shop and house from his widow, and we've been here ever since."

Merlin's father used a poker to shift the coals around the blade. "A little more air … That's it. Funny how life changes you. Now I'm the one known as *An Gof*, 'the Smith.' I can still hear the old man whistling."

"Hadn't you ever thought about being a smith?"

"Oh, like most boys, I was fascinated by the heat, sparks, and ringing of the anvil. But no, I hadn't thought about it. You see I … You don't know this, but I was the youngest son of a chieftain."

"Really? My grandfather was a chieftain? Where?"

"Rheged, north of Kembry. The fortress of Dinas Crag. I hear my oldest brother, Ector, rules there now. My father wanted me, as the youngest, to be a leader in the church and had me trained for it."

"Why didn't you tell me?" All the years his father was unwilling to visit the chapel surfaced in a fresh light. Fear sank like a rock into Merlin's stomach as he waited for the typical lash from his father. But this time it was different.

Owain stepped away from the forge and walked over to Merlin, who kept working the bellows, but slower now.

"Part of my life has been locked up, for I don't know how long." He placed a hand on Merlin's shoulder.

Merlin's fear ebbed away.

"But now I'm free, and my soul can move. For the first time my father's faith, and my son's faith, is now mine."

"When did Grandfather leave the old ways?"

"I don't know, but he was the first in our family. I prepared for the church because it was expected. Ah, but I failed him in that! I wanted to be a warrior like my brothers and spurned his desire for me to be a monk and serve the church. I told the abbot and left."

"Was he angry?" Merlin asked.

"As a churchman, he understood. I'd — "

"No, Grandfather, was he — "

"Ahh ... very angry, yes," Owain said. "But he didn't disinherit me at that time."

The light from the forge dimmed, and Merlin pressed the bellows faster to keep it going. "In leaving the abbey, did you reject God?"

"Not really. Just being a monk." His father returned to the forge and scooped fresh char-wood around the edges. "As the son of a chieftain in Kembry, I had certain privileges, among which was meeting others of my rank. And higher. One became a fast friend. He was a lad three years younger than I, named Uthrelius, the son of High King Aurelianus."

Merlin dropped the bellows handles. "You and Uther are friends?"

The smithy was deathly silent, until his father said, "Not anymore. But I served in his war band before we parted. And a bitter parting it was. He was just a prince then. Now a score of years have gone by." Owain turned away from the forge, and his voice became wistful. "Many years ... and he is High King and I am nothing. Nothing but a blacksmith."

"But you're *more* than that, Tas," Merlin said. "And you *can* be more. It doesn't matter what you do with your hands. It's your character and faithfulness. Your honesty."

"Sometimes I doubt it. Uther certainly won't think so."

Merlin hadn't considered what Uther would think. "Will he even remember you? Does he know you're in — "

"Bosventor? No. He doesn't expect to see my face tomorrow. Nevertheless, he won't have forgotten. But I hope time will have lessened his rage at me for deserting the war band."

"And that's why we're here. In the smithy."

His father pulled the blade out to check its color.

"Yes. And I hope I'll have my most excellent sword for him. Normally I'm angry when a man says he'll pay for an elaborate weapon like this and then disappears. But now I'm glad. We'll give it to Uther ... and may he forgive me."

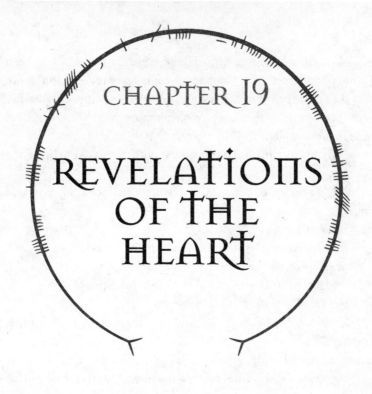

CHAPTER 19

REVELATIONS OF THE HEART

Ⲛatalenya screamed.

Vortipor jerked backward. "Thunder of Taranis, don't do that!"

He stepped forward again with his arm raised, and Natalenya shrieked even louder.

His upraised hand reached out ... and grasped a cast-iron pot from where it hung from the ceiling above her. "See, I'm just getting this for your mother."

Natalenya's shoulders trembled as she exhaled.

One of the servants peered through the doorway, then hurried away.

"Why did you shout?" Vortipor asked, cracking the knuckles of his right hand on the hilt of his dagger, which hung from his belt. "You have no need to fear me."

Natalenya stared at him. His young face had already been bronzed and lined from years spent out in the wind and sun. If not for his sparse beard over his youthful chin, he'd appear twice her age. But his eyes ... they lingered on her more than she liked. *A wolf,* she thought, *who has no bone to gnaw.*

"W-why does my mother need the pot?" she asked to break the silence.

"To warm up honey. And everyone else, including you, was busy."

"I see."

"She seems to have no end of jobs for me." He stretched his neck down and peered at her, scum on his lips showing in the sallow light. "Why'd it take so long to take that wine to my father?"

Her face flushed. "I ... I was delayed."

He shook his head. "I see now. Did they tell you something, perhaps?"

She lifted her chin. "No!"

Natalenya's mother walked into the room and cleared her throat loudly.

Vortipor whirled to face her.

"There is the pot," her mother called. "Come along. The honey isn't getting any warmer."

The two left the room together, but before he turned the corner, Vortipor grinned at Natalenya, and his teeth seemed to her sharp and leering.

In the corner of the culina, she sat on the bench next to the shuttered window and prayed for help. How could her life change so in the course of a few hours? Was her father really going to promise her to Vortipor? If only her mother had a say. But no, her father only made decisions in consultation with his moneybag.

And what of her father's and Vortigern's talk about the High King? Were they considering treason? She had never known her father to speak that way, so it didn't make sense. He was a man who loved high positions, and as long as he could harvest coins from the people, he seemed happy enough to let those above him have their way. Sure, he had sought advancement but never through disloyalty.

And Vortigern? He was brother-in-law to Uther. Surely she had heard him wrong.

Even so, she would keep her eyes and ears open just in case.

One thing she did understand, though, was that if Vortipor was like his father, she would loathe him.

A great sob knotted up in her chest. Taking a deep breath, she closed her eyes and envisioned stuffing her fears into a bag and carrying it down a long hallway lined with closed doors. Soon she found an empty room, threw the bag in, and locked it away. Like all the other emotions not allowed in her father's house.

But then, while standing in the imagined hallway of her heart, she heard a voice call from the distant end of the corridor.

Who was this? She stood on her toes, looked through the bars, and took in a sharp breath. It was a ghostlike image of Merlin. He stood there, tall and nearly as strong as his blacksmith father, his golden torc shining in the torchlight below his shoulder-length, curly black hair. He smiled at her, his fine teeth showing, and her heart was drawn to him.

But it was hard to look at his injuries. The pupils of Merlin's eyes were scarred, and the eyelids disfigured. From there, long gouges emanated across his cheeks, temples, and forehead. Even though the scars were no longer red, their depth set Natalenya's teeth on edge.

Whatever happened, it must have been excruciating. Despite these wounds, he was noble, faithful, and strong in spirit.

He reached out to her, calling her name.

In a fluster, she opened her eyes. Why was he there, locked up in her heart? She'd always pitied him, one of the many disabled people who lived on the woodland moor. But had she ever really known him or considered him? Certainly not until the events of the past week demonstrated his amazing strength to stand for what was right. Despite his blindness.

And that was the real issue. Could she marry someone blind?

Truly love someone so deeply scarred? Yes, she realized now that she could. Oh, but how could he provide for her and a family? For the present he could work for his father, but after Owain died, what then? Merlin could never be a tradesman on his own. And *her* father would never approve. Never.

She wanted to run away and not come back. If she stayed, she'd be forced to marry Vortipor. Either way she'd lose her mother — her helper, teacher, and friend. Her whole life seemed to be crashing down around her, and these thoughts swirled in her head until she felt dizzy.

Finally gathering her wits again, she wiped her eyes and straightened her skirt before marching out of the room. There in the great hall, the men loudly gathered around the hearth, where Trevenna handed out wheat-coriander cakes brushed with honey.

But Vortipor was talking with his father, and his glance met hers before she was able to avert her eyes. He whispered to his father, whose smile quickly faded. His mouth became a hard line beneath his thick mustache as he clenched his fists, drew a long knife, and stabbed the wheat cake in front of him, slicing it in two.

Natalenya did her best not to notice, but her heart beat wildly.

Her father marched into the room dressed in his leather cloak. "Vortigern, are you ready? Mórganthu said after sunset. Come, let us see this Druid Stone again."

"Men of Britain." Vortigern's voice thundered through the hall. "We go to water our horses before sleep and to look upon this Stone once more. Gather!"

Before they left, Vortipor rushed over and seized three honey cakes. He stuffed them into his broad mouth, and many precious pieces fell to the floor to be trampled by the men.

The last one out the door, oddly enough, was Vortigern, who as the battle chieftan normally would have led the men from the room. Before closing the timbers, he faced her. And she trembled, for his gloomy eyes bored into her and seemed to say, *Beware, Natalenya ... beware!*

Owain used a poker to push the bright coals away from the sword, and then he clamped the tongs onto the blade. "We're ready for another time at the anvil."

The leather-wrapped handles felt familiar in Merlin's hands, and the heat of the sizzling sword warmed the air.

His father positioned him so the glowing blade was over the anvil. "Ready?"

Merlin tensed his legs, back, and arms. "Ready."

After hammering for a while, his father hid the blade back in the coals, and Merlin returned to the bellows.

"Tas?" Merlin asked. "Why'd you leave Uther's war band? That would have been exciting — to serve a prince."

"Dangerous, I'd say. We helped keep the northlands clear of Prithager and Eirish, and we did it well while their raiding parties were small. But they sent a large force against us."

Amazed he was finally hearing some stories from his father, Merlin asked, "How many?"

His father shifted the coals. "They had a thousand to our three hundred. Hotter, Merlin ... That's better."

"What'd you do?"

"Ah, we were up in Guotodin, with no help nearby and our route south cut off. So we retreated northeast to the closest fortress. Atleuthun was the old king at Dinpelder, and he was a sometime ally to Uther's father. We went there for help — stayed two days preparing for the coming foe — but in that time I fell in love."

"Mother?"

"Yes. Gwevian was the king's daughter."

Merlin stopped the bellows. "I never knew!"

"It's true. She was so beautiful. All that red hair down to her waist. You should have seen the braids she could make." Owain paused, and Merlin marveled at his father's peaceful, almost wistful tone.

"But Atleuthun's house was pagan, so I shared the knowledge of

Jesu with his daughter. She not only believed; she fell in love with me even as my heart was drawn to her."

"Why was Uther angry about that?"

"Slow down," his father said. "But keep the bellows going. It was Atle who was angry, and that was the crux. Something perplexing about that man and his son, but I never put my finger on it. It wasn't long before I was thrown in Atle's dungeon, and Uther and the men had to leave with neither the king's warriors to help nor food. And an enemy thrice their size approaching from the southwest."

Merlin worked the bellows mechanically, his thoughts centered only on his parents. "What happened?"

"King Atle tried twice to kill your mother for her refusal to deny Jesu. The first time he threw her from the highest cliff of the fortress and —"

"What?"

His father rattled among his tools. "Yes, it's true. To the glory of Christ, she lived, and not even a scratch marked her fair skin. She told me later she felt invisible hands protecting her."

Merlin thought of the angel he'd seen in his own visions. "What did Atle do?"

"You mean what did *I* do? Because of the miracle, a servant snuck down and released me, telling me the tale. The woman was old and hunched over, but her heart was gentle."

"So you got out."

"I made my way to Uther's camp, where he was girding for battle." His father sighed. "But we couldn't agree. I wanted him to help *me* save Gwevian, but he named me a fool for getting them shut out from Atle's fortress. Instead, he wanted me to help him in the coming battle. To stand by his side."

"I see."

"Ah, I was thick even to ask him, and all of us were in trouble because of Atle's wrath at me. At me!" His voice suddenly rose, and he hurled a tool, which clanged against the rock wall of the smithy.

Merlin jumped.

"And in the end I failed him. I left on the eve of battle to go to her."

One thing still didn't make sense. "You said Atle tried to kill Mother again —"

His father groaned. "Yes. But this time his magicians tried to sacrifice her to his pagan water god. He bound her and set her adrift in a leaking boat as the tide rolled out."

"How did God save her?"

"This time through me. One last hammering, and I think we'll be ready for shaping the blade with the grinding wheel."

The work at the anvil passed quickly, as only the blade's tip and one troublesome spot near the guard needed light work. His father viewed the blade by the forge's light and grunted in satisfaction. "Ready for the grind."

In this step Merlin sat on a stool near a small grinding wheel. He spun the wooden handle by hand while his father guided the blade, dipping it in water every so often to cool it. This step revealed how excellent his father's hammering was, as very little excess metal needed to be removed. Two different grindstones were used, the second one finer and flatter. After this his father smoothed the blade by hand with two small, flat rocks, one limestone and the other agate.

"Only one small spot where my hammer mark shows, but in spite of that, it's one of my best swords."

"May I hold it?" Merlin asked.

His father gave him the long, round tang. Even though the blade wasn't fully sharp, it was still dangerous, as the wolf discovered when Merlin killed it. He held the sword carefully and felt its heft, smooth metal, and bevels. "Beautiful."

"Now for the hardening. Bluster them bellows, and we'll be done in no time." His father put the blade back into the coals and pulled out three glowing pokers, which he had placed there earlier. The familiar hissing sound filled the room as the pokers were pushed into the slim barrel of quenchant to warm it in preparation for the blade. His father used a recipe for the hardening quenchant passed on secretly by Elowek: sheep fat mixed with beeswax, salt, and snake blood.

When the blade had been heating for a while, his father asked him, "Would you get the hardening stone? It's about time to test the blade."

Merlin let go of the bellows and turned to the stone wall behind him. Feeling with his hands, he found a small, squarish rock about waist level. Working it out of its hole, he reached into the crevice, grabbed the wire inside, and pulled out a small metallic stone threaded onto it. Here was their secret lodestone, which his father employed to judge the proper time of quenching so the blade would be as strong as possible. This was another trick Elowek had taught them.

The lodestone was a miracle in that it was attracted to the iron like a thirsty horse to water. And only when the blade was at its perfect heat did the lodestone stop being drawn to the metal. Elowek had bought it at great price from a blacksmith in Lundnisow, and Merlin was never allowed to take it out without his father's permission.

Merlin handed the lodestone to his father, found the bellows again, and resumed lifting, pressing down, lifting, pressing down until his father called to him.

"We're ready. The lodestone says the quenching should happen now."

Merlin backed up against the wall and waited, because this step was dangerous to both the blade and anyone standing nearby. Once, flaming grease had exploded from the barrel and caught his shirt on fire. He never forgot the burn or the word-whipping from his father.

And sometimes a blade would crack or bend beyond repair. His father suspected either uneven heating prior to putting it in the fat or an inner fault of the iron, which was shipped in from Brythanvy especially for their swordsmithing. Merlin remembered that once a blade had shattered into eight pieces when quenched. Holding his breath, he sent a prayer to heaven on his father's behalf.

"Here we go ..."

A great sizzling and a smear of flames shot out of the darkness of the barrel. Bitter smoke of burnt fat and wax swirled around Merlin.

After several moments, the flames died down, and his father pulled the blade from the barrel for a quick inspection before returning it to the fat. "Perfect. No cracks. No warping," After a longer wait, his father tested the hardness of the blade with a file, and then whooped. "Done!"

"Before we temper it, can you tell me what happened to Mother in Atle's sinking boat?"

His father sighed, set the sword down, and pulled his stool close to Merlin. "The tide headed out as I watched from some brambles. To save her I left my sword and armor behind, and, with only my dagger for protection, I ran out past the warriors and dove into the waves."

"Didn't Atle and his men try to stop you?"

"In those days I was a fast swimmer," Owain said.

Merlin could hear the pride in his voice. It made him proud too, to imagine his tas speeding through the water to save the woman he loved.

"By the time they retrieved their bows, I had swum too far away, and they didn't have any boats nearby. I climbed in, unbound your mother, plugged the leak as best I could, and she and I both bailed. We had neither oars nor sail, so we drifted for two days."

"Atle didn't come after you?"

"Yes, he did, but a fog rose on the water. His men searched for hours, rowing and sailing back and forth. Sometimes they were so close we could hear their oars strike the water — but they didn't find us. It was a tense time, but we eventually escaped and struck land. We came upon an abbey, and a good monk gave us shelter."

His father paused, and the light of the forge lit up his eyes. "We were married ... sweet Gwev and I. Yes, we were married ... and lived there in hiding for a year. You were born in that abbey."

"Now I understand why you fled south, to Kernow," Merlin said.

"We couldn't stay near Atle, and I couldn't show my face to Uther or my father. So you're right. Kernow was as far away as we could get without going to the Eirish lands of Lyhonesse."

Merlin looked toward his father with awe. "You saved her. You—"

"No! I just postponed her death. I ... I failed her. At the lake, she ..." He broke down and fell to his knees. "Dear God."

Merlin wrapped his arms around his father's heaving chest. "I know, Tas. God showed me in a vision. You did your best. It was the Druid Stone that killed her. The Stone, do you hear? It was at the bottom of the lake."

His father became still. "The Stone?"

"Yes."

Owain roared as he rose, breaking Merlin's grip. "We must stop this. Mônda and Ganieda are still there, worshiping it. We've got to get them away from it."

"But Tas, she tried to have you killed."

"No, she just doesn't want me to leave her. And by God's strong arm, I won't!"

"Tas, you need to leave her. She's Mórganthu's daughter, and she'll never change. Save Ganieda, sure, but with Mônda it's hopeless—"

"Drop such talk. I have to try. Once when you were young, Mórganthu tried to convince Mônda to sacrifice her life and blood to these pagan gods, and I stopped it. I can't abandon her now, and I won't fail her like I failed your mother. Get your staff. We're going."

"But the sword—"

"We'll finish it when we return. Let's go."

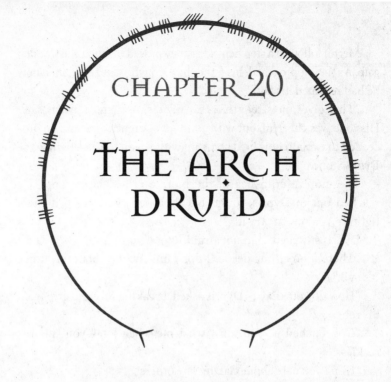

CHAPTER 20

THE ARCH DRUID

I t comforted Merlin to have his father lead him as they walked through the darkness to the village green. And through that slight touch on his father's shoulder, Merlin sensed some excitement in Owain's stride. The indecision was gone. Even if Merlin didn't think Mônda would leave the druidow, he was happy his father wanted to try. And his father was proof that a person could be transformed. Who knew what God would do?

The bright smear of a bonfire appeared to his right, and voices drifted across the field.

"I don't know what everyone is doing at this hour," his father said. "I thought it would be quiet."

"Do you see Mórganthu?"

"Too many people around the Stone to tell, but I would guess he's here. The monks are just inside the gate. Let's head in their direction."

Merlin followed a step behind as they passed through the wooden gate. As they approached, his father hailed Dybris and explained how he had regained his faith.

"That gives me strength ... for my task tonight," Dybris said. His tone was cheerful, but with a hint of apprehension, and he proceeded to explain how he'd come up with a plan to Christianize the Druid Stone.

The more Merlin heard, the more alarmed he became. He reached out to Dybris, found his shoulders, and gripped them tightly. "You mustn't try it!"

Dybris stiffened. "I'm not afraid."

"There's something deeper I don't understand about the Stone. It's evil."

"How do you know?" Dybris asked, breaking Merlin's grip from his robe.

"I've touched it. You must trust me when I say your plan is reckless."

"Don't you care about Garth? The others?"

Merlin's face grew hot. "My back is still sore from my flogging. Don't tell me — "

Someone stepped in between them. "Peace, Merlin ... I think our enemy will bury us all if we don't stick together."

Merlin steadied his breathing and turned toward the voice. "And who is this?"

"Crogen, our new abbot," Dybris said.

"May God bless your leadership," Merlin said, pressing the back of his hand to his forehead.

"And may God give us all wisdom tonight."

But *was* Dybris's plan wise? Merlin weighed it in his mind, and it continued to gnaw at him. When he had touched the Stone by accident, he'd encountered a depth of evil and darkness he hadn't known was possible. The Voice's words still echoed in his memory. What would the Stone do to Dybris? Prontwon certainly hadn't foreseen its power.

"Dybris?" Merlin asked. "Since you are firm in your decision, who is going with you?"

"No one."

Crogen cleared his throat. "This is Dybris's plan, and his alone. The others are more careful of the Stone's power. And from what you say, rightfully so. As their abbot, I will stay with them, and we will pray."

Merlin took a deep breath and looked at Dybris. "Then I'll go with you."

"What? You're against this."

"Even if it's dangerous, you shouldn't go without support."

"But there's no need. You couldn't — "

"Help? My blindness is exactly why I want to come. I can't see the Stone, and that makes me safe from its enchantment. You might need someone like that helping you."

Owain took Merlin's right hand. "Are you sure about this? I need to find Mônda. I had hoped you'd come with me. Help me know what to say."

"Come with us, Tas. We'll find her afterward, together."

"I don't dare." His father's voice quavered. "The Stone's hold over me is still too fresh. Go with Dybris, and I'll find Mônda. With the bonds broken, I'm strong enough for that."

Shouting rose from the crowd across the field, and Merlin listened carefully. "What's happening?"

"It's Tregeagle," Merlin's father said. "He's laughing as he walks from the Stone, and he's holding a gold platter the size of two horseshoes."

"Who are the warriors?" Crogen asked. "The High King's men?"

Dybris pointed. "The tall one there that Tregeagle's talking to is Vortigern — "

"I guess battle chieftains must be grim," Crogen said. "But Tregeagle giddy? Never witnessed such from him."

Dybris stepped forward. "I shouldn't delay. Merlin, are you sure you want to come?"

Merlin paused. Was he sure? Like large black spiders, revulsion for the Stone crept up his legs. He wished he could forget the Stone and these people. He and his father could move away and start a blacksmith shop somewhere else. What had these people done that he should risk his life for them? Look how well that had turned out with Garth.

He wanted to refuse. The words were on the tip of his tongue. But all around the pasture, the druidow began chanting, then the voices of the villagers joined in. And the drums beat.

Merlin could feel it. Change. Change that would sweep across Britain, erase the name of Christ from the people's memory, and bring suffering and bondage in its wake. There was nowhere to run. Bosventor was the place this unholy fire could be stamped out, and he might be the only one who could confront its flames.

So did Dybris's plan have any hope?

Very little, Merlin guessed. Yet even a sputtering candle stub of hope was better than none. If the plan failed, then their actions would still make a statement. And for that alone, Merlin would take the risk.

He cleared his throat and stepped forward. "Yes, I'm certain now."

Owain watched Dybris and his son walk off in the direction of the crowd. How had Merlin grown so much? One day he was no higher than Owain's belt, and the next he was a man. How many years had they lost in between? True, they'd worked together all that time, but Owain had pushed his son away on every level. Now he understood part of the reason, and he determined not to let the precious time they had left slip from his hand.

As Merlin and Dybris approached the outer edge of the mob that worshiped the Stone, Owain longed to rush after his son and support him. Yet he dared not go near the Stone — at least not yet — for its memory still burned in his mind.

He turned away. He needed to find Mônda. But anger toward her flared up in his heart like buried coals exposed to the air. Mônda had kept his spirit tied up — away from God — and as Merlin said, she had immediately run to her father's side. Didn't she deserve her fate?

But something nudged his heart. He had been guilty too. He'd pushed God away ever since Gwevian had drowned and so had made his heart ripe for Mônda's plucking. Did *he* deserve God's love?

Owain thrust his anger away. He had been given a second chance, and his shame was consumed in the heat of that love. God's love. Merlin's love. Now it was his turn to reach out.

Sending up a short prayer that he'd find Mônda at some distance from the Stone, he circled the throng and watched for someone with the dark, flowing hair of his wife, being vigilant to avoid any sight of the blue flames.

Passing by Uther's warriors, he overheard Tregeagle and Vortigern talking.

"Did you ever see the like?" Tregeagle boasted. "This plate was tin! Made right here on the moor. But see it glitter now."

Instead of answering, Vortigern sniffed the air through his moustache and turned to face the Stone. His eyes became glassy, and a leer spread across his face.

Owain turned away lest his own gaze be drawn toward the Stone.

He walked past the two men and saw Mônda standing near the back of the crowd. He called, but she didn't answer. He stepped next to her and gulped at his mistake. This was some black-haired druid wife, toothless and dour. Her arms and face bore many scars, proof she'd partaken in many rituals. Owain shuddered as he realized *this* could be Mônda's fate, or worse, if he failed to bring her back.

As he strode away, someone tapped on his arm.

He spun but immediately dropped his defensive stance. *My Ganieda!* She looked up at him, her pretty nine-year-old eyes filled with fear. "Mammu is sick. She's over by the meeting house. Please hurry!" She turned and sped away.

Owain sprinted after her as she ran to the south edge of the pasture. She darted past a small cluster of men and approached a campfire that had collapsed into embers. There Owain found his wife sleeping fitfully on a bed of dried grass. Her face was pale. Too pale. He bent down and felt a burning fever on her forehead. "Mônda, it's me ... Owain."

She opened her eyes halfway. "Wha'?"

"I'm here."

She turned her head, and her hair fell near a live coal that had tumbled from the fire. "Owain?" she sputtered.

He scooped her hair back and flicked the coal away. "I came to take care of you."

"It hurts." She pulled up her left sleeve, and the skin was bloody where her covenant band had circled her arm. Pus wept from the sores.

Merlin held on to Dybris as they stepped through the now chanting crowd. How the villagers had learned this gibberish, Merlin could only guess.

Reaching behind him, Dybris handed Merlin a bag. "Can you carry this and hand it to me when I tap you?"

"Sure. Let me put my hand on your shoulder so we don't get separated. Is it much farther?"

"Twenty paces."

Merlin took a few careful steps. "Is Mórganthu near the Stone?"

"No."

Merlin peeked past Dybris, and a blur of blue light shone from inside the Stone. "If possible, don't look at it," Merlin said.

"I'll try not to."

"And don't touch it."

"I won't."

"And—"

"Shah! We're almost there."

Someone stepped in front of them. "Halt! Why do you approach the Druid Stone?"

"We come to worship," Dybris answered.

"A monk? Do you think I'm a fool?"

"We're here *to worship*. Let us pass! Are not all welcome?"

The man paused, then shrugged his shoulders and waved them on.

"I didn't say *whom* I was going to worship," Dybris whispered as they stepped closer. "We're before it now. Let's bow and pray to *our* God. I won't look until I have to."

Merlin dropped down and kept his eyes shut so he wouldn't see even a glimmer of the Stone's fire. Alternating waves of heat and cold flowed through the ground under his knees, and he realized with rising panic how close the Stone lay. Remembering his last encounter, he brought his hand to the back of his neck and prayed for Dybris.

He also prayed that Garth and the villagers would have their eyes opened. That God's Spirit would halt the mockery of the Stone. That Christ would be exalted.

Dybris double-tapped on Merlin's knee.

Unstringing the bag he'd been given, Merlin reached in and drew forth a sealed ceramic pot and placed it, cool and heavy, in Dybris's waiting hand. Next he pulled out a brush with a short wooden handle and passed that forward as well.

Standing on the outside of the circle near the drummers, Mórganthu spied a monk and Merlin wending their way through the crowd toward the Stone. *Whatever that boy is planning, he shall pay dearly for the attempt.*

Garth tugged at Mórganthu's robe. "I'm all done with stackin' firewood, Ard Dre. Am I free now?"

"More. More wood." Mórganthu reached out to push Garth's insistent hand away, but he missed as his gaze followed the two intruders.

"But Ard Dre, I've already gotten enough. The pile's a great heap!"

"Get wood," Mórganthu yelled at him. "Get wood, you stray dog!"

Garth shut his mouth and ran off.

"Anviv! What do you make of those two who speak with that ignorant guard?" Mórganthu pointed to Merlin and the monk as they were intercepted by one of his druidow.

"That, my father, appears to be a meddling monk and the blind beggar of the smith trying to make trouble."

Mórganthu ground his teeth. "I had hoped today's message to the abbot would keep them away. But they come again, and I dare not call the Eirish warriors here with these brutish men of Uther's about."

"Then what *have* you prepared for these pests, Father?"

"Our spies tell me that nearly all the monks are present. It is time to show our strength."

Anviv licked his lips. "And if they do not respect us, O Father?"

"Tonight is the warning. Tomorrow evening there will be an end unimagined."

Anviv laughed. "You mean — "

Mórganthu whistled. Immediately, two men walked up. Mórganthu whispered in the ear of the first, and he raced away.

The second man stepped forward, and the light of the bonfire fell upon his brown cloak and hooded face. Mórganthu smiled. It was crooked-nosed Connek, the perfect man for tonight's work.

Speaking into his ear, Mórganthu pointed out Merlin.

Connek nodded and slunk into the darkness.

"Give me the armband!" Mônda said. "Where did you put it?"

Owain held out his empty hands. "It's gone. Merlin destroyed them, and we're free."

"Nooo!" Mônda tried to scratch him, and he backed up.

Three druidow appeared out of the darkness and gazed at Owain.

Startled by their sudden appearance, Owain readied his hand at his dirk and locked eyes with the largest of them.

"Just lighting these," the man said as he held three torches to the embers. "We're not looking for trouble. We've a job to do." The torches flamed up, and the men left, heading east into the darkness and away from the gathering.

Mônda screamed again, causing Ganieda to cry.

"Come with me," Owain pleaded. "All three of us can heal. Jesu will help!"

"I won't," his wife spat. "I'll never leave the druidow again."

—✦—

Connek slid closer to Merlin. Stopping just short of the inner ring, he concealed himself next to a twiggy druid with a gray tunic.

What are the fools doing? Connek wondered. Had Gold-neck and the monk started worshiping the Stone too? Or maybe they were just trying to make their own gold coins without permission. No problem, then, for Connek would steal those as well.

Merlin tilted his head slightly to the left, revealing the edge of the torc. The fine metal glittered in the stone's blue flames. All it would take would be one prick of his blade in the right place ...

Connek watched Merlin and the monk for several moments as they knelt in front of the stone. Then Merlin pulled some object from a bag and handed it to the monk. Connek wasn't sure what they were up to, but he decided it was high time Merlin got what was coming to him. He smiled at the thought as he edged closer to his prey.

—✦—

When Dybris saw the flames subside and sink back into the Druid Stone, he knew it was time. He stood and called out, "All of you, listen to me!"

The crowd hushed and the drums stopped.

"You have worshiped this Stone and turned away from the Living Christ who bled for you, but I now Christianize the Stone in your presence!"

Many of the people shouted.

Dybris uncorked the pot and dipped his brush in. Raising the wooden handle, and without glancing at the Stone, he stooped down to its dark surface and pressed the brush against it. Quickly, he painted a large white cross on the top, dipping three times into the colored pigment.

Dybris raised his arms, brush in hand.

"What you worship in confusion, I proclaim to you in truth. Christ is Lord of all. Your Stone has no power over Him, and this sign I have made confirms His Lordship. Continue to worship, but do so to God and not to the false powers of the earth or sky!"

As he finished speaking, a deep rumbling sounded from the Druid Stone, and Dybris eyed it cautiously.

Connek's heart pounded as he pulled the knife from his sleeve. Just a moment more, and the kneeling fool would be dead. A knife in the back, a grab for the torc, and he'd run off into the woods. The opposite direction of those snail-footed warriors, who had stupidly left their horses tied up on the other side of the field and wouldn't be able to catch him.

And then Mórganthu's three gold coins would be his as well. Connek tensed his legs. With a burst of rage, he lunged forward. His clenched fist aimed the death point of the knife straight at Merlin's back.

A sizzling blue flame exploded from the Stone.

The next thing Connek knew, he had been laid out flat on the ground with an incredible weight across his chest and neck, with coarse wool stuffed in his mouth.

People yelled all around him.

Straining, Connek heaved the smothering weight off and found it was the monk. The Druid Stone must have blown him away from Merlin. Rat tails! There was still enough time to make a kill. Connek searched frantically for his knife, but it was nowhere in sight.

The bellowing increased even as the flames blazed up from the Stone. Connek turned to face it, and the freshly painted cross smoked away in one swift moment. Not even a trace was left behind.

Even without the knife, he could still steal the torc! He stood just as the angry crowd surged forward.

"Stand back!" Merlin shouted as he swung his staff to ward the people away.

Taking his last chance, Connek dove under the whirling stick and slid a finger under the golden torc.

But the mauling crowd thrust him down, and his prize was lost. A bare, smelly foot stepped on his face, and Connek fought to free himself from the mob. They beat Merlin and Dybris as the frustrated thief pulled his brown hood over his stinging face and slunk away, cursing.

Owain heard the uproar and looked with alarm at the sudden riot.

He handed some coins to his daughter, told her to take care of her mother, and ran toward the pulsing mob. A few steps behind the warriors, he dodged around Crogen and finally passed Tregeagle and Lictor Erbin, both of whom fumbled for the gold coins the magister had spilled in the confusion.

Vortigern blinked as the throng of villagers began to block his view of the Stone, breaking its hold upon him. His chest felt free now of the pincerlike vise, and he gulped in the air like a greedy man.

Someone tugged at his leather jerkin. "Highest Battle Chief, hear me!" a round monk shouted in front of him. "Stop this riot!"

He shook his head. He longed to punch the man's face, plop his tubby form to the ground, and continue to look at the Stone and dream again about the glorious future. But the villagers were shouting now, kicking and punching. And thoroughly blocking his view of the marvelous Stone.

"Why should I meddle?" he demanded.

"Because I'm the abbot, and if you don't, I'll tell the High King of the beating, and that you did nothing to stop it!"

Vortigern snarled and pushed the insolent monk away. Who was he to tell Vortigern what to do? But then, the man made *some* sense. Uther would arrive in the morning to inspect the fortress — and to receive the fealty of these unruly people.

Rot. What a mess! It would go badly for him tomorrow if the people didn't learn to respect his men, for they were truly his, even if not in name. Besides, he wouldn't be able to stare at the Stone again unless he got everyone out of the way.

"Blades up!" he shouted as he pulled his hand-and-a-half sword from the scabbard on his back. All the warriors who had blades did the same, and the sound of ringing steel filled the air. Others brandished their spears.

Shouting a war cry, they rushed right past the monk and into the crowd. Pushing the people away like saplings, the warriors broke into the center.

⊢—

Merlin huddled before the onslaught, covering his head and protecting his face, but it was no use. Time blurred as each blow found its mark.

Then his assailants inexplicably fell back, leaving Merlin dazed and bruised. He struggled for breath as someone blew a battle horn and the shouting died down.

His ears ringing, Merlin climbed to his knees just as his father arrived.

"I'm here, Merlin —"

Above, Mórganthu shouted, "My people, my people! Why harm these two? Cannot our Druid Stone defend itself?"

Amid the murmurs of the crowd, Merlin heard Crogen instructing monks to pick up Dybris and carry him away.

Mórganthu waved his arms. "Back now and sit, my people."

The gathering quieted.

"Vortigern, I thank you for stopping this small altercation. You may withdraw your men. We are at peace again."

Merlin's father whispered, "We need to get away."

As Merlin stood with his father's support, he found his limbs sound, though sore.

The warriors tromped out of the circle, followed by Merlin and his father, who made it to the open grass beyond the crowd.

"Since you again see the powerlessness of our enemies," Mórganthu shouted, "I call the uncommitted to join us. Come! Who will show their fealty to the Druid Stone and the safety, happiness, and treasure it offers?"

Merlin heard an excited buzz as many of the villagers went forward and, following Mórganthu's instructions, bowed before the Stone.

"Who went?" Merlin asked as he discovered a bleeding scrape on his left forearm.

"I can hardly tell in the dark, but among the thirty or so who went forward, I saw ... wait ... it's Tregeagle. Mórganthu's welcoming him and Erbin, and they're bowing down."

Merlin's thoughts went out to Natalenya. "What will Uther do tomorrow when he finds the magister has given his allegiance to the Stone?"

But before his father could answer, a man rushed onto the green from the road, yelling, "The abbey's on fire!"

Merlin turned, and there beyond the dark eastern arm of the Meneth Gellik, he saw smears of an orange glow billowing out into the night.

PART THREE

BLADE'S EDGE

Hammered with muscle and bone soon breaking,
Swathed in hellfire the black void quaking,
Pierced by hard light the demons shaking,
Quenched in blood the tempter awaking,
Smoke and death, there the bright sword vies.

CHAPTER 21

THE HIGH KING

D ybris moaned as someone pressed a cold rag to his forehead. "Finally awake, eh?"

It was Brother Neot, whispering.

Dybris sat up but regretted it as his head throbbed and his stomach soured. "Where's Merlin?" His voice rasped.

"Wherever ... and better off than you. *He* protected his head, but you couldn't, you fool."

Dybris stretched his neck and regretted that as well. "Go away."

"Crogen has forbidden me." Neot wrung his rag into a wooden bowl.

Touching his face carefully, Dybris determined that the left side of his head was swollen, and his eyebrow had a scabby mass. "Where is he?"

"Outside. Weeping."

Dybris's tongue felt thick as he sipped water from a bowl. "Tell him I've woken."

"Dreamer! He doesn't weep for you. The druidow burned our abbey last night."

Dybris looked around the room. He'd thought this was an abbey building, but a glance confirmed that above him hung the ragged thatch around the hole in the roof. Faint light from the morning sun seeped through, revealing the stone walls of the village chapel and his brother monks sleeping in soot-stained garments on the dirt floor and on wooden benches.

"Ah, now you see, don't you, the results of your *fine work*. Herrik ran to us for help, but it was too late. We and a few villagers brought water from our spring, but the fire wouldn't be slaked." His voice turned bitter. "All our years copying the Scriptures are nothing but ashes."

Dybris covered his face. "Nothing saved?"

"Just the scrapings of food stored in the cave. But that means nothing since neither parchment nor quill survived." Neot's voice broke. "And it's your fault!"

"Oh, God!" Dybris cried out in prayer.

A quiet knock sounded on the chapel door.

Neot rose, answered, and stepped outside.

In the dim light, Dybris hadn't seen who had come. He was about to rise and investigate when Neot opened the door and entered with squinting, smoldering eyes.

"Now it's worse. Troslam, the good weaver of our village, tells me there was thievery and death last night."

"You can't blame me for — "

One of the monks turned over in his sleep, and Dybris hushed his voice.

"For stirring up these troubles?" Neot whispered. "Yes, I can. All restraint has been thrown off, and only God knows the depth of last night's transgressions. Never in all my years in Bosventor has there been a murder, and now three men lie slain. Priwith the potter was stabbed in his own bed, his house ransacked and his valuables stolen ..."

Dybris stood, and his bruised limbs protested the act. He had to get away from Neot and speak with Crogen.

"Then Troslam caught Stenno sneaking in through a window. In the struggle, the weaver slew him while defending his family. And don't you dare leave." Neot pulled Dybris's hood and forced him to sit down. "Drink the cup you've filled. Last of all was poor Brunyek, our simple oat farmer, whom Troslam found while on his way here. Thrown into a ditch along the road, his back stabbed and his bag of coins missing."

Pushing Neot's hands away, Dybris limped to the door. "Stop blaming me for the sins of the Stone! This I tried to stop, while you did nothing."

"You don't deserve to be in our order," Neot yelled as the other monks awoke.

"That is for Crogen to decide." Dybris slammed the door behind him as he hobbled out into the sunrise.

Downhill he found Crogen sitting on a rock that jutted out from the hillside like an old tooth. His sooty, tear-stained face was uncovered, and he looked unblinking to the western hills, where dark clouds gathered.

"It ... it is burned up," the abbot said quietly. "Completely gone. Day has brought it to light, and who of us will survive these flames?"

━━━┼━━━

Merlin rose, still tired from the failed efforts to extinguish the abbey's flames. Yet a new sense of urgency gripped him as he remembered the unfinished sword and the imminent coming of the High King. In the house, he woke his father and they devoured the day-old barley porridge along with a few hard biscuits.

After pushing the bowls to the center of the table, they walked to the smithy with purpose in their steps.

"After you fell asleep last night," Owain said, "I heated the hoof shavings and left the blade to temper overnight. It should be ready for us to clean and then attach the handle." He went over to where they kept a waist-high barrel, removed the lid, and fished through the hot shavings with a pair of tongs until he found the blade and pulled it out by the tang.

Merlin turned the handle of the grinding stone while his father removed the scale created by hardening the blade. After that, Owain smoothed the transition to the ricasso near the tang with a set of handmade files.

Next they ground the tang so the bronze guard, handle, and pommel fit snugly. These pieces had been poured from liquid metal two months ago using a split clay mold Merlin's father had carved.

A craftsman from Fowavenoc had inlayed red glass into the pommel as well as the guard. Owain explained that the center inlay of glass bore a triskelion design — a triple spiral. Merlin surmised from this that the craftsman must have been a Christian, for the triskelion design had come from Erin with missionaries who used it to represent the Trinity.

All Merlin could see, however, was the flash of red when the sun played upon the surface of the inlays. Red like blood and fit for a king who must rule by the justice of his blade.

When all the pieces fit, they wrapped wet leather around the blade to protect it and then heated the tang's tip to a bright apple color. The guard, handle, and pommel were tapped into place, and Owain hammered the tang tip flat into a small recess in the pommel. In this way, the sword was made whole and, barring some catastrophe, would not come apart.

Using the reflected morning light to reveal flaws, Merlin's father examined his work and said that he could find nothing disagreeable.

Merlin took the blade then, and he felt all the bevels and edges, tracing each detail of the hilt with his fingertips. He finally tested its weight and balance as he swung it with both hands in the center of the shop.

"This is the best work you've ever done, Tas. An expert blade to rival the finest in the kingdom!"

"They say an old blade's always better than a new, so we'll see.

Many's the dying warrior who cursed his smith. The ones that bent or broke taught me more than the ones I did right. Only through fire, quench, and battle is any man and his work truly known."

"Shall we sharpen it?"

"Aye. And carve 'OAG' onto the handle to mark it as one of my blades. There's just enough time before Uther arrives."

"What will you do if the High King won't receive it?"

His father sat down heavily. "I haven't decided. Very little that I have is precious enough to show my sorrow. What else could I offer to make amends? There's a puzzle to think on."

Merlin swung the sword one last time before offering it to his father. "Will Uther give the monks justice for the burning of the abbey? Mórganthu better not show his face."

"If I know Mórganthu, he'll be there."

Merlin winced. "Then may Jesu and the king help us."

In all of Dybris's years as a monk, he had never felt the way he felt this morning. Standing there beside the road with the other monks as they awaited the arrival of the High King, he was utterly embarrassed. Aching, swollen, bloodied, unshaven, and with spilled pigment on his robe, he wanted to crawl back to the chapel.

Oh, he'd protested to Crogen, but the new abbot said they all must appear before the king. Of course, yesterday Dybris just *had* to choose the white pigment, and when the Stone's iniquitous power had knocked him away, he just *had* to spill the pigment all down the front of his robe.

Why hadn't he put the stopper back?

Ah, to have only soot on his robe like the others — but no, it appeared some malignant bird had stood on his head and offalled him.

Fie!

For all that, the arrival of Uther mab Aurelianus, High King of the Britons, would have been a grand affair if not for the somber mood of the people of Bosventor. Oh, the other monks eagerly anticipated the justice they'd receive against the druidow, but the villagers were downright glum.

One man, whom Dybris hadn't met during his brief time at the abbey, stood near and complained to those around him, hooting, "A crock o' ants, he is! Tregeagle cares nothin' but fer tribute, and Uther'll be the same. You'll see."

The others nodded, and an old woman said, "Ah, Uther'll not care for tributes when he gets a sight o' our Stone!"

The Stone. What *would* Uther do with the Stone?

So when the battle horns blasted and people turned to see Uther's war band rounding the side of the mountain from the east, Dybris prayed for deliverance from the Stone and its curse.

Uther rode up in his gilded chariot with a friendly smile but a stern gaze.

All around Dybris the people averted their eyes from Uther's face, yet still they spied at the silvered shirt of iron rings that hung down past his waist and over his gray leather trousers. This was all held fast with a thick brown belt, buckled and tied, from which hung his sword. Over it all Uther wore a plum-colored, embroidered cloak pinned on his right shoulder with a silver brooch.

Longer still the villagers stared at his golden torc. Thick and intricate, it shone brightly on the man's sturdy neck, and its ends each carried an eagle's head with amethyst eyes. Uther's shaven face was handsome and rugged, and his thick brown hair fell down past his shoulders. His left hand, gauntleted in dark gray, gripped the reins of twin chestnut horses as he raised the other, bare, in a blessing to the people that went unreceived.

"There," one of the brothers whispered, "look at his shield!"

Dybris hadn't yet noticed it or the signifier who held it, standing as he was in the chariot close behind Uther. The shield was blazoned with a great golden boar in the honor point and wreathed with a knotwork of blood-red vines.

To Uther's right in the chariot hunched an old man, long-bearded and hoary. He was unarmored, yet he wore fine garments of green covered with a great black cloak. In his hands he held an ancient wooden harp whose bronze strings glittered in the morning light. At his throat rested a twisted white-gold torc, and its ends were formed as heads of moor cats, each with a sparkling white eye.

Behind Uther's chariot, two palfreys pulled a light wagon. Holding the reins in the center sat a thoughtful Igerna, queen and covenant wife of Uther. Her dress of blue-and-green plaid was simple and yet showed signs of an expert seamstress. Over this she wore a light-brown traveling cloak with a silver brooch that matched her husband's. Her hood was raised over her flaxen-red hair to keep off the morning chill, and a thin gold torc, clean of ornamentation, glinted at her throat.

"See the babe!" a woman next to Dybris said.

"Wait till Mórganthu shows *him* the Stone," another answered. "Won't he jus' love it?"

Dybris sidestepped away from them to see the new heir to the throne, Arthur, who sat nestled in the queen's arms. He was dark of hair and, Dybris thought, bright of eye for one so young. The boy, by all accounts not a season past his first winter, looked out with a tender shyness, and Dybris smiled to behold his countenance. Here sat the future hope of Britain's protection. How many armies would those chubby legs lead? Which judgments would his pursed lips speak? What number of enemies might those small hands slay? Or would he die in youth as countless princes had done throughout history?

O God, Dybris prayed, *guide and guard this little one. And if he is not your chosen one for our land, please raise up another to take his place and protect us from our enemies.*

The horses paused for a moment to eat some grass, and Igerna spurred them forward. Only then did Dybris notice that on each side of the queen sat the two royal daughters, Eilyne and Myrgwen.

Eilyne, coming to the age of womanhood, sat stiffly in her plaid of maroon, green, and white. She glanced at the people but did not smile. Myrgwen, not yet ten winters, giddily waved at the monks and leaned over the edge of the wagon. Her older sister reached behind their mother and pulled her back, but the younger kept waving.

After the wagon rolled past, a troop of twenty warriors rode by, each bearing the pin of a small golden boar on their variously colored cloaks. Firm of face, they scanned the gathered crowd and moved to follow their king.

Combined with Vortigern's men, Dybris reasoned, that would make around forty warriors in all. Not many, considering this was the High King, but it was logical, since his purpose was to check the fortifications and beacons — and to recruit Gorlas, the king of Kernow, and raise up men to join the fray. Uther's main host, it was told, lay eastward, where the Saxenow threat grew.

Neot coughed and turned to Crogen. "Now then, didn't Uther's father kill Vortigern's grandfather in battle? How can one serve the other?"

"It is a wonder to behold, I say. The battle took place because Vitalinus had, while steward, assassinated Aurelianus's father, Constans, and stolen the High Kingship."

"How did they reconcile?" Neot asked.

"Blood-bitterness lay between the families until Uther chose Igerna as his bride."

"And she is Vortigern's sister?"

"I have it on good authority that he secretly courted her after they met on a bridge one day when he was on campaign. Oh, she refused him, you can be sure."

"But changed her mind?" Neot asked.

"She saw the practical side … bringing the two houses together and healing the blood-feud … But they say she soon fell in love as well."

"And why do *you* know all this?"

Crogen's head tilted slightly, and he sighed. "Ah, Neot, a scribe like I … I wrote a history, you know. And now I'll have to write it again."

Merlin somewhat reluctantly passed back the wool-wrapped sword to his father as they entered the village green near midmorning. It had been a privilege to carry it along with his small harp, which hung over his shoulder.

"Uther's here," his father said, "and we've made it just in time. He and his wife are on a bench atop the Rock of Judgment."

"Are the druidow here?"

"Only a few guarding the Stone."

Finding a place at the back near the monks, they sat down on the long grass. Merlin found his father's hand, which trembled upon the cloth-covered hilt of the sword.

"It's been a long time since I've seen him, but Uther's barely changed. Stronger, with more hair, but he hardly looks different from when we parted."

"And so, splendid lord," Merlin heard Tregeagle say, "this man, this Pennar, has been seized by the men of Garrinoc. They would have tried him themselves, but their magister has died. Hearing of your coming, they sent him for your judgment rather than bothering Gorlas."

"So it is better to bother me, then?"

"Esteemed lord, they considered your judgment of the more lasting type. It seems Gorlas has trouble making up his mind on such matters."

"I am innocent!" Pennar pleaded, and his chains clinked as he held his hands out to Uther.

"What crime is he accused of, Magister?" Uther asked.

"Cattle thievery, my lord. Caught with three steers in his possession."

"Did anyone witness the crime?"

"No, splendid lord, but — "

"Then how in a Pictish winter am I to judge? Surely someone — "

"I can speak, my lord," spoke the nasally voice of a man who shuffled from the crowd and bowed low.

"And who are you?"

"I am named Kudor, my highly estimable majesty, and it was my cattle he stole. I lay asleep on a cold night and woke to hear bovinous lowing. Desiring still my warm pallet, I ignored it. In the morning, three of my prized cattle had been stolen, and the footprints led to my neighbor's house."

"And did you find your three cattle there?"

The man belched. "No, goodly lord, there were but two."

"Two? What of — "

"I can explain, my lord," Tregeagle said. "One had already been roasted."

"What do you say, accused?" Uther demanded. "Do you deny this?"

"No, my lord," Pennar pleaded. "Kudor owed me the cattle these last four years. When I lent them, he'd just moved to our village, was poor, and I took pity."

"Slander!" Kudor said, but Uther held up his hand.

"Pennar," Uther asked, "why did you not bring this before your magister?"

"I did, my lord, but he was old and did nothing before he passed away, and King Gorlas failed to appoint a new magister. This winter my other cows caught the bloaty shakes and had to be burned. With no milk or meat, and little grain from a poor harvest, my family starved — "

"Punishment of the gods, my lord," Kudor snorted.

"Pennar, have you proof of this debt?" Uther asked, leaning forward on the bench.

"Kudor's left forearm has three small scars marking the debt in the usual way."

Kudor laughed as he rolled up his sleeve. "I paid it back two years ago. As you see, my lord, the lines are cross-scarred, signifying payment."

"A lie," Pennar claimed. "Never did I crosscut them. If the magister were alive — "

"Silence!" Uther said.

No one spoke for a while, and Merlin asked his father what was happening.

"Uther's examining Kudor's arm, and by its girth I'd say that man hasn't missed any meals."

"Kudor," Uther said. "I see the debt scars and the payment cross-scar, but what scar is this from under your sleeve?"

"That, my lord? A mere scratch."

And Merlin heard him cough. Twice.

"Lift your shirt, man," Uther said.

"My shirt?" Kudor's voice turned shrill. "How will that decide the present case?"

"Lift your shirt."

"No sense, no sense, I say!"

Uther's bench creaked as he rose.

"Merlin," Owain said, "Uther's jumped down from the rock, and the man's backing into the crowd. Hah! Uther grabbed him by the scruff of his tunic and is hauling him back. Wait ... Uther's limping. I've never seen him limp before."

Kudor blubbered as Uther ripped the man's shirt off.

"As suspected!" Uther said. "Not only has he been whipped for thievery, but — if I can tell from the different ages of the scars — thrice. Vortigern," he commanded, "inspect the back of the accused."

"It is clear, my lord. No scars."

"I protest," Kudor screeched.

Uther's bench groaned as he sat down again.

"He's conferring with his wife," Merlin's father said.

After a few moments, Uther rose again. "The accused is to be set free. Kudor's cross-scar is recent, and he tried to hide his past thievery."

"Thank you, my lord," Pennar said.

"Colvarth! Where is my bard?"

"Tas," Merlin whispered, "I didn't know there was a bard here. What's he like?"

"It's the same man who served Uther's father. I wouldn't have

235

thought him still alive. And his beard's twice as long since last I heard his harp."

"Colvarth," Uther said, "write a declaration of this man's innocence and my judgment that Kudor is to pay an honor price quadruple the theft."

"No ... I'll have nothing left!" Kudor pleaded.

"His family will be in poverty," Pennar said. "Please, High King, change the judgment—"

"Have him whipped? Are you a fool?" Uther asked.

"Please. Just lessen the fine ... in Jesu's name."

Uther paused. "Because you claim this by the Christ, Pennar, the honor price will be reduced to double. Colvarth, please write that down."

Colvarth's quill scratched on parchment as the bard wrote out the High King's decision. Then he spoke to the king, slowly. "Is ... that all, my king?"

"No. Record as well that our merciful Pennar is to be the new magister of Garrinoc."

Colvarth coughed. "King Gorlas might not be ... pleased with the appointment. Is it not ... better to ask him first?"

"Certainly not. Pennar will do nothing but please our Gorlas, and I will tell him myself when we see him."

Pennar fell to his knees. "Oh, my great lord, I don't deserve—"

"Nonsense. We need able men in leadership. Mercy. Action. Faithfulness. Loyalty. Wisdom. All these I seek. Rise, Pennar. Shake off your bonds and instead receive this bronze torc of office from my hand."

"Merlin," Owain said, "it's my time. Before Uther goes on to something else. Come with me to the front. Here's the sword. Hold it till I call."

They wended around the crowd, and Merlin felt his father's sweat drip down to their joined hands. Merlin's stomach felt as if he'd swallowed a frog. Would Uther think his father had been faithful? Loyal? Wise?

"Sit here," his father told him. "And pray."

CHAPTER 22

THE MOST CHERISHED GIFT

Owain ground his teeth and offered up an awkward prayer. How could he do this? He must be stupid to think Uther would forgive him for his desertion. He had spit on their friendship the day he'd run after Gwevian. Couldn't he have trusted God to save her *and* obey Uther? Had a right decision even existed?

But Owain had chosen her, and God in his grace had given them a few sweet years and a son of high character. And then she had died, leaving a rift in his heart that might never heal.

Uther had just taken his seat again, and Pennar stepped away with a timid smile.

Now was Owain's chance.

As he lifted his foot to take the first step toward the High King, Owain's heart quailed. If he didn't step forward, then Uther would never know his adversary stood in the crowd. Owain could slip into obscurity. Take his sin to his deathbed. Who would know?

Merlin would. And God would. Owain had been hiding for eighteen years, and the time had come to stand in freedom, whether Uther condemned or forgave him. Merlin had stood before Tregeagle and received punishment unjustly, with grace and strength. *Shouldn't I be willing to receive my own rightful judgment?*

He strode forward, and it was one of the hardest things he'd ever done.

Before the inattentive Uther, Owain fell prostrate with his face to the horse-scented grass, saying, "Great Lord Uther. Your humble servant comes for your judgment."

"And what complaint do you bring?" Uther said casually. "Has someone stolen *your* cattle?"

The villagers laughed.

"No, my lord. Rather, someone has a complaint against me."

"A complaint against *you*? Where is your accuser? Maybe I scared him off." This time it was Uther who laughed, and his wife tried to stifle her own mirth.

"My accuser is present, my lord, and he will soon make himself known."

"Then accuse yourself," Uther teased. "Ha-ha. Never did a man do that — except maybe Colvarth here!"

"My crime is that I forsook my friend and let him face death. And I did nothing to help."

Uther stopped laughing.

"This is a serious thing before God," the High King declared as he rose and limped slowly across the shelf of rock. "How do you plead?"

"Guilty, my lord."

"Do you have anything to say for yourself? Why would you do such an ignoble thing?"

Owain's legs shook. "Great lord, if I may be so bold as to beg a question ... Have you ... have *you* ever had a friend forsake you?"

Uther stopped. And paced again. Faster.

Owain saw through his fingers the king limping back and forth and his gaze darting. His lips curled in one silent word: *Owain*. He mouthed the word again. Soon the High King scanned the heavens and closed his eyes in a scowl.

Owain stood before Uther. "It is I ... Owain ... and I beg your forgiveness and mercy."

Uther turned and pointed at him. "You," he roared. "Deserter! You dare come before me?"

He jumped down, grabbed Owain by the tunic, and pulled him within inches of his face. The smell of mead was upon Uther's lips as he snarled and threw Owain backward.

Shocked by Uther's onslaught, Owain failed to catch his fall, and his breath was jolted away. The next thing he knew, he felt a blade at his throat and Uther's knee on his chest.

"Traitor! Why did you leave? You had us thrown out of Dinpelder, and then you left," Uther hissed. "I've waited for this day."

"I left for love."

"And where was your love for me? For Barthusek? For Abrans? Their bodies and twelve-score more were eaten by crows while you ran away to what? Your *love*!" He spit out the last word.

"Her father tried to murder her. I had to — "

"You had to *what*?" Uther raged. "Make him so angry he'd send *his* warriors to attack our rear guard while the foe bled us at the front? Did you know he did that?"

Owain felt the blade bite into his throat. "She almost died!" His heart beat wildly, as if the ocean itself tried to burst from his chest.

"I almost died! I hobble because of that day. And with every step, I curse your name."

"What could I have done?" Owain asked, and he felt hot tears escape his eyes and run down to his ears.

"Stood by my side!"

"We both might have died. And Gwevian as well."

"Die with me, then!"

Igerna knelt beside her husband with a steady hand on Uther's sword arm. "Mercy, Uther," she pleaded. "Did you not risk all for *me*? For my love?"

"That was different." Uther swore, but the blade backed off, and Owain dared a breath.

"What price for *our* love?" she asked Uther. "What would you do to save *my* life?"

Uther leaped off Owain and away from his wife. He threw his sword into the tall grass and yelled on his way back to the Rock of Judgment, "A thousand Prithager! And you wouldn't stand beside me. Ahh! The death I saw that day."

Owain sat up and wiped his eyes. "I'm sorry ... I ask your forgiveness." His gaze shifted briefly to the crowd, which looked on as if in shock.

Igerna returned to her place on the bench and looked to her husband, pity and hope reflecting in her eyes.

"As a token of my sorrow," Owain said, "I bring you a gift."

He called Merlin, who stood and stepped over to Owain. Receiving the sword from his son, he unwrapped it and held it carefully by the blade with the hilt aloft. Reflecting the morning light, its newly polished steel blazed forth before the silent crowd. Its bronze handle glowed warmly, and the red glass inlay on the guard and pommel shimmered before the High King's startled eyes.

"My lord, I failed to be the blade beside you, so I now offer you *this* blade. I am but a smith now. A swordsmith. And I give to you my most excellent work."

Stepping forward, Owain placed the hilt in Uther's hand, then backed away.

Uther looked vacantly at the blade ... and then his shoulders began to shake. He raised the sword up, and shouted, "I should strike your head off for all you deserve." He threw the sword down on the Rock of Judgment with a clang and turned away.

Sadness rolled through Owain as part of his soul dashed away with the discarded sword. It had been bitter parting the first time. Could he bear it twice? How could he show his sorrow? Was there anything to break through Uther's pain?

Movement from behind caught Owain's eye. Colvarth, the old

bard, took a step forward, holding his harp and staring with luminous eyes. At Owain? Or someone else? Who *was* the man looking at?

Merlin.

The bard gazed at Owain's son, who was sitting on the grass and had unslung his own small harp from its bag. Merlin's eyes were tightly shut, and he silently fingered the strings as if to relieve the pressure of the situation.

Colvarth. Yes, of course. An idea buried deep within Owain sprang to life. A chance, though slim. Owain raised his voice. "My king! If you cannot forgive and if you cannot receive my sword, then in sorrow and grief I offer you my most cherished as a gift."

"What can you offer me?" Uther said, not bothering to turn around. "There is nothing more precious than your life. Begone from here, or I will take it from you."

"My king, please ..."

Uther turned in a rage. "I said — "

"I offer you my *son!*"

The king faltered.

Like a partridge from the brush, Merlin burst upward and gripped Owain's shoulder tightly. "Tas," he whispered, "what are you doing?"

"What I do is for your best. You'll be provided for when I'm gone."

Worry lines knotted his son's brow. How had Merlin aged so much in these few short weeks? Would he be grateful for being placed where his needs would always be met? His future had always weighed heavily on Owain. One day his own arm would fail by injury or old age, and he dreaded to see his son a beggar.

But what *would* happen if Uther agreed? Owain prayed he would allow Merlin to serve Colvarth, as the two were so alike in spirit. Otherwise, his son would be forced to do menial chores at Uther's fortress in Kembry. Owain consoled himself that at least the work wouldn't be harder than smithing. If only they'd spoken about it. But he'd not fully foreseen this, and now it was too late.

"Your son?" Uther asked as he surveyed Merlin.

"Yes."

"How is it he wears a torc of such majesty? And yet ... and yet ..."

The High King stepped closer and peered into Merlin's disfigured eyes. "Are you the son of Gwevian myr Atleuthun? Though you have suffered, you bear the face of that house."

Pride coursed through Owain as Merlin answered the king with shoulders square and head high. "I am of that lineage, my lord. And though not wholly blind, I am told eyes are ever deceptive. I also know God's strong hand holds more boons than just sight."

"Well said." Uther answered. "And what are you called?"

"In the tongue of the Romans, I am named Merlinus, but my mother named me Merlin."

"Where is your mother?" Uther stepped back and scanned the crowd. "Is she present? It's been many years since your father and I stood upon the great rock of her house."

Merlin blinked a few times and then answered. "She is dead, my lord. Fourteen years."

Uther looked to Owain for confirmation. Blinking back tears, Owain nodded in confirmation. The king closed his eyes, tightened his lips, and nodded.

"I see," he said. "You have both suffered."

The king limped back to his bench and sat down. "If you entered my service, young Merlin, what would you do? How could you serve me? You cannot — "

"Fight?" Merlin answered. "No, I cannot. But I am strong and can do tasks that many hands are unwilling to do. I can garden. I can haul wood and work a bellows. I can hoe out dung. I can — "

Colvarth stepped forward, and Owain's heart swelled with hope. The bard straightened as far as he was able, raised his thin hand, and in his slow, halting manner said, "Nay, son born of the wild-water ... you are not fit for such tasks! You shall be a ... bard. Wisdom shall grace your speech, and angels ... dance upon your harp. Though now you see not, Merlin, yet in the darkness you shall ... light the

242

path of Jesu for all the kings of the world. And though humble, yet in God's strength you shall ... uphold your people!"

As if struck, Uther looked at his chief adviser. "What are you saying?"

"A prophecy, my king," the bard said.

"Can you be sure of this?"

Sticking his bristly white beard out, Colvarth took one of his long fingers and tapped Uther on the chest. "So has the ... voice of the Most High spoken. Do not doubt, my king. Though the young man is ... beyond the usual age, yet I will teach him."

At that moment the druidow made their appearance.

Preoccupied with the discussion, Owain hadn't heard their approach. They marched four abreast onto the green until all one hundred or so stood around the Druid Stone. They turned to face Uther and the assembly.

Owain looked for Mônda among them but did not see her. He had to find her soon to make sure that she was being cared for properly, even if it meant visiting the camp of the druidow. Though it seemed a futile effort, he had to try once more to persuade her to forsake her pagan ways and follow Jesu.

Mórganthu stood serenely at the front of the gathering wearing a green linen robe with a leather belt. Around his neck hung a large silver amulet shaped like a crescent moon lying with the horns pointing upward. Close by stood a half circle of seven druidow, including Anviv, and their robes were similar to Mórganthu's.

Uther's eyes opened wide, and he asked Colvarth, "My bard, what of this? Vortigern mentioned they were here with some rock, but so many? Do you know these?"

Colvarth stared at the druidow, his eyes neither moving nor blinking.

"Colvarth," Uther said, shaking the old man gently. "Do you hear me?"

"Yes," he said.

"Speak, man!"

"Ah, my king. I see the sickle ... and it is sharpened for a harvest of woe!"

"But do you know them?"

"In your father's time, before he ... claimed the Christ, I helped lead and dwelt among these druidow. Though I am not familiar with all, yet I know ... Mórganthu, their leader, for his thirst for power and devotion to the ... old gods is unsurpassed."

"So he is the one you've told me about. What am I to make of this?" Uther asked.

"It is a challenge. The people ... have them give fealty to you and your heir. Do it now before Mórganthu speaks and ... tries to draw their hearts to himself. It is his way."

Uther hesitated but finally went to his wife and spoke to her. She called for her eldest daughter, Eilyne, who brought the young Arthur.

The High King stood upon the bench above the people and called to them, arms outstretched in welcome. "Citizens and Britons! Hear your High King. I have come to visit you, not only to have your fortifications inspected, which aids in your protection" — the people turned and murmured assent — "but also to receive your fealty."

Dwarfed by the large frame of Uther, the bard spoke next. "Each of you, come forward and kiss the leather of the High King's boot ... and the boot of his son. And so receive his protection."

The crowd mumbled and looked to one another. A few of them shrugged their shoulders and stepped forward. Until Mórganthu raised his voice.

"People ... my people! Do not give fealty to the High King. He neither honors your gods nor worships them. All who call on his foreign god will be cursed." Mórganthu struck the Stone with his staff, and from deep inside the blue light gleamed.

Most of the villagers turned and walked toward Mórganthu, their arms stiff and their heads swaying slightly as drums began to beat beyond the Stone.

Owain held his breath as he looked to Uther and saw rage flash in the king's eyes and play at the corners of his mouth.

CHAPTER 23

THE BLADE STRIKES

Owain saw Uther baring his teeth. Colvarth tugged on the king's belt, whispered in his ear, and then pointed at Mórganthu.

"Vortigern," Uther called, and his battle chief attended him at once. They conferred for a moment, and then Vortigern summoned half the warriors. These stepped forward and slid their steel from their sheaths.

"What's happening?" Merlin asked in Owain's ear.

Owain placed a hand on his son's shoulder. "It looks like Uther's going to confront Mórganthu."

Merlin blew out a short breath. "How could he not? This is treason."

"Aye." Owain watched as Uther reached to pull his own sword from its sheath but found it missing. He jumped down and kicked among the tall grasses for the blade, which he'd thrown there, but not finding it, he returned to the Rock of Judgment and — to Owain's delight — picked up the new sword. The sunshine blazed off of its lustrous surface as Uther tested its weight and balance.

He seemed satisfied, and Owain told Merlin the news.

Uther stalked off, stiffly, toward the druidow with Vortigern and his twenty warriors behind. The other half stayed behind in vigilant guard over Igerna and the children.

Onward they advanced, as fast as the High King could move with his uneven stride. How the sight of that limp pained Owain now, but he pushed the thought aside. Taking Merlin's arm, he followed the king's company at a distance as the villagers parted to admit the wave of armed men.

The advance of fierce-eyed warriors sent a panic through the ranks of druidow. One druid in a brown cloak tried to run but smacked into another, and both fell. Yet another druid ran sideways near Vortigern, and the battle chief shoved him face-first into the dirt. Only the center held as Mórganthu pulled Anviv and his robed druidow close to the Stone.

Owain had fully expected to see blood, but none was shed. The warriors had bluffed their way through, and now Uther stood before Mórganthu, whose eyes flashed as he stood firm, staff held at the ready.

"You call for rebellion, druid. Leave this island and let your name never be spoken of again. You will be forgotten, and your gods along with you. I command it."

"It is *we* who are in power here," Mórganthu answered with a sneer.

Uther pressed the tip of his sword through Mórganthu's beard and brought it near the man's heart. "You are a fool. Take your magician's rock and go."

"We *will* take it. In truth, we have come to remove it back to the Gorseth Cawmen. Tonight we light the Beltayne fires after the double descent of the moon and the Seven Torches, and then" — Mórganthu smiled — "and then ..."

"What?" Uther demanded, now pushing the blade against Mórganthu's chest. "You waste your speech calling on the old gods."

"Our gods have power, and woe to any who oppose." Mórganthu spit on the sword.

In response, Uther sliced the chain of Mórganthu's crescent-moon amulet, and it fell to the dirt. "You test my patience. Leave this place now!"

Mórganthu glared at Uther as he picked up his amulet. "You malign me because you do not believe. You malign me because your criminal of a bard does not believe. But the Druid Stone is before you, O doubter. Look and behold true power!"

And as Mórganthu stepped aside, he struck the Stone twice with his staff, and from its surface blazed a blue fire higher than Owain had ever seen.

Uther eyed the Stone in surprise.

Merlin pulled closer to Owain. "Tas? What's happening?"

"I'm trying not to look at the Stone, but Uther sure sees it. We should've warned him."

Uther's face lost all expression. His hands and arms relaxed, causing the tip of the new sword to descend until it touched the grass.

Anviv stepped up to the High King and mocked him, saying, "Ha! You see, O father, even the *mighty* Uther falls before the power of our Stone!"

Owain shuddered and turned to Merlin. "We have to stop this. Uther's become enchanted."

He stepped forward, but Merlin pulled his arm. "No, we need to pray! I'm convinced that's the only way to save him."

"He has to look away from it." Owain shook off his son's hand, but before he could take another step, Merlin wrapped his arms around his father's chest in a powerful hold, restraining him.

"Father God, we pray for our king, the king you have appointed to rule over us. Free him from this sorcery ..."

Owain tried to agree in his mind with the prayer, yet the events before him fought for his attention.

Anviv waved his hand in front of Uther's face. "Where is your *strength*, O forceful one? Where is your *justice*?"

Uther blinked.

Anviv almost danced around the High King. "His majesty ... servant of the Stone!"

Uther's lips twitched, and he shook his head.

Mórganthu tried to pull Anviv back, but he ignored his father.

"Fall prostrate, mighty king," Anviv jeered up at Uther's face. "Touch the Stone of Abundance, and then kiss the foot ... kiss the foot of the arch druid!"

A rage crept onto Uther's face, and he jerked backward from the Stone as if escaping the talons of an invisible beast. Lifting his new sword, he swung with astonishing speed, and in that deadly arc, he sliced through Anviv's neck.

Owain gasped as the head and body fell to the ground at the same instant, the face of Anviv frozen in mockery, and his copper torc rolling away, bloody, on the grass.

"What is it, Tas? Has Uther — ?"

"No ... he didn't ... he didn't touch the Stone."

Owain fell to his knees, and his tongue caught in his throat. He'd seen much worse before, but it had been a long time.

"What? Tas!"

"Anviv is dead."

Mórganthu fell stricken beside the body of his son, his beard trailing in the blood as he picked up the fallen head. All the druidow retreated from Uther, who still held his sword at the ready, his eyes aflame.

"Noooo!" Mórganthu cried, and tears rolled from his eyes.

Uther pointed to Anviv's head with the sword. "What of this wolfish druid? Let the dead die!"

"He ... was my son," Mórganthu shrieked.

The High King stepped back, his mouth pressed in a firm line and his warriors gathered silently around him.

Mórganthu smoothed back Anviv's hair, his hand leaving a slick of blood across the strands. "A curse ... on you, Uther mab Aurelianus ... a curse on your life! May Belornos drink deep of the blood of your house!"

Mórganthu stood and called the druidows to him. They picked up the body and torc of Anviv while others took up the leather tarp with the Stone suspended inside.

Mórganthu turned to the speechless villagers and said through his tears, "Come this night, O people! Bring your animals for purification to the Beltayne Feast and the Night of Fire. There, with smoke, we will cleanse ourselves from the rot of" — his voice broke — "this *High King* and his false god. We will have roasted meat, bread, and drink in abundance for all. And we will dance and dedicate ourselves to Belornos ... and the Stone which he sent."

All around, the people nodded, but the thought sickened Owain. How could they be so easily led astray?

With Mórganthu in the rear, the druidow departed the village green as quickly as they had come. Before passing through the gate, Mórganthu pointed at Uther and mouthed words that couldn't be understood. Then cradling the head of his son, the arch druid departed with wailing and cursing.

And there, even as storm clouds blew in from the west, Owain saw Garth walking alongside Mórganthu and holding on to the old man's belt.

Merlin's frustration rose as the moments went by. What had just happened? Being nearly blind was tolerable during mundane activities, but it stretched his patience to breaking when important events rolled past all around him. And his father explained all too little.

Then someone called his name. "Merlinus! It is Uther speaking. As of this day, you are my servant. Take my sword and clean it."

With a deep breath, Merlin let go of his father's reassuring shoulder and walked toward the voice until he stood before Uther.

"This weapon has served me well. Clean it, and I will receive your fealty."

Merlin reached out his hands, palms open, and Uther placed the heavy blade there.

As Anviv's blood smeared from the sword onto Merlin's left hand, he felt dizzy, and the ground fell away from his feet. Everything in his weak eyesight turned to a soft whiteness, and waves of mist beat upon his face.

Upward he felt himself fly, and Uther's new sword became heavy. Merlin gripped its hilt with both hands but feared he'd lose his hold in the quickening rain.

Suddenly the rising motion ended, and he fell. With a great shock he crashed onto a hard surface. When Merlin opened his eyes, he found himself lying, wet and cold, at the edge of a small glade within a vast forest. And his eyesight was clear.

In the center of the glade stood a giant boar, grunting and snorting as he thrashed his feet in every direction to crush a mob that was attacking him. His massive bristled back reared eight feet high, his regal snout jutted two feet long, and along his flanks rippled muscles of incredible strength.

Merlin lay in awe, transfixed by the magnificence of the creature. Surely none like it existed in all creation. Outward from his mouth curved two tusks, each the length of Merlin's forearm. Each swipe crushed or impaled an attacker — but these weren't men!

Thousands of ratlike creatures, all carrying ropes and running on two legs. One belt-high creature scrambled past Merlin, its stinking fur coated in slime and a fang-toothed smile upon its face. Merlin watched in horror as they skittered around the boar, trying to bind his legs. The boar slew dozens of them, but for every one he slew, ten more took its place, and the boar was soon bound and cruelly stretched upon the forest floor.

Out from the shadows stalked a stranger, taller than Merlin, and he held a bronze sword. He was a beast in man's shape, with yellowed skin, and his nose almost as long as the rats'. His pupils were a goatlike horizontal shape, and from his jagged teeth hung strings of raw meat. Antlers grew from his skull, and his head was covered with a mane of thick, silver-green hair.

A forked tongue slithered in and out of his mouth, and he

turned to face Merlin. "Gettest thou gone, briiight one. Keep not Kernunnosss from his prey. It is I who claim the throne of the Lord of the Forestsss!"

Kernunnos jumped at the boar and drove his blade into his back.

The boar shrieked in mortal terror and thrashed wildly.

The fallen leaves became slick with blood.

Bile rose in Merlin's throat. He wanted the boar to escape and turn on these vile hunters. He pulled Uther's sword from where he had dropped it on the grass and tested it, sharpened to a deadly edge by his father just that morning. He stepped forward to save the boar.

By then Kernunnos had leaped around the great animal, and he lifted his bronze sword above the taut belly.

Merlin winced as he looked to the anguished face of the boar, who strangely was able to grunt the plaintive words of "Hhheelllppp. Hellpp maaay."

It was Merlin's last chance. He ran forward and yelled, "Stop ... You will not harm this creature!" A half-dozen rats died under his swinging blade, and the rest backed away. He jumped into the center and started to sever the rope holding down the boar's forelegs.

Before he could finish, however, Kernunnos ran toward him. "I warned youu, and ssso your flesh shall be feasssted as well!"

Their swords struck with a clang.

Again and again their blades met, and each time Kernunnos pushed Merlin back by the ferocity of his attack. Whenever Merlin tried to gain an advantage, his sword met either empty air or a slicing parry. Kernunnos pushed Merlin toward the rats, who now sported flint-tipped spears.

In desperation Merlin charged, but his foe jumped to the side.

Merlin tumbled to the ground with Uther's sword flying from his hand. In panic, he stretched out and touched his fingers to the hilt.

He was too late.

Kernunnos had planted his foot on the flat of the blade, and try as he might, Merlin couldn't wrench it free. The amber-colored blade of his enemy jabbed toward Merlin's face, and the rats trussed him and hung him by his hands from a tree.

He kicked at the silent rats until he spied Kernunnos. Once again, the beast stood at the chest of the boar. This time he held Uther's sword.

"No!" Merlin yelled.

Kernunnos's goat eyes burned with glee. "You cannot ssstop mee, briight one, and now I use your own sssteel. There is only one Lord of the Foresssst, and I will have reeevenge!"

Uther's blade plunged into the boar, who squealed in agony and arched his bristled back to pull away, but in vain. He shook his head, and blood poured from his mouth.

Kernunnos slit the boar down the front, and the rats rushed in to gorge their appetites.

Merlin wept, yet through his tears he beheld an angel in a blinding white robe. He spoke, and his mighty voice shook the trees.

"BEWARE EVIL, MERLIN!"

The angel disappeared in a flash of light.

And Merlin's last memory before losing consciousness was Kernunnos slipping toward him through a haze. Before his face he held Uther's bloodstained sword pointing to the moon.

CHAPTER 24

OATHS UNTAKEN

With a start, Merlin found his blotched eyesight had returned. In his hands he still held Uther's sword. His arms throbbed as if he'd been holding it for hours.

"Merlin?" said a voice nearby. It was gravelly, and the person spoke slowly.

"I'm here."

"It is I ... Colvarth, and I hold a rag for you to clean the blade."

Merlin felt a wet cloth touch his left hand. Taking it, he wiped down the sword until the metal felt clean and cold, finally drying it with the other end of the rag.

"Let us ... take the blade to Uther, and when he is ready, he will ... ask you to swear fealty."

Thunder sounded in the distance as Colvarth took Merlin's arm and led him back to the Judgment Rock, where Uther again sat before the villagers.

Merlin held out the sword, hilt first, and Uther received it.

"My thanks, Merlin. You are dismissed for the moment."

Colvarth directed him to a place on the grass next to Owain, who spoke to him. "Why the trouble cleaning Uther's sword? Are you well?"

"I have a heavy burden. I can't it explain now."

Apparently he had missed some proceedings, for Abbot Crogen spoke. "And so, my lord, we ask for justice as well as help regarding the burning of our abbey."

"Do you have witnesses against the druidow?"

"Yes, my lord. Two of our number witnessed three druidow lighting fire to the thatch roofs. Brother Melor and Brother Herrik, please step forward."

Uther examined them, asking details of how they knew the torch wielders had been druidow. Then he called for other testimony.

To Merlin's surprise, his father stepped forward.

"Yes, my lord, I was here on the village green last night prior to the burning of the abbey, and three druidow wearing the same clothing the monks described lit torches in my presence and ran eastward toward the abbey."

Uther asked a few more questions, then, apparently convinced by the answers, he dismissed Owain. "My judgment goes against Mórganthu and the druidow. Tregeagle, approach."

The magister stood before the High King.

"Tregeagle … as I must meet Gorlas at Dintaga, I charge you to exact the equivalent of five gold coins from the druidow as recompense to the monks of Bosvenna Abbey. You may collect cattle, clothing, coins, or any other possession of theirs."

"Assuredly, my lord, without delay."

"That is well," Uther said. "And to assure the good abbot of your faithful collection, I ask you to pay him now."

Tregeagle gulped loudly. "Now, splendid lord?"

"Yes, of course. From your treasury."

"But —"

Uther sat forward. "You are planning to make Mórganthu pay, are you not?"

"Yes, but —" Tregeagle stammered.

"Is there a problem?"

"Splendid lord … I did not bring such a sum."

Uther stood, holding his new blade in the air as if he was inspecting it. "Assuredly you did."

Merlin's father whispered. "He's taking his sword and slicing Tregeagle's belt …"

The belt fell ringing to the rock, and some of the coins rolled away.

Owain laughed. "Tregeagle's going to faint!"

"Take five and pay the good abbot."

"My lord," Crogen protested, "three would suffice."

"Five," Uther said. "You must purchase supplies as well as pay the workers. And this amount still does not cover the lost years of work on the Scriptures. There is *no price* that can be put on such labors."

Tregeagle groaned as he knelt to pick up his severed belt and scrabble after the lost coins.

Merlin could imagine how red his face must be as the magister slowly stood and dropped the coins into the abbot's hand.

Tregeagle turned to leave, but Uther called him back. "Five. Your ability to count has grown stale, my magister."

"Ah … yes, lord." Tregeagle turned back to Crogen, dropped the final coin clinking into Crogan's hands, then stepped off the rock.

"God's blessings be upon you, my lord," Abbot Crogen said once Tregeagle had gone.

Uther took a happy, babbling Arthur in his arms and sat down again. "Merlin, step forward so I may receive your fealty of servitude."

Merlin let out his breath and bowed his head. How he wished that his father hadn't pledged him. Why now — right when the two of them had finally grown close? A few steps, a few words, and his life would change forever. There would be no going back. He would have to leave Bosventor, his friends, and his family. Was this really the penance that Merlin's father had to pay? Couldn't they work this out some other way?

Colvarth coughed next to him, and the moment of indecision passed. Would Merlin really become a bard? *A real bard?* He knew it would take years of training, but a sudden excitement coursed through his heart and danced down his arms to his fingertips. This was something he could do, even if he was blind. A faint strum of harp strings floated through his mind, and he saw a vision of himself wearing a finely made black cloak pinned with a silver brooch and standing before a king. The chieftains of Britain as well as those of the heathen Saxenow feasted before him, and all looked upon his countenance as he played a song of wisdom and power. It was a sad song — a song of treachery, deceit, and tragedy — but the truth of its notes shone forth like an unquenchable torch.

In his vision, Merlin gazed upon a handsome young man who stood nearby wearing leather armor laced with iron scales. He had dark hair, and he smiled devotedly at Merlin. The young man's face seemed familiar, but from where he didn't know.

The vision faded, and the blur of Uther's form appeared once again.

Colvarth placed a hand on his shoulder. "Are you ... ready, Merlin?" he asked.

Merlin nodded.

Colvarth led Merlin to the foot of Uther's bench, where he bowed and repeated the old man's words.

I beseech thee, High King,
and deign thee to bless with thy right hand.
The fealty of my mouth,
that I may speak well of thee.
The fealty of my heart,
that I may follow thee.
The fealty of my arms,
that I may fight against thine enemies.
And the fealty of my legs,
that I may go where thou commandest.

Merlin paused and swallowed before he said the last words.

For all my days will I serve thee and defend thee,
along with thine heir, and all that is right under Christ,
on the Isle of the Mighty.

As instructed by Colvarth, Merlin found Uther's boot and kissed the fresh-smelling leather lacing. Then, reaching up, he found the dangling boot of young Arthur, small yet strong. As he kissed it, he wondered what kind of man Arthur would become. His life was bound to the boy's now, for better or for worse. For a moment panic sprang up in Merlin's heart. So young — still just a babe, in fact. What if Arthur grew to be a tyrant of a man? What of Merlin's vow then?

Even as the question rose in his mind, his heart knew the answer. He would serve Arthur no matter what type of leader the prince became, but he would never compromise fealty to God, even if it cost him his life at Arthur's hand. Yet in the capable care of his parents and Colvarth, the boy might grow into a godly High King, and for that Merlin prayed.

Uther raised his hand. "I receive your fealty, Merlin. And may the Lord Jesu bless your future service. Know that as I carry the mercy of Christ, I also carry the sword of God's vengeance against all who do wrong, including oath breakers."

Colvarth helped Merlin find his place on the grass before turning to the assembly. "Who will ... likewise swear fealty, either to serve as a warrior to ... fight the Saxenow or as a Briton grateful for the High King's ... protection?"

Merlin saw a small number of blurry forms rise and step forward. His father, sitting next to him, spoke the names in Merlin's ear as each approached the Rock of Judgment. The monks. Allun the miller. Troslam and Safrowana. Kyallna the widow. Trevenna and Natalenya. And the char-man. Finally Merlin's father rose and went forward as well. But the rest of the villagers remained sitting on the grass, murmuring in angry whispers.

"No more?" Colvarth called. "Do you understand that … you refuse your High King?"

Lightning flashed, striking the Meneth Gellik, and thunder rolled down the hillside.

Uther handed his son to Igerna and stood. Merlin heard the ring of metal as the High King pulled his sword once more from his belt. With it in his hand, he limped back and forth on the rock, and his feet scraped against it each time he turned.

He uttered a curse and then spoke to the people. "You think your Druid Stone more important than your king. You think yourselves safe here on the moor, far away from the coastal raiders, and that you need me not."

The people quieted as the anger of the king rose.

"You are wrong," Uther said. "I have seen the babes gutted by our enemies, the Saxenow! I have seen fathers begging for bread with their eyes gouged and gone. I have rescued the men and women taken as Pictish slaves to the northlands. I protect you while you sleep in safety on your straw."

The people murmured again, but no one else came forward to take the oath.

"Do you hear? I have just come from raising Kembry, and they have sent most of their men, food, and weapons. All they could spare, because they know how dire the threat is. And now I have come to raise Kernow, and in two days I will meet King Gorlas to receive his help. Who will fight with us? Stand, men! Stand and join the battle!"

Merlin felt a few raindrops fall as another lightning bolt split the sky. The explosion was deafening, and it seemed the world dimmed for a brief moment.

"Citizens," Uther called. "I give you one last chance! But before I do, I will show you a goodly example. There is an expected individual who has not yet sworn fealty to me, and thus I call forward Tregeagle, who will show his fealty to the one who protects his subjects."

Tregeagle shuffled forward and bowed upon the grass before the Rock of Judgment where the king stood. "Speak, splendid lord. What shall your servant swear?"

"We will begin with the usual. Proceed."

"I beseech thee, High King," Tregeagle began, "and deign thee to protect me even as I swear fealty to thee and thine heir."

Uther paced. "That is good. Now, swear that you utterly reject and hold in contempt this foolish druid Stone. Ha! Swear to crack it in half the next time you set eyes upon it!"

But only the rising wind answered the High King.

"Speak!" Uther commanded.

"I cannot, my lord," Tregeagle mumbled.

Uther's voice rose in mountainous anger. "What bewitchment is upon this village?"

Merlin suddenly felt all the hairs rise on the back of his neck, and his scalp felt as if scores of tiny worms crawled across it. The last time this happened was when Prontwon died. *The lightning!*

Uther roared in fury, and standing on the very edge of the Rock of Judgment, he raised his sword straight up, ready to slash it down and kill Tregeagle.

"Stop!" Trevenna and Natalenya shrieked.

Merlin burst forward. Holding his staff level, he charged the dark form of Uther. Surprising the High King, Merlin struck him full on the side and upset his balance so that they both tumbled to the grass.

Immediately lightning struck at the same spot where the High King had stood.

Everyone was blown back by its force. Screams and shouts coursed from the villagers. Arthur cried.

Twice more it struck, slicing the sky like an angry whip. When the booming finally faded, the air itself tasted burnt.

Uther turned and tried to pull Merlin up by the shoulders, but Merlin refused to rise. "My lord, I expect your judgment for daring to strike you."

"You saved my life." Uther heaved Merlin up and laughed. "*Karo-Righ* I call you, Merlin. Not servant but friend of the king!" The High King then stooped to help his wife up, with the bawling Arthur in her arms, just as hail poured from the sky like countless angry bees.

The villagers scattered as Uther and his retinue ran toward the village meeting house.

"Tas?" Merlin yelled through the driving ice. "Where should I go?"

"With Uther," Owain called. "I'll be at the smithy!"

Merlin felt Colvarth's hand on his arm, and together they made their way to the cramped meeting house. At the door someone jostled them from behind to get out of the hail.

"Vortigern," Colvarth said. "I did not see ... you following us."

CHAPTER 25

MYSTERIES UNBIDDEN

U ther pushed his way behind a table at the back of the crowded meeting house, evicted a warrior from the bench, and sat down. The air stank of sheep manure and wet leather, but that was the least of his concerns. It was those druidow, curse them! *They* were behind this village's impudence. Colvarth had told him about these meddlers, but Uther had never expected to run into so many. Certainly not in this wee village. If its mountain fort hadn't been on the main line of beacons, Uther would have never even come.

And he wouldn't have visited Kernow at all if that contentious King Gorlas had simply joined him against the Saxenow. Their former rivalry for Igerna's love made things difficult.

Nowhere had people refused Uther fealty. And they always loved Arthur! But here, they scowled. Refused him honor. Wouldn't join the fight against the Saxenow. But why did it gall him so? Igerna chided him about his pride, but wasn't he the High King?

Should he just depart? Spit on their mud? But he couldn't afford to break the line of beacons. Not with the Saxenow building their strength on the eastern shore.

Maybe Tregeagle could ... *Tregeagle!* That two-faced, money-grubbing druid lover.

Uther was in a precarious position. If he captured the Tor by force from Tregeagle, he could spare only a few men, and Vortigern said the place was a trap without better stonework and new timber. It would be simple for the druidow to take it over after he left.

And the Stone? Dreamlike feelings had come over him when he'd looked at it. A vision had appeared of himself conquering his enemies, even besieging Rome to take it back from the barbarians. Oh, how he'd longed for *that* since last year when Odoacer had conquered the empire's capital and deposed Orestes and his young son Romulus Augustulus. Uther the emperor ... Yes, the Stone had thrilled him!

But then he'd felt an icy claw begin to scrape his neck, the pain slicing into his heart. And if it hadn't been for the vexations of Mórganthu's son, that fool with the reeking breath, Uther might not have pulled his eyes away. Moreover, hadn't he called out to the Christ? He could barely remember now. And if Colvarth was right, this village's bewitchment was just the beginning of the arch druid's plans. Uther needed a council. And quickly.

But first he needed to get away from the village. Set up his tents on some defensible hill. Give his horses room for action. And the sooner out of this cramped, smelly roundhouse, the better.

"Ho! Battle chief. Pack us up to move," Uther called through the dark press of men.

Vortigern pushed through the warriors. "For the Tor?"

"No. We will find no proper welcome there. Our magister has left his loyalty in the dust."

"Here isn't bad. The horses have grass — "

"Not in the village."

"Don't you like it?"

"No. And you?" Uther said, arching his eyebrow.

"Eeeh." Vortigern shrugged. "But it's raining."

"That has never stopped you before. Move."

"Shall we head to the other side of the mountain? From the Tor, I've seen hills and a lake."

"Fine."

In less than half an hour, the whole company was on the move to the other side of the mountain. Once they arrived, Vortigern pointed to a flat hill between the lake and the marsh.

Uther surveyed the land and nodded. There, with the rain falling lightly, the warriors raised his campaign tent and soon had their own tents set up as well.

The rains quickened again, and before Uther closed his tent flap, he gazed out over the long marsh to the west. Out on an island, he spied a stone tower surrounded by ruins. It stood perhaps twenty-five feet tall, and at its top a single dark window opened eastward.

Peculiar. What was a tower doing in the marsh?

"Vortigern," Uther called.

No answer.

"Vortigern!" Where was that slumber-loving battle chief?

Merlin, who had come with Colvarth, tapped with his staff until he stood behind Uther. "Can I fetch him for you?"

"There is a tower on that island yonder. Tell me its history."

"No one knows for sure, my lord. It goes back further than the founding of the village."

"How old is Bosventor?"

Merlin closed his eyes. "I am told that around a hundred years ago, monks from the coast escaped inland to avoid sea raiders. People followed, and they rebuilt the Tor."

"Rebuilt?"

"The Romans had built the fort to run the tin and copper mining."

"The tower in the marsh," Uther asked, "is that Roman too?"

Merlin paused before answering. "Our lore says not, my lord. Some say it was built by a tin merchant before the Romans conquered

Britain, but no one really knows. We call it Pergiryn's, the tower of the pilgrim. The isle is named Inis Avallow. My sister and I have picked apples there."

Uther parted the tent flap and gazed once more across the marsh. As Uther studied the tower, a light flashed from its window. "What was that?" he exclaimed. "Did you see it?"

"No, my lord. I can see colors and things moving, but my vision is blurry—"

Uther felt the heat rise to his cheeks when he realized he'd asked such a question. "I see a light from the tower ... from the window."

Merlin paused. "Others have also sworn they saw a light in the tower, but no one has been to the top to know what it could be. There's a floor up there, I am told, but the stairs have all rotted away."

Uther, suddenly hungry, closed the tent flap despite his curiosity. He had no time for such mysteries. There was a rebellion to deal with, and he needed food.

"Fire and meat!" he called. "Colvarth, where is my venison?"

Garth couldn't believe the druid wives were making him pluck chickens. Clean this. Pluck that. Chop these. Bring more wood. Always more wood!

It wouldn't be half bad if they'd let him sneak a bite here and there. But after his second scolding, they refused to allow him near the roasting meat unsupervised again. Even Brother Loyt back at the abbey used to give him treats here and there.

"Stop yer dreamin'," a greasy-mantled woman shouted at him as she plopped two more scalded chickens in the dirt. "Keep on pluckin', or yer next meal will be a plate o' piney cones!"

Garth sighed.

With a loud thunderclap, it started raining again. Muttering, Garth got up, pushed his bench farther underneath the pine tree and clopped it against the trunk. After retrieving the half-plucked chicken and the two new ones, he sat down again.

Two men interrupted his grumblings as they walked down the side of the tree-shaded hillside about three stone throws away. They had come from the circle, and Garth recognized Mórganthu on the left.

Ah, that'll be my way out o' this miserable feather tuggin'. The druid wives won't dare yell at me while standin' next to the arch druid. In his excitement Garth jumped up and poked his eye on a pine needle. He stifled a yell lest he attract the attention of one of the women, and rubbed his lid as he fell back to the bench. When he could see again, he looked out at the two figures talking in the distance.

Garth froze. The other figure was one of the monks! The brother stood with his back to Garth and had his hood up, making it impossible to tell who it was. But why was a monk talking with Mórganthu? Good thing Garth had been smart enough not to embarrass himself. The last thing he wanted was to talk to one of those bagpipe-stealing … Well, *maybe* he'd make an exception if it was Brother Loyt coming to bring him some steaming, buttered, and oh-so-perfect bannocks.

Better yet would be old Kyallna shuffling over with a steaming pot of her glorious soup. Then he wouldn't have to bother with those monks at all. He needed to visit her house again soon. Real soon. Garth's stomach gurgled as he picked up the chicken and slowly started plucking again.

Mórganthu and the monk conferred for quite awhile. Then the arch druid gave something to the monk, one of those bronze tubes with a wooden stopper. Just like the tube of oil Dybris used to anoint people. Didn't the monk have his own oil?

And come to think of it, this monk was really tall. In fact, half a head taller than Mórganthu. *Not like any monk I know. An' why is there a strange bulge on his back? Looks almost like he's hidin' something under his cowl.*

Soon they parted. Mórganthu walked back toward the circle of stones as the monk ran northward along the ridge.

But the abbey and village weren't that way.

"Have them chickens cleaned?" The druid wife startled him. She bent down and snickered. He hadn't even finished the first. "No midmeal for you," she said as she stomped off. "What a lazy louse. No parents and won't work a lick!"

Garth almost started crying, but he bit his lip instead.

"How much time has passed?" Crogen demanded as he closed the door to the chapel.

"Not long, Abbot. Two hours at most."

"Two hours, Neot! Do you know what this means?"

Neot wrung his hands. "I know exactly. Herrik never came back with us from the meeting with the High King."

"How could you have missed him?" Crogen said. "I know I've been visiting Troslam — and Dybris took off after Owain — but can't you *count*, man?"

"I realized too late while preparing our meal at the chapel. Herrik could be anywhere."

"But he was the one caught drawing the Stone!" Crogen beat his chest. "Oh, Jesu, forgive me, for I shouldn't have taken him to the village green while the Stone was still there."

"He's been dragged away by his heart, and his blood will be on his own head."

Crogen collapsed to a bench. "Oh, Neot, what have I done?"

CHAPTER 26

ADVICE UNHEEDED

Merlin felt a cold draft of air as a warrior with a haunch of freshly killed deer entered Uther's campaign tent. In no time he had it on a spit over the crackling fire.

Colvarth excused himself, and Merlin spent the next hour conversing with Uther, Igerna, and their daughters about life up on the moor. Eventually the conversation turned to Owain, but Merlin detected a hint of anger lingering in Uther's voice and changed the topic to the recent appearance of the druidow.

Soon the meat was ready, and Merlin sat before the fire eating roasted venison, whose aroma filled his senses. The bone was so hot, however, that he had to hold it with the edge of his cloak. Eating it brought a warmth that eased the tightness of his stomach, and the grease felt good on his lips.

Nearby, Igerna spoke quietly to her husband. "You drink too much mead, and only on the eve of battle do I see you eat this heartily."

"A battle? It may be. Colvarth's prayers will soon be said, and we will hold council about these druidow."

"And their Stone?"

"Yes."

"What stone do you mean, Mammu?" Myrgwen asked. "Do you mean the rock you and Tas sat on today?"

"No, Myr, not that one—"

"The black one with the fire," Eilyne said from beside Merlin. "The one the druidow dragged away after Tas ... judged that scofflaw."

"I didn't see," Myrgwen said, and Merlin heard her scraping a bone with her knife.

The whole family ate in silence awhile, except young Arthur, who babbled earnestly as he chewed his own meaty portion.

Even though Merlin knew better, he felt as if everyone must be staring at him and his scars. It was different to eat with a family not his own, especially the High King's. And Colvarth's absence only made it worse.

Eilyne broke the silence. "If that man had hurt you, I'd have—"

"Shah." Igerna said. "Your father took care of it."

"I'd have run to help with my knife, and—"

"Enough. Let's not dwell on what might have been."

Uther raised a hand. "Eilyne, your father was not in danger ... but I receive your love, and who knows? One day we may need your protection."

The tent flap opened once more, and cold rain blew across Merlin's neck, sending a shiver down his spine.

"Colvarth, welcome!" Uther called. "You must be famished."

The bard sat on Merlin's left. "Not so much, my king. My stomach ... is delicate tonight."

"Eating like a bird again?"

"A bird with a ... song I would say." Colvarth's harp strings hummed as he brought his instrument from beneath his cloak. "But first I have called your ... battle chief and his chieftains here, my lord—"

The flap opened yet again, and a group of men entered.

"Merlin, I would like you to meet my war chieftains," Uther said.

Merlin stood, reached out his hands, and greeted each warrior as he walked by.

"I'm Rewan," the first said, and his hands tapped Merlin's briefly before he walked on.

"I am named Bedwir, friend," the second said, shaking Merlin's hands.

"Sydnius, from the moor originally," said the third, and his hands were thick and strong.

"Vortipor," said the last as his wiry hands squeezed hard. A little too hard.

Eilyne and Myrgwen moved closer to Merlin to make room for the men, who found seats around the fire. While Merlin and the family hastily finished their meal, the men chatted about a score of flopping fish some warriors had just caught using a boat from the village.

"Did you see Sethek spear 'em?" Bedwir asked. "He's promised to smoke one for me."

Sydnius burped. "Ah … been a long time since I've smacked lips with a good fish."

"Vortipor," Uther interrupted, "how long till your father comes?"

"Uh … I think he gets water down at the lake, my lord."

Uther stood and began pacing. "Does anyone know if he received the summons?"

"Yes, my lord," Vortipor said.

Uther swore. "Then where is he? A council of war, and my battle chief is fetching water?"

"My king?" Colvarth said. "I suggest we begin and … test his thoughts when he comes."

"Obviously we have no choice. Daughters, time for you both to go."

"It's raining outside, my love," Igerna said gently. "Couldn't they stay in the tent? The girls won't bother anyone if they sit out of the circle."

"Please, Father," Eilyne said.

"Yes, please," Myrgwen echoed.

Uther stopped pacing and considered. "One interruption, and you will have to leave." He sat down next to his wife. "So, with Vortigern gone, my war chieftains will have first voice. What think you of our situation?"

Rewan spoke, flipping a gleaming knife in the air and catching it again. "I say we *make* the villagers bow."

"And how do we do that?" Sydnius said with a mocking tone.

Rewan pointed his knife at Sydnius. "By the edge of my blade."

"Is that what we want? Blood could turn more of them away, and a forced allegiance is no allegiance at all."

"And if we don't," Rewan shot back, "they'll ignore our High King. And then they'll refuse to pay Tregeagle their taxes, and Tregeagle won't pay his — "

"But won't the druidow spread the news everywhere?" Sydnius countered. "Imagine ... all through the land, the High King threatens Britons at knifepoint to force fealty!"

"How about the opposite?" Bedwir asked. "Give a feast. There's plenty of game here."

"Are you serious?" Rewan asked.

"Really, I am. We stay a few extra days and make 'em happy. Get that harpist to play, the pretty one we heard last night — no offense, Colvarth. Find a few more musicians, and we've got a dance."

"An' you'll pay for the mead, now won't you, Bedwir?" Sydnius elbowed him in the ribs.

Uther held up a hand. "And what do you suggest, Sydnius? You do not seem to like any idea."

"I say get out. It's just a mood they're in, nothing more. I grew up near Guronstow, and the people up here don't think they need outsiders for protection, being so far from the coast and all. But they'll come begging for your help the first time they're threatened."

"Hmm," Uther said. "And you, Vortipor, what would your father say?"

But Vortipor was silent.

Uther sipped some mead. "Go on. I can tell you've been thinking about this."

"He would say ..." Vortipor began. "He *might* say that we ... we should make an example of one of the villagers. You killed a druid, so now take a villager who's ignored you and let the birds eat his flesh."

Uther laughed. "Tregeagle, yes."

"No, no, not Tregeagle!" Vortipor said along with a curse. "Someone else. Lower down."

"How is that different from what *I* said?" Rewan asked.

"You don't force them *all* to give fealty. Just show justice to one and let that sink in — "

"And?" Uther interrupted.

"Maybe ... after meeting with King Gorlas ... we see if they've changed their minds."

Merlin almost spoke but held his tongue. Vortipor's idea was brutal. Yes, the people were culpable before God, but there was a power here that was beyond them. And how foolish everyone's advice was. No one had considered the enchantment of the Stone.

"Colvarth," Uther called.

The old man yawned. "Yes, my king?"

"What do you recommend? Share from your granary of wisdom."

"From myself, but little seeds, my lord. But I have ... prayed to the Almighty regarding this circumstance, and He has ... reminded me concerning an old lay. I will share it, if it please you."

Myrgwen shouted from the side. "A ballad! Colly's going to sing a ballad."

"Shah," both her mother and Eilyne warned.

"What ballad will you give us?" Uther asked.

"It is ... 'The Lay of Tevdar, King of Kernow,'" the bard replied. "Do you ... recall it, my lord?"

"I heard you play it once before. Many years ago in my father's hall."

"You would have been about ... Myrgwen's age."

"I know the gist, but I have forgotten much. Go ahead. We will all enjoy it."

"Yes, do sing, good bard." Igerna said. "This has been a difficult day, and I would appreciate the wisdom God has given you."

"Then," Colvarth said, "this is how it wends."

Merlin heard the harp strings pulse high to low as Colvarth tuned his instrument, humming. When the bard was satisfied with its sound, he began to play, and his method was unlike Natalenya's. Where she would often comb the strings as if her harp were a horse's mane, Colvarth struck them perfectly and with such vigor that Merlin could feel the vibration on his cheek and ear.

He closed his eyes so he could concentrate on the music, and each note appeared before his mind like a beautiful tree in a forest, with budding leaves bursting from each branch and stem. As the melody progressed, Colvarth created variations like honey flowers springing up between the trees, each blossom with a fresh and succulent scent.

The flowers reminded Merlin of Natalenya and the flower in her hair. Ah! What would she have given to hear Colvarth play? What would Merlin give if he could have her sitting beside him, holding his hand as she had done when they parted from the dock?

Colvarth raised his voice, gravelly but strong, and sang to the melody of the harp:

> *Come hear the river rushing down unto the salty sea.*
> *And hearken to this olden tale of Tevdar's sad decree.*
> *One hundred fifty years ago upon our dearest shore,*
> *In Kernow when the pagan ways held sway on field and moor.*
> *Tevdar was king in Kernow, his fortress grim and bare.*
> *And Vuron, druid — white and thin — was counsel to him there.*
> *Dynan also, the battle chief, with golden hair, adored;*
> *The dark king's brother — a twin — firm of shield and true of*
> *   sword.*

A ship appeared upon the key, with passengers of five.
They brought the faith of Christ to preach — in Kernow for to
   strive.
Gwinear, and sister Piala, sailed from their Eirish shore,
With Erth and Uny, brother's true, and sister Ia, more.
Gwinear the tall, their leader strong, asked king if they could stay,
But Vuron raised his voice and said, "Depart — be on your way."
But king, he smiled, for he had spied Piala, pleasing maid.
And in his passion, he gave them — near his fort — land and aid.

Colvarth's voice quieted while his fingers played on. Merlin found himself lost in the melody until the bard's words flowed once more.

And Dynan truly fell in love — with Ia, light and fair.
Spurned gods, he gave himself to Christ, and did his troth
   declare.
But Tevdar followed Piala, he listened to her pray.
He feigned false interest in her Christ, to see her eyes of gray.
And in his ache, Tevdar was fey — ignored his people's needs.
Rival kingdoms did raid their land; the king forgot his deeds.
So the people left the old gods — and turned from Vuron's way
To hearken to bold Gwinear's words. The druid had no sway.
Gerrent, a chieftain tough and brave, he took the wine and bread,
And bending knee to his new God, he yelled for the king's head.
Vuron, he came and warned the king, who said a dead dog's howl
Cannot change the courses of the moon. So Vuron left to prowl.

Colvarth added lower notes to the tune, and his voice not only quieted, but took on a darker timbre. Everyone leaned in closer to catch the words.

So walking lone to scheme, he cried, "The fool, he does not know —
The realm will fall and bring on us a never-ending woe."
But then a plan the druid made — to rid the kingdom of
These Christians who upset the land, or wastrel king in love.

If Christians die, what did he care? The land would be so free.
If Tevdar died, he would appoint a better of his tree.
He slithered off to meet Gwinear and told him of the king—
That he would be with Piala at dusk his love to bring.
Gwinear, in anger, told Vuron, his sister she was chaste.
And Tevdar she would never wed—a pagan in distaste.
Gwinear, he planned to meet the king, no marriage to bestow.
He would decry it should not be and told the druid so.
Vuron, he crept unto the king and of Piala lied—
"She wants you, king—seek out her house at dusk and go inside.
But her brother Gwinear she fears, and so she will pretend
To protest you as through a veil, but will her love extend."

Now the deeper notes filled in more of the melody, and Merlin could imagine Colvarth's fingers flying across the strings. As the bard raised his voice again, someone stood, and based on the uneven pacing that commenced, Merlin guessed it was Uther.

"Now take her like great king you are, and so together go."
The king he smiled and up he got, his strength for her to show.
At dusk Tevdar marched to her church—her dwelling by the Din.
Found her on knees in solemn prayer and entered there within.
She stood in fear, surprise, and dread, for vast unkind was he,
Who tried to take her rough away, despite her struggling plea.
Gwinear burst in, and with his staff pushed broaching king away.
Tevdar drew sword, cut off his head—poor Gwinear he did slay.
Piala fell and wept aloud and held her brother dear.
The head, it spoke a prophecy— "King Tevdar's death is near."
Piala rose and took his knife— the king she tried to kill.
And on king's sword she fell and died—the poor maid's blood
*   did spill.*

Colvarth's old voice softened, sorrow emanating from the pulsing harp strings. And even as he slowed, the High King increased his pacing.

Vuron, he called the king to fight, for Christians would attack.
Tevdar decreed that they should die. No warrior did he lack.
On spear they lifted Gwinear's head and hastened to the
command
To kill the followers of the Way and cleanse all Kernow land.
Three hundred died in weeping wails, as they would not recant.
They clung to Christ and to His Way — king would no mercy
grant.
Tevdar went to Ia's brothers — soon Erth and Uny died.
And then to Ia, Christian fair — to murder Dynan's bride.
But there at Pendinas so strong, brave Dynan's fortress tall,
They saw the army of Gerrent pour forth from his great hall.
The king, he called for brave Gerrent, to single combat fight.
Sharp blades they drew, yet ere a step — Gwinear's head fell
to smite.
Tevdar's iron helm was broken in — skull crushed in gory bed.
Vuron swiftly fled far away. Gerrent was king instead.
So ends this olden tale of woe — of Tevdar's sad decree.
Yet Christ, he came to this great isle, with pow'r to set me free.

The notes fell away into silence. Uther stopped his pacing, but still no one spoke.

Surely, Merlin thought, *the druidow and the Stone can be dealt with before bloodshed such as this occurs.*

Colvarth broke the silence. "These things, my king, may be ... taken figuratively. As this ballad is ordained for this telling, it is ... possible the people in it represent persons here. Surely Vuron the druid would represent ... Mórganthu."

"Then who am I?" Uther inquired. "Tell me, Colvarth. Set before me the plain meaning of your riddle."

"I intend no ... riddle. But as you, Uther, are a Christian, you could be Gerrent ... maybe Dynan ... or maybe Gwinear. The ballad does not say, but the ... bards before me have passed on the lore that Gwinear was an ... Eirish prince before coming to this land."

"Then who is King Tevdar?" Uther asked. "Who dares slay Christians?"

"These things are ... mysteries known only to God. Perhaps there is no one in such a role. Surely there is ... no king greater than thee on the Isle of the Mighty, and — "

The tent flap opened, interrupting Colvarth, and a man stepped through.

"Vortigern!" Uther exclaimed. "My battle chief rises from the dead."

"Do not mock me, my lord." Vortigern said as he stamped his feet and shook water from his cloak all over Merlin.

"We hold a council of war, and where have you been?" Uther demanded. "Your shoes and breeches are soaked. Did you wade for your water?"

"Me?" Vortigern replied. "Sure, I went for water ... and found Sethek's horse stuck in the mud."

"Then Sethek should have gotten it out."

Vortigern shrugged. "He was fishing."

The High King walked up to Vortigern. "You were summoned *here*. Attend your duties in the future, or you will not hold them for long."

"Yes ... my lord." But Merlin caught a subtle contempt in the battle chief's voice.

"Sit down, Vortigern." Uther turned and continued pacing. "Colvarth just finished a ballad, and I was about to hear from my new adviser, Merlin."

As Vortigern found a place beside Vortipor, someone threw a few more logs on the fire, and all chatter subsided.

Merlin felt every eye looking to him.

"As the solitary resident of Bosventor present, Merlin, you know better of the druidow' recent dealings. Tell me. Of all the advice given, which is the wisest?"

Now it was Merlin's turn to pause as he realized his words had the ability to sway the decision of the High King ... and possibly result in bloodshed. Although he had to speak, the weight of his words pressed upon his tongue.

"My lord, if I may be so bold — and no offense is meant — none of the advice your war chieftains have given would remedy the present troubles."

Protests arose from the warriors, but Uther silenced them and told Merlin to proceed.

"The villagers are not the root of the problem. My advice to you is to heed Colvarth's ballad, for it has revealed the true source of your trouble."

"The druidow," Uther stated.

"No, my lord."

"Explain."

"Do not the druidow follow Mórganthu?"

Uther must have looked to Colvarth, for the old man answered in the affirmative.

The High King paced again. "I will have Mórganthu slain. It is simple, what you suggest."

"But that is not my advice, lord," Merlin said. "The real question is whom does Mórganthu follow?"

"Is there another druid greater than Mórganthu?" Uther asked. "I will have him *and* Mórganthu executed."

"In Colvarth's ballad, Vuron did not want his pagan gods to lose power. But Mórganthu now follows his pagan gods through the Stone, my lord."

Uther stopped pacing. "The Stone? Can this be? It is just a rock, strangely inspiring and amazing though it is."

"This is a mystery, my lord, but the Stone is no mere rock. Somehow it lives, plots, and hates. And it desires to enchant not just Bosventor, but every Briton."

Exclamations of surprise burst from those around the fire.

"All of the *Britons*?" Uther asked as he knelt before Merlin and looked him in the face. Merlin blinked at the smell of mead as Uther's words softened. "How do you know these things?"

"I have touched the Stone, my lord. The Stone hates the Christ whom I serve, and so it tried to slay me. Yet I live."

"I have faced the armies of chiefs and kings, but never have I fought such evil." Here the king lowered his voice. "Colvarth, is this beyond me?"

The bard cleared his throat. "I think not, my Lord, although ... I cannot know for sure."

"Can it be destroyed?"

Merlin had pondered this question and spoke up. "The Stone will oppose you because you claim the Christ, and Mórganthu now hates you because you slew his son. There is danger. But perhaps God sent you here at just this time to defeat it, on Beltayne before the enchantment spreads. Both strength and caution are needed, my lord, for Mórganthu has Eirish warriors in his service."

"Warriors? How many?"

"I have personally met at least six, but I don't know their true number." Merlin stood, and there before them all, he proclaimed, "My lord, take your men and ride to the druidow' camp. There you will find the Stone in the center of the Gorseth Cawmen. Scatter the druidow and cover the Stone with animal skins. Then take it away to be destroyed. But heed well this warning: no one should touch the Stone or look at it. To do so is perilous."

Silence filled the tent as Uther resumed pacing back and forth.

Merlin, feeling awkard to have spoken so boldly, sat down. His face felt the heat of the fire, and he began to sweat. What would Uther do? Surely he'd reject Merlin's advice, coming from someone so young and inexperienced in matters like these.

Vortigern commented on how hungry he was and began to eat a hunk of venison. For a long while his chewing and Uther's pacing was all that could be heard.

Finally, Uther began walking around the circle, pausing now and then as if deep in thought. When he passed behind Merlin, he stopped.

Merlin held his breath, waiting for the king to speak. He wanted to leave the council and make his way home in the rain. He had made a mistake, and now Uther would reject his service for what it was — that of a fool.

But Uther placed a hand on his shoulder. It was strong, steady, and reassuring. "This plan of yours, Merlin, this I will do." Uther grasped Merlin's hand and bade him stand.

But Vortigern stood too and interrupted Uther. "My High King, grant me the boon of leading your men on this mission."

"And what of me?" Uther picked a log from a pile at the edge of the tent and slammed it sparking onto the fire. "Am I infirm that I cannot — "

"I think only of the safety of my sister, your wife, as well as your children."

"You are a fool, Vortigern! Of course I would leave some of our warriors to guard them."

"How many would you leave?"

"Five … perhaps ten."

"That would weaken our forces considerably. We are battling not one man but many, and there are an unknown number of Eirish warriors. Uther, listen to me. No warrior will guard your family better than you. I urge you, my lord, to stay with them in a safe place and send forth the rest of us."

"My family is safe here … Igerna, you agree with me on this?"

Merlin did not hear a response, but Vortigern spoke for her.

"You see, my lord … my sister is concerned. It is not her habit to be so near a battle. Your children are in danger. Stay with them."

Young feet pattered to Uther, and his two daughters clasped their father around the waist.

"Please, Tas," Eilyne said, "don't let them hurt us!"

Uther said nothing, and Vortigern continued.

"Your heir, my lord, is worthy of your personal protection. Arthur is in grave danger, is he not?"

"I'll protect him," Myrgwen cried. "I'll die with him if I have to."

Uther turned. "Colvarth? What do you say?"

The bard spoke from beside Merlin. "I know not the better course, my king. This is ... for you to decide."

"Merlin," Uther asked. "What is your opinion? Shall I go with my warriors or stay with my family?"

"My king," Merlin said, distrust for Vortigern rising in his throat. "I stand by what I have said. You are here for a reason. Lead your men."

"Please, oh, please, Father, don't leave us!" Myrgwen nearly shrieked.

"Vortigern ... if I follow your plan, where would we go?"

Vortigern walked behind Merlin and opened the tent flap. Uther stood beside him after extricating himself from his daughters.

"There, my lord," Vortigern said. "The island in the marsh with the old tower. The locals call it Inis Avallow."

"Yes, the tower." Uther opened the flap farther so he could see, and Merlin felt a chill breeze blow through his hair.

"There your family will be safe under your watch while I scatter these traitorous druidow. The men already borrowed a fishing boat from the village. You can use that to take your family across."

"The light from the tower ... Did you see it just now?" Uther asked.

"Eeeh ... I saw nothing."

"Wait ... I see an entire stone fortress there," Uther exclaimed. "The tower is just part of it! The walls grew out of the ground before my eyes, with beautiful stonework surrounded by blooming orchards ... and there is a man in the window beckoning me."

"My Uther," Igerna said from his side — she had walked there so silently Merlin hadn't heard her. "I see nothing but the ruined tower. You have been drinking too much — "

"I have not. There — do you not see him?"

"There is no such man," Igerna said. "Come, sit down by the fire again."

"No. Do not speak like that. You have made it fade from my vision. But the light is still flashing ... from the window there at the top. Vortigern, surely you see this?"

"I do not, my lord."

"What is this I have seen? Surely something is there! I had desired to explore its ruins before, but now I must go."

Merlin felt uneasy with the king's tone. What had come over Uther? Had the Stone enchanted him without Merlin knowing?

Vortigern coughed. "My lord, you could explore the ruins ... yes ... while I lead the warriors and do as your young adviser ... *Merlin* ... has suggested. Just after the evening meal, before dark. I will take the men to raid the druid camp after you are all safely on the island."

Again Merlin heard a hint of disdain in his voice, but Uther didn't seem to notice.

The High King's hand found Merlin's shoulder. "It is a good plan."

Merlin bit down on his tongue, unconvinced.

CHAPTER 27

CONSEQUENCES

A light rain was falling when Merlin left the council. As he tapped his way toward home to collect his belongings, according to Uther's command, he thought about the plan the High King had chosen. No matter how he turned it over in his mind, he couldn't make peace with how his own recommendation had been changed by Vortigern.

Logically, what Vortigern said made sense. Having Uther protect his family on Inis Avallow freed up many warriors, who could spread out and help disperse the druidow. And what better place than the island in the marsh?

But somehow it sat bitter in his mouth, like a blackberry plucked green from the bushes south of the smithy.

And why did Uther prefer exploring the ruins of the old tower while enemies raised their scornful heads? If only that hallucination hadn't come over the man, he might have explored the ruins *after* the Stone's destruction.

As much as Merlin wanted to protest, the High King had made his decision. But what of the Stone? Would Vortigern capture it and bring it to Uther to be destroyed? Some inner voice warned Merlin against trusting the battle chief, and his concerns about the man grew.

When the High King had sent Merlin off, he'd ordered his newest adviser to report at first light, ready for travel. As if everything would be settled by morning! Merlin wondered why Uther had even asked his opinion, since he seemed so set on ignoring the facts before him.

In this frustrated mood, Merlin had to find his way south from Uther's camp. Not a hard task when he could navigate by the position of the sun, but with these dismal clouds, he had to be careful to stay on the narrow path that wended between the mountain and the marsh.

Sure, Vortipor had offered a ride on the back of his horse, but Merlin had refused. If Vortigern smelled of pride, then Vortipor reeked of it. "Need a ride on my stallion? You might fall in the marsh and drown otherwise." And he had laughed.

About halfway to the village, Merlin heard a woman call his name.

He turned, and her voice called again, somewhat breathless. "Merlin! I've been praying ... since you went off with the High King ... waiting for you to come back."

He smiled and held out his hands in greeting. "Natalenya!"

She ran to him and, to his great surprise, fell into his arms, sobbing into his tunic.

For a moment Merlin stood there, stunned. Why would she weep? Why come to *him*? He thought his heart might leap out of his chest.

"My father betroths me to Vortipor tonight. To be married in *Junius*."

Vortipor? How could Natalenya marry that foul-mouthed, cruel ... "That's terrible," he said and instantly realized his mistake, for her crying increased until her arms shook.

Merlin tentatively cradled her head. The rain-fresh smell of her hair filled his senses.

"Unless you *want* to marry him ..."

She pulled back a little, and even with his poor eyesight, he thought he saw a fierce light in her eyes. "Never!"

Merlin was taken aback. Maybe he wasn't the only one who disliked Vortipor. But did she mean it? The man was, after all, someone important. "He's the battle chieftain's son — "

"I don't care."

A weight lifted that he hadn't entirely realized was there.

"But what can *I* do?"

"Help me!"

"How? I can't sway your father."

"Hide me. Don't make me go back. He's not himself to make a decision like that."

"They'll hunt for you."

She buried her face against his chest once more. "Not if I *couldn't* marry Vortipor." And her tears soaked into Merlin's tunic right over his heart.

"Natalenya ... you'd have to be married for that to happen."

She wrapped her arms around him and held to him tightly. "Yes."

The word struck him with greater force than if he'd been hit by the Druid Stone's lightning. She couldn't mean she wanted to marry him.

Hope and joy flared within him, only to drown in an ocean of frustration over his blindness. He was nothing — a glorified beggar at Uther's table. If the king's house didn't bestow enough provisions for him, could he subject her to a life of toil? His heart beat like a galloping horse, and he wanted to shout, but his words slipped out one by one, like dry pebbles dropping to the ground.

"Natalenya, I love you, I do. But I can't guarantee I can provide for you."

She looked up at him. Touched his scarred face. "I don't care. We'll find a way."

Yet the true reality of their situation pierced him like a deadly arrow. "Vortipor ..." He pulled back, shaking his head. "I serve the High King now, and his son after him. I'll be near them for years and years. Maybe for the rest of my life."

"What do you mean? You serve your father."

The tremor in her voice nearly undid him, but he forced himself to speak. "No. He pledged me to Uther." He paused, and a realization struck him. "But you were there!"

"When?"

"Just before you swore fealty with your mother."

"We'd only just arrived." She fell silent, and he felt her soft hand slipping into his.

Merlin didn't know what to say.

"I never dreamed you'd serve Uther," she said at last.

"I leave tomorrow."

"You can't."

"I've sworn my service. If you came with me ... If we were ..." Again he shook his head. "You'd never escape Vortipor and his father."

Natalenya pulled her hand free and turned away. "You don't want me."

"That's not true — "

"You're afraid of Vortipor. I understand."

"No — "

"You'd rather I marry another."

"Natalenya, I — "

Merlin stopped. He didn't have the words. Why had his father pledged him to serve Uther anyway? His blindness, always his blindness. It ruined his life and sucked away his joy, causing even his blessings to become deep sorrow. If only he'd known of Natalenya's predicament and her feelings yesterday, he would have told his father to recant his promise. He wanted to tell her how much joy she'd bring him, but his words turned to ashes in his throat.

"Don't worry. I'll figure something out." Her voice trembled.

He reached out, but she'd stepped too far away. "Maybe there's another way," he said.

"Maybe."

"Natalenya?"

"Yes?" She turned back to him, but her voice sagged with weariness where before it had sprung with hope.

"Stay. I'll help. But first I need *your* help to destroy the Stone."

"The Stone." She stepped closer but didn't take his outstretched hand. "Very well, Merlin. Let us see to this Stone."

Merlin wanted to ask about the aloofness in her voice, but thought better of it. "I'll explain my thoughts as we walk to the smithy. Hopefully my tas is still there."

The rain stopped falling as they walked down the path. Eventually they entered a wooded area where the thick foliage darkened the already-dull light. The underbrush had almost taken over as well, and fronds of unseen bushes groped at Merlin's legs. From their right, where the soggy smell of the marsh floated through the trees, a flock of crows began to caw loudly.

Merlin wanted to explain his plan to Natalenya as they walked, but he felt awkward and focused instead on trying to keep his pace even. As the path narrowed even more, her steps came closer, and he feared tangling his feet with hers.

Something rustled a bush ahead of them, and the crows amplified their calls.

Merlin stopped. "Did you hear that?"

"What?"

The sound faded, and with it even the crows ceased their rancor so that the woods became silent as death.

"Let's keep moving."

Sweat formed on Merlin's brow, and he wanted her to take his hand and guide him as they ran down the path to escape the woods. But he *had* to keep his composure in front of her. It was probably just a squirrel or some feral cat in search of its prey. The worst part of it was that in such dim light, Merlin's eyes were almost useless.

Now the sound came from behind them, and Merlin stopped. Willing his pulse to stay even, he turned to listen.

Natalenya sucked in her breath. "I heard it."

And there, in the mottled light, Merlin peered at a dark shape slipping from the bushes.

Natalenya screeched and grabbed his arm. "A wolf!"

Fear blazed in Merlin's chest as he held out his staff to Natalenya. "Take this and get behind me." He snatched his dirk from its scabbard, his heart was pounding so hard that he could barely hear the slow, stealthy approach of the creature before him.

"There are two now. They're — " But her words were cut short by a scream. "Merlin!"

He tried to turn and help her, but the wolf in front of him snarled as it leaped in the air. The shadow fell upon Merlin so fast that he had no time to do anything but raise his left arm to ward the gaping jaws.

Why did they keep hunting him? There were plenty of young deer in the woods, especially in springtime.

The wolf's teeth ripped into his elbow, sending a shock of pain that stunned him. The beast was heavy, and it pulled Merlin down and forward until he fell into the bracken.

Letting go, the wolf snapped at his throat, its stiff claws on his chest.

Merlin panicked and thrust his dirk upward, but the thick fur prevented the tip from penetrating deeply.

The wolf pulled back and yelped but then dove forward once more. It snapped at Merlin's neck, its warm saliva dripping on him.

Natalenya screamed again, and this gave Merlin a rush of strength.

He yelled and plunged his dirk into the beast's neck.

The wolf yelped as Merlin rolled its spasming body off him and then stood. To his right, he heard the whir of his staff being swung at another snarling beast.

"It has my skirt!" Natalenya cried out.

He lunged forward and tried to stab the creature, but it jerked to the side. There was a ripping sound as material tore away.

Merlin lunged again, but the wolf retreated and then began growling.

"Run!" Merlin said, holding out his hand.

"Where?"

"The smokehouse!"

Natalenya seized his hand, and together they sprinted down the path. But Merlin could hear growls behind them.

"How many?" he asked.

"Four!"

They burst into the open as the woods fell away from the path. But still the wolves pursued them. Merlin's scars stung as flashes of memory burned in his mind.

"How much farther?" Merlin asked, gasping.

"Almost there."

A wolf ripped into Merlin's cloak. He pulled the hood over his head, threw it at the beast, and tried to keep up with Natalenya.

"Merlin, run!"

The smokehouse roof appeared like a dark splotch on his right, and he could smell the smoldering fire that preserved racks of fish in its back room. They ran toward it, but he forgot the steepness of the slope leading down to it, and he stumbled and rolled.

Natalenya frantically banged on the door. "Megek!" she yelled, but the old man who smoked the fish didn't answer.

Merlin regained his footing and crouched, ready to use his dirk. Three of the wolves appeared over the hillside and hesitated before two of them slunk off to the side, perhaps to circle around and attack from behind. Were they that intelligent, or was some evil directing them?

"Merlin, I can't reach the latch!" Natalenya called.

Merlin turned just as the blur of a wolf jumped at her back. She shrieked and went down.

Only a few feet away, Merlin sprang at the creature, being careful to differentiate the gray fur from Natalenya, and thrust his blade into its back. The blade slid off a rib and sliced deeply into the wolf's chest. Despite this, the wolf still tried to snap at Natalenya, and so Merlin stabbed it again and then threw it off.

Natalenya was crying.

"Are you hurt?"

She grabbed onto his arm with a shaking hand and pulled herself up. "Just a few scratches. I bunched up my cloak to keep him from biting me. The latch ..."

Merlin reached up to find the wooden handle and pulled the string to lift the bar.

He let Natalenya slip inside first, and then he entered, banged the door shut, and dropped the bar. The room was dark and reeked of fish. Merlin suspected that Megek's barrel of guts was ripe and ready to be closed up, rolled over to the woods, and dumped. The old man had apparently finished for the day and gone home.

Natalenya caught her breath and then broke the silence. "Thank you."

"I'm just glad you're safe. If anything happened to you, I couldn't live with myself."

"You risked your life for me."

Merlin gulped. "It's me they're after. If you hadn't been there to help me find my way ..."

She raised her hand and touched his face. "That would have been terrible."

Merlin reached out, and she embraced him, her tears flowing freely. Time fled away as he held her close and breathed in the smell of her rain-soaked hair.

Then a wolf began scratching at the door and sniffing. In the distance one of them howled.

Merlin released Natalenya and backed away, awkwardly aware of their situation.

"How do we get out of here?" she asked.

"We fight them."

"We already tried that."

"Not this way." He oriented himself in the gloom, walked forward, and ran into a worktable. Sliding a hand along its slimy, fish-sullied edge, he made his way to the wall that cut the crennig in half. From there he found the door that led to the preserving side. It was warm to the touch, and smoke leaked through the cracks.

He tried to see what was in the room, but it was too dark. "Is there any wood here? There should be a pile — "

"Sure, just to your left."

He reached down and took two branches, then ripped off his torn left sleeve in two parts. After tying some material around each branch, he opened the door and then had to step back, for a cloud of noxious oak-fired smoke filled the air and made him cough. Inside, Megek had lit a great fire in a stone hearth and then smothered it partially with stones. If the fire had been brighter, Merlin would have been able to see the rows and rows of fish hanging from the ceiling.

Taking a deep breath, he ducked into the room and inched his way forward until he found one of the drip pans by kicking it. After wetting the makeshift torches in the greasy liquid, he shoved the tips in the fire. It didn't take long for them to light, and moments later he made his way back to the workroom, closing the door behind him.

He handed a torch to Natalenya, opened the smokehouse door, and stepped outside, torch first. Two wolves were there, and they stopped growling and backed away.

"Wait!" Natalenya called. "What if the torches go out?"

"I've still got my dirk, and the smithy isn't far. We can run if we need to."

Natalenya stepped out next to him, one hand holding Merlin's staff and the other grasping the torch, which she thrust toward the wolves.

"You watch behind and to the sides," he said, "and I'll wave my torch out front."

Merlin stepped into the well-worn path that his feet had almost memorized. Just a short distance to the large rock next to the pine, and then the path turned south. But the wolves harassed them, and their progress was slow. Three times Natalenya had to shove her torch into their faces, and Merlin had to use both his torch and his dirk to keep them at bay. If he wasn't already wet from the rain, he would have felt the anxious sweat trickling down his back. He felt foolish for risking their lives in this way, but what other choice did he have? There wasn't much time before Vortigern would attack the druids.

Finally the wolves slunk away, discouraged, and Merlin breathed a sigh of relief.

It was just in time, for the rain began again and the torches went out.

With the wolves gone, Merlin and Natalenya walked along in silence until they arrived at the old oak door of Merlin's home. He found the iron lever his father had crafted and paused to feel its comfortable curve. After he left with Uther in the morning, how long until he returned home? When would he feel this handle again? Suddenly every mundane detail about his life became special. The straw mattress where he slept in the smithy. The sound of his sister as she pranced about the soup pot. Their old horse, Kapall. Even Merlin's broken mug.

And Natalenya. How he wished he could marry her. But all these things were slipping away. He would spend his days away from his family, unmarried and blind.

The door opened with a jerk. Someone jumped out and tackled Merlin, pressing the air from his lungs as he hit the ground. From somewhere above, Natalenya gave a short scream.

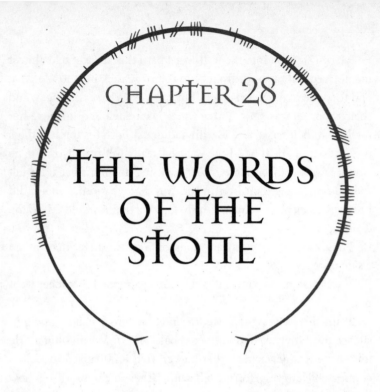

CHAPTER 28

THE WORDS OF THE STONE

M erlin fought back against his attacker, trying to free his arms.

"Got him!" the man yelled.

Extracting an arm, Merlin struggled to push the attacker off, until he recognized the voice. He sucked in a little air and said, "Tas ... it's me."

"Merlin!" His father let go and stood, then pulled Merlin up. "Why in the name of Rome were you fiddling with the latch?"

"I wasn't ... I was just coming home." *Maybe for the last time.*

His father scraped some mud from Merlin's shoulder. "Didn't mean to scare you. We thought someone was listening at the door again. He got away last time. Hello, Natalenya, come in out of the cold."

Natalenya brushed against Merlin's arm as they entered, and he felt her shiver. Dybris greeted them from the table beyond the hearth, and Natalenya sat down opposite him. Before Merlin joined her, he retrieved a wool blanket from Ganieda's bed and awkwardly laid it over her shoulders. She reached up to clasp it together, and their hands brushed. Her touch lingered for the briefest moment, and though Merlin felt that he was forgiven, it did little to ease the hurt muffling his heart.

"Merlin, your father and I have been discussing what to do about the Stone, but we don't agree," Dybris said without seeming to notice the exchange before him.

Owain coughed as he sat down, throwing Merlin a warm, wet towel. "I see you've been in trouble again. Use that to wipe the blood off your arm."

Merlin had already forgotten about the wolf attack, and he pulled up what was left of his sleeve to wash his wounds. Thankfully none of them were deep, for he had killed the wolf that quick. But all of this was unimportant, and he forced his attention back to the problem threatening them all: the Druid Stone.

"What are your thoughts?" he asked the men.

"I say we do *something*. Like drop it in the marsh," Dybris said, "but Owain thinks I'm hopeless."

Merlin's father slapped the table. "I never said that."

"Both of you, wait," Merlin said. "On our own this cause *is* hopeless. But if we had help, we might destroy the Stone."

"But who would help?" his father said. "All I want to do is save Mônda and Ganieda."

Merlin put his hand on his father's shoulder. "We can do both, Tas. What if the High King's men planned to attack the druidow tonight?"

"Shah, then," his father whispered. "You're telling us something you shouldn't."

Dybris clapped his hands. "That means we're free. If Uther attacks, we need only wait."

Merlin sighed. "I wish it were so. Vortigern arranged it so he leads, while Uther guards his family."

"Do you lack confidence in him?" Dybris asked. "Surely the High King's battle chief—"

"Vortigern can't be trusted," Natalenya interrupted, and her words were woven with fear. "I overheard him speaking with my father, and I doubt his loyalty to Uther."

Merlin took stock of this new information, confirming his own suspicions. "The truth is this: we can't rely on Vortigern to destroy the Stone. So we need a second plan."

Merlin's father slid his bench closer to the table. "What do you suggest?"

"You and Dybris should go to the circle of stones, and as soon as Vortigern scatters the druidow, steal the Stone in the confusion. Then we four will destroy it. We must act now, or we'll forfeit the chance. It wants to enslave us all ... or kill us if it cannot."

Dybris made a humming sound, as if in thought. "And if Vortigern doesn't show? If you can't trust him—"

"In that case, we'll have to figure something else out."

"And how will we take it away?" Owain asked.

"We can cover it," Dybris said, "with the same skins they use. That way we won't see it or touch it."

"And Merlin and I can bring your wagon," Natalenya said, "and wait for you."

"Let's not forget Kapall," Merlin's father said. "He's still limping. I doubt he could hobble that far."

Merlin sighed. "We'll need to find another horse to pull the wagon. Can we trust Allun? His mule would be perfect if he doesn't need it for milling tonight."

"Sure," Dybris said. "I've spoken with him recently, and if there's anyone besides Troslam who has his head on straight—"

"Do you think he'd let us?" Natalenya asked.

Owain leaned back and tapped the wall. "I'm sure he would."

"What worries me," Dybris added, "is how to avoid getting caught."

Everyone sat in silence. The druids guarded the Stone, and it would be difficult to get close without being discovered. To take it away would be even more difficult.

"What if you disguised yourselves?" Natalenya asked.

Dybris laughed. "To look like druidow? What would Crogen say?"

"And how to you propose we pull that off?" Owain asked. "You want us to cut blue scars on our arms? Without those, we'd be dead. We couldn't even wear long sleeves, because they don't hide their scars."

"It'll be dark ... What if you painted them on?" Merlin said. "Surely Troslam and Safrowana have blue dye."

His father got up and paced. "Sure, and we'll learn the secret druid talk in the next hour too — "

"We have to do something, Tas!"

"And what if Vortigern takes us for real druidow? I don't want a sword through my neck."

Dybris patted his partially bald head. "I'll just show my tonsure and vouch for you. No worries."

"If you think you're gong to save me with your bald spot, I have plenty of worries."

"The plan isn't perfect, Owain, but I can't think of anything better. We'll go to Troslam's to dye our arms while Merlin and Natalenya borrow the miller's mule. Let's try."

Merlin's father resumed his pacing.

Just as Merlin prepared to speak again, a twig cracked outside the window on the other side of the house. His father ran, knocking his shin on a stool. He slammed open the door and sprinted outside, Dybris close behind.

Someone yelled, and then silence. After awhile the two men trudged back inside, and Merlin's father swore. "Slipped in the mud and let him get away."

"Was someone spying on us?" Natalenya asked.

"Yes." Owain pulled off his mud-slicked tunic.

"He must be fast," Dybris said. "I didn't even see him run into the woods."

Merlin took the tunic and laid it near the hearth. "Who would eavesdrop on us?"

"Don't know. Didn't see very well either time, but he was wearing brown. Maybe a monk ..."

Natalenya took hold of Merlin's arm. "A monk? Why would a monk spy on us, and how much did he hear?"

Dybris sat down, and his bench squeaked like his voice. "I can't answer that. I can't answer that. Let's pray."

As the druidow finished their evening meal, Mórganthu and one other druid passed like dappled shadows through the gray-skinned trees until they arrived at the glade where the circle of stones lay. Mórganthu paused, gazed at the Stone, and wrinkled his brow deeply.

The druid tapped him on the arm, but Mórganthu slapped his hand away.

"Ard dre, you have not answered me yet. We are ready now for the wicker fires of Beltayne. Shall I proceed with your plan?"

With a crooked finger, Mórganthu wiped a tear from his cheek. "Yes, yes. So sorry for my silence. Gather half our number, and do not stray from my words."

The druid nodded, then headed back the way he had come.

Striding from the eastern side of the field, Mórganthu stopped six feet from the Stone and glanced around to verify his solitude. Then, jingling his wand of seashells, he circled the Stone southwise to follow the course of the sun. His gaze was always fixed upon the Stone, and he chanted in the druid tongue.

After passing five times around the Stone, he stopped, pulled a fish from a bag, and set it on the Stone. Then he knelt. "O great Belornos, I give you this offering and beseech thy counsel. Allow me to approach thy Stone of Abundance!"

A blue flame emanated from the Stone, engulfed the fish, and consumed it.

Mórganthu crawled forward until only inches separated his hands from the Stone. "O Stone of Abundance, I ask to touch thee and receive the counsel of Belornos!"

The blue light radiated even more brightly before him.

Mórganthu closed his eyes and carefully placed a hand on each side of the Stone, where they immediately stuck as if frozen. He chanted again, but the words slurred as his mind faded into the flames.

The blue glow pulsed, and Mórganthu jerked his head up, eyes wide and pupils dilated.

"That is *not* the agreement I made with him," he yelled.

Instantly a few flames burst from the top of the Stone.

Mórganthu cried out until they faded.

"I will perform *part* of thy command. They will all be killed, but not her. That was the bargain!"

Flames burst forth again, and Mórganthu shrieked. When they subsided and he could breathe again, he asked, "You, you would make me break my potent oath to such a man of consequence?"

The flames leaped even higher, and Mórganthu screamed. "*Mercy!* Mercy, please, I relent. As you command, O Voice, they will *all* die!"

Flashing blue fire exploded from the Stone, scalding Mórganthu's hands and nearly igniting his hair before flinging him onto his back.

Garth dashed from the woods, knelt beside Mórganthu, and cradled his head. The boy flicked away blue cinders that burned in Mórganthu's hair.

"Ard Dre, are you all right?"

Mórganthu groaned and tried to sit up. He would have failed if Garth's hands hadn't been there for support. "My son. My only son, you are here …"

"Sorry to disturb you, but as I get no midmeal, which is right cruel in my 'pinion, I was sent to say *he* wants to see you."

Mórganthu blew on his bleeding hands. "Who?"

"The warrior wearin' black an' such —"

"What? What is his name?"

Garth rubbed his stomach. "He'd have come himself, but he's stuffin' his cheeks with loaves an' chicken. I asked him for a bite, but he — "

Mórganthu struck Garth across the face, leaving a red welt. "What is his name, you fool!"

Garth yelped and jumped away. "An Eirish warrior. McGoss."

"Help me ... Help me to stand."

Garth drew near to support the arch druid as he found his balance but flinched when Mórganthu's hands reached out to him.

"Belornos told me I would need him for this task, and he already comes?"

"What did you say, Ard Dre?"

"Nothing. Nothing! Ignore an old man's wandering tongue. Now fetch him. Tell McGoss I am ready."

As Garth ran off, Mórganthu called after him. "And when you have told him, be a kind son and bring the long rope from my tent."

That sea rat McGoss! I don't even get a bite o' food for runnin' his message, and the brute twists my ear purple until I promise not to tell anyone about his secret meetin' with Mórganthu. Garth's left ear felt twice the size of the other.

And he still had to get the rope for Mórganthu. Then he could hide from those evil eyeballs of the druid wives.

His stomach growled as he unstrung the flap to Mórganthu's tent, a place forbidden to him ever since he'd joined the druidow. But Garth knew special delicacies lay inside. After the previous evening's meal, Mórganthu had brought out a small barrel of dried strawberries and passed them around to his inner circle. Did poor starving Garth have a sweet strawberry plopped into his mouth? Not even one sliver.

As he stepped into the warm tent, he peeked out at all the druidow sitting beyond the campfires laughing and talking. Garth grinned as he tied the flap closed again, his stomach near to rolling in anticipation.

As he turned around, his gaze was drawn to the drooping tent's ceiling. There hung hundreds of bones, each etched with the same kinds of lines Garth had seen on a few of the standing stones around the circle. One of the druidow had told him the writing was called *ogham*, but he didn't understand a lick of it. Some of the bones were old and gray, while others were yellow with pink ends where flesh had been cleaned off.

A wind blew over the tent, causing its cloth roof to wave and sending the bones clinking into each other. Garth stuffed his thumbs in his ears and ducked toward the center of the tent, only to run into the head of a white bull and its rolled-up hide. The dark eye sockets glared at him, and the sharpened horns pointed at his throat like daggers.

Recoiling from the bull, he found the pile of rope on the right side of the tent, which he'd bring to Mórganthu soon enough. For now, he ran to a wooden chair at the back of the tent, behind which sat a number of barrels. The chair itself was carved with fanged, winged, and scaled beasts. One of them was a snake with horns.

Pulling his gaze away, Garth reached for the largest barrel and pulled off the lid. Inside he found nothing but wooden stakes and scraps of torn tent cloth. Opening the next largest, he discovered it to be empty except for a smattering of dried oats in the bottom.

Kneeling down, he picked up a smaller barrel and felt its weight. Garth smiled. This one must have the strawberries!

He opened the lid, and a terrible smell belched from the barrel. He wanted to close it immediately, but he wondered if some strawberries had gone bad. Waving the lid made the smell dissipate a little, so he peeked inside. He was surprised to see a white-haired animal skin on top. More of the bull's hide? Reaching in, he took hold of the hairs and pulled it out.

And then Garth screamed.

CHAPTER 29

THE SECRETS OF THE TOWER

U ther picked Myrgwen up and placed her in the boat next to Colvarth. Oh, how she'd grown. Just last harvest he could still throw her in the air and catch her, to her squeals of delight. But since he'd returned from his military campaign, he realized the days were numbered for such play.

Igerna smiled at him as he passed her a basket of food. She sat there in the back of the boat next to Eilyne — they were both so pretty. Arthur sat between them. Uther couldn't have been more proud of his son. *What a warrior he'll make!* Descended from two High Kings, he would grow wise and proud. Uther looked forward to teaching him how to fight and how to lead.

Finally ready, Uther was about to push the boat out into the water when Vortigern walked down to the bank and held out a draught skin.

"Here," the battle chief said. "The last and best mead. Caught Rewan sipping it and thought you could ... enjoy it while you're on the island."

"My gratitude!" Uther smiled as he tucked the skin under his arm. It would do him good against the chill. "And do not forget. After you scatter the druidow, take the Stone to the fortress and occupy it. I want Tregeagle powerless in the morning."

"Already planned. What will you do with him?"

"Evict him. He can lick the chunks of his broken Stone for all I care."

Vortigern clucked his tongue. "Eeh. He won't like that."

"I don't care. That fool of a magister is lucky to still have his neck."

"True."

"We'll stay on the island till morning, but have Sydnius row over with word of your success. I'll be glad when this is over."

Vortigern rubbed his hands together. "Ah, let me push you."

Uther climbed into the boat, and Vortigern shoved the prow away from the boggy shore. As the craft floated off into the marsh, Uther took a sip of mead and watched his battle chief ascend the bank to the join his already-mounted men.

"Good-bye, brother," Igerna shouted. "May God fill your horn with every blessing!"

But Vortigern must not have heard, for he didn't turn or wave.

Garth sat, shaking and staring into the face of a man's cut-off head. He began to scream again, but at the last moment muffled it with his sleeve. He didn't want to be discovered going through Mórganthu's things. Because no matter how much he wanted to drop the head, his fingers wouldn't let go.

And he recognized the face. *Old Trothek!*

On the man's right cheek lay the same large mole Garth remembered. And even with his face puffed hideously green, his beard cut short, and his jaw slack, the man's identity was clear.

Trothek had opposed Mórganthu, true, but he had seemed kind, even caring. Why would Mórganthu have his head in a barrel? Had the arch druid killed him?

Garth despised that evil High King for cutting off Anviv's head. Didn't this make Mórganthu evil too? Nothing seemed to make sense anymore.

The wind blew again, and the bones noosed to the tent roof jangled their ominous music. Garth's hand shook, and he almost vomited as he set the head back in the barrel.

Good-bye, Trothek.

No sooner was the top in place when a voice called outside the tent.

He chucked the barrel behind the chair, swabbed his hand on the grass, and ran to the rope. Flinging himself under the side of the tent at the back, he yanked out the coil of rope and tried to make himself as small as possible.

"Who's there? Who be shouting?" the voice called again from the other side of the tent.

Garth saw the fabric quiver, but then he realized the man was walking *around* the tent. Garth froze. The dark shape loomed near the corner. All Garth could think of was his own head in a barrel, and he fainted.

Bedwir kicked his horse in the flanks to catch up to Vortigern.

As the most recent war chieftain chosen by Uther, he calculated the risk of angering Vortigern by questioning the man's obedience. Bedwir could lose his position, even his place as a warrior. Maybe even his life.

He'd seen how Vortigern punished those who had crossed him. But how could he ignore the High King's clear command? *Deal with the druidow and then destroy the Stone*, they'd been told. So why did Vortigern skirt around the mountain and head to Bosventor? The druidow weren't in the village tonight.

Finally reining up near the battle chief, Bedwir shouted, "Vortigern! Sydnius says the druid camp is across the stream. Where are we going?"

"To the Tor. Uther said we take the Tor *first*."

"What?"

"We'll leave the horses there!" Vortigern shouted. "You think we can sneak up on the druidow riding horses?"

"Who said we should sneak up on them?"

Vortigern pulled his sword and chunked out a small chip of wood from Bedwir's shield. "No more questions."

Bedwir fell back, swallowed his anger, and checked his damaged shield.

Riding up the long path through Bosventor, the warriors approached Tregeagle's house. The magister had just climbed into his wagon while his wife stood at the door of their house instructing a servant. Vortigern rode ahead, had a quiet word with the magister, and pointed to the fortress on the hill.

Tregeagle pointed as well, a sly smile on his face.

A few more words were exchanged, and then the magister squinted, nodded at Vortigern, and called his wife to join him.

Vortigern backed his horse up and looked at his men.

What is Vortigern's game? Bedwir knew Uther planned on ridding the village of Tregeagle in the morning, so why engage the traitor in friendly banter? He wished he'd been there the night before and met Tregeagle himself.

Bedwir and his men rode their horses to the side of the path, allowing the magister to thunder past with an impenetrable look on his face.

Vortigern raised his arm, and the men followed him up to the fortress, where a guard stood by the open gate.

From where Bedwir sat on his horse, two-thirds down the line, he saw Vortigern dismount and speak with the guard, who stood up as tall as he could and thumped the ground with his spear. They appeared to be arguing fiercely.

Finally Vortigern laughed long and hard with his hands on his slim waist. And then, quick as an adder, he smashed the guard across the chin with his forearm and knocked him down. Leaping on him, the battle chief sunk a freshly drawn dirk into the man's gut and up into his lungs.

Had Vortigern gone mad? Killing a man who hadn't even attacked him?

The guard gasped, his hand jerking as his spear rolled into the mud.

Vortigern remounted and rode whistling through the gate.

When Bedwir's horse trotted by, he glanced at the guard lying there, barely breathing and calling for help with quivering, silent lips.

After tying up his horse, Bedwir ran back to the man at the gate. "Do you want water?" he asked, instantly regretting the words. Though what was he to say? The man was dying.

But the guard nodded, the dust around his eyes wet with tears. Bedwir pulled out his waterskin and gave him a sip, which he choked on at first but was able to swallow.

"I ... said ... he could ... not come in ... with horses ... The hay was ... for the goats ... I ... spoke well of Uther ... but ..."

Bedwir was shocked. This guard was loyal to Uther.

The man vomited blood, and Bedwir helped turn his head. "Die ... die ..." he choked.

"I know you're dying ..."

"No ... my name's Dyffresyn. Tell ... wife ... children ... love 'em, and ..."

But his words failed, and the dim light in his eyes faded like two stars eclipsed by the reaching fingers of a coming storm.

Then someone kicked Bedwir.

"Get up!" Vortigern yelled. "And stop dribbling on the dead."

━┼━

As Uther pulled the now empty boat farther up the muddy shore, he could see his family, followed by Colvarth, ascending the bank of the large island. Blackbirds called from the shore, and the croaking of the frogs meant the evening was upon them.

He thought about hiding the boat from prying eyes but surmised there was little danger and decided to lash it to a tree. Who would suspect that the High King and his family had gone to the big island in the marsh?

Uther grabbed the tie rope and attempted to pull it out, but he found it wrapped around an anchor. Pulling the anchor out, he saw that it was none other than the rusty head of a pickaxe that had lost its handle long ago, probably cast away by a tin miner and procured by a local fisherman. Winding this twice around an apple tree, one of hundreds that covered this end of the island, he gave a tug to make sure it was secure.

As he turned back to survey the marsh, he unstrapped the mead skin from his belt, removed the stag horn stopper, and took a quick sip. Whether he looked south beyond the broad end of the island or north beside the long shoreline, all he set his gaze upon were reeds and sedge grasses clumped amid lethargic water channels. The receding rains and the stilling of the winds had brought forth a mist that rose upon the marsh in twisting, white fingers.

Ah, the fishing must be excellent here! Not since his youth had Uther found time to enjoy the simple pleasures of life, such as fishing. All these he'd denied himself since taking on the mantle of leadership, both as a warrior guarding the people of Britain and later as High King when his father, Aurelianus, had died — Jesu bless his spirit. An old tune his father had hummed one rare day when they did fish came to Uther, and he whistled it now.

Looking back east past the marsh, he scanned the immediate hills, where his campaign tent stood among the warriors' smaller tents, and a distant ridge far beyond them, where a faint line of smoke rose. This marked the camp of the druidow, no doubt, and their pagan stone circle. Soon Vortigern would carry out swift justice there, and this shortsighted rebellion would be over.

Taking a longer swig of mead, Uther found that the drink flowed across his tongue more sweetly than what he'd become accustomed to on the trail. But as Vortigern declared, this was of premium stock.

He replaced the stopper and slung the skin over his shoulder. Hefting the extra tent from the boat, he limped up the thick, grassy shore, where his family waited for him. Myrgwen ran and hugged his waist while Eilyne balanced on a log nearby. Igerna, smiling, sat on a large rock holding the food basket and young Arthur. The boy leaned forward from her lap, grabbed a twig, and broke it from a length of dead branch sitting at her feet.

Uther patted Myrgwen on the head. "Where's Colvarth?"

"At the tower."

Igerna stood and reached out her left hand to him. "Shall we follow?"

Soon they approached the ruined blocks of a small fortress, and within that, the old tower. Dark granite stones lay scattered across the ground as if a giant of old had risen from the marsh and broken them with massive hands. Moss clung like leeches to their northward faces, and Uther imagined the centuries of wind whistling across the flat marshlands that had worn smooth their other sides.

Although Uther had passed many flower-adorned apple trees while walking up to the ruins, here their ancestors stood as dead sentinels to a distant age. Each tree bore its fate gauntly, back bent and withered, broken branches outstretched in a fruitless, mocking display.

He found a level place hidden behind a large brush-covered stone and set their temporary lodgings up while Igerna gathered the old applewood for a fire. This gave him time to sip more of the sweet mead as well as study the tower, a marvel of engineering. Uther had seen plenty of fortresses in his time, either supervising their construction or else besieging them. The stones had been fit expertly as the tower tapered from a base of sixteen feet wide to — what Uther estimated — about eight feet wide at the top. Its height rose to nearly forty feet, and vines choked each other on their way to reach the crown like moldy skeletal arms protruding from a grave.

The stout wooden roof had long ago fallen to ruin, and yet enough remained to show a semblance of its conical shape. Uther walked to the doorway of the tower, which remarkably stood three feet up from the ground. "Colvarth, anything of interest?"

The bard poked his nose out from the slim stone archway, and his voice echoed. "Nothing much, my king. But come see ... for yourself."

Uther stepped up onto the high threshold of the doorway and pulled himself through. Blinded for a moment by the swift change to near darkness, he tried to step down and lost his balance. With his bad knee he fell hard onto a rock and then headlong to the dirt.

Colvarth rushed over. "My king! Are you all right? The floor is ... higher inside, and rough."

Uther's knee screamed with pain and his head spun. He rolled onto his back and looked upward, straight to the top of the tower. The top floor Merlin had spoken of had rotted away, and now nothing remained but an empty shell.

A man appeared above him, ghostlike, emerging from nowhere and walking down an invisible stairway. He wore an embroidered sapphire robe with white-gold trim, and at his waist a jeweled belt held the scabbard of a dagger. A *druid?* No, this wasn't the blade of a Briton; it was arched like those of traders he had seen from the eastern lands.

But the oddest thing was the man's face. Though his gray beard hung down to his waist and his eyes wrinkled with wisdom, his cheeks were smooth, his lips young, his nose unmarred, and his forehead unlined. By all accounts, he bore the marks of a youth.

Uther pointed at the man and tried to speak, but his throat was stiff and wouldn't utter a sound.

Colvarth patted him on the shoulder. "A nasty ... tumble ... yes. Rest awhile, my king."

The man in Uther's vision reached the bottom of the unseen stairway, put a finger to his lips, and, kneeling, drew the cross of Jesu in the dirt. Then he descended right into the ground as though it didn't exist. Just before his head sank from sight, he stared straight at Uther, and his eyes held a secret and sorrowful longing.

With that he disappeared.

Uther's knee suddenly felt no pain, and his tongue loosed. He jumped up, almost knocking Colvarth over. "Did you not see him?"

"Arthur is ... outside, my king."

"The man, dressed in blue." Uther looked up again to the top of the tower. The angled daylight filtered through the bones of the roof, and the empty window sat like an eye to the outside. Nothing else could be seen. No floor to stand on. No metal hung there to reflect sunlight to onlookers.

Nothing. So what *had* he seen? The flash of light from before, this he could have imagined. But twice now he'd seen the man in blue. What of him?

The ground! The man had descended through the ground.

Uther swallowed a long draught from the mead skin and then felt dizzy for a moment. Soon the feeling passed, and he sank to his knees at the spot where the sign of the cross had been only moments before and dug frantically in the soft soil with his knife. "Colvarth, bring Igerna and the children. Bring them here!"

Waking with great shivers, Garth looked up into the eyes of Caygek, who bent over him with concern on his face, his long blond beard almost touching Garth's nose.

The druid's hand brushed dirt from Garth's forehead. "Are you unharmed?"

Garth blinked.

"Why are you so white?" Caygek asked. "I saw you go into Mórganthu's tent. Something there scare you?"

Garth shook his head, then changed it to a nod.

"You hollered. No one else paid any mind — too much talk about tonight. But those who keep their ears open get to question the thief. So ... did you see Trothek?"

Garth nodded again, this time firmly.

Caygek's eyes became soft. "He was my friend, and I'm sorry you had to see him that way. The arch druid killed him when the moon was under the foot of the Druid constellation, perhaps twelve days ago. Slit his throat and cut off his head before us all."

"Why?" Garth croaked.

"Because Trothek opposed his plans," Caygek answered. "It's painful to think about, but it's exactly what a warrior does with his enemy. Doesn't Mórganthu gain Trothek's wisdom by keeping his head?"

Garth had heard of such practices but never imagined it could happen here in Bosventor. Sitting up, he pulled the coil of rope to his chest. "I've got to go! Mórganthu's waitin'."

"Then go, but come back, and we'll talk some more."

Garth stood up, shaking.

"Garth."

"Yes?"

"Beltayne is tonight, and I must warn you of what Mórganthu might do. Fifty of our number just left at his orders, and I don't know on what mischievous errand. We have to be careful. Stick with me, and I'll keep you safe and look after you. A few of us will be waiting at the big pine beyond the ridge. Do you know the place?"

Garth nodded, then walked off through the woods with the heavy rope draped over his shoulder. With each step closer to Mórganthu and the stone circle, he envisioned the arch druid's hand tightening the rope around his neck. He was nigh to blubbering when he finally arrived.

"Stop! Stop your crying!" Mórganthu yelled.

Garth closed his eyes, but a few more choked moans escaped his lips.

Moments later he felt the sting of the arch druid's hand across his cheek. "Such a slug, you cannot even bring rope without crying! And here I have a special job for you."

Garth swallowed. Wherever he looked, Trothek's ghastly face floated before him.

"Garth! Look at my personage. Did you not grow up learning to handle a boat?"

"Y-yes."

"And are you not familiar with the marsh?"

"A little ... sure."

"Which parts, would you say?"

"Well ... close to the village, anyhow." As he thought of the marsh and his few but wonderful times fishing there, the image of Trothek faded.

"Are you familiar with Inis Avallow? The island with the tower?"

CHAPTER 30

THE PLOTS OF MEN

Natalenya's proposal bothered Merlin. "Are you sure you're willing to get Allun's mule alone?" Yes, he had asked her for the second time, but he had to be sure.

"If you're wondering whether I can handle it, I've hitched up my father's horses many times, and I drive them myself whenever my mother and I go out alone."

Dybris finished putting on one of Merlin's old tunics to replace his monk's robe. "But this is a dangerous night to be out alone. We've all planned for Merlin to go with you, and he's more than willing."

"I insist," Natalenya said. "Merlin is needed more at the circle of stones than in the dusty old mill hitching up a mule."

What Merlin found the most agonizing was wondering whether she was still mad at him after he had fumbled her hints at marriage. What a fool he'd been. What he wouldn't give to tell her how he really felt.

"Fine," Dybris said as he opened the door and stepped through. "We'd better go, then."

Owain joined him outside, but Merlin hesitated.

"Here … will you wear my torc?"

"Why?" she said, her voice softening. "It's a gift to you from —"

"The druidow will recognize me with it on." Truly, though, he just wanted her to keep thinking of him. "And let me lend you this … It's a small knife my father made for Ganieda."

"You think I'll need it? I can run pretty fast, you know."

"Just in case."

Before taking the blade from him, she pressed both of her hands around his. "You'll be careful?"

"Yes. And you?"

She nodded, and Merlin saw the motion by the light of the lamp. And her hands felt good — small but strong. The only hand he could properly compare them to was his younger sister's, since he couldn't remember his mother's and had never held Mônda's. And yet Natalenya's hands weren't like his sister's. Ganieda's were thin, almost frail, always wiggling and cold, but Natalenya's hands firmly and purposefully held his, and the warmth spread up his arm until he began to sweat.

"You'll leave after you eat? Tas set out a mug of blueberry-leaf tea for you, as well as some oatcakes."

"Thanks."

"Well, the tea is a bit tart, and the oatcakes are dry. You can have some smoked meat —"

She laughed, finally taking the blade. "I'll be fine."

Outside Dybris coughed, and Merlin paused awkwardly on the threshhold, then he turned, closing the door behind him. As he joined his father and the monk, he heard her drop the bar in place to secure the door.

Merlin was glad she was going to rest and eat, for she hadn't had a meal since morning and had grown more weary the longer they discussed their plan. But though her hands had trembled, she'd never wavered in her intent, and Merlin respected her mettle. Whatever her father was, Natalenya was of quality, something Merlin was beginning to understand.

As the men began their journey, Merlin put a hand on his father's shoulder so they could keep a better pace, but Owain grumbled at him. "Tell me again — why are we going to the Stone?"

"Because we need to destroy it."

"This is madness," his father said, and Merlin could imagine his scowl.

"You agreed to the plan."

"But I don't have to like it."

Was his father afraid of the Stone? Deep down, Merlin certainly was. Were they all fools?

Dybris, who always seemed hopeful, joined in the conversation. "Come now, the plan is simple. Have faith, my friend."

Owain pushed Dybris away and walked faster. "I do this only for my wife and daughter."

"I know what we wish to do is not without great risk, but we do it for the villagers as well. For Prontwon's memory, and for Garth. I didn't mean to anger you."

"I'm not angry. I just don't have much hope."

Is there hope? Merlin wondered.

Dybris stopped talking, and since Owain tended to like silence, Merlin said nothing either. Soon they dropped in at the miller's shop. Allun barely looked up when they made their request for Natalenya to borrow his mule. A large grindstone lay across two wobbling benches, and the miller was studiously dressing the stone using a long metal file.

"We're going to disguise ourselves as druidow," Dybris explained. "Natalenya will visit in a bit to hitch the mule to Owain's wagon and hide in the woods. Merlin, Owain, and I will sneak into the druid camp and steal the Stone. Then we'll destroy it, and its enchantments will be gone forever."

Allun swung aside the thick timber boom so he could see them better. "Surely you jest," he said, filing away and making the benches wobble. "You're not going to meddle with that pagan Stone, are you?"

Merlin hoped the miller wouldn't now recant his permission to use the mule.

"I agree," Owain said, "it's a foolhardy —"

But Dybris cut him off. "We have to free the people."

"Well, that'd be a good deed," Allun said. "Hardly a soul's been by to grind since that Mórganthu showed up. Thought I'd take the posey time and get the grinders workin' better."

Merlin's father bent down and looked under the benches. "Hey," he said, "the nails in your benches have worked themselves almost completely out. I wouldn't do much more without hammering 'em back in."

"Ah, they do that every time. I'll hammer 'em back in after I'm done tonight." He stood and banged his head on the boom. "Ow! Drat that timber. I keep pushin' it away, and it keeps swinging back."

"So ... may Natalenya borrow your mule?" Merlin asked.

"Sure, nothin' to grind anyway. Plewin's in the back field eatin' her favorite spring blossoms. Get her anytime. Jus' bring her back when you're done."

Thanking the miller, the three left and walked uphill toward Troslam and Safrowana's house. Merlin felt increasingly uneasy and wondered if they were being followed. Perhaps the man who had spied on them earlier at the house was still on their trail. He asked his father and Dybris to keep a lookout for anyone suspicious, but they saw no one. Then Merlin realized why he felt so uneasy, and he motioned for them to stop.

"What?" Dybris asked.

"All the villagers are gone. Listen. It's too quiet. Do you see any smoke?"

"Except for Troslam's house up the hill and the mill, no. And none of the crennigs have a fire lit."

They hastened up the hill, and Owain banged on the weaver's door. "Troslam!"

Merlin heard the sliding of wood before the door jerked open.

"Shah, Owain! You needn't scare us." The weaver's voice held an anxious tone.

When Merlin shook the man's hands an old memory flashed before Merlin — the weaver was tall with a golden beard.

Troslam turned to Dybris and with an exclaimation, fell to his knees. "Brother Dybris! I didn't recognize you without your robe and with your face bruised. I thought — "

"What?"

"I thought you'd been taken away!"

"Taken?"

Troslam practically sputtered. "The druidow came, not more than half an hour ago, with knives and spears, and took the brothers away."

Dybris sucked in a breath.

"They surrounded the chapel and broke the door in. Led them away, with the villagers following. Taken to that awful Stone, I'd guess."

Merlin closed his eyes in disbelief, and Dybris grabbed onto his shoulder for support.

—┼—

"Inis Avallow?" Garth asked. Mórganthu's question seemed odd. "Yes, Ard Dre. Even I know where *that* is."

"Well, my warriors do not, and I want you to lead them through the marsh. We have procured two boats from fishermen who ply their trade on its northern waters, and this works well, for we do not want you to be seen passing through the village, nor do I want you stumbling through Uther's camp."

Only then did Garth notice all the Eirish warriors standing around. That beast McGoss glared at him through those dark-slitted eyes of his.

"Are ... you sure, Ard Dre? Can't someone else lead 'em?"

Mórganthu raised a hand.

Garth flinched, imagining a flashing knife. "I'll lead 'em! Don't — "

Mórganthu brought his hand down and smiled warmly. "When you come back, I will let you have some of those strawberries you begged me for last night. Would you like that?"

"No! No, sir!" Garth shook his head wildly.

Mórganthu's eyes narrowed. "And why not? They have come all the way from Brythanvy."

"I ... I ... wouldn't want to spoil me supper."

"Yes, yes, a glorious feast tonight. I nearly forgot in my, shall we say, anticipation."

———✦———

With a druid leading them, Garth and the Eirish warriors had set off at once. At first Garth walked in the middle of the group, but unable to keep up, he soon found himself trailing behind.

McGoss joined him. "Keep yer lips tight," he hissed. "Let on about me an' the ard dre talkin' secret, an' I'll stick ya." He lifted his cloak, and underneath glinted a long notched dagger.

Garth swallowed and nodded. He tried to catch up to the others, but McGoss yanked him back. "Keep close."

Northward they marched over the hills. At one point they walked by a path leading down to the right, which Garth recognized as the way to the char-man's camp. If only he were with Merlin now, fetching coal, instead of with these foreign warriors. If only he still had his bagpipe.

McGoss poked him in the back. "No laggin'."

Soon they turned down the hillside to the stream and forded it at a shallow spot where some old tin dredgers lay on the bank. From there they cut westward across the hills until they came to the northern reaches of the marsh. Their druid guide uncovered the two boats hidden among the reeds and then returned to camp, leaving Garth alone with the warriors.

One of them put a hand on Garth's shoulder. "So welcome, little druid. I'm named O'Sloan, and now it's yer turn to lead."

"To the island?" Garth asked.

"Aye. And back. But there's a mist rising, so ya better be a good scout."

"Navigator."

"Whate'er. Jus' don't get lost, aye?"

They split into two groups, with McEwan, McGoss, and Garth in the first boat, and the others in the second.

Garth saw why he'd been picked to lead them: these men knew nothing about boats, made clear from facing the wrong way to not knowing how to use the oars. And the huge McEwan nearly tipped over their boat and dumped Garth in the water.

"We're *kern* warriors, fightin' men, ya see," O'Sloan called. "We know horses — but we taint taken time for silly boats."

They arranged themselves in the dinghies, then Garth demonstrated the action of the oars to McEwan and to O'Sloan in the other boat. After a few tries O'Sloan figured it out, but the giant made Garth's boat turn in circles.

"I'd rather paddle wit' me hands!" McEwan declared, and Garth bit his tongue to keep his comments private until the oaf picked up the habit.

Garth directed them southward into the slow central current of the marsh. The fog had thickened considerably, but he found solace in the fact the island was nearly impossible to miss, even in the creeping darkness.

"An' why're we goin' to Inis Avallow?" Garth asked.

From the back of the boat, McGoss's eyes were like icy daggers.

"To catch a little mouse," McEwan said, and his laughter boomed across the marsh.

"Shash-en!" someone called from the other boat.

McEwan clamped his lips shut.

"No, really, what are we doin'?" Garth asked.

"Ya mean ya don't know?" McEwan turned his head to look at Garth and smiled, his large teeth gleaming through the mist. "We're goin' fer revenge on the High King."

Still getting over the shock of Troslam's news, Merlin considered their situation while Dybris prayed silently for the safety of the brothers.

Owain waited until the monk said his amen before speaking. "Does this change our plans at all?"

"Are you backing out?" Dybris asked.

"Never. But it's just not as simple now."

"We need to free the brothers as well," Merlin said.

Safrowana appeared and grasped their hands in greeting. When she saw Merlin's arm, she gasped. "What happened?"

"It's not that bad —" Merlin began.

"Imelys, fill a bowl from the water bucket and bring a rag," Safrowana called. "Yes behind the drying rack … That's it."

The girl brought her mother the bucket and watched Safrowana clean the wound while Merlin described the scuffle with the wolves.

"The cuts aren't deep, like you said. But they sure gave me a fright."

"As if there isn't enough to be fightened about." Imelys said.

Owain stepped over to their hearth and took a deep sniff. "Always glad to walk into a house where goat-leek soup is simmering over a slow fire."

Only then did Merlin notice the pleasant aroma that filled the room.

"You'll have to excuse our blacksmith," Dybris said. "I can personally attest that this man hasn't eaten a warm meal in quite a few days."

At this, someone short stepped into the room from the back of the house.

"Kyallna," Owain called. "I didn't expect to see you here."

"Came 'cause o' the troubles last night," she said, hobbling across to join them. "Brought the soup along. Help yourself!"

She reached up and pinched Merlin's cheek. "If you see that

chubbins Garth, tell him I've got some more soup. He's welcome. Such a dear, sweet one, that boy."

Merlin smiled at the old woman. "Thank you, Kyallna. I'll certainly tell him about your offer if I see him." He placed an arm around her shoulders and addressed Troslam. "With your permission, we'd like to borrow some dye." And then he spoke at length of their plan.

"You're welcome to any dye," Troslam said, "but I'm afraid we're out of blue. We just used our last woad leaves and madder root to make purple."

"How long will it take to make more blue?"

"Well, we won't get more woad till fall when the merchant comes through. We could try some bluestone, but it'd take hours to make it dark enough."

"Purple?" Owain asked.

"Hmm." Dybris paused, then shrugged. "Guess it'll have to do. So what shapes do we paint?"

"Anything. Beasts, knotwork, symbols. Just leave off the crosses — "

After Owain and Dybris finished painting their arms and hands, they each painted one of Merlin's arms, and then they all stood near the fire until the coloring dried to the touch.

"I'm glad the color darkened," Owain said as he picked up his cloak. "Most will think it's just blue, especially at night."

Before they departed, Dybris raised his hands to heaven and sanctified Troslam and his family.

Blessed shalt thou be in thy crennig;
Blessed shalt thou be in God's woodland;
Blessed shalt thy children and babans be;
Blessed shalt thy planting and harvest be;
Blessed shalt thy spinning and weaving be;
Blessed shalt thou be when thou comest in,
And blessed shalt thou be when thou goest out.

Troslam bowed. "Thank you. We'll pray for your safety and success this night."

The three men stepped out of the house to find an overcast gray sky frowning upon them. Merlin pulled his hood down, concealing his face in shadow. Behind he heard Troslam drop a wooden plank to bar the door.

"So, Drybris," Owain said, "you think the druidow will be fooled by that portly blue boar you drew on your arm? His tail is so long you'd think a snake was biting his rump."

"Hah! No worse than the moons you drew. They're so squashed they resemble Brother Loyt's bannocks."

"Let's hope they don't look too closely," Merlin added.

They set off down the path, and after a short distance, they came to the chapel.

"Tell me what you see, Tas," he said.

Merlin's father described the violent scene before them: The latch had been ripped from the wooden door, and the shattered end of a brass sickle knife had been jabbed into the center. Inside the chapel, one of the overturned benches was smeared with blood.

Dybris ran in and fell to his knees. "Let's go," Owain called. "Drawing crosses in the bloody dirt won't help if Mórganthu starts killing the brothers."

Dybris followed him outside, and without a word they walked downhill through the deserted village and turned east at the main road. Rounding the mountain, they hurried past the ruins of the distant abbey to the rushing stream and crossed the Fowaven bridge.

Owain pointed toward the hills and the smoke rising from the druid camp. "We should slip into the woods that way. You lead, Dybris, since you've scouted their camp."

Dybris agreed. Merlin grasped his father's arm as they left the path to trudge up a steep heather embankment. Beyond that, Dybris led them into a thick stand of pines. From there they turned straight north and, walking through the trees, paralleled the stream to a point below the druid camp.

As quietly as possible, they started to climb the hill, but after only a short distance, the monk's steps faltered.

"What is it?" Merlin asked his father.

"Someone's been murdered," Owain answered. "He's covered in blood, and by the look on his face, he died painfully."

Dybris let out a mournful wail and grabbed Merlin's arm for support.

———✠———

Natalenya tucked Ganieda's knife into her belt and then tugged at the crennig door until it closed with a groan.

The black, lifeless shadows of night was gathering in the deepest parts of the woods surrounding the path. She set out, but a slight rustling from the bushes to her left brought her up short. A snake crossed right in front of her, its chisel-shaped head sliding before its slow, thick body. Natalenya froze, her stomach tightening in a knot. But it passed by without noticing her, and once it was gone she walked slowly, warily, fighting the urge to break into a sprint. She reached up and touched Merlin's golden torc, which lay upon her neck, and found her courage once more.

Since Merlin and the others hadn't come back, she reasoned, then Allun must have agreed to lend his mule. Although Plewin was stubborn, Merlin had assured her that he pulled anything, including wagons, with an untiring and sure-footed stride.

When she arrived at the mill, all was silent and the building appeared dead — its sad roof sagging, the high windows desolate and grim. Was this where all the villagers gathered to have their grain milled and share the latest gossip? Where had everyone gone? Where was Allun?

She scanned the field beyond the ghost-white stone wall, but the mule wasn't there. *Plewin must be inside the mill eating a trough full of grain,* she mused. Merlin had said Allun fed her that way when he had extra.

Natalenya walked toward the mill, gravel crunching under her boots. Pausing at the door, she pressed her ear against the thick wood and listened, but she didn't hear anything. Allun didn't appear to be there. *Too bad I didn't borrow one of my family's horses before father and mother left in the wagon,* she mused. But there was nothing she could do about it now.

A cold gust of wind blew, and the door creaked on its hinges. It was open. Unlocked.

She pushed on the rough wood of the door, determined to get the mule. Merlin was counting on her. They needed the wagon to transport the Stone. To destroy it. *Right.*

Natalenya stepped into the mill, and the darkness swallowed her. She waited a moment to let her eyes adjust, and then, off to the right, she saw the silhouette of Plewin in her stall.

She took three steps forward but then froze in her tracks.

The door behind her closed.

Then she heard the bar fall into place.

An evil laugh echoed through the room.

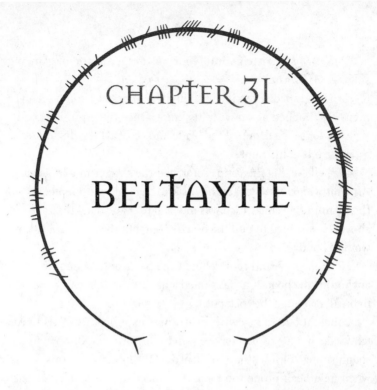

CHAPTER 31

BELTAYNE

U ther slashed the knife down again and again, then threw the softened dirt out of the ever-widening hole. There in the tower, alone, he could hear his panting breaths echo off the walls.

There must be something here. The man in blue wouldn't have disappeared below the earth at this spot if something hadn't been buried here. Hopefully it wasn't just the man's bones.

Uther continued digging until, with a start, he felt a tap on his shoulder.

"My ... king, your queen stands here, and your ... children. I have brought them."

Uther looked up for an instant, and a wave of dizziness distorted his sight. When had Colvarth and his family climbed through the door? He nodded to his wife and took a long sip of mead, some of it sloshing off his chin and into the damp hole.

"Something here." He pointed. "A man went into the ground."

"You saw someone go into your hole?" Igerna asked, glancing sideways at him.

Uther blinked. Even if she thought him crazy, he *had* seen the man. He chopped again with his knife. Once the ground was sufficiently loose, he dropped the blade and scooped the dirt onto the growing pile at his right.

In the hole, his fingertips scratched the surface of a large rock. *Ah, that will be trouble.* Taking his knife again, he attempted to jab the surrounding soil, which was much harder and drier than the soil above. He strained to pull the boulder out, but the monstrous thing wouldn't budge.

He looked up and remembered the pickaxe he'd tied up as an anchor for the boat. If he fashioned a handle for it, he might be able to break or wedge the rock out.

Uther stood, and a swirl of darkness engulfed him. His knees felt weak, and he groped for the wall of the tower, holding on to the rough stones until his sight returned. He'd experienced this before when he'd been prone too long. As expected, it soon passed. *Just moved a little fast, that's all.*

"I'm going for the anchor from the boat," he mumbled as he sat on the threshold of the doorway and swung his legs out. Maybe fresh air would help.

After walking down to the muddy bank, he stopped to view the rising fog and the sinking sun. If he wanted to find what the ghost man desired, it would be easier before the light failed.

He cut the pickaxe free from its rope and tied the boat directly to the tree. On his way back to the tower, he spied the dead branch lying next to the rock where Igerna had sat with Arthur earlier. Picking up the limb, he whacked it on the stone to test its strength, which didn't disappoint. Next he compared its thickness to the hole in the rusty pickaxe and found that a little whittling would make it a perfect match.

Magnificent!

Back inside the tower, he joined his family and Colvarth, who were all sitting on a linen cloth in a corner, eating cold venison and barley bread. Taking a few nibbles of the bread his wife offered, he noticed the worry in her eyes — her brows two trembling arcs tethered tightly in the center. Ignoring this, he whittled the end of the thick branch until he could fit it in the hole of the pickaxe. Taking the branch out again, he worked a deep notch on the end with his blade. Fitting the pickaxe head on again, he chose three wedges he'd whittled off and hammered them into the gap with a rock. But his hand shook, and since Igerna was watching him like a concerned mother, he walked to the other side of the room to finish the job.

Why does my hand shake so? he wondered. *Perhaps it's only hunger. I simply need to eat more bread.*

Colvarth joined him and studied the pickaxe with a curious eye. "My ... king. What is the purpose of this ... digging? You attack the ground as if to slay it. And now the pick?"

"You think I make a grave, eh?" Uther tucked his shaking hand behind his back.

"No, I do not." Colvarth's words faded, and his face contorted, eyes bulging out. His skin changed to blue and then white.

Was the world going mad? Uther closed his eyes and shook his head. When he glanced again, Colvarth's face appeared normal. "Say this prophecy," Uther whispered. "Whose grave is this? Who is buried here?"

"Speak not of such things!" And Colvarth turned away.

———✦———

Garth's feet were cold and wet before McEwan finally heaved their boat onto the gritty shingle. He tied the rope to a bent cypress tree that leaned out from the bank, its roots sucking at the mud and slime. Even though the island was quite large, finding the northern landing had been harder than Garth expected, what with the fog so thick. The white dampness filled his lungs, made his throat itch, and clung to him like the shreds of a ghastly cloak as he stepped ashore.

Although he loved to fish here, he'd never been on the marsh at dusk, and it was nothing like the open, and rolling ocean he longed for. Out of the mist, birds squawked from sharp beaks, their chirrups ethereal and their eyes unseen. The frogs croaked so loudly that surely each would be found and plucked from its hiding place by the bill of some gray heron of death. And all the while the insects wailed a song of mourning as the gloom sped its way over the marsh.

While McEwan was distracted, swinging his stout club, McGoss pinched Garth's shoulder and whispered, "Remember, no tellin', or I make fish bait out o' yar guts. Hear?"

Garth held his breath and nodded.

The warriors in the other boat finally pulled ashore, disembarked, and began whispering to each other in low Eirish murmurs. Garth tried to draw close to them, but O'Sloan pushed him away. "Stay wit' the boats."

Alarmed to discover he'd be left alone, but equally fearful of going with them, Garth pulled his cloak more tightly over his shoulders. "W-when will you be back?"

"Soon enough. How far is the ruined tow'r? I canna see it."

"Ten throws of a stone, I'd say. Take the trail through the apple trees."

The six warriors walked off into the mist, and soon the only evidence of their existence was the fading sound of their footfalls.

Garth was utterly alone.

"Why?" Uther called after his bard. "Why should I not ask? You declared my digging a grave. Is it the grave of the man I saw?"

Colvarth turned back and, glaring up into Uther's eyes, tapped his long finger onto the king's chest. "Speak of what you hope to find … Tell me."

"You ask what I do not know. Something unexpected. Something powerful, maybe." With these last words Uther's lungs felt smothered, and he took a deep breath.

"Are there not enough ... strange things in Bosventor? Is the Druid Stone not ... enough?"

"Maybe Jesu has sent something good." Uther wheezed out the words. "Holy, even. Here in this very dirt where the man in blue drew the sign of the cross."

"I saw nothing."

"Are you my fool or my bard?" Uther yelled. "I have seen this!"

His words echoed through the tower, and Myrgwen and Arthur both cried. The fog had thickened outside, and Eilyne gaped at its sallow entrails leaking through the open doorway.

"Leave me alone, all of you. Go back to your meal. I am ... digging."

Colvarth bowed and, shuffling back to the broken circle of the family, sat in silence. But Uther could feel the bard's eyes on him still.

In anger, Uther raised the newly joined pickaxe over his head and, with a mighty blow, split the rock into three pieces. Finding the iron head still tight, he swung in earnest at the harder soil surrounding the rock, and in no time he threw the pieces of the offending stone to the side.

After pausing for a long sip of the mead, he dug again in earnest, and within a short time, he'd deepened and widened the hole until he could stand in the bottom. There he alternated between digging and throwing the dirt up in great handfuls until his arms dripped with soiled sweat and his eyesight dulled with the failing light.

"Uther, cease!" Igerna said from above. "What madness has come upon you?"

Setting down his pickaxe, he swallowed a last, long gulp of the frothy mead and flung away the skin. Mead had never tasted so refreshing. He needed to reward the man who brewed it.

Climbing out of the great hole, Uther looked at his wife and beheld two of her standing before him. He moved his lips to tell her that something was buried here, but no words escaped. Igerna tilted toward him. The very air reeled, and Uther collapsed in the dirt.

His eyes dimmed, yet he could feel his hands shaking.

All around him, people shouted, yelled, and shrieked.

＋

The brutality of the murder shocked Merlin.

Dybris fell to his knees.

Merlin's father stood in front of Dybris and pulled out his dirk, tested its edge, and then returned it to his scabbard. "Who is it?"

"It's our Herrik! Those cursed druidow took all the monks captive" — he spat — "and they weren't satisfied with their victory, so they blazed the hillside with our blood."

"Without his robe, I didn't realize he was a monk."

"The devils stole it. Left him to die cold and bare, and now the wolves have gnawed his flesh. Even his hands are gone ..."

Owain knelt to examine the body. "That's odd. I don't remember long swords among the druidow, but this chest wound is sliced straight through. See the blade's exit on his back, here? It's a wide cut too. Not a slim blade, that."

Merlin fumed at the injustice of Herrik's death. Why did the druidow have to kill him? How many more bodies would they find on the path?

"Just last night," Dybris said, "our new abbot had thought me excessive when I looped my old dirk onto my belt. And now look at this! O, God, protect them. Protect them all." He rose and then hastened to a small spring gurgling from the hillside.

"What are you doing?" Owain asked. "We can't delay."

"I'm wetting a cloth." And with it, Dybris came back and cleansed the blood from Herrik's face. Next he took his bronze flask of oil and anointed the man's forehead, Merlin assumed, with the sign of the cross.

Then the monk lifted his voice in prayer.

None exist like the Almighty,
The goodly God of love and cheer,

Who rides in power upon the sky,
Bringing help in thy time of fear.
He forges gates of iron and bronze,
And fills thine heart with strength by day.
He is thy shield, thy swift spearman,
The sword sending pagans away.
He will drive out thine enemy,
And destroy thy foe in the land.
The living One is thy refuge,
Under thee is God's kind, strong hand.
Blessed be thy soul, O my friend,
Go in God's peace — safety be thine.
Rising from earth to high heaven,
Be morning dew wisped by sun's shine.

Dybris choked out the last words.

Wash him, wash him — his soul, his sins.
Take him, take him — his heart, his breath.
Bend him, bend him — his way, his will.
Keep him, keep him — his life, his death.

Rising, he picked up fist-sized rocks and placed them around the body.

Owain grabbed Dybris's arm. "We haven't time."

"Then we haven't time for anything." Dybris shook Owain away. Taking more rocks, he added them to the others.

"We can come back later," Merlin offered.

"There may not be a later. I pray this is the last soul who dies this night, but we know not what awaits us. Help me."

Merlin moved to help, looking to his father as he passed by. Owain shook his head at first but later joined the others. Together they quietly gathered and raised a small mound of stones over Herrik's broken life.

"It's enough," Owain finally said, and Dybris slowly nodded.

Merlin rose, then followed the men up the hillside. He wiped his tears and tried to concentrate on the blurry path ahead. Dybris guided his steps as they approached the top of the hill and the circle beyond. The path widened, and Owain led them into the darkness of the dense woods, where they hid behind some bushes and observed the druid gathering.

Within the circle of gigantic stones, a large number of druidow stood murmuring.

"Tell me what I'm seeing," Merlin said, hoping to learn something that would enable him to be of some small help later on.

"There are seven druidow in green robes," his father said, "and they all have drooping hoods that conceal their faces. They're chanting around Mórganthu, who is standing in the center of the circle near the Stone.

Near their hiding spot, druidow began to beat broad wooden drums.

Boom! Boom!

"Just beyond the ring," Owain continued, "stand two large wooden constructions in the shape of cages, at least ten feet high and about five paces from each other. Young timbers serve as posts, and these have been interlaced with smaller branches. The druidow are depositing bundles of branches around the cages to build a pile of tinder."

The judgment of wicker. Merlin had heard antiquated tales of Beltayne, when the druidow of old burned to death prisoners of war or any they considered criminals, all as sacrifices to their pagan gods. Then, leading cattle and followers between the burning victims and through the evil smoke, the druidow claimed cleansing and protection from witchcraft.

But who were in the cages? Merlin squinted, but it was too far away for his scarred eyes to see. "Are the monks — "

"Yes," Dybris said. "Those accursed druidow have locked them up." He let out a muffled sob and grabbed Merlin's shoulder. "Do you see Mônda or my daughter?" Owain whispered.

The monk let go of Merlin and peered through the bushes. "There are hundreds of villagers milling about. I don't know them well enough to pick them out."

"Let me know if you do. Hah, there's Tregeagle. In front of the villagers on that ridge."

"We've got to do something about the cages," Dybris said.

"We will," Merlin said. "but not this very moment. We need to think."

"They could burn the monks to death while you sit there pondering!"

"We have time — they won't do it until it's perfectly dark. And Vortigern hasn't attacked yet." Merlin turned to face west. The sun hid behind a thinning line of gray clouds, but from its position, barely half an hour remained before it would drop below the hills. "We have to get close to the Stone so we're in position to take it when the attack comes. Then we free the monks."

"Won't Vortigern do that?" Owain said.

"We can't count on it."

In the center of the circle, druidow began to move.

"What's going on," Merlin asked.

Dybris quietly parted the bushes and looked toward the circle. "The green-robed druidow are holding up brass sickle knives and chanting. Now Mórganthu is raising a bronze cauldron, and one of the druidow is stepping forward. Mórganthu handed him the vessel, and he's holding it aloft like Mórganthu and walking toward the west. He's skirting the drummers ... and pacing straight toward us!"

Boom! Boom!

"He's coming. Don't move."

Chanting loudly, the druid found the path leading to the spring and floated past them down the hillside, his verdant robe billowing in the fading light, and the small bronze cauldron held out before him.

"Can you see his face?" Merlin asked.

"What? No ... His hood is pulled low," Dybris said in a hushed voice.

"Now's our chance," Merlin whispered. "He's getting water. Tas, take care of him and come back with his robe."

"That's crazy," his father said.

"The sun's nearly down, and we don't have much time. You can get near the Stone."

"Are you certain?"

"What else can we do?"

"Don't rightly know. So I'll give it a try," Owain said as he unsheathed his dirk.

Dybris grabbed Owain's tunic. "Don't kill him!"

"Shah, get your hand off me. No time to talk."

"Enough bloodshed. Are we no better than they?"

"What?" Owain asked.

Dybris untied his leather belt and pulled off his sheathed dirk. "Bind him instead. We are Christians."

"Fine. I'll do it if I can, but I won't make any promises." Taking the belt and a clublike branch that had lain next to Merlin, Owain snuck down the path after the druid.

Dybris slid his own dirk inside the waist of his pants.

Moments later, they heard a sharp crack down the hill.

Merlin winced. "Did the druidow notice?"

"They didn't seem to."

Boom! Boom!

Soon Owain returned, dressed in the green druid robe, and he held the bronze cauldron, now sloshing with water. "I stuffed a stick and moss in his mouth. Hope your belt holds."

"We'll slip around near the monks," Merlin said, "and free them when Vortigern attacks. Once that's done, we'll come help get the Stone."

"Be quick about it, and pray for me. I'm not strong near the Stone."

Dybris nodded.

Owain stepped forward into the glade and walked toward the circle of stones.

Merlin placed a hand on Dybris's shoulder. "How can we get to the monks?"

"It won't be easy. Even in the woods on the other side of the circle, we won't be close enough. If the druidow light the fire at the base of the cages, there'll be no time to free the brothers before the flames are too strong."

Boom! Boom!

Crouching uncomfortably, Merlin shifted his weight, and a dry twig broke under his foot. A branch! They could gather branches and bring them to the wicker cages. He told Dybris of his plan, and soon they had each scraped together enough fallen wood to make a bundle.

They were about to leave when Dybris grabbed Merlin's tunic. "Wait! Your father just passed the cauldron to Mórganthu. He's bowing, and now he's joining the other green-robed druidow as they march around the Stone."

"Mórganthu ... what's he doing?"

"He's frowning. He might suspect."

Merlin's head began to throb. They had to act quickly.

An entire hour had been lost waiting at the Tor, and Bedwir drew his sword for the twentieth time, tested its edge, and shined its broad length in the gray light. When would that gluttonous Vortigern get off his backside, put out his fire, and set his welcome cup down? Bedwir wanted to kick him in the teeth.

So for the first time since they had arrived at the Tor, he plucked up his courage and approached Vortigern to complain. The lanky battle chief leaned upon a large pile of hay, sipping mead and wolfing down roasted goat. He tapped a small wooden chest resting at his side and then whacked his son, Vortipor, on the shoulder.

"You didn't!" Vortigern laughed. "Never knew *that's* what you did when I sent you to battle in Brythanvy. Be careful who you tell that to!"

"Vortigern," Bedwir said, but the battle chief paid him no mind. "Vortigern!"

The mead cup stopped midsip and the battle chief's eyes turned to Bedwir.

"Vortigern, the sun will be down soon. We must attack."

"And who says?"

"I do ... and ... and others."

"Sit on your sword or something. My son is telling a grand tale."

"But what of Uther's command? What will he think of our delay?"

Vortigern stood and, dusting the hay off his cloak, drew his sword.

"Worry what *I* will do if you interrupt again."

Heat rising to his face, Bedwir spun on his heel and stalked away.

Malicious laughter continued to swirl around Natalenya.

She spun and drew her small blade with a shaky hand. "Who's there?"

The sneering voice of a man spoke from the darkness, "Welcome, rich rat spawn of Tregeagle! Despite the scratched one missing, I'm glad you've come."

"Who are you? What do you want?"

The man stepped forward, and the fading light fell across his malevolent face. His hair was wet with sweat, and he had pockmarked cheeks and a thin, pointed nose.

Natalenya backed away. "I don't know you."

"But you've heard my name. Connek — robber among thieves, future master of thugs, and present slitter of throats." He pulled out a long, rusty knife and rubbed his calloused, dirty thumb on its edge.

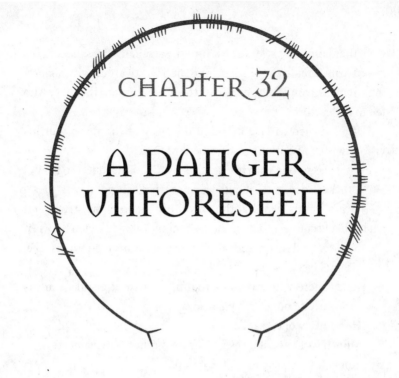

CHAPTER 32

A DANGER UNFORESEEN

Someone lifted Uther's head and called to him. The voice echoed as if from a mountain peak.

"Uth ... ther ... a ... wa ... ake ..."

He tried to sit up but couldn't, his arms flailing in the darkness. His lungs felt as if they were full of water, and he gasped for breath. Forcing himself up to find some air, he opened his eyes as dim light crawled through the doorway like a glowing leech.

"... warriors outside ... stand ... fight!"

Warriors? Here?

"... danger!"

Colvarth. My family!

A shadow passed through the doorway. The person supporting him screamed, and he finally recognized the voice. *Igerna!*

He burst upward with newfound strength and tried to draw his sword, but he pulled it only halfway before someone grabbed his right arm from behind and clamped onto his neck.

Uther jammed his left elbow into the assailant's ribs, freeing his sword arm. Arcing the blade behind, he was rewarded with a piercing shout. Turning fully, he thrust the blade through the man, who fell to the earth.

Uther turned to face the high doorway of the tower, but his vision twisted as dark forms climbed through.

What was wrong with his sight? Why did his head feel so heavy?

"Uther ... look out!" shouted a voice from behind.

Thrashing his sword at the oncoming shadows, he struck and felt his blade connect. But without warning, he was clouted between the shoulder blades, and the ground rose up, jamming into his face.

"Uther!" Igerna screamed.

He lay there with his ribs groaning, sputtering soil from his mouth. Someone pulled his blade away.

"He's a lively one," said a voice.

"More'n we were told, yes," boomed another. "Are ya hurt?"

"Some. Cut me arm. 'Ere, tie 'im up."

Uther felt himself lifted and trussed until he could barely move. He opened his eyes, but everything was upside down and skewed.

"McEwan, get 'im to the boat. We'll get the boy."

Those behind him screamed as Uther was hoisted up and lifted through the doorway. His head hit the rock-hewn sill, and everything flashed to nothingness.

Offering a prayer for his father's safety, Merlin pulled his hood down and picked up his bundle of sticks. He followed Dybris with a hand on the monk's arm as they skirted through the trees to the other side of the circle of stones. But they stopped short once they stepped from the woods, and Merlin didn't know why.

"There's a bunch of druid wives ahead," Dybris whispered. "They're watching the proceedings."

Boom! Boom! the drummers pounded.

One of the wives turned toward them. "You're a wee bit late with those," she called.

Dybris shrugged his shoulders, and he and Merlin both walked as naturally as they could into the open, carrying their bundles of sticks to the first wicker cage.

"Give me your bundle and then stay here a moment as I shove a path to the door," Dybris whispered.

The monk wedged himself next to the cage door and placed the bundles down.

One of the imprisoned monks spoke angrily. "Can't you see there's enough?"

"Peace, Migal," Dybris said. "I'm here to free you. Be quiet and pray."

A soft whisper spread through the wicker cage, and Merlin could tell that hope had been rekindled among the monks. Dybris hummed as he pretended to rearrange the stick bundles and then returned to stand by Merlin's side.

Dybris leaned over and spoke in a low voice. "The door's small, two feet by three, and made from saplings. It's secured with strong tendons."

"Be ready to cut it open at any time," Merlin said. "I'll block if they try to stop you, but I won't be able to hold them for long."

"You there!" a druid called from behind. "Pay attention. Can't you see Mórganthu's about to wash the Knives of Sacrifice?"

Merlin nodded in the man's direction and then whispered to Dybris, "Tell me what's happening." He was concerned for his father. How long could he keep up the ruse?

"The green-robed druidow have raised their sickle knives and are circling Mórganthu, who is holding the bronze water cauldron."

Merlin heard Mórganthu begin to chant in his dark tongue, and then without warning, the arch druid let out a piercing cry, and all the druidow joined in. Merlin almost plugged his ears but stopped himself just in time. Instead, mimicking Dybris, he raised his fist and shook it.

"One of the green-robed druidow is marching to Mórganthu. Now he's bowing ... Uh-oh!"

"What?"

"Mórganthu is pulling the druid's hood back. The man looks surprised. Mórganthu's nodding to him, and now the druid is standing. He just sliced his sickle through the water."

Merlin heard the man shouting:

The Sky and the Reddened Earth bear witness,
The Sun and the Thirsty Moon bear witness,
The Rocks and the Reckless Wood bear witness,
The Living and the Soon Dead bear witness!
I bring this Knife — first from Foulness,
I plunge this Knife — second through Water,
I take this Knife — third to Clarity,
I bind this Knife — fourth for Sacrifice!
To thee, Great Belornos, I bring this Knife
From Spring's Bone unto Summer's Blood
To make an Eternal Servant for thee
To offer to thee an Unending Life!

Merlin shuddered as Dybris continued his description. "The druid is joining his comrades, and the next druid's approaching to repeat the ritual. He's bowing down, and Mórganthu's lifting the man's hood and studying his face."

Acid gurgled up into Merlin's throat. "Which one is Tas? Can you tell?"

"No ... They all look the same."

Merlin held his breath and prayed once more.

Owain stood and walked forward, trying to act as much like the other druidow as he could. But he knew Mórganthu suspected. Thankfully he had the brass sickle knife ready, and he'd use it to end that murderer's life before he'd let himself be caught.

He approached the arch druid, hood down, and knelt with every muscle tensed.

Mórganthu's hand reached down, and just as it touched the hood, Owain sprang, slashing the sickle knife at the evil druid's throat.

Mórganthu was faster than a rat, and his right hand caught hold of Owain's wrist, diverting the blow so that it barely scratched his forehead. At the same time, Mórganthu's other hand gouged at Owain's eyes in taloned madness.

But Owain was stronger. He slung his head away from the fingernails and rammed his shoulder into Mórganthu's stomach.

Both men sprawled to the earth.

Owain raised his knife to strike.

Stunned, Mórganthu flailed his left hand out and, to Owain's horror, it landed upon the Stone. White lightning burst from the craggy surface, shot through Mórganthu and into Owain.

Owain felt instant torture spread through his body. His limbs stiffened in excruciating pain. Such burning! The brass knife fell from his hand in a white-hot lump. His vision faded as his beard began to smolder.

⊢—

As Dybris described the fight, Merlin's heart felt as if it would pound its way free from his body.

"There are *imposters* among us!" Mórganthu shouted. "Everyone must be tested!"

"Go!" Merlin urged Dybris. "Cut the door open!"

Dybris ran back to the first wicker cage and began hacking at the tendons securing the doors.

Merlin stood guard, preparing to block anyone who challenged them.

"Dear God, help me!" Dybris prayed as he hewed at the stubborn strings. "Why didn't I have Owain sharpen this old thing?"

Shouts rang out, and Merlin turned to face the onrush. But the sun was almost gone now, and in the grayness, he didn't see the first druid coming. A shoulder knocked into him with just enough force that he fell backward over a pile of twigs. By the time he scrambled to his feet, it was too late. The crowd of druidow had surrounded Dybris and flung open the door of the first cage. Laughing, they threw Dybris in with the other monks.

Merlin reached for his dirk, preparing for a fight, but the druidow didn't seem to notice him. They shut the door, and new tendons were brought to knot it closed. With the door secured, they lingered around the cages, leering at the unfortunate prisoners and hurling insults at them.

Trying his best to blend in with the crowd, Merlin decided it was better to bide his time a little longer and find some way to save his father and his friends.

Brother Neot's voice rose from within the cage as he addressed Dybris in his typically sarcastic tone. "Spectacular rescue, that."

Mórganthu came over and stood close to the woven branches of the cage. "Oh fool, oh impudent fool," he mocked. "One dupe of a blacksmith to sacrifice to the Stone, and now I have one more monk to burn in the Beltayne fire!"

Garth retreated to the boat and climbed to the very center of the middle seat. He'd withdrawn here, he told himself, not because the mist scared him — oh no! — but because it was warmer sitting on wood and more familiar being in a boat.

Sometimes the water splashed among the reeds near the shore, and Garth tried not to imagine blood-sucking creatures slipping into the marsh and encircling the boat.

After what seemed a very long time, stone-scraping and sliding noises echoed from the island. A dark creature lumbered toward him out of the fog.

Garth yelped, whirled around, and rowed furiously away. A few anxious moments passed, and he was just about to take a deep breath when he heard a voice rumble behind him, so close he jumped and almost dropped the oars into the water.

"If ya're goin' to row away, ya best untie the lash first!"

Garth turned, and McEwan laughed at him with his foot on the rope, still tied to the bent cypress. On his shoulder hung a bound man — the High King. McEwan chucked Uther like a rag doll into the other boat, and the body fell roughly among the seats and extra ropes in the front.

Garth tried his best to picture Anviv's death at Uther's hand, but the image of Trothek's severed head appeared instead.

Three more Eirish warriors walked out of the mist, with O'Sloan leading. His left arm bled profusely, and the blood had soaked his tunic, as well as a cloth-wrapped bundle he carried. Garth gripped the side of his boat as O'Sloan stepped in and set the heavy bundle on Garth's lap.

"'Ere. Take care o' this till we return. McEwan! Grab those ropes so we can tie up the others 'afore we leave."

McEwan pulled out extra rope from both boats.

"So McGoss was killed?" one of them asked.

"Weren't ya there?" McEwan boomed. "We risked our bellies, and where were ya?"

"Leave 'im alone," O'Sloan said. "I told 'im to stay outside and keep watch."

McEwan coiled the ropes. "Och, then, 'twasn't McGoss who died, that worthless lout. We left *'im* back to guard the ladies an' the ol' bard. 'Twas Gilroy that the High King killed."

O'Sloan groaned, holding up a bloody blade. The same one the High King had killed Anviv with. "Slit 'im through the heart. A perilous blade, this one."

Taking the ropes, the warriors climbed the shingle and disappeared into the fog.

"Sit and keep watch," O'Sloan's voice called back.

Alone, Garth looked down at the wrapped bundle in his lap.

Pulling the thick, bloody cloth aside, he was startled to see little eyes staring at him, wide with fear.

"A littl' one!" Garth shouted.

He pulled the blood-soaked cloth back farther, and the child's dark hair emerged. The boy wriggled his right arm free and, reaching up, squeezed Garth's nose. In his other hand, he held a small crust of barley bread, which he alternately chewed and sucked on.

"Hello to you too," Garth said. He inspected the child and found no wound on him. The blood must have been from O'Sloan's injured arm.

"If I know rightly, then yer Arthur, and over there's the king." Garth pointed, and that was the first time he noticed the man's head wound, a dirty gash that bled down across his eye and forehead. He didn't appear to be breathing.

Garth picked up an oar with his free hand and prodded Uther across the divide between the boats, but the man didn't stir.

"Yer father's dead, Arthur. That's a bad thing. An' I know, 'cause I lost me tas too."

Memories of Garth's own childhood flooded back. Fishing with his father on the wind-rolled sea. Hauling the full nets up the beach and sorting through their daily catch. Throwing clams at his father and being chased into the waves. Selling the fish together at the village market.

At night they'd sit by the hearth, his father playing the bagpipe in the soft flicker of the fire. They'd eat oat porridge together and talk long after dark, with the starlight shining through the shutters of their small seaside crennig.

And his father would tell him stories about his mother, who had died when he was born. Garth cherished those memories the most.

Then he recalled the fatal day his father drowned. Garth had been sick and unable to go along. That morning a black gale had blown in from the west, piling the foaming waves high and white across the Kembry Sea.

His father never came home. Days later another fisherman discovered his father's boat capsized and half sunk.

Garth teared up, and Arthur's little hand reached up to touch his wet cheek.

"Yer all alone now, Arth. Me father's buried in the sea, an' yours'll be buried on land, and you'll ne'er see 'im again."

Anger rose in Garth. Why did they have to orphan young Arthur? Why did those warriors kill the High King? Sure, he'd slain the ard dre's son — but hadn't the ard dre killed Trothek without reason? Death. All around him. And the blood from Arthur's wrappings smeared on Garth's hands. What would the ard dre do to this boy?

Then, finally, it all made sense: Uther had killed Anviv, and the ard dre would kill Arthur. A son for a son. Mórganthu would put the child's head in some barrel or stick it on a spear. It was *wrong*. And if Garth allowed it, the child's blood *would* be on his hands.

"Thy path is twisted. Get thee gone," a voice called from the fog of the marsh.

Whipping his gaze toward the sound, Garth saw a thin island floating toward him. Moss clung to it, and reeds grew from its prow. But it was a boat, and a man paddled it.

"The cock has crowed," the man said as he peered at Garth with bloodshot eyes. "Take hope and go before the bear is bled!" His patchy gray hair was slimed down upon his ragged tunic, and his eyebrows had been replaced by thick scars, as if he'd been burned long ago.

This must be Muscarvel, the one all o' them scary tales were about. He's sure scarin' the wits out o' me!

The marsh man raised a rusty sword with astonishing speed and swung within inches of Garth's nose. "I say flee with the young one like a *piskyn*."

Garth bumped backward, set Arthur down at his feet, and raised an oar for protection. "Leave me alone, you!"

Arthur lost his bread crust and began crying.

Muscarvel swung again and chopped off the tip of the oar, its wet splinters flying into Garth's face. The crazy man laughed as he leaped to shore and sliced the rope holding Garth's boat to the cypress.

"Must away! Tombs for the noble, life to the living." Muscarvel tossed his blade under a bush, waded into the water, and shoved Garth's boat away.

The old man swam and pushed the boat until the fog hid the island. "Come not back. Death stalks in the shadows," he croaked.

"All right, I'll go! But leave me an' me boat alone!" Garth swung his oar and cracked Muscarvel on the head.

The old man sank beneath the water and was gone.

"So which is it?" Connek laughed. "Will you toss me that torc or shall I slice your throat?"

Natalenya almost forgot to breathe as she prayed for God's wisdom and strength. She clutched the knife Merlin had given her. Masterfully forged by Merlin's father, the blade was really quite small, and yet it felt solid and comforting in her hand. But what good was it? Could she really fight Connek and win? Could she ward off all his blows?

She looked into Connek's malevolent eyes and wondered if she should give up Merlin's torc. What *was* Connek's game?

"I'm going to count to five …" Connek said.

Natalenya looked around quickly to see if she could climb out one of the windows. But they were all too high, and in the darkness, she couldn't see anything to climb on.

If any hope remained, she wouldn't find it by protecting Merlin's torc.

What about Allun? Was he lying in the shadows with his throat slit? And what about the mule? She should already have been on her way to the druid camp with the wagon to help transport the Stone.

"Give me the torc, hag. I'm not takin' any chances this time, an' I prefer to keep its gold braids clean when I cut your ripe neck open. There's a reward out for you too. Did you know that?"

That was all Natalenya needed to hear. Without hesitating, she unclasped the heavy torc from her neck. *God, I need Your help!* "Where do I throw it?" she asked, stalling for time while she gauged the distance between them and the weight of the torc.

"Here. Right into my itching, happy hand."

She hurled it right at Connek's head, and then ran.

Connek cried out as the torc bounced off his face and fell into the darkness. "You witch! I'll cut your fingers off when I catch you!"

If she could make him chase her in a circle, she could unbar the door and run out — but then she still needed the mule. What was she to do?

Wary footsteps padded toward her from the darkness.

She backed up, and her foot fell into the depression where the mule walked in a circle to turn the top grindstone. It was enough to orient her. With a burst of speed, she ran the track to the other side of the stones. Reaching to steady herself on the mill, she was surprised to find the upper stone missing. Allun must have set it on his benches. The miller was always a busy man but had more time to talk while dressing his stones, and Natalenya sometimes chatted with him and the other ladies of the village on those occasions.

Hearing footfalls behind her, Natalenya continued around the circle until she cracked her hip into the upper millstone, rocking the supporting benches. Pain shot through her leg, and she cried out.

Behind her, mocking laughter filled the air. "You're trapped. Turn an' get yer due!"

Natalenya reached out to her right and felt the wall of the crennig. To the left, then. She jumped onto the bottom millstone ... and ran into Allun's workbench, covered with files and tools. Many of them fell clanging to the stone below, along with her knife.

"No way out, you rich brat!"

CHAPTER 33

AN END
UNIMAGINED

U ther awoke. Besides his head feeling as if it had been bashed with a war hammer, his whole body ached, and his hands, tied behind his back, were numb and swollen.

He opened his eyes and found he could see out of only one, as drying blood had smeared across the other, gluing it shut. He tried focusing, but the world around wouldn't hold still. Finally he realized he lay in the bottom of a boat, and the rocking he felt was nothing more than gentle waves under the hull. A slight breeze blew and thinned the fog somewhat, but even then the final gasps of daylight couldn't pierce the gloom.

"Stay thine hand, O Boar of the Britons. Thou art safe from my biting jaws," spoke an unfamiliar voice.

The stranger bent down and peered into Uther's good eye. "Thou needest not strike thy boggy servant in the pate. I mean no harm to thee or thy kin."

Water dripped from the man's grimed forehead, and the smell of the swamp rolled off him. "Bah," he shouted in Uther's face, making him jerk. "The rotten trees ha' taken thy torc, they have."

"What?" Uther groaned, realizing his neck ached and his legs were twisted across the sharp edge of a thwart.

"I'll get it back, curse them. A king should die with his torc on!"

"Don't want to die. Cut my bonds."

The man's mud-caked nose came in and out of focus. "Shah, 'twill take only a moment, but it's too late. They come to slurp the mire off this glacking frog's bones!"

Uther heard footsteps on the rocks, with shouting and confusion.

"The other boat — it's gone!"

"The wee scout's taken it."

"Hey! Who's that old'un crouchin' next to the High King?"

The man bent one more time and winked at Uther. "A task for me from thy good God!" He ran away, swinging a rusty sword. "For the Boar of Britain!"

Uther tried to lift his head to see, but his neck was too stiff. Cries and shouting echoed forth. Steel clashed. Someone screeched.

"He cut me, the limmer. Kill 'im!"

A short shriek pierced the night, then all was silent.

"What now, O'Sloan?" came a voice. "We canna all fit in one boat, not w' McEwan, an' we already staved in the king's boat."

"Lookit, another one, there! Must be the wild man's. 'Tis a carved-out log that could carry two."

"That'll do us, sure, now that we're rid o' McGoss."

"Dinna say his name agin as long as I live."

"Sorry. 'Tis fool hard ta believe his evil deed. An' that poor bard."

"Shah, I said. We judged the traitor by our good laws, and sure, I'll speak no more o' it. You, then, get in the log boat an' see if it sinks or nay."

Uther used all his might to arch his back and untwist his legs.

A man shouted. "Thar's a snake in the log boat! I'll nah go in there."

"We'll have to ferry o'er in two trips, then, what with Gilroy's body 'n all."

"But the boy's gone 'n stole the king's heir. Sure 'n the ard dre'll have our heads."

Uther's addled brain tried to comprehend these tidings. His heir? Were they talking about Arthur? Anger surged through his limbs, but he couldn't break free of his bonds.

"He'll take a fury to us, sure," one of the Eirish warriors said. "But we've got the High King, and we'll be rewarded well. The ard dre has special plans for this one, I ken."

Merlin found a place to sit on a rock just outside the stone circle — reasonably close to the wicker cages and not too far from where his father lay tied to the Stone. There, as darkness finally spread over the hilltop, he pulled his hood down and prayed.

The drumming ceased, and the druidow stopped their ritualistic nonsense. In front of him, Merlin heard many footsteps approaching, so he hunkered down a little farther. The nearby crowd parted, and a man holding a torch stepped forward with his green robe rippling in the rising wind.

"At last, at last you have come back from the island," the man said, and Merlin recognized his voice. *Mórganthu*. "And as promised, you have brought my enemy for judgment and sacrifice!"

"Aye, 'tis true, Ard Dre," said a voice on the right, "but we've lost two warriors, and I'm wounded along with O'Rewry."

Merlin tried not to move or draw attention to himself. The man speaking was one of the Eirish warriors, and the faint smell of the damp marsh wafted from where he and his companions stood.

"It dinna go as ya told us it would."

Mórganthu snorted. "And what could have gone wrong? Surely the young and weak presented no obstacle? Tying them up as I instructed was not difficult, hmm?"

"It dinna work that way, Ard Dre. McGoss dinna follow yer

orders. And by the look on his face, he dinna think we'd do it, but we judged him by our laws, and now that murderer is dead."

Mórganthu clucked his tongue. "Really? I never thought him capable of that."

Merlin's ears pricked as a man rasped out the words, "Let me go ..."

Did Merlin know that voice? His poor eyesight frustrated him.

"And where is the heir of the High King?" Mórganthu inquired. "I do not see him here."

"He cried too loud," the warrior on the right said, "and so ... we drowned him in the marsh."

At this news, Merlin felt as if a massive hand had grabbed his throat and squeezed. Were they talking about Arthur ... was he dead?

Mórganthu cursed. "You were told to bring him alive. Alive! Where is his body?"

"He ... he slipped and we lost him."

Merlin hung his head and gulped back his rage. How could the world change so drastically in so few hours?

"You drown the babe and then lose his body? You will pay for this disobedience!"

"Ard Dre ... if it helps, we've brought this torc and blade as a gift for ya."

"Ah, finally! The torc has finally come back to the keeping of the druidow ... Yes, to bestow on one who is worthy. And the blade, yes, I see. Vengeance. Very appropriate. At least Belornos will be pleased with *this* new servant tonight!"

The rasping man struggled against his bonds. "Where's my wife? My children? What have you done with them?"

Merlin's heart sank. The man was Uther! And now Merlin's burden had increased. How could he — alone and blind — save his father, Uther, and the monks all at once? Indecision and fear began to tear at his soul like twin demons bent on destroying him.

"Oh, do not struggle, my bound one. You will see your queen

and family soon enough. Bring him to the Stone and place him upon it." And as Mórganthu walked away, he laughed long and loud.

Natalenya felt Connek's blade slash forward and rip the back of her dress, cutting a thin line across her shoulder blade.

With both hands on the tall workbench, she kicked backward and hit Connek in the stomach. Thankfully she had two brothers who had, through their rough play, taught her to hold her own. Turning to her right, she vaulted onto the upper grindstone, causing its supporting benches to creak under her weight. As she slid off the other side, she banged her head on the swinging timber boom and crashed to the ground.

"Die, and I'll have my reward!" Connek shouted as he charged up and heaved his weight against the huge grindstone to topple it onto her.

Natalenya shook her head to clear it as the benches groaned and the wood splintered above her. The heavy stone tilted forward.

Terror drove her to roll away, find her feet, and grab the low timber boom. With all her strength she heaved it in Connek's direction. "Leave me alone," she yelled.

As the boom swung forward, a thud echoed through the room, and Natalenya heard Connek fall.

"I'll get you, you rich hag!" Connek yelled from the ground.

She backed away from the grindstone and saw a glint of golden light reflecting off of something underneath the benches. *Merlin's torc? It must have landed there after hitting that despicable Connek's face.*

"The torc … It's under the grindstone!" she called as she made for the door.

Glancing back, she saw the thief stoop down and lunge underneath the stone. "I'll have it!" He grabbed the torc and laughed. As he scrambled forward, one of his knees hit the leg of a supporting bench, and with a great bang, the wood cracked and the stone fell.

Natalenya stood in shock as the dust settled. He was dead. He had to be. The stone had crushed him just behind the neck, and from there the thief's blood began to pool in the dirt.

Tears sprang to her eyes, and she broke down, releasing all the panic and horror she felt. She hadn't meant to kill Connek ... just slow him down. She hesitated a moment, then walked forward, knelt, and extracted the torc from his hand. Then she placed it around her neck once again, and its golden curve weighed heavily upon her. She wanted to take hold of Connek's dirt-encrusted hand and pray for his soul, but she couldn't find it in herself to do it. Maybe one of the monks could do that before they buried him.

Natalenya retrieved the knife Merlin had given her and placed it back in her belt.

Someone moaned over by the mule stall, where Plewin munched a manger full of grain.

Allun ... he's hurt!

She quickly lit a rush lamp and found the miller tied up in a corner near the stall. After untying him, she offered him a sip from his waterskin.

Allun took a long drink, then sat up stiffly. "I thank you," he said after a moment. "That crooked upstart attacked me." He peered at Natalenya in the dim light. "He knew you and Merlin were coming. Planned on catching you here. But I kept my mouth shut that Merlin had already been here and gone. I prayed you'd come with one of your brothers, or someone else. Are you well? He didn't hurt you?"

"A scrape or two, that's all." But her heart was still fluttering.

"You're a brave lass, you are. I'll throw that miscreant's body in the ditch, I will. Take Plewin if you must, but be careful out there tonight."

Knowing her time was short, she helped the miller to his feet, untied the mule, and then thanked him before leaving. As she stepped out into the darkness, Natalenya shuddered, for the moon was already slipping below the horizon, signaling the start of the druidow's Beltayne feast, and she had to hurry.

Owain lay on the damp ground next to the Stone and struggled against the ropes that bound his feet and hands, but he couldn't loosen their chafing cords. A stranger had been placed upon the Stone next to him, but since Owain faced away from the gleam he couldn't see who the man was. Yet even with his back turned, Owain felt heat pulse from the Stone's craggy surface, followed by cold, and then back to heat. On and on. The druidow circled with continuous chanting while the drums beat a slow cadence once more.

Owain studied the wicker cages and wondered where Dybris and Merlin were hiding. Still watching from the bushes where Owain had left them? But his hopes burned away when he spotted two hands with purple-blue designs holding the posts of the nearest woven cage. So one of the two had been caught, and probably both, considering Merlin's blindness. They were all likely to die before that sluggish Vortigern came. Die before Natalenya even knew they'd been captured. Moisture dotted Owain's eyes as he realized that Mônda would live out her remaining days without seeing the light or knowing his own love properly.

And Ganieda. Young, impressionable, and with so many needs. What would become of her? Already Owain had seen her taking on her mother's hatred for the worship of Jesu.

And Merlin would die too, caught in a trap of fire that he couldn't escape.

The man next to him groaned and struggled and finally spoke. "Igerna!" he cried. "Myrgwen ... Eilyne! Someone help me!"

Owain swallowed back bile as these words hit him like a hammer in the gut. The man was Uther, and with him held hostage, what could Vortigern do? Would he even discover the king in time? And even if he did, how could he attack and free them all with the life of the High King at stake?

Owain moaned and closed his eyes as a stronger chill crept from the Stone, and the icy flow began to sap his hope away. He ground his teeth and thrashed his body to break free.

Uther spoke, but his words carried no strength. "... have lost ... lost all."

Owain rolled onto his back and squinted at Uther's face. "No! There is hope while we live."

The king's body shifted, and his head turned slightly, recognition flickering in his eyes. "Hope, Owain?"

"Vortigern is coming," Owain whispered. "He'll rescue us!" *Though the odds of that decline by the moment.*

"Yes. Igerna's brother." Uther's voice gained resolve. "Goodly Vortigern."

"Do you remember that night near Uxellum when we were pinned against the cliff? We were barely nineteen winters. Your father sent us to patrol in the mountains north of the wall, and the Picti caught us from above."

"The Picti. They ... threw spears down and dropped rocks ... and—"

"And we hoisted you up. Ah, you routed 'em! Sixteen to one, and they ran at your wrath!"

"I remember." Uther strained to sit up but rose barely a finger's breadth before collapsing against the Stone.

"You were unstoppable when the battle frenzy came upon you."

"Brewygh died with a spear ... through his skull. Couldn't let anyone else die. Didn't want you to die."

Owain coughed as the chill sank deeper into his flesh. "Uther, do you forgive me for leaving you for Gwevian? I couldn't stay with you both, and I need you to understand."

"It's hard, Owain—"

"I need to hear you say it. I've needed it all these years. I'm sorry I failed you and the war band, but the new love that God kindled had to win out. Her father would have murdered her."

Uther rolled his head to the side and looked at Owain. Blood dripped from the gash above his eye. "We were like brothers, you and

I, but … I've learned to love now too … Fierce Igerna … faithful Igerna … Never see … my flower again.… Nor my children." And then quietly, Uther said, "Owain, I forgive you … Sorry it's ending like this."

"It's not over. Don't say that!"

Uther groaned against his bonds. "I don't want to die. The Stone … it hurts. A voice is telling me I'll die … will worship it, yet it burns!"

"Fight it. Don't give in — "

"Burning my soul …"

"Call on the name of God — "

The pace of the chanting druidow quickened, and the drums boomed louder. The seven torch holders snaked in and out of Owain's vision.

With a flourish, Mórganthu reappeared, Uther's sword belted at his side, and his golden knife protruding like a fang from his hand. Speaking in the druidow' tongue, he circled the Stone like a cat.

Uther's groaning increased as the Stone's sickening glow poured like smoke from underneath him. "It burns … it *burns!*"

"Battle, Uther! To battle!" Owain turned away from the Stone. Even then, like massive tongs it tried to turn his head, and he mounted every ounce of strength to resist.

Mórganthu, his head uplifted and darkness in his eyes, raised his voice. "All! All who have come to serve Belornos and the gods of the druidow! Do you hear me?"

The people shouted back to him.

"This is the night when the moon descends to join us. The night when it slays the Seven Torches. Behold! The time of the otherworld is upon us!" And Mórganthu pointed to the west, where the moon was disappearing below the horizon with a constellation of seven stars beside it.

Merlin was listening to Mórganthu's ravings when a man sat down to his right on the same rock. Merlin stiffened and turned his head slightly away to keep the man from seeing his scars.

"I've been watching you," the man said.

Merlin swallowed. "Whatever for? Nothing better to do than bother a fellow druid?"

"You're no druid, and you were with the monk before he was caught."

Merlin's left hand went quietly to his dirk.

"Don't worry, though, I won't give your secret away."

Merlin took a breath. "Why?"

"My name's Caygek, and I'm one of the leaders of the filidow. We don't support Mórganthu or what he's doing here. It goes against the laws of the wider order as they've been taught for the last hundred years."

Hope surged in Merlin's heart. "So you'll help me?"

"I have men in position around the Stone, and they're ready to intervene when I give the signal."

"You'll free my father ... and the High King?"

"If we can."

"And then the monks."

"The monks ... no. They've been judged and are considered criminals, not a sacrifice. The two at the Stone, however ..."

This didn't make sense to Merlin, and he gritted his teeth when he spoke. "You have to help me save them."

"Why? I'm already risking my neck to try and stop the sacrifice. If my companions and I are alive by this time tomorrow, we'll all have Grannos to thank."

"The monks are innocent. They've done nothing deserving death."

"Perhaps."

"*Perhaps?*" Merlin could barely contain his outrage.

"Like all other monks, they're responsible for turning the people away from the old gods. For that slander, we druidow have an unforgiving hatred, and these monks are to be an example."

Merlin scoffed at these words. "Can't the old gods defend themselves?"

"We are their instruments of justice."

"Don't you see that killings like these have caused you to lose support? Fear cannot long hold a people in bondage, and if these monks die, then the news will spread, and you will all be driven out completely."

"Perhaps."

Tensing his fists, Merlin turned his head away. "I can't save them on my own. I'm blind."

"Ah, so *you're* the famous Merlin, the one who keeps Mórganthu gnashing his teeth late into the night. Yes, I've heard about you. Well, then, let's just say that it's the ones who have sight who make the decisions."

"Fine, then. Leave me alone to my prayers."

"Not so fast. That doesn't mean I've decided not to help you. I happen to know that if word got to Mórganthu that *Merlin* had ransomed the monks, then that just might agitate him to an early grave. It might even direct his wrath in your direction. And that, my phony druid, is something that interests me. Ransoming is something we allow by law."

"You want me to pay you … to do what is right?"

"I have a few extra men I could call into service, but if you don't have the money …"

Merlin squeezed the bottom of his bag and tried to remember the number of coins there. "How much do you want?"

"For that many men our law would suggest the ransom be, say, half a gold coin."

"*What?*" That was an impossible price.

"Fine, a quarter of a coin, which in silver would be — "

"Go get your gold from the Stone."

"From Mórganthu? Ah, now you see the problem of the filidow, the least-favored of our order."

"I only have five screpallow."

Caygek laughed. "You too? What about your torc?"

"You want me to cut a chunk from it? I can do that, though I'd need to do so later. I don't have it with me."

"No, no. I'm jesting. Don't even think about marring such a priceless thing. Five screpallow it is."

"You're serious?"

"The rumor doesn't need to say how *much* you paid us, does it? I'd dearly like to see Mórganthu's face when he hears about it."

"So you'll help?"

"For the right to rub salt into Mórganthu's wound, yes."

A great weight lifted from Merlin's shoulders as he handed over the five coins. "Thank you."

"No promises, hear? We filidow are heavily outnumbered. More than likely we'll all be dead before the moon sets."

———✠———

Bedwir was nearly giddy when Vortigern finally marched them on foot out of the Tor's gate. Down the Meneth Gellik, through the village, and northeastward on the road, they eventually drew nigh to the road leading to the burned abbey. A shame, that.

From there, with the sun behind the mountain, Bedwir could see torches moving in an eerie circle a half league across the valley and through the woods.

The armed company advanced down the road to the stream and up again until they took a snaking path into the forest. Soon the noise of drumming reached their ears, and Bedwir began to sweat. Was it because of their long march or the closeness of the air? Or was it due to the coming battle? Enemy warriors in daylight, fine. But magical druidow in the dark amid an ancient pagan circle of giant stones — that was different.

When the druid's chanting could finally be heard, Bedwir halted his contingent of men.

"Vortigern says we're to wait in silence," the man in front of him whispered. "The battle chief goes alone to scout out the situation. He says to listen for the sounding of his horn."

Bedwir stood on his toes and craned his neck. About ten paces in front, the cloaked shadow that was Vortigern faded into the trees.

"This is *Beltayne* night," Mórganthu shouted to the crowd, "when we light the wicker bonfires filled with the enemies of our gods. When we purify ourselves, our cattle, our children, and our spirits through fire and smoke from all that pollutes, in order to protect ourselves from witchcraft."

What a hard time Merlin had listening to this. At any moment Mórganthu might give the signal to burn the monks to death or sacrifice Uther and his father, and what could *he* do? Nothing. Sure, prayers escaped his lips in continuous pleading to God, but Merlin's soul, spirit, and body all urged him to action. He couldn't just wait —

Boom! Boom!

Merlin's throat closed up when he saw the blur of large torches being carried toward the wicker cages, ready to light the mounds of tinder on fire.

"You, my people, you have been bewitched by these practitioners of a foreign god! I ask you, what is done with witches?"

Mórganthu chanted now in the common language of Kernow, and all the people joined with him.

Flames blaze and burn the witches!
Fire! Flames! Destroy the witches!

Boom! Boom! smote the drums.

Behind him, Merlin detected a sound he had not heard in the druid glade before ... the slight jingle of ring-mail. He turned and, out of the corner of his good eye, saw a shadowy figure marching into the circle of stones. Whoever it was pushed aside any druidow who stood in his way. Merlin's heart flip-flopped as the man walked straight to Mórganthu and the Stone, a shining sword on his back reflecting the light of the moon. Was it Vortigern or one of the other warriors?

"A word, master druid!" the man's deep voice boomed.

"You intrude here," Mórganthu said in a sneering tone. "Your work is done. Begone!"

"I need assurance."

"He is here, on the Stone."

"Alive?" the man said, his voice rising in pitch.

"Yes. Yes, of course. We have our own ways."

The hooded man paused, then asked, "The heir? Where is he?"

"Drowned in the marsh, his body lost. A trifle, I assure you ... I cannot prove his death."

"Trifle, you say? And Igerna? Where is she?"

Mórganthu turned his back to the man and lowered his voice so that Merlin barely heard his answer. "I am told she and the daughters are dead, as well as that chief offender of a bard."

Uther let out a desolate cry, and Merlin's heart broke for him.

Mórganthu turned back to face the warrior. "It seems one of these imprudent Eirish warriors could not control himself. But if it is of any comfort, the offender was slain by my own hand."

In great rage, the man lunged forward, and everything became confusion. It appeared to Merlin that the warrior picked Mórganthu up and threw him to the ground. "You tell me *he* is alive while my sister is *dead*?"

The warrior, whom Merlin now knew was Vortigern, reached down and snatched something from Mórganthu, and when he stood again, there shined in his hand the reflection of red, inlayed glass.

Merlin recognized what he held: the sword Merlin's father had made and given to Uther.

"He will die now," the warrior cried out, "but not by *my* blade."

Merlin had up until this point sat in mute shock, listening to the two men argue. And all the time he was waiting for Caygek's men to intervene and save Uther's life, and the life of his father. But these filidow, cowards all of them, were waiting for who-knew-what signal, and Merlin could wait no longer. Vortigern's threat drove Merlin to his feet.

He drew his dirk and rushed headlong at Vortigern, who leaned over Uther and the pulsing blue Stone — with the blade poised to kill the High King.

"No-o!" Merlin yelled, and he swung his blade wildly, hoping in the darkness to beat Vortigern back.

Uther musn't die ... he musn't!

Vortigern swore. "Get back, druid!"

Their blades met, and the superior power of the hand-and-a-half longsword his father had made almost knocked Merlin's shorter blade from his hand. But the weight of the longsword had caused it to swing too far, and though Merlin had every reason to fear death, a frenzy to save Uther drove him in closer. He grabbed Vortigern's sleeve with his left hand and slammed the point of his blade into the man's ring-mail.

But the tip didn't go through, and Vortigern took the pommel of Uther's blade and cracked Merlin over the head.

"Out of my way."

Merlin's feet failed first, collapsing out from under him as a great clanging and thudding reverberated through his head. He felt weightless, and the only knowledge he had of hitting the ground was the taste of dirt as he coughed and yelled in pain.

———†———

Blades clashed next to Owain, and one of the men stepped on his hair, making him flinch. When the fight was over, and one of the men writhed on the ground in pain, the warrior stepped over to the Stone where Uther lay. There, looking up at the man, Owain saw into his hood, and the shimmer of the torches revealed Vortigern's bearded face. His neck bulged red, and spit frothed through his moustache.

"No!" Owain cried. "No!"

Without a glance in Owain's direction, Vortigern plunged the blade through Uther's heart.

Uther's mouth opened in a mute scream, his eyes wide, his face wracked with pain. As he exhaled his last breath, he whispered, "Jesu, have mercy..."

Owain squeezed his eyes shut as furious smoke rose from the Stone and lightning streaked across the sky. When he opened them again, he saw Vortigern fling the bloodied blade away. Turning from the murder, the battle chief covered his eyes with his hand while great tears streamed down his face.

Owain tore his gaze from the traitor, and it fell on the face of his friend, lightless eyes staring in death. *Great Uther. Dead. And the heir as well!* Despair again threatened to take him, and he drew in great gasping breaths, struggling to keep it at bay.

Mórganthu, now on his feet again, rose to his full height and called out, "Druidow! Sons of the wood! Slay this man who dares interfere with the divine rights of the sacrifice of Belornos!"

From all around Vortigern, the druidow advanced, holding blades, axes, and spears with shaking hands.

Vortigern drew his broadsword, brought his great horn to his lips, and blew long and loud. The dark woods echoed with thrumming feet, and in less than ten heartbeats, his warriors burst onto the field.

"Havoc! *Havoc!*" Vortigern shouted. "The king is dead. Druidow have slain the High King! Come to my aid, my warriors!"

CHAPTER 34

A LAMENT UNSPOKEN

Colvarth tore his tunic and wept until his vision blurred and he could no longer see the pale face of his dead queen. Eilyne and Myrgwen wept with him, hugging their mother and wailing.

The nightmarish images of the attack whirled through his head as he stood. He'd been so shocked with how swiftly Uther had been taken that Igerna's cries barely reached his ears.

"Colvarth!" she'd shrieked. "They've taken Arthur!"

It all happened so fast. The men had stripped Arthur from Myrgwen's arms and left the tower. All, that is, except for the one Uther had slain and the dark one guarding their escape.

But instead of joining his fellows when the rear was secure, this foul warrior had advanced upon Igerna and lunged at her with his sword, only to find two girls and their slim blades between him and his prey. The two daughters had defended their mother with all the fierce determination and inexpert skill they could muster, but to little avail.

"Get awa'!" the man had shouted, waving his sword as if to shoo away flies buzzing over his supper. "I'll ha' me reward o' gold, nay matter the cost!"

God, pardon me for not acting more quickly. Treachery of this kind against women and children was against the ancient laws of the land — even the laws of the Eirish — and Colvarth, his bones shaking, simply had not fathomed the danger.

He should have acted sooner. *My Father ... forgive!*

Eilyne snarled in righteous defense of her mother and had tried to stab the man. But McGoss, or so they named his fetid face, had clouted her with his fist and thrust her aside.

Myrgwen likewise had advanced to face him and was tossed into the rock wall.

"You whelps'll die proper in a moment, once yer mither's dead!" McGoss bellowed, circling her with blade thrusting and swinging.

Her own dirk in hand now, the queen defended herself fiercely, even slicing his elbow once, but the warrior simply outmatched her.

Only then had Colvarth woken from his fright. Grabbing the pickaxe, he wounded the murderer in the leg before being kicked into Uther's freshly dug hole.

By the time Colvarth had crawled out, the queen, God save her soul, was dead.

And by grace alone had Colvarth and the unconscious girls escaped the man's blade. For at that moment the other four Eirish warriors had returned, more quickly than McGoss had apparently expected. Caught in his despicable act, McGoss pled with them, but they hacked him dead in lawful judgment — and left again as Colvarth sobbed into his beard.

"Ah, God!" Colvarth cried as he kissed the wet cheek of little Myrgwen, now bereft of her mother ... the queen who should have lived to see her godly lineage.

Eilyne still held her blade, and she ran at the mutilated body of McGoss, screaming. Colvarth grabbed her and held her back. "He is dead. Leave his ... judgment to God, my lady." He took her blade and held her sobbing shoulders tightly. Ah, she would have been a good sister-guide to young Arthur.

"Arthur," Colvarth cried aloud, half scaring himself. "They've ... taken him!" The heir was alive, and so might Uther be! A fool upon fool to abide with the dead queen while the living might be helped!

"Stay here with ... your mother." And he made them promise. "I will see what may be ... done for your brother."

He clambered through the door and clopped off into the night. Following the muddy tracks of the warriors, he passed the ruins, dodged through the forlorn apple orchard, traced his way through a forest of poplars and pines, and finally found his way to the northern tip of the isle.

There he found the warriors standing on the shore with Uther bound in a boat. They were pushing the lifeless body of a peculiar, wild-haired man into the bushes.

Colvarth hid behind a large tree and overheard them talking in anger about how someone named Garth had stolen young Arthur out from their clutches and slipped off with one of their boats.

Oh, when Colvarth heard this news, a song of praise almost burst from his lips! Stifling himself, he prayed that whomever this Garth was, he would take good care of Arthur until the old bard could find the young prince.

Hunching down on his aching knees, Colvarth pulled his black cloak close about him and waited until the warriors ferried themselves off the island in two trips. Standing again with difficulty, he went back to the tower with hopeful steps. Maybe God's goodness remained despite the terrible evil of this night.

As it was dark, the girls would be afraid. He went to their camp and, finding the small metal fire chest, opened it and blew upon the coals until they glowed. Taking an oil-soaked torch they had brought, he lit it and climbed back into the tower.

"It is I," he called but received no reply. The dim torchlight landed on the girls' sparkling tears, bringing forth his own grief yet again.

The elder of them gazed at the appalling scene. "What will we do?"

"We should build ... a cairn over her," he said, his words echoing inside the tower. But with what? Stepping to the door, he peered out, and while there were stones aplenty, they were nearly all too heavy for an old man and two young girls to lift through the high doorway.

Their best option was to bury her in Uther's pit. Although less dignified than a cairn, it was far better than leaving her to whatever wild animals might live on the island.

Let that *be the fate of McGoss's bloody remains!*

He glanced back at the girls and realized this was a task he would need to take on alone.

With tears clouding his vision, he climbed down into the hole to retrieve Uther's pickaxe. There amid the soft soil, his foot hit something hard. Thinking it a stone, he paid it no mind until he stepped on it again and heard a hollow sound.

What's this?

Kneeling, he felt the shape of the object and brushed soil from its surface to reveal silverish metal, which he suspected was pewter, for it had no tarnish or rust.

Shoving the torch's handle into the dirt at the side of the hole, he dug and found a box no wider than two handbreadths. But the soil was hard, so he took out his small eating knife and chopped the dirt all around until he could pull the object free. Intricate patterns were inscribed on its sides, one of which held the sign of the cross surrounded by the likeness of two trees he did not recognize.

Realizing that he was studying the hinged side, he turned it around and saw on its front not a cross but words in an unknown script. The box was shut fast with some sort of mechanism loosed only by a missing key of clever design.

The box did not weigh much, but he heard faint jostling within. Had Uther been right that this was something holy? Surely the sign of the cross meant it had been owned by a Christian.

Climbing stiffly out of the ditch, he set the box down. His eyes traveled to the reason he had entered the pit's depths. "Eilyne, Myrgwen, I need you to ... stay near the wall." *How I wish they were not present for this task.* With a heavy sigh, Colvarth lifted the queen and moved her into the makeshift grave. With great care, he folded her arms in a pose worthy of her grace and nobility.

As he climbed out and gathered dirt to place over her body, Eilyne screamed.

"Nooo!" She pushed Colvarth away, embracing her mother and weeping. Myrgwen stood at the edge of the grave, her face having lost all expression and her eyes glassy.

Colvarth tried to comfort Eilyne, but it was a long time before the girl's furious grief was stilled.

Together, the three gently covered the queen's lifeless form, watering the earth with their tears. Colvarth was already composing a worthy tale of her life and a lament over her death.

"O God," he spoke aloud. "Let Thy Day of ... Judgment and Resurrection come! Yes, come, O Lord Jesu."

As he scratched the last of the soil over the grave and picked up the silver box, he realized Uther may have truly received a godly vision.

But why had the king acted so strangely? And how had these Eirish warriors known the royal family was staying on the island?

Slow as Colvarth considered himself in his old age, his suspicions finally roused.

Picking up his torch, he searched the inside of the tower and found Uther's discarded mead skin. Colvarth threw away the stopper, sniffed, and wrinkled his nose. Pouring a droplet of the liquid on his finger, he tasted it and was surprised how its sweetness preceded the slightest touch of bitterness.

Was there something wrong with it? A poison, perhaps?

Colvarth dropped to his aching knees in prayer, for Uther and his son, and when he rose, the light of the torch seemed brighter.

Who had given the drink to Uther? Ah, yes, now he remembered. Vortigern.

Before he left with the girls beside him, Colvarth laid upon the grave a thick branch of old, weathered applewood, scrawled with a message written in both Latin and Ogham:

> *Here lies Igerna myr Vitalis,*
> *High Queen of the Britons and the faithful wife*
> *of High King Uther mab Aurelianus,*
> *buried along with her two daughters, Eilyne and Myrgwen,*
> *and her young son, Arthur.*

"Why did you write that?" Eilyne asked as they climbed out from the doorway. "It's not true."

"Because," Colvarth said, "though I am ... old and slow, the nose of this fox can still smell a wolf. It is my plan that you two be kept safe, and may the ... goodly God help our Arthur too."

Owain wanted to weep at the death of his friend, to mourn, yell, and thrash about, but events occurred too quickly. As Owain lay tied next to Uther's body, still upon the Stone, the last howls of Vortigern's battle horn died, and his warriors stormed onto the field.

Then three things happened at once.

First, panic set in among the villagers and druidow. The guardians next to the wicker cages ran to join the battle, but not before dropping their torches into the tinder. The flames ignited the wood and began to spread.

Second, Vortigern attacked Mórganthu, who picked up the sword of the High King and fought back. So deft was Vortigern, however, that Mórganthu would have died if not for the arrival of a brightly dressed Eirish warrior. With gray-streaked hair and a long beard covering a silver torc, the warrior swung at Vortigern from the side. Realizing his danger just in time, the battle chief parried the blow and backed away.

Last, a druid in a green cloak and blue tunic appeared at Owain's side with a long iron blade of good quality. Owain's body tensed as the sword hovered over him.

"Get it over with," Owain said. "Your dark arts can't touch my soul."

"Shah," the man whispered. "I'm just trying to see the ropes. You want me to free you or not?" He sliced off the cords binding Owain's arms.

"What are you doing?"

"Cutting your bonds. Name's Caygek."

A thrill went through Owain. *Freedom!*

"Hold still. By Crom, these are tight."

"You don't even know who I am ..."

"You're Owain, the village blacksmith, and Merlin's father. I know that much. And I, like some of the other druidow, know these sacrifices are wrong."

Owain looked to the wicker cages. The flames had climbed high on one side, while the other smoked and hissed. Dark forms moved nearby. "My son! And the monks — are you freeing them?" he shouted.

"Your son is sitting up over there, and yes, we have water. Now quiet," Caygek hissed. "You'll bring death upon us all."

Owain spotted Merlin near a large rock. To Owain's joy, his son stood up shakily and began to make his way toward the Stone — just as another man ran toward them from the crowd, clutching something to his chest.

Owain jerked his head, expecting Mórganthu or one of the robed druidow, but it was Tregeagle. The magister bowed next to Owain and shoved Uther's body off the Stone. With shaking hands, he spilled hundreds of coins onto its glimmering surface. "Chance to ... get ... gold. Gold!"

Free at last, Owain thanked Caygek. He got up on one knee and tried to stand, but his limbs felt wooden.

Dybris ran to him through the crowd, dodging warriors who mistook him for a druid. Merlin followed close behind.

"Owain, the Stone!" The monk tore his tunic off and threw it over the top.

Tregeagle yelled.

Owain kicked the magister in the side, sending coins spinning through the air like overweight moths. Tregeagle himself flipped onto the grass beyond the edge of the leather tarp, which was still under the Stone

Owain had wanted to do that for some time. He pulled a Roman-style blade from the stunned magister, fancy looking but of poor steel, and tucked it into his own belt. Together, he, Dybris, and Merlin unfolded the tarp, hefted the Stone, and took off toward the woods. For its size, Owain had expected the Stone to be heavier, but it swung between them easily, and they made good progress.

As they passed through the first line of trees, a cry arose behind them. Tregeagle stood amid the torches waving his arms and yelling.

"They've taken the Stone. Stop them!"

The three dodged under pines as they loped toward the road. Behind them people shouted, and Vortigern's battle horn sounded.

"Faster! They're following us," Dybris called.

"Where will Natalenya be?" Merlin asked.

"The road? I don't know!"

✦

Natalenya finished hitching Plewin to the An Gof family wagon and then pulled herself up into the seat.

Taking the reins, she called, "Hy-mos!" and the mule began plodding forward at what felt like a snail's pace. *Can't she go any faster than this?*

She snapped the reins harder, and Plewin jolted forward, but the wagon gained little speed. *I guess she's just slow.*

As she was passing the village green, Natalenya saw something ahead on the road shimmering. All she could see was a dark shape coming toward her. Then the darkness lifted, and she saw a cloaked man waving at her. He had white hair, and he was holding a harp. Uther's bard!

"Colvarth!" she called.

The dark figure hobbled toward her. "God be praised, young lady! No time ... to explain, but Uther's been taken, and Arthur ... is missing."

"Taken? By whom?"

"Eirish warriors, I think ... sent from Vortigern."

"But those warriors are bound to Mórganthu."

Colvarth shook his harp in anger. "In league, then! God ... save Uther. But Arthur was taken from them to safety, and I ... must find him. They spoke of ... a Garth who protected him."

Natalenya's heart jumped. "Garth!"

"You know him? Where ... is he?"

"If he's turned away from the druidow, I don't know where he might be."

Colvarth's white hand gripped the side of the wagon. "Can you help me find him? I have the ... two daughters of the king hiding in the bushes, and ... I *must* find Arthur and get them all to safety."

"I'm sorry. There's no time. Merlin is trying to destroy the Stone and is waiting for me. Troslam, the weaver. He'll help you ... And he can hide the girls." Natalenya quickly gave the bard directions to their house.

"What does their crennig ... look like?"

"It's the oldest house on the mountain, so the wall around their field is higher than the others, almost a full eight feet tall for protection. If you don't find help there, go farther down the road until you see the chapel."

"I go! Whatever breath I ... have, I pray."

Natalenya reached out and grasped the old man's hand for a moment, and then she was off.

Holding tightly to the leather tarp, Merlin ran as fast as he could without tripping, while the mad shouts drew closer. But his heart was divided, and only necessity had forced him to leave Uther's body behind. Merlin hadn't stopped Vortigern, and now Uther had been murdered. Merlin had failed, and with every step he wished he could go back and defend the king once more.

When the trio burst out of the trees and onto the road, Merlin fell to the ground, and this set his head to throbbing again. Owain pulled him up while Dybris straightened the tarp and looked around frantically for the wagon.

"Natalenya's not here."

But Merlin heard a faint whinny. "That way," he called. "Horses!"

Southward they ran down the empty track, full of shadows, with the swinging bulk of the Stone between them.

After turning a bend in the road, Merlin followed along as Owain and Dybris changed their direction.

"The magister's wagon is here," Owain said, "and Trevenna's at the reins."

With the shouting in the woods growing louder, they dashed toward her.

"Trevenna! We have the Stone!" Dybris called. "We need your wagon to take it away and destroy it."

But Trevenna was weeping and didn't seem to hear. Merlin looked back just as the torches of the druidow burst onto the track.

Dybris called once more. "Vortigern has slain the High King! We need your help."

"Vortigern? Slain the — "

"Yes!"

"Take it. Go!"

They heaved the Stone into the back of the wagon, and Dybris climbed in after it.

Trevenna stepped down and stood helplessly on the side of the road.

"Come with us!" Owain implored as he helped Merlin clamber to the front seat.

"I follow my husband," she said, and she walked off into the dark forest, away from the oncoming torches.

An arrow whizzed past Merlin's ear as Owain turned the horses southward, then slapped the reins on their haunches. Off they bolted, but Dybris yelled as a druid grabbed the back of the wagon and pulled himself over the rail, clunking into the box.

"He has a knife." Dybris called. "Do something!"

"Take the reins!" Merlin yelled.

"I've never driven horses!"

"Then here's a blade. Take care of him."

"Me?"

There was no more time for talk as the druid climbed forward and raised his flashing knife toward Owain's back. Then the wagon hit a hole and lurched to the side. The long steel blade jabbed into the padded wooden seat.

Merlin smashed his elbow back and connected with the druid's stomach while Dybris tried to wrest the knife from the man's hand.

But the druid pulled free and raised his knife for another strike. Owain leaned forward. "Get him!"

"God forgive me!" Dybris called as he plunged Merlin's dirk into the druid, who screamed and fell backward onto the covered Stone.

The road snaked downhill, and Owain slowed the horses so they could manage the first curve. "Throw him out."

Dybris hesitated. "I should help him."

"We need to go faster," Merlin said, for even with his weak eyesight, he could see the dark woods and hillside floating with scores of torches.

"Not fair ... they're not taking the road."

Owain gave a short, dry laugh. "What'd you expect? Throw the druid out."

Merlin climbed to the back and helped Dybris heft the body over the side of the wagon.

"Will we make it?" Merlin asked when he returned to the front.

Owain snapped the reins faster. "If we get to the bridge first. Do I smell smoke?"

At the back of the wagon, a sizzling sound rent the air. Merlin turned and saw the tunic covering the Stone catch fire.

"Y-mo!" Owain shouted and whipped the horses into a frenzy as they descended the hillside for the final run leading to the bridge. Smoke trailed behind, and more flames began to shoot from the Stone.

Merlin gripped the rail. "The wagon's burning!"

"As long as we make it to the smithy."

"The smithy?" Dybris asked.

"Where'd you think we were going? We've got to break the Stone."

"But we're — "

"Hold on, here comes the bridge!"

With a shock, the wagon hit the wooden planks and began vaulting over the bridge. Merlin's head pounded as the ancient timbers groaned, and one of the wagon's wooden rear wheels came down with a shattering crack.

The horses pulled the wagon beyond the bridge and a few paces more, but the wheel was broken and sent spokes and splinters flying. They tipped, and the horses plunged to a halt.

Behind them, the hillside swarmed with torches.

Natalenya thrashed the reins until Plewin moved again, as fast as she would go. Eastward Natalenya traveled until she rounded the bend toward the road that led to the ruined abbey. From there she descended toward the stream. Below her, the hillside across the valley was filled with torchlight.

She tightened her grip on the reins. She wanted to turn the wagon and go back, but Merlin was counting on her, so she flogged the mule until the wagon bumped down the slope.

Wait! Was that a bonfire on this side of the bridge? *No, it can't be!* It was her father's wagon on fire, and the horses were running off. Merlin and Dybris were waving at her.

But do they have the Stone? Yes! It was at the center of the flames, and the wagon was broken.

"Natalenya!" Merlin shouted as he and Dybris ripped a board from Tregeagle's wagon. "We have to get the Stone into your wagon. Circle around and drive Plewin alongside."

"Where's Uther?" she called.

Merlin choked out the answer. "Vortigern killed him."

In shock, Natalenya directed Plewin to circle up to their wagon.

"They're coming," Dybris yelled.

Natalenya looked back at the hillside, and a multitude of torch bearers approached, calling to one another as their din grew louder.

Owain ran over to help Merlin lift a sideboard off the magister's wagon.

"Dybris, we need to lever the Stone over!" Merlin called.

The wagon shook beneath Natalenya, and she smelled burning leather as the Stone rolled into the back. The sounds of shouting grew as Merlin climbed in beside her.

Dybris and Owain dove into the back of the wagon.

"They're at the bridge. *Go!*" Owain shouted.

Natalenya snapped the reins.

The mule, chewing grass beside the road, refused to budge.

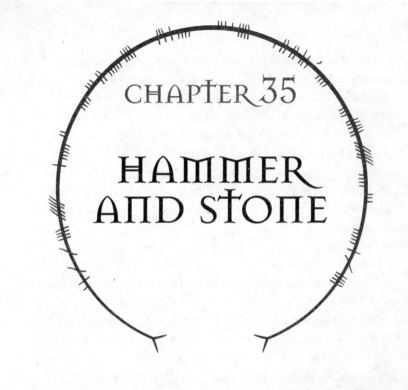

CHAPTER 35

HAMMER AND STONE

H is feet weary and his arms aching, Garth sat down on a rock at the edge of Lake Dosmurtanlin and placed Arthur on his knee.

The child gazed up at him with wide, dark eyes.

Such a quiet kid — he rarely peeped — but Garth could tell what he was thinking just by looking at his stiff lips and upraised eyebrows. "I know yer hungry too. An' since yer barl's et up, you must be famished. There's food back at the druid camp, but you don't want to go there, oh no!"

Shifting on his rock, he looked out to the misty water. "Aww-wn, Garth! What'll you do now? No friends. No tuck. Nothin'."

Arthur's little hand reached out and pinched Garth's cheek.

"You sure do that a lot. Why, only last week a grandmum here in Bosventor did just that. Pinched my cheek, she did, an' called me a *Ker-onen*! As if I was a crock full o' honey, I guess."

Memories interrupted his words — memories of the first time

he and Merlin visited her house. Like a distant tune piping over the mountain, the smell of her rich broth with mushrooms, leeks, and lamb filled his head. A soup pot. A friendly fire. Bread baking in a little pan. Rose vines climbing the stones outside of her stout little home. The old lady smiling like he was her long-lost great-grandson. And her big thumb and finger pinching his cheek.

Well ... he could do without the pinch.

"Arth, yer onto somethin'! Kyallna was her name! Maybe she has some soup on her hearth! Said I could stop by any time I wanted. Now there's a *real* friend!"

Standing up, he pulled little Arthur to his chest and set off with a bounce in his steps toward the mountain. Working his way around the western side, he arrived on the outskirts of the village and hiked to the upper road.

But the town was not as he'd left it. All of Bosventor was silent, and the only sound he heard was the neighing of many horses coming from the Tor. No one was on the road. No one stood at any of the doors. No light could be seen. Even the hearth fires had died.

"Somethin' odd, Arth." He walked down the road past empty crennigs that leered at him with dark, weasel-eyed windows.

"Here, this is her place, Arth, but it doesn't seem like anyone's home." He walked down the rosebush-lined path, and his pants caught on a thorn. Freeing himself, he stepped to the door and knocked, but no sound came from within.

"Not home. Now what are we gonna do?"

Then he smelled something more wonderful than roses. And it lingered on the air for just a moment.

"Food on *someone's* hearth, an' no mistake!" Garth stood up tall and sniffed. Not detecting anything, he walked back to the road to get away from the nose-numbing flowers. He cradled Arthur's head at his shoulder and turned around a few times, inhaling.

"This way." And off he marched westward. The next house was dark and quiet, but the following crennig's chimney wafted faint tufts of smoke.

Garth remembered. "Sure, an' this is the weaver's house." Marching up to the door, he rapped on it loudly. "Anyone," he yelled. "Open up!"

A heavy bar was lifted and the door swung wide.

Garth peered into the darkness and was met by the tip of a spear thrust through the collar of his tunic.

"And who are you?" said a deep voice.

⊹

Merlin could only stare at the coming wave of torch-bearing druidow as the mule snapped up more weeds and chewed.

"Give me the reins!" his father shouted from behind. Natalenya stretched them out, and Owain pulled hard to lift the mule's head.

But the beast kept crunching her prize.

Pounding feet echoed across the old bridge.

"Get your blades out," Dybris called.

Merlin bent his head in prayer but had only a moment before sparks from the Stone showered him. It was as if its dark malice knew of his call to God and was trying to stop him.

Numerous embers bored into his neck and hair, and the pain bit deeply even after he brushed them away. He pulled Natalenya down as more flickered past. One flaming cinder landed on the mule, and in terror she dug her hooves into the ground and jolted the wagon forward at such a startling pace that Merlin's father fell next to the Stone. The last of the sparks blew upon him, and he yelled.

"They're here," Dybris shouted. "Owain, *get up!*"

Running feet beat the ground next to the wagon, and Merlin turned to see the advancing men.

"Keep that mule moving," Owain shouted.

Some druidow pulled themselves into the wagon, and Merlin drew his dirk to protect Natalenya.

"Don't wrestle 'em, Dybris. Throw 'em out!" Merlin's father called.

"I'm trying!"

A piercing yell split the night.

"One down!" Merlin's father called. But his voice became choked. "Dybri —"

"Jesu, help us," Dybris called.

Frustration rose in Merlin as the confused shadows of his father, Dybris, and the intruders mingled behind him.

A thud, a pounding of feet, and another yelp.

"He was one of Vortigern's warriors," his father called, his voice shaky. "He would've sliced my gut if you hadn't come to my aid."

The wagon raced toward the village, and despite the rushing wind, the smell of smoke pricked Merlin's nose.

"It's happening again!" Dybris yelled. "The wagon's on fire."

Garth jerked back and yelled, causing Arthur to cry.

The man pulled the spear away. "What's this?"

Garth gaped like a dumb fish as a little crowd of people peered out at him. Beside the man with the spear stood an old and wizened man. And there was the weaver's wife, Safrowana, holding a rush light. Behind her stood three girls — as well as Kyallna, the soup-mum!

But the two men he'd never met. The bearded man holding the spear wore a finely woven dark-blue tunic, a match to Safrowana's. The old man was about Garth's height and wore sea-green clothes and a black cloak. At his throat lay a white-gold torc, and his hair and beard were like frosted ocean waves.

All of them stared in awe as if Garth were a ghost ship.

"Garth," Safrowana exclaimed. "God be praised, come in, come in! We were just praying for you."

"Prayin' . . . for me?" Garth thought it a joke until he saw the old man's eyes dancing with delight despite his craggy brow. And then two of the girls, each wearing fine dresses smeared in blood, ran forward and took Arthur from him.

They were crying, but these were happy tears.

The soup-mum came and put a warm arm around his neck. "You've come back to your Kyallna. Ah, my dear one, my sweet keronen." And she pinched Garth's cheek. "You're thinner than last I laid eyes on you. Come sit at the hearth, as I've brought over me soup!"

Garth dodged another pinch and was about to slip inside between the adults when he changed his mind about sneaking in. He bowed to her. "I was ... was hopin' for that, mum. Smelled it down the road, I did, as me tummy's sore an' rumblin'."

The old man gripped Garth by the elbow. "First, you and I need to talk for a ... minute." Because of his grip, Garth expected the old man to be angry, but instead there was joy mixed with sadness on his face. Garth went with him through the back room of the house and out into the weaver's high-walled pasture, where a few sheep grazed quietly.

Sitting down on a rock, the old man stared at Garth with piercing eyes. Garth found a spot next to him, if only to avoid his stare.

"I am named ... Colvarth. I am Chief Bard of the ... Britons, and I serve the High King. How did you come to the island to save the ... life of Arthur? Did you come with that peculiar man whose boat I borrowed?"

Garth shifted. "No ... no, sir! I ... I guided the Eirish warriors to the island, but didn't know their purpose till too late."

"You have brought great ... evil upon everyone. But know this," Colvarth said as he put a hand on Garth's shoulder. "Where evil and calamity lurk, there ... God is hiding as well, ready with His grace, planned long before the world began. I praise Jesu that the ... Almighty took hold of you. Great good may yet ... come of your deed."

"I'm sorry, sir!" Garth stammered. And he wanted tears to flow to show his remorse, but his stomach hurt too intensely. "It's all my fault."

"Not so," the bard said. "Uther's battle chief, ... Vortigern, bears the true blame, for I think he has betrayed his king into the hands of the ... druidow. Now Arthur is found, and I must gather those who will try to save the child."

"Uther's own men betrayed him?"

"Not all, no, but they are led by ... Vortigern and will be deceived."

"A traitor!" The image of Uther lying dead in the boat came back to him, igniting his anger. "Where're the king's warriors? I heard lots o' horses up on the Tor. Could the horses be theirs?"

"Doubtless it is true. They were told to take the ... fortress, so perhaps they are there now. We must be very ... careful."

A woman opened the back door and dashed over to Colvarth. She fell at his feet, panting and weeping. At first Garth thought it was Natalenya, but he soon saw this woman was older, more careworn.

Colvarth took a cloth from a bag at his belt and handed it to the weeping woman. "Trevenna, wife of Tregeagle! A night ... of tears, is it not?"

"King's ... bard ... I ... saw my husband ... running ... Came as quickly ... to find help ... Took the high path over the mountain ... Troslam saw me.... Help."

"Slow down, my ... daughter."

"I am told ... the High King ... is slain by Vortigern!"

Colvarth grimaced and closed his eyes. "It is as I feared."

"Owain, Merlin, and Dybris have ... taken the Stone to destroy it ... And now my husband ... all the warriors ... they and the druidow are in pursuit!"

Colvarth stared unblinking. "Uther's ... warriors? Preventing the Stone's ... destruction? Now I see, yes, the false source of ... Vortigern's betrayal. It is as Merlin feared."

What's Merlin gotten himself into? What've I gotten into?

Trevenna wept again. "Colvarth, anyone —"

But her words were cut short as shouts echoed from the village below.

Garth sat up straight. "What's that noise?"

"I hear ... nothing," Colvarth said, cocking his head to the side.

Garth ran to a granite boulder lying next to the wall, and hoisting himself up, he gazed down the mountainside. There, far to the east, was a wagon being pulled down the road by a large horse. The wagon box blazed out orange flames, and in the center sat a dark object with a deep-blue glow that pierced the night.

"The Stone!" he shouted. "They've got it, an' they're takin' it away in a wagon."

As Garth looked at the Stone, even at such a distance it seemed to grow and fill his vision. Closing his eyes, he turned his head away. "The nasty thing's callin' me, but I'm *not* listenin' anymore!"

Trevenna and Colvarth joined him next to the wall.

Merlin's there, Garth thought. The memory flooded back of the great debt he owed Merlin for taking his whipping. He heard again the ripping of Merlin's shirt and remembered the bloody gashes striping his friend's back. His friend's back. His friend.

And Garth now saw what he'd missed before. Scores of men running after the wagon, some bearing torches.

"They're bein' chased, just like you said, ma'am!"

The door creaked open behind them, and Kyallna hobbled out with a tray holding three ceramic mugs of steaming soup. Taking one, she held it out to Garth. "Here, love, to fill yer empty stomach."

Garth snapped up the mug. Holding it close, he sucked in the aroma of wild garlic and goat, letting it dive deep into his lungs.

He sighed, and his mouth began to water.

He lifted the wooden spoon to his lips — but let it splash down again.

"It's not right!"

"But you haven't tasted it, love." Kyallna's puckered face looked up at him.

"Not the soup, ma'am. I mean it's not right for me to eat while my friend Merlin and the others are in danger."

The wagon was gone from his sight now, but the entire road, far below, was filled with the shouting men, both druidow and Vortigern's warriors.

Carefully handing the soup back to Kyallna, he licked his dry lips. "I've got somethin' to do!" He jumped down from the rock and ran back into the house. There at the hearth fire, he snatched three burning branches, ran out the front door past the startled weaver, and disappeared into the night.

—✦—

"Dybris, do you see the bar for the doors?" Merlin yelled.

But the monk was helping Merlin's father carry the Stone inside the smithy. Using two leather aprons, they placed it upon the great anvil.

Natalenya ran over to a workbench and pulled the bar from underneath it. She placed the bar in Merlin's hands, but he hesitated. "You should go," he said. "It's not safe."

Natalenya turned to face him, and the flickering light from the newly lit forge reflected off her cheeks and forehead. "I'm not leaving you."

Outside, the yelling of men could be heard in the distance.

He dropped the bar into place, and her hand found his and squeezed.

"Merlin!" his father called. "We need your help holding up the Stone. Natalenya, keep watch through the crack between the doors."

Merlin found his way over to the anvil and grabbed the corners of the leather apron from his father. He could feel the heat of the Stone before him, and from deep within he heard a rumbling. His father set a chisel on top and smashed his hammer down upon it.

Clank!

And again.

Clishink!

Ten more times Owain drove the chisel into the Stone, each blow becoming wilder than the last. Merlin knew his father's strength and expected chips of rock to fly, but nothing happened.

"Is it breaking, Tas?"

"No!"

"There are torches outside," Natalenya called. "They've come. I can see druidow and lots of warriors. Even the villagers."

The Stone flared up with a bright blue flame, and Dybris yelled.

Merlin backed up as the burning tentacles of fire pulled at his fingers.

Owain threw the chisel down and took up his biggest hammer. He waited for the flames to die down and then smashed down with all his strength.

Crack!

Once more.

Cracsh!

Again and again his father's iron-forged arms tried to split the Druid Stone asunder, but the sound of the hammer blows did not change, and Merlin could tell that the Stone hadn't fractured.

His father gasped. "It's not breaking!"

The wood of the doors groaned and then splintered.

"They're trying to smash in," Natalenya yelled.

Owain called to Dybris, "Take this sword. Everyone else push benches against the doors. If they break in, we're outnumbered ten to one."

Garth ran up the stony path toward the fortress with all the speed he could muster. His empty stomach groaned, and his lungs burned like the bundle of three ember-tipped branches he held. But up he climbed without fail, passing Tregeagle's shadowed house, until he arrived at the first ring of the old earthworks. There he sat behind a boulder to rest a bit, keeping the branches lit by fanning them.

"'Never let your fellow sailor down', me father'd say, an' he'd be happy I was helpin'."

Far to the west, lightning ripped the heavens.

"Better do this before it rains!"

Garth stood and faced the fortress, whose staved wooden walls seemed to soar into the night sky. Studying the top of the walls and tower, he couldn't see anyone on lookout. He listened, and the multitude of horses neighed as before. He bent over — hopefully unseen — and snuck around the outside of the wall to the right, where the ground was higher.

Now where did I see that huge pile o' hay inside the fortress? He thought back to the time when Merlin had taken him to the tower for a tour. Before he'd borrowed the wagon ... well, stolen it, to be truthful. If only he had done right back then.

Ah, he remembered where the hay was. Inside the wall, right up against the timber-built tower! Finding a high spot near a bush, Garth held the branches close together upside down and blew them to flame. He closed his eyes and uttered his first prayer in a long while.

Scrunching up his nose, he threw the first branch over the fortress wall. The second branch went wide, hit the wall, and fell. The third went over like the first. Garth scampered to the one that fell, backed up, and lobbed it over.

Then he ran back down the hillside as fast as he could without tripping in the dark.

Bedwir stood next to two other warriors, and at Vortigern's orders, they slammed their shoulders into the doors for the tenth time. At first the doors had moved and cracked, but now something heavy halted their momentum.

"What about the other door?" Vortipor asked his father.

"Eeh, these double doors look weaker. Grab the tree trunk, you softies!" Vortigern roared. "We'll get that Stone or you'll break your backs."

Bedwir looked at Vortigern in confusion. *Get the Stone?* Uther had commanded it destroyed. And why had Vortigern forced them to make this mad chase after calling off the attack on the druidow, who now stood idly by, chanting their twaddle?

A voice rang out, "The Tor, look at the Tor!"

Bedwir glanced up to where the warrior pointed, and there, halfway up the mountain, flames and smoke surged upward from behind the fortress walls.

"A fire! Our horses!" the warriors shouted.

Vortigern cursed and blew a blast on his horn. "Save the horses. Everyone up the hill!"

———✠———

Garth watched with glee from the shadow of Troslam's house as the hay inside the fortress caught fire and flashed a glow upon the tower. Soon the flames roared up the central tower itself. Within moments the fortress gate was drawn up and the horses driven out, followed by a few guards. The flames climbed higher, and soon there must have been fifty horses galloping around, neighing and kicking.

A few found the path downward, away from the blaze, and others followed.

Garth glanced down the hillside at the warriors heading toward the blaze and danced a little jig. "Yes!"

Numerous horses raced onto Troslam's road, and four of them slowed to a trot nearby. Ah, they were beautiful stallions. Shiny coats all, and high striding as well! Two brown, a bay, and a black. They seemed lost.

Garth stepped out and grabbed their reins. He coaxed them forward and led them to the weaver's high wall and wooden gate. Finding the gate unbarred, he swung it wide and brought the horses in.

"Good *hobbhow*, go and eat grass!" He barred the gate from within the yard and ran back inside the house, to the surprise of all. Finally, he took up his mug, still warm from where Kyallna had placed it on the hearth, and sat down to his soup!

———✠———

The beating on the doors ceased.

For a moment no one moved or spoke as Merlin and the others waited for something — anything — to happen. When no horns

385

blew, no battering ram burst through the door, and no fire lapped at the walls, the four of them slid into motion once more.

"Merlin, get around to the bellows and work 'em double fast," Owain said. "Maybe I can break the Stone if we heat it."

Avoiding the still-pulsing rock, Merlin made his way around to the bellows and set to work. Just that morning he had gripped these warm handles, but now it seemed like months ago. He looked out the iron bars of the window, and there, surrounding the smithy, floated hundreds of hazy torches like the lanterns of dead spirits. The druidow' chanting hung eerily in the air.

Up and down he pumped the bellows, and the air blew through the forge, causing the coals to spark and dance. When they glowed hot and red again, Owain and Dybris picked up the Stone by the leather aprons and, shuffling over to the forge, rolled it onto the mound of flaming charcoal.

The room darkened as the Stone blocked the light of the forge. Merlin tried to pump with even more strength, but the bellows just wouldn't blow any harder.

His father told Dybris to guard the doors, and Natalenya made her way over to Merlin. "Can I help?" she asked.

Her voice was tired, and he sensed fear there — the same fear that filled his heart. What if they couldn't break the Stone?

In answer, he took her hands and placed them on the left handle of the bellows, situating his own hands so they could work together. "On the downstrokes, put your weight on the handle." Her pressing barely helped, but having her hands near his comforted him. If he could only see her, hold her gaze with his own and forget for a moment their danger.

Upward and downward they drove the bellows, and heat filled the room. Never had the forge been jammed with so much coal, never had the fire been so hot. This kind of heat would swiftly scar any iron with a white, sparking heat. What of the Stone?

"What's happening, Tas?"

From deep within, the Stone glowed whitish-blue.

"It's changing color, but I don't know if that's good. I'll try to break it again."

Without warning, the doors splintered as if someone had hit them with a massive war hammer.

"They've got a battering ram!" Dybris yelled.

———✦———

Five druidow backed up McEwan as they heaved the tree into the center of the double doors. This time the stubborn timbers cracked and pushed inward a little.

McEwan smiled.

But just as the tree slammed into the doors for the second time, a long sharp blade sliced out of the crack and almost nicked his forearm.

McEwan yelled as he dropped the tree. "Ard dre, they ha' long blades in there!"

Mórganthu walked forward to survey the situation. "Trivial, trivial, I say. Are you not my finest warrior?"

"Sure, an' I'm your last one. O'Sloan an' the others fell at the circle!"

"The easier to reward you. Kill those inside, and I will give you triple the price of the finest *kern* warrior."

"But if me hand is cut off—"

Mórganthu forced the tip of his staff into McEwan's chin. "Do you fear *their* blades? A smith, a monk, and an imbecile?"

"I fear none if I got me own good club. But when the doors bust open, I'll ha' naught but a lug o' tree."

"Nevertheless, I command you to break them down. The Stone calls to me. Kill those inside and bring it out!"

McEwan grimaced but nodded his assent.

Backing up until he was out of the blade's range, he and the druidow picked up the tree again and, with one mighty heave, rushed at the door.

CHAPTER 36

THE FORGE OF SUFFERING

erlin paused at the bellows and yelled, "Is the Stone breaking?"

"No," Natalenya answered. "Nothing seems to hurt it."

Again the hammer clanged against the Stone. Merlin's father backed away from the smoking forge and sucked in cleaner air.

Off in the distance, thunder roared and shook the smithy.

"They're coming," Dybris yelled.

With a loud boom, the doors cracked.

"Use the sword!" Merlin's father called as he slammed the hammer into the Stone, causing flames to shoot upward from the coals.

"Too late to—"

This time the blow from the battering ram snapped the bar in two, and the doors burst inward. Chunks of wood flew across the room as the workbenches overturned.

Merlin released the bellows and drew his dirk. As he moved forward, he squeezed Natalenya's trembling hand. "Pray." *I'll need it.*

But she was already whispering for help.

As the dust settled, a huge shadow moved into the doorway, blocking the blur of torchlight before shoving the workbench aside with a mighty thrust.

Dybris swooshed his sword and yelled as a club hurtled down. The monk clunked to the ground just as Merlin's father jumped into the gap.

"Have at you, brute!"

There was a clash as the sword bit into the club. Merlin stepped closer, trying to keep track of the dodging shape of his father and the lumbering form of the giant.

"Stay still, *gwer!*" the Eirish voice boomed through the smithy. "I'll bash yar head just like the monk's."

"Not while I'm — "

The giant's long leg shot out and kicked Merlin's father, who collapsed to the dirt. The warrior then yanked him up and threw him across the room over the blazing forge. Owain landed on top of the bellows with a crack.

Merlin took his chance. He dove forward with the point of his blade and jabbed it into the giant's side, biting deeply.

The man bellowed in rage and slapped Merlin down with his meaty hand.

Merlin rolled and stood again with his dirk ready.

But the intruder was gone.

"The bard stabbed me!" he shouted as he ran off into the darkness.

The light of the room dimmed as the druidow continued their dark chanting. Thunder echoed on the western wind, and the Stone began to hum. At first the noise tickled Merlin's ears like a fly, but soon it grew to the sound of a great beating of wings.

He covered his ears as a violent wave of freezing air blasted at him from the Stone. Merlin bit back a cry as the skin on his face dried and cracked, and his hands blistered in the burning frost. The Stone blasted another icy wind, and this time, like raking claws, it drew blood from his skin.

He could faintly hear Natalenya's voice, but the exact words were caught by the howling din.

Merlin tried to rouse himself by walking, but his legs felt as if they were trapped in heavy snowdrifts. He lifted his arms a little and discovered they too had numbed beyond feeling. His lungs deadened, and a heavy sleep crept upon him. With detachment he felt his dirk drop from his fingers and clang upon the frozen dirt at his feet. He strove to think, but his muddled thoughts drifted away like snowflakes.

The chanting grew louder outside. Soon the footfalls of a man echoed through the doorway, and a dark shadow filled the expanse.

"O blind one, is that *you*?"

Merlin turned toward the silhouette. *Who is speaking?*

"I'm ... here," Merlin said. "May I ... help you?"

"Yes, yes. I have arrived to claim that which is my own from the smithy."

The smithy? Is that where I am? "The shop's here. Tas ... can assist you. Do you need something ... forged?"

Laughter filled the room. Mocking. Poisonous. "No, no. I am not here for the services of your father. I am here to slit your throats and throw your bloated bodies onto the heap of this wasted Christian age."

"Who ... are you?"

More laughter. "Do you not know? The Stone has indeed frosted your thoughts! Allow me to introduce myself." And the man stepped forward so the light from the forge danced across the whitened grave of his face. "I am Mórganthu mab Mórfryn. I hold the sword that slew my only son, Anviv, and if I have heard rightly, you and your father are responsible for its making."

Mórganthu lifted the gleaming blade to strike.

Merlin tried to move, run, block the blow, but his limbs hadn't thawed enough. He could only watch helplessly as the sword flashed down.

With a great yell, Merlin's father jumped in the way. And despite Owain's attempt to parry the blow, Mórganthu's blade struck, biting deeply into the slope between Owain's shoulder and neck. He cried out but did not fall.

Blood spattered Merlin's face, and he winced. "Father," he called, but his voice felt weak and his lungs hurt.

Owain raised his own blade again and thrust at Mórganthu, who warded off the blow and stepped back.

Merlin sought to force his legs to move toward his father, but it was as if gravel grated his bones.

Wheezing in anguish, Owain beat off blow after blow from Mórganthu as their blades clanged together, but each parry showed his diminishing strength.

Mórganthu lunged, and when the blade missed its mark, the arch druid yelled, "Die! Die, my enemy!"

With great concentration, Merlin began to move forward.

"Merlin, here's your blade!" Natalenya's voice shook with fear. One of her warm hands rested on his neck, and the other pressed the dirk handle into his thawing hand.

"Your father's bleeding—"

"Get back ... behind the forge."

"What can I do?"

"Stay safe and ... ask God to strengthen us!"

Merlin dragged his feet forward, his dirk ready.

His father pushed Mórganthu into a workbench, and tools clacked to the dirt. Yet in a flash Mórganthu sliced his blade down again, and his father howled in pain.

Merlin tried to run, but he stumbled on his still-numb feet. As he fell, he saw a red flash from the pommel of Uther's sword. Reaching toward it, he grabbed hold of Mórganthu's wrist as he plunged to the man's feet, almost pulling the druid down with him.

"Let go, you lout!" Mórganthu scratched at Merlin's scarred face with his free hand, leaving new gouges.

But Merlin raised his dirk and, in one swift stroke, severed Mórganthu's hand.

Uther's sword fell to the ground, and Mórganthu stood in utter shock as a flood of crimson poured forth. He then began to scream, the shrill tones filling every nook of the room. Finally, shoving the stub of his arm under his tunic, he ran from the smithy.

As his wails faded, the room suddenly lit with a fierce blue light. Merlin climbed to his knees just as flames from the Stone shot high into the air.

Natalenya shouted.

Merlin sheathed his dirk and fetched Uther's sword, prying off the sharp-nailed fingers of Mórganthu's hand. This was the sword his father had made. The sword with which Merlin had killed the wolf. His blade until the day he could surrender it to Arthur. He rose to his feet and attempted to reach Natalenya beyond the forge, but the blaze blocked his way.

"Natalenya!"

"Merlin, help!"

The blue inferno of the Stone rose above him now, and the thatch roof caught fire.

"Get out through the window," he yelled. "It's behind you!"

"I can't," she screamed. "There are iron bars, and I can't pull them out."

Coils of sapphire flame hunted for Natalenya, who cowered, coughing.

Merlin felt for his father's hammer on the anvil's stump and hefted it to his chest together with the sword. "O God, help me!" he cried as he dove at the flaming Stone. The exposed parts of his arms and face reddened, and his clothing began to char. The flames licked against his face, and his hair smoldered. Above him a torrent of thunder shook the smithy's walls.

None of his father's tools had destroyed the Stone, but he had to save Natalenya. He jabbed the point of the sword against the Stone and pounded on the bronze-forged hilt with the hammer. But the blade couldn't pierce the pockmarked surface.

Evil laughter swirled around Merlin as he hammered harder.

Natalenya called across the rift of flames, but he couldn't make out her words.

With every blow the pain increased in the hand holding the sword. The skin curled, and his shrieking fingers caused the sword to shake to the side. It would have dropped to the floor, except Natalenya, standing now, reached through the flames, clenched his hand, and raised the sword up again.

Cries escaped her mouth, and her hand flinched in pain.

Merlin struck a ringing blow with the hammer, and lightning burst from the Stone. Merlin's whole body wrenched forward into its searing tendrils.

The smithy darkened, and Merlin felt himself falling. But there was no floor.

Natalenya, Dybris, his father, the flames, the Stone, the smithy — all disappeared as he tumbled through a whispering murk.

Into a place of distant echoes he fell, finally striking the ground hard with his left shoulder. He wanted to open his eyes to see the blur of his surroundings, but he needed to rest until the throbbing in his bones subsided. He felt his hands to see how burnt they were and was surprised to find them well.

He sat up, opened his eyes, and discovered that everything around him was in perfect focus. At his side lay the sword, and he found comfort in gripping its handle. Glances around revealed he had fallen into a massive cavern of dark rock where dim lights floated. Were they torches held by the druidow, or something else entirely? Beyond the lights, on the far side of the cavern, plumes of smoke wafted from a large hole in the wall.

A faint, moaning voice rippled across the chamber. Soon a chorus of other voices joined. Wailing filled the cavern, and Merlin stopped up his ears to the dirgelike cries. One of the lights hovered closer, revealing itself to be a large, headless body, white and ghost-like. Its bones cracked and shook, and its arms carried Natalenya's limp body.

Merlin bounded to his feet. "Set her down!"

Lifting his sword, he tried to stab the headless creature, but it ignored his futile thrusts and glided over to the center of the cavern.

A granite pillar covered with a blue cloth — the same as in his previous vision — ascended from the ground, and the specter draped Natalenya upon it. Her pale form lay where the drinking horns had once stood. Her disheveled locks hung down upon her bloodstained and tattered dress.

Burning bile filled Merlin's throat, and he sprinted forward. "Natalenya!"

More headless phantoms appeared, and each one bore a dark chain. Merlin swung his sword at them as they passed.

One spun around and lashed him across the mouth with its sharp shackles.

He fell to his knees licking blood.

The dead creatures sped to Natalenya. They anchored the chains to the granite table and fettered them around her wrists and ankles.

Merlin lurched upward and ran at the table, shouting and scattering the phantoms. He tried to slide the chains off Natalenya but found they bit cruelly into her skin. He struck a chain five times with his sword, but the links only bent.

Blue light poured from a giant hole in the cavern wall, and the smoke thickened. An ear-splitting roar shook the ceiling until stones and stalactites crashed to the floor.

With rocks pelting down, Merlin whipped his cloak and arms over the woman he loved.

Then he saw the dragons.

Two enormous winged dragons crept from the hole and slid toward him — one red and the other white, their goatlike horns curving away from the sides of their heads behind fanged jaws.

Considering their massive size, their arms and legs were small, but the ends of each held a set of dagger-sharp claws. Their muscles rippled in spectacular power as they slithered toward what he now realized was an altar.

Toward Natalenya.

Merlin's chest squeezed tightly on his heart, and he could no longer take a breath.

The red dragon was much smaller than the white, though faster. Thick, jagged scales covered its body, and from its mouth blazed a purple flame. Even at a distance, the heat smote Merlin, and sweat ran down his forehead, stinging his eyes.

The dragon slid closer and snatched one of the specters from the air. With black liquid dripping from its fangs, the dragon crushed it into a pile of shattered bones.

Merlin jumped between the dragon and Natalenya, holding out his trembling sword. He tried to yell at the beast, but the words choked in his throat.

The dragon noticed neither him nor his puny sword as its dark and silver-gold eyes gazed upon the altar and its chained prey.

Closer and closer it approached, crushing rocks as it came. And farther back, the head of the white dragon reared up, surveying the scene.

Overwhelmed with fear, Merlin felt blood drain from his face, and his arms were like dead branches tied at his sides. An angel appeared before him in a blinding white robe. His voice was strong yet no more than a whisper in the great cavern.

"STRIKE EVIL, MERLIN!"

Then the angel faded from sight.

Merlin gulped, furrowed his brow and, embracing his own death, bounded at the creature. When he came within striking distance he tried to jab it in the snout.

Cla-rack!

The sword only glanced off its scales.

But the dragon reared up and studied him with narrowed pupils.

"Who ... art ... thou?" it questioned as a long forked tongue flickered through its teeth.

"I am Merlin, servant of the High King of the Britons, and you shall not have her!"

"High ... King?" It laughed, and its snorting roar shook the cavern. "This night ... we feasted on his blood ... and we will gorge ... on *thine* as well!"

The white dragon slithered forward, now alongside the red. Behind them, a movement caught Merlin's gaze. A woman climbed out through the cavern hole and hobbled toward them. At first he thought she was Mônda, but while Mônda had black hair, this woman's tresses waved reddish gray over her rags. A cruel thrall ring lay bound upon her neck, and a long chain fettered her to the wall of the cave. Scabbed gouges covered her body, and her hands were broken and smashed. The woman's eyes gazed vacantly, yet as she lifted her oval face to behold him, tiny sparks of forgotten hope and wonder were kindled.

Rage welled up in Merlin. *This should not be!*

For the sake of the chained woman's freedom, as well as Natalenya's life, he thrust his sword before him and called out, "In the name of the Christ, I command you, serpents. Go back to your vile hole and set these women free!"

The red dragon turned to look at the hag and snarled, "The old servant's ... time is dead ... and we will swallow her. The young one ... shall take her place."

"By the power of the living God, you shall have neither!"

The white dragon clicked its claws together as black liquid dripped from its teeth. "We are hell and death ... None shall deny us!" It inhaled deeply, bright-green fire licking from its nostrils as air rushed in.

Merlin lunged sideways just as the dragon spewed forth a torrent of emerald flame. The back of Merlin's hair became singed, and his cloak caught fire. Whipping the burning material off, he lunged at the white dragon, whose underside was exposed.

Merlin jabbed with all his strength, but the blade clacked uselessly against the white scales, jarring his shoulders so hard that his teeth cracked together.

The creature roared in anger and raked its claws across Merlin's chest, sending him skidding across the cavern floor. Pain took his breath away, and before he could stand, the dragon was upon him.

Its white lips curled back. Its gaping jaws struck down.

Merlin yelled even as he lashed out with his blade. The sword bit deep into the soft flesh above the teeth, and the beast recoiled as a six-inch, bloody fang fell smoking to the ground.

The white dragon screamed and thrashed away, hitting its head on the rock wall and shaking the entire cave.

Merlin stood just as the red dragon's tail snapped forward and slammed him prone to the ground.

Still holding his sword, he tried to rise to his knees, but his vision tilted and he fell over, dizzy.

The red dragon's maw clamped down on his legs and stomach.

Merlin cried out as he was lifted high into the air, his chest, arms, and head hanging from the creature's mouth. But before the teeth could sink into his flesh, he gripped the sword with both hands and chopped at the eye of the dragon, who lowered its lid and began shaking and ripping Merlin's body.

In a last, desperate attempt, Merlin pried the point of the blade inside the eyelid and thrust it deep into the socket.

Roaring, the beast arched its back and let go of Merlin, who held on to the sword and attempted to drive it yet farther into the eye, even as he was whipped like a mere plaything. He lost his grip on the sword and fell against the side of the granite altar where Natalenya lay.

The red dragon crashed to the ground. Howling, it scratched at the blade with its claws, pried it out, and flung it away, along with a gory, glowing mass that was once its eye.

Snorting purple flame, the beast convulsed and clawed the ground.

Merlin's blood poured from his wounds as he staggered to his feet. Natalenya moaned beside him, and he turned to her and took hold of her hand.

Then his eyes failed and the cavern disappeared.

My hands ... like searing fire.

Merlin opened his eyes and saw the haze of white-blue fire engulfing him. In his right hand, he felt the dead weight of the hammer, and in his left he held the handle of the sword — point down upon the Stone — with Natalenya's flinching fingers wrapped around his.

The smithy! The Stone!

With the pain fierce beyond imagining, Merlin raised the hammer and struck the hilt of the sword again with all his strength. Twice more, until the blade pierced and inched into the Stone. A great rumbling filled the room even as the fire swirled back inside, bringing relief to his burning skin.

He smashed the hammer down four times more, and the sword thrust through and out the bottom. A furious wind blew, roaring away from the Stone as if all the storms that had ever blown upon the moor had been hoarded inside and released in an instant.

Merlin tried to hold on to the blade's hilt, but the wind blew him backward and across the room. The hammer dropped from his fingers, and he fell hard against the broken doors of the smithy.

His head ached, and he gripped the splintered bar of the doors as the pain intensified. Merlin shut his eyes tightly. Even so, stars swirled and danced, blazing such bright and painful arcs that soon the pure light of the sun seemed to fill him.

The light came together and formed the shape of a man — no, the angel — who stepped near the forge. and, with a shining bowl, poured crystalline water upon Natalenya. Walking to Merlin, he poured more water upon Merlin's head and hands. He called forth words that shook the air. "By the will and power of the Lord God, you are healed."

The burnt skin on Merlin's hands mended. He opened his eyes, and colors swirled and danced before him. Bright red and blue. Orange. Even green. The tints blended and separated, coursing past him until finally coming into focus. Clear and bright the world seemed at first, and even as his vision of the angel faded, his new eyesight remained.

For the first time in seven years, he could truly see in the waking world. There was neither blur nor haze nor confusing shadow. He touched his eyelids and cheeks and felt his same old scars, but the wounds upon the eyes themselves had been healed.

His joy and wonder faded as the dark scene before him appeared. The broken smithy. The fire consuming the timbers and thatch of the ceiling. Natalenya pulling herself up from the ground with shaking resilience. The Stone, dark and silent, with the High King's sword thrust through.

Dybris lay near, groaning and gripping his head. And Merlin's father! Four feet from Merlin, he lay deathly still in a green druid robe, with blood draining from a deep cleft at his neck.

The angry tongues of fire spread upward through the thatch, and while smoke began to fill the room, the heat threatened to burn Merlin's newly healed skin.

"Natalenya!"

She looked at him in shock, her dress charred and soot-stained from their ordeal.

"Go to Dybris," he said. "We need to get out!"

Merlin grabbed his father's wrists and dragged him out the broken doors of the smithy. Natalenya was close behind as she tugged at the monk's legs.

All around them lay the druidow and villagers, thrown down where they had stood, their torches snuffed but smoldering. For a moment Merlin feared that the destruction of the Stone had slain them, that he and his companions alone survived. But no, they were moaning, barely stirring. *Lord, let them finally be free of the Stone's enchantment.*

The thunder-driven wind fed the roof's crackling flames. His father coughed weakly, and Merlin pulled him into the garden just far enough from the smithy to be safe from the fire. Natalenya followed with Dybris.

Merlin ran his hand through his father's red-slicked hair and pressed his ear to his father's chest. "Stay with me, Tas."

His father opened an eye. "Merlin ... failed you again."

"No, you saved me! And we destroyed the Stone — "

"We did ... good."

"We'll have time now — "

"No."

Tears streamed down Merlin's face. "Tas!"

"Garth's bagpipe ... in the house ... traded for it with the merchant ... Needed his horse ... reshod ... It's in a basket near the grain ... Unfair Tregeagle forced it ... to be sold. You — "

"No! You give it to Garth. You'll get better!"

But Owain wasn't looking at him anymore. His eyes viewed the stormy sky, and the deep lines of his face relaxed. "I see family ... friends ... kin ... my clan ... beckon from a feasting hall ... high in the mountains."

"Who? Who do you see?"

"My younger brother ... he's there. My mother, she stands so straight now. But" — his bloody brow furrowed — "Gwev's not there."

Merlin choked on a sob. "Mother's not there?"

"No, but I go ... my father so tall ... strong ... He holds for me the welcome cup."

"Tas!"

"Love you ... son." With those last words, his eyes dulled, and Merlin felt his father's heart flutter to a stop.

"Tas!" Merlin pounded the ground with his fists, and his whole body shook in great sobs. He lifted his father, now limp, and tried to sit him up. He listened at his father's chest and raised his head only to have it fall back down into his cradling, shaking embrace.

Natalenya put her arms around Merlin, but her consolation was interrupted by the screaming of a woman who ran toward them. "O-wain!"

Mônda. Her hair was unkempt, and her sunken eyes were gripped with fear. Her left arm puffed out of her sleeve with a scabrous infection.

Merlin's sister, Ganieda, wasn't far behind. She stared in disbelief at the bloody scene of their father's death.

Mônda kissed her dead husband's cheek until her lips were covered in blood. "No, you are mine!" she cried. "You can't die." She clawed her broken fingernails through her hair, then standing, she shrieked and ran off into the darkness.

Ganieda grabbed Merlin's sleeve and shook him. Her face contorted and her lips trembled. "You destroyed our family. I hate you. I will hate you forever!"

And she dashed away after her mother.

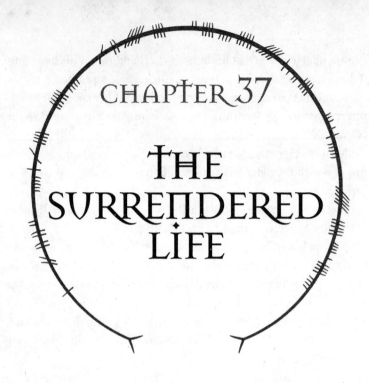

CHAPTER 37

THE SURRENDERED LIFE

The flames from the smithy roared upward, and cinders had landed on the thatch of his family's crennig, lighting it on fire. Merlin wiped the tears from his eyes and squeezed Natalenya's hand. "Stay here. I'll be right back."

He ran toward the house.

Natalenya picked up his walking stick. "Merlin! You forgot your staff—"

"I don't need it." He hurled himself through the doorway. For the first time in seven years, he saw his family's home, but there was no time to tarry. He hurried to the back of the house where his family kept baskets for keeping grain and other things, throwing lids to the side. But he couldn't find the bagpipe.

In the corner lay an uncovered basket with a chicken nestled on top, and Merlin ran toward it in desperation. The bird squawked as he shooed it away, and underneath lay Garth's bagpipe in an open woolen sack. It seemed like years since Merlin and his father had spoken of the bagpipe as Garth's only memory of his dead father.

Now Merlin was an orphan as well, and what memory would he treasure? Smoke leaked into the house, and flames shot through the thatch.

He had to choose, and fast.

Sprinting to the wall by the table, he selected his father's personal long sword, one of better quality that his father prized. The cross-guard was of braided iron in the shape of ox horns, and its tapered blade made singing arcs when slashed through the air. With Uther's blade now embedded in the Stone, Merlin would need a serious weapon to protect himself. And his dirk could be put to better use.

Next he grabbed his harp from its peg near the table and slung it over his shoulder. From there he spied one of his father's rings sitting near a pot of stale goat milk and took it. He had felt it many times on his father's left hand, though it was but a simple thing of cast pewter with a small white stone.

The room was now half filled with smoke. Ducking over to the hearth, Merlin pried a stone from the floor and snatched a bag of coins from his father's hiding spot. He rushed out the door and into the fresh air just as the roof timbers caught fire. Before looping the longsword's scabbard onto his belt, he slid off his dirk and held it out to Natalenya. She stood, and Merlin looked into her eyes for the first time.

Hazel-green they were, her lashes long and dark, and her soft eyebrows knitted together in confusion as she looked up at him.

"I never knew," he said.

"What?"

"How beautiful you are."

"Can you ... can you see me?"

"I think God healed us both after we drove the sword into the Stone."

She looked at the hale skin of her hands and back to his eyes. "You *can* see!"

"And I'm so glad."

She hugged him, and he kissed her on the forehead.

"None of that now," said a voice. And from the darkness stepped three men. Two were monks, and the third was Troslam, holding a spear. He had aged in the years of Merlin's blindness, but his golden beard and ready smile were the same.

"Colvarth sent us," he whispered as he looked at the villagers and druidow lying insensible all around. "And he'll be glad you're alive. But ... what of the Stone?"

"It's destroyed."

Both monks dropped to their knees and bowed their heads, prayers of thanks escaping their lips. Troslam's eyes shone as he embraced Merlin.

"Did Colvarth find Arthur?" Natalenya asked.

"Shah," Troslam said, and his voice turned even quieter. "They're hiding in the woods by the lake. Colvarth asked us to lead you to him."

"Dybris is hurt, and I need to" — Merlin's voice broke — "bury my father."

The two monks, whom Merlin didn't recognize, rushed to Dybris. Troslam bent down and examined Owain.

"I'm sorry, Merlin, so sorry. But Colvarth urgently needs you."

"I'm not leaving till a cairn is raised. Help me."

Troslam nodded, and together with Natalenya and the monks, they brought pieces of stone from the wall and stacked them over Owain's body.

With each rock Merlin laid upon the pile, the tears poured until he could cry no more and his voice turned hoarse. Natalenya rested her hand on his shoulder, and he found comfort in her soulful gaze.

Troslam lifted a large rock and laid it on top. "We need to leave now."

Merlin looked at the cairn and the progress they had made. Sure, his father had been covered, but it wasn't enough! Did Colvarth not expect him to honor his father? A burial and mourning usually lasted a week. With Uther dead, wasn't Merlin released from his vow?

But did Merlin's vow extend to Uther's son? What *had* he vowed? And then he remembered his words:

> *For all my days will I serve thee and defend thee,*
> *along with thine heir, and all that is right under Christ,*
> *on the Isle of the Mighty.*

The roof of the smithy collapsed, and flaming thatch wisped all around Merlin. Everything he knew had ended, and yet he was afraid to step forward into his new duty. The future of the people of Britain. Merlin's future. Natalenya's future. And the future of Arthur, so young and vulnerable.

But with the Stone's destruction, wasn't the danger gone?

If Vortigern's craving for the High Kingship led to Uther's murder, then Arthur was in peril. Merlin felt the whole of Britain's future press upon his shoulders like a millstone. Did Colvarth also feel this weight? The old man shouldn't bear it alone.

"I'm ready to go."

Natalenya looked from one to the other and finally rested her eyes on Merlin.

"You're not — ?"

"Coming back? No, I don't think so." He had lost everything, and his heart felt so empty. Yet she looked at him with such tenderness. He took a step toward her and held out his hand. "But though I don't know where I'm going, I can provide for you. Will you come?"

She took his hand. "Where you go, I will go, and your people will be my people."

"We need permission."

Troslam coughed. "Natalenya, your parents are at the lake too, for a different reason. Come, and you can speak to your mother."

"And my father?" Natalenya asked, her lips quivering.

"I'm not so sure. But we have to go, and carefully. Vortigern could be anywhere."

Horses' hoofs sounded upon the road.

Merlin knelt and kissed a rock on his father's cairn.

"Good-bye. I love you, Tas."

The monks stayed behind to tend Dybris while Merlin and the others fled to the woods. Troslam guided them, and they dodged from shadow to copse, skirting the mountain. Soon they arrived at the eastern end of the lake, as far as they could get from Uther's camp and the few sentries guarding the tents.

Troslam urged them into a deep thicket, where some horses were tied to the trees. Colvarth stepped forward to greet them. The bard held young Arthur, who slept upon his chest. "My ... Merlin, you have come! What news ... of the Stone?"

"It's destroyed, and God has graciously restored my sight."

Colvarth stepped closer and peered up into Merlin's eyes. "May He be praised, and ... may He deliver us from our present danger as well."

"Vortigern?"

"Yes. We must flee north ... to Kembry, you and I and this ... little one."

"An' don't forget me" piped up someone from the dark. Stepping forward and pulling the hood of his cloak back, Garth poked his beaming face out.

Merlin grabbed him in a hug and lifted him off his feet. "Garth! I heard you saved Arthur. You'll have to tell me about it."

"Nothin' to be proud of," Garth said, his voice squeaking.

Merlin set him down, and Colvarth patted Garth on the shoulder. "He has done a ... noble deed, but now we must make good our ... escape."

Natalenya stepped out from behind Merlin and approached the bard. "I would ask, Chief Bard, for the privilege of accompanying you."

"Ah! But this is a ... dangerous journey. Why would you ask such of me?"

Merlin smiled. "Because where I go, she goes."

Colvarth's eyes twinkled. "It is agreed, then, and I could use a ... ah ... woman's delicate help with my young ... charge."

"But there is one problem," Merlin said. "We need permission from Natalenya's parents. We were told they would be near, but I don't see them."

Troslam cleared his throat and turned to Natalenya. "Your father is at the lake, and your mother with him."

"Is something wrong?" Natalenya asked, and her smooth brow wrinkled with worry.

"Come and see."

Natalenya held tight to Merlin's hand as Troslam led them through the trees until they arrived at the northern shore of the lake, where Trevenna sat on a rock. About twenty feet beyond her, Tregeagle knelt at the water's edge.

"Go," Troslam whispered. "I'll meet you back at the horses."

Natalenya ran forward to her mother, and the two embraced. Trevenna's eyes were dry, but the salt of tears had left trails upon her face.

Tregeagle, seeing his daughter, limped over and hissed at Merlin. "A mock upon my fortune has come! A scourge to my treasure and a darkness to my lamp."

"Father?"

"What did you and your sick smith of a father do to the Stone? It doesn't ... it doesn't call me anymore. The power is gone, and I am ruined. *Ruined!*"

He turned back to the lakeshore and began examining a large rock. Then he threw an iron coin onto it and wailed when it didn't turn to gold. Natalenya bit back a tear as she realized what her father had become.

Trevenna pulled Natalenya closer, and they whispered together.

"He thinks to find another stone. Mórganthu had told him it came from the lake. Now he won't rest until he finds another."

"Mother ... Merlin is leaving with Colvarth."

"Vortigern. Yes. The bard told me."

"May I go with him?"

Trevenna's eyes grew wide.

Merlin dropped to his knees before her. "My sight has been restored, and I want to marry your daughter ... with your blessing."

"And take her into danger?"

"There is danger here," Natalenya said. "Vortipor expects to be trothed to me tomorrow."

Trevenna looked down at her shoes, torn and gray with mud. "Yes, you're right."

Merlin held out his hands. "I love your daughter."

She stared into Merlin's eyes and burst into a weeping smile. She reached out to them both. "Your father has no blessing to give, and so go with the consecration of God and my own."

Natalenya kissed her mother. "And what will you do?"

"My place is with your father, for good or ill. Tell of my fate to our kinsmen in Oswistor, especially my uncle Brinnoc. Have them send aid in my time of need."

"And my brothers?"

Trevenna's face grew sad. "Rondroc's joined with Vortigern, and Dyslan ran off when he was told he was too young. Pray for us all."

✝

Merlin led Natalenya eastward along the shoreline.

"Shouldn't we go through the trees?" she asked.

"I need to say good-bye. It'll only take a moment."

"I don't understand."

Merlin tugged her hand. "Follow me?"

The clouds were clearing, and the stars danced in the sky. They stopped at a place between two water-lapped boulders. Merlin knelt down and pulled scrub grass away to reveal a smooth white stone.

Natalenya crouched down next to him. "What is it?"

"My father placed this here in memory of my mother, Gwevian. She drowned many years before your family moved here."

"I'm sorry."

Merlin prayed for his mother's soul, then, standing with Natalenya, he spoke aloud. "Good-bye, Mother."

The waves of the lake rose and splashed the boulders.

Merlin lifted his hand but didn't detect any change in the wind. Natalenya moved closer.

Soon the water boiled just beyond the rocks.

He stepped in front of her and yanked his father's sword from its sheath, falling into a defensive half crouch.

The water bubbled, and a dark shape broke the surface, rising before them.

Natalenya pulled at Merlin's arm even as his heart beat swiftly. Though much evil had come to his family at this site, yet he wasn't afraid. "No. Wait."

The creature glided through the water toward them and stopped at the shore.

It was a woman.

Her skin glimmered with a silver hue, and her long red hair hung down to the water. Her emerald wrap glittered, and upon her neck rested a torc of gold inlaid with pure, bright stones. Her slightly webbed hands were held out in greeting, and she smiled at Merlin and Natalenya.

He fell to his knees as though struck, dropped his sword, and reached out to her. The woman took his hand and raised him back to his feet.

"Merlin," she said, and the sound of her voice jumped through the air like a spring of water in a full and happy rush from its dark confine.

"I ... I ..." was all he could say.

"Ya need speak nothing. It is I, yer mother, freed from my long years of slavery. Ya have broken the power of those who took, changed, and held me in service. It was I in the vision, the woman in chains. I was to die after a new servant had been chosen." At this she nodded to Natalenya. "Until ya freed us both."

"Mother ..." He shook his head. "But ... that wasn't real. I know it felt real to me, but that was a vision. It didn't happen, right?"

"A vision is a great mystery. Perhaps but chaff blown to ya from God to reveal the deep things of the world. And so heed the vision and beware! Ya think the Stone is slain, but 'tis not so, for the Stone is not what it appears to be."

Merlin rose, and looking upon the cherished face of his mother, he embraced her. "Father died," he choked out.

"I know. But ya canna hold me. I was changed by the Stone to serve it all these long years, and though I am free, I must go back to the lake. I am bound to live here amid the waters until the day God takes me home or changes me back."

"And I ... we must go."

"There is little time. But I must lay charges upon ya. First, protect the babe and ensure he is taken to safety. Then, and only then, go to my father Atleuthun's fortress in the kingdom of the Guotodin and undo that which has been done."

"How will I know what to do?"

"Ya will know."

Merlin nodded.

"Ride now and do not delay!"

She kissed him and smiled at Natalenya, then dropped below the waters until no trace of her remained.

✝

The bushes clawed at their faces and arms as Merlin and Natalenya pressed through to reach the horses. Troslam stood ready with his spear, while Colvarth and Garth held the reins of their mounts.

"You have been ... slow, and we must flee!" Colvarth said as he handed Arthur to Natalenya. "Many leagues must separate us from ... Vortigern before we make camp."

"I beg your forgiveness, bard, yet I have one last thing." And turning to Troslam, Merlin said, "My sister is running loose, and Mônda cannot take care of her. Would you and Safrowana find her and see that her needs are met?"

Troslam bowed to Merlin. "Colvarth has temporarily put into my care the two orphaned daughters of Uther and Igerna — to keep them secret while you flee with Arthur — and we will have little room in our house. Yet you have saved our village, and I will do so as if she were my own daughter."

"Here is my father's money. Take it for Gana, and her mother if need be. Here also is my father's ring. If necessary, use it as proof that I've given you authority to take care of my sister."

Troslam nodded.

The small group led their horses through the trees and brush until it thinned enough to mount. Since the horses were all stallions, bred and trained for war, they needed a firm hand to get them to obey. Riding hard, the company turned north upon a track that followed the dwindling stream, and they stayed to this path until it ended at the main road, which ran through the northern part of Kernow. Here they turned east.

When they were far away from Bosventor, and no sign of pursuers had been seen, Merlin finally breathed easier and knew that it was time. He leaned over and tapped Garth on the shoulder.

"You know, I've never left Kernow before."

"Me neither, at least if you don't count boatin' for fish."

"Garth … I have something for you."

"For me?"

"How would you like *this* back?" And Merlin handed over the woolen sack he'd kept carefully tucked under his arm since they'd left Bosventor.

"What's this?" Garth asked. He set the reins down on his horse's mane and opened the bag. His eyes squinted in the darkness, and he blinked. He looked at Merlin. He looked in the sack. "Oh, my bagpipe! How did you — ?"

"My father bought it from the merchant —"

"Oh, my *bagpipe*!"

" — before he left the village."

"Oh, *my* bagpipe ... Thank you, oh, thank you!" Garth dug into the sack and began assembling the instrument. Suddenly he shouted.

Colvarth and Natalenya turned and looked.

Garth beamed at all of them. "Look at this everyone!" And there in his hand he held two perfect chicken eggs.

Setting them in the hood of his cloak, he put the drone to his shoulder, filled the bag with air, put it under his arm, and began playing the two chanters until his face turned red.

So they went, sqwonking and squeaking, down the road.

And Merlin smiled.

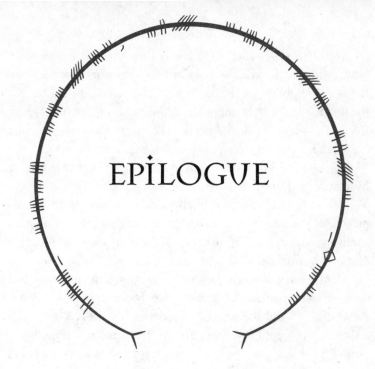

EPILOGUE

B edwir turned the body over — already stiff and reeking — and pried open the man's bag to see if it contained any valuables. Finding nothing but dried, dusty meat, he kicked the sack away and wiped his hands. He hated the job of sorting through the belongings of the dead. Especially when wolves and crows had been devouring the bodies. Yet the morning sun had barely risen when Vortigern had ordered everyone to search the dead from the previous night's battle.

So here he was at the cursed circle of stones, grubbing through the clothing and bags of dead druidow. And if Vortigern himself had not personally come to bury Uther, Bedwir would have begged off the gruesome task and found someone to fix his boot instead.

But Uther! What a calamity for the druidow to sacrifice him on the Stone. If only Vortigern had known. If only they hadn't waited for nightfall but attacked sooner. Who would have guessed?

And the loss of young Arthur was almost more than he could bear. Sydnius delivered the news just an hour since that they had found the High King's family slain and buried on the island. For the first time in his remembrance, Bedwir had witnessed Vortigern weep. His sister, nieces, and nephew all shared the grave, but who buried them, nobody knew.

Colvarth was surely dead too, but no one could figure out where his corpse lay. Drowned in the marsh, some said.

In love for his lost lord, Vortigern and some select warriors picked rocks from a wide area and built a mighty cairn over Uther south and west of the circle of stones. All while Bedwir and the other luckless warriors dealt with the dead.

Ah, these druidow held curious possessions. If Bedwir found one coin for every five carved stones or oddly painted strips of bark, he was lucky. And the weapons were mostly useless. Once upon a time, some would have been fine instruments of war but were now chinked and rusty with old handles. These proud people had become destitute.

He found a pile of three men and began separating them. The bottom man had a long char-colored beard and was dressed differently, brightly. *Must be Eirish.* Maybe a chance to find something useful. First Bedwir took the wiry silver torc from the man's neck and then pried the sword from his hand. It was beautiful! Gilt, with flashes of small gems in the hilt, and a sharp edge.

Using the sword, Bedwir cut the man's bag from his belt and shook it. The sound of coins jingled, and he pulled the bag strings open.

The man moaned, and Bedwir jumped back. The man's fingers twitched, and he looked up with a yellowed eye. The Eirish warrior was alive.

"Help me ..." he whispered, but a gaping hole bled from his abdomen, and his embroidered shirt was covered in blood.

Bedwir stood. "Vortigern! One of the Eirish warriors is alive!" Only Vortigern was just out of earshot, and another passed the word on to him.

Everyone rushed over, and when the battle chief arrived, he drew his sword and held it near the man's throat. "What do you know of the death of the queen?"

The man opened a bloodshot and shrunken eye. "Just planned to take ... king and the child ..."

Vortigern pushed the blade against his skin. "And the child? Where's his body?"

The man's eye flitted back and forth.

"Tell me!"

"Alive ... taken by ..."

Bedwir gasped. Arthur was among the living?

Vortigern kicked the man. "Who? Who took him?"

"A boy. Garth ... Garthwys ... stole him from us ... and ya ... yar the — "

Roaring in anger, Vortigern drove his blade into the warrior's throat, silencing him forever. He turned to his massed warriors. "Have you seen anything unusual? Anyone riding off?"

One of the warriors recruited from the village stepped forward. Rondroc by name, if Bedwir remembered. "Last night I was stationed at the camp and heard horses beyond the lake."

Rewan thumped the man on the chest. "The horses were everywhere, blast you! It took hours to gather them."

"But I saw people, and strange lights. I heard them riding off to the east. My father even told me that Merlin was there."

Vortigern shoved him against one of the massive stones. "Is this truth?"

The young man nodded and was knocked to the ground for his answer.

Vortigern unclasped his horn and blew it loudly.

"Everyone get mounted! We'll find those who took Arthur hostage — and then I'll have my justice."

Acknowledgments

Nothing difficult can be accomplished alone.

To God, who "rescued me from the dominion of darkness and brought me into the kingdom of the Son he loves, in whom I have redemption, the forgiveness of sins." And to Christopher Board and Gary Thomas Wood, who first told me the good news about Jesus Christ and his love for me.

To Robin, my wife, best friend, joy of my life, and my number-one fan. This book could not have been written without you. To Adele, my faithful daughter and writing buddy — your fascination and understanding of the ancient world has kept me on track. To Leighton, my amazing son — thank you for your devoted support, your love of swords, and for applying your 3D artistry to helping promote *Merlin's Blade*. To Ness, my cheerful youngest — your friendship, smiles, and love of books inspires me to keep on writing.

To my mother, who passed away during the editing of this book. Thank you for choosing to give me life. Your love has been a shining light that saw me through many dark days. Thank you, also, for sharing your priceless library of old British, Scottish, and Irish books. My novels would be that much poorer without them.

To my sister, Wendy, for all of your tireless genealogy work, without which I never would have known we were descended from a Cornish blacksmith. To my brother, Stuart, who encouraged Leighton and me to learn bladesmithing. And to all my other family members, you know that I care for you even if busyness and distance have gotten in the way.

To my in-laws, Dick and Carol — your cheer and love have been immeasurable during the last six years of writing.

To my growing-up friends, Mark and Richard — you helped me become strong in the faith and righted my ship more than once.

✦ ✦ ✦

The rough path to publication has also been smoothed by the many new friends I have met along the way. This is to them. If I have forgotten anyone, may God credit you doubly!

Tegid, you have been a great advocate and encourager. Your generous confidence in the value of my tale spurred me on to keep writing and working toward publication.

To L. B. Graham: our regular author get-togethers have been nothing short of sanity saving. Thank you for the friendship, commiseration, critiques, belief, and help.

To Wayne Thomas Batson and Christopher Hopper — you guys are awesome! Your crazy wisdom and timely backing have helped make the difference. To Scott Appleton: thank you for helping clear a path through the jungle of publishing. To Douglas Bond: your careful attention to detail and historicity are an inspiration. To S. D. Smith: many thanks to a true friend and brother — may your quill and quiver never be found empty.

And thanks to my other helpful critiquers: Brandon Barr, Keanan Brand, Marcus Goodyear, John Otte, and Daniel Struck. Your selflessness helped make *Merlin's Blade* a better book. Thanks also to Jeff Gerke and Randy Ingermanson — you both got my novel on the right track with your expert advice.

To Jeffrey Overstreet: thank you for being a kindred soul on the playground of paper and pen. Thanks also to Stephen Lawhead for your unique and expert critique. You have inspired me more than you can know.

To all the Holy Worlders — you're a fantastic bunch, and I appreciate all the help you've given to a new author like me. To the Lost Genre Guild — may this novel be one more signpost on the road to our genre being found by the masses. To all the ArthurNetters — I appreciate each and every discussion about Arthuriana, and I continue to be corrected and enriched by your scholarly points of view.

To all my reviewers at Authonomy.com, especially Nichole White — thanks for the great suggestions and encouragement.

To Nick Burns and everyone at Burns Family Studios — thank you for including Leighton and me as extras in *Pendragon: Sword of His Father*. To be the author of an Arthurian fantasy who has appeared, even if briefly, in an Arthurian film is a rare privilege.

To all my loyal blog followers (you know who you are) — thank you for believing in me and my writing during the long years that it has taken to get to this point. Your faith has finally been rewarded.

To Rebecca Luella Miller and the Christian Science Fiction and Fantasy Blog Tour participants — one more of us has now graduated from fan to author. I appreciate all that you do to promote Christian fantasy and sci-fi. May there be many more graduates, and may the tour increase in influence and strength!

To Les Stobbe, my agent beyond extraordinaire — you have accomplished a miracle and my thanks will always be with you. To Jacque Alberta, my editor at Zondervan — you fought hard for *Merlin's Blade*, improved it greatly, and confirmed that King Arthur still lives on in the hearts of people everywhere. To all the other Zondervan staff, I am grateful to you for helping refine and promote *Merlin's Blade*.

In memory of Phyllis Mary Angove, *Studhyores Kernow* — your bardic and scholarly legacy still lives as an inspiration to our family.

And finally, to Mrs. Sitts, wherever you are. You were the first to recognize my writing in the eighth grade when you requested a copy of my first book. It took nearly twenty-five years for me to start writing, but here it is. At long last.

A PORTION OF
BOSVENNA MOOR, BRITAIN

Dinas Camlin
5 LEAGUES

Guronstow
3 LEAGUES

Dintaga
5 LEAGUES

CHAR MAN

GORSETH CAWMEN
CIRCLE OF STONES

LAKE
DOSMURTANLIN

Fowaven River

BOSVENNA
ABBEY

Kildentor
3 LEAGUES

ISLAND OF
INIS AVALLOW

MUSCARVEL

MENETH GELLIK
MOUNTAIN

THE
MARSH

THE TOR

MAGISTRATE

BOSVENTOR

CHAPEL

DOCKS

MEETING
HOUSE

MILL

SMITHY

VILLAGE
PASTURE

2000 FEET

The Village of Bosventor
Inis Avallow & The Kernow Peninsula

THE TOR

HIGH PASS OVER THE MOUNTAIN

THE MARSH

MAGISTRATE

TROSLAM & SAFROWANA'S HOUSE

CHAPEL

DOCKS

MEETING HOUSE

MILL

VILLAGE PASTURE

SMITHY

1000 FEET

THE MARSH

NORTHERN LANDING

KEMRRY SEA

DINTAGA

ISLAND OF INIS AVALLOW

DINAS CAMLIN

AREA OF DETAIL AROUND BOSVENTOR

BOSVENNA MOOR

APPLE TREES

KERNOW, BRITAIN

SOUTHERN LANDING

LYONESSE

OLD TOWER & RUINS

300 FEET

9 LEAGUES

PRONUNCIATION GUIDE

The following helps are for British names, places, and terms and do not apply to Latin. If you find an easy way to pronounce a name, however, feel free to ignore the following. Your first goal is to enjoy the novel, not to become an expert in ancient languages.

Vowels

a	short as in *far,* long as in *late,* but sometimes as in *cat*
e	short as in *bet,* long as in *pay,* but sometimes as in *key*
i / y	short as in *tin,* long as in *bead,* but sometimes as in *pie*
o	short as in *got,* long as in *foam*
u	short as in *fun,* long as in *loom*

Consonants — the same as English with a few exceptions:

c / k	hard, as in *crank*, not like *city*
ch	hard, as in Scottish *loch*, or *sack*, not like *chat*
f	*f* as in *fall*, sometimes *v* as in *vine*
ff	*f* as in *offer*
g	hard as in *get*, not like *George*
gh	soft as in *sigh*
r	lightly trilled when found between two vowels
rh	pronounced as *hr*, strong on the *h* sound
s	as in *sat*, not with a *z* sound

GLOSSARY

Pronunciation Note: The goal is for you to enjoy reading *Merlin's Blade*, and so, where possible, easier spellings have been chosen for many ancient words. For instance, the word *gorseth* would more properly be spelled *gorsedd*, with the "dd" pronounced similar to our "th." This is also true of the decision, in some words, to use "k" instead of "c." The goal is readability. A pronunciation suggestion has been provided for each word. Again, please relax about how you say the names. If you are a language purest, then indulge the author, knowing he is well aware of the depth, history, and complexities of the Brythonic and Goidelic languages represented here.

Also, since this spiral of Arthurian stories begins and ends in Cornwall, Cornish has been chosen as a basis for many of the names and places. Though Welsh, Irish, or Scots Gaelic could have each served for this purpose, Cornwall is the nexus of the story line.

Historical Note: Although many of the following explanations are based on history and legend, they are given to aid your understanding of *Merlin's Blade*, and thus are fictional. If you feel inspired, you can research Roman, Celtic, and Arthurian literature for a deeper appreciation of how they've been uniquely woven into the entire Merlin Spiral series. An asterisk has been placed next to those words that will yield a wealth of information.

Agricola* — (ah-gri-CO-luh) The Roman general who conquered much of Britain. His full name is Gnaeus Julius Agricola.

Allun — (AL-lun) The miller of the village and owner of Plewin the mule.

Anviv — (ON-veev) The son of Mórganthu, Mônda's brother.

Armorica* — (arr-more-EYE-kah) The Roman name for the northern and western provinces of Gaul, including the interior. This includes modern-day Brittany, France.

Arthur* — (AR-thur) The son of Igerna and Uther and heir to the High Kingship. His sisters are Eilyne and Myrgwen. He is one-and-a-half years old in *Merlin's Blade*.

Arvel — (AR-vel) During the prologue of *Merlin's Blade*, he is a young hunter on the moor who witnessed a meteorite crashing to earth. Literally "one who is wept over." He is later named Muscarvel.

Atle /Atleuthun — (AT-lee / at-lee-OOH-thun) The king of Guotodin in the far north when Owain visited there; his fortress was at Dinpelder. He is Gwevian's father and Merlin's grandfather. In legend he is known as King Lleuddun*.

Aurelianus* — (ow-rell-ee-AH-noos) The former High King, Uther's father, and Arthur's grandfather. He slew Vitalinus Gloui to revenge his father's murder.

Bedwir* — (BED-weer) A chieftain under Vortigern.

Bel's High Day of Fire — The druid rite performed near the beginning of May each year. Also known as Beltayne*, it is dedicated to the druid god Belornos.

Belornos — (bel-OAR-noss) An ancient god of the Celts, personal god of Mórganthu, and god of the underworld. In *Merlin's Blade* he is represented by the moon in the night sky. Normally spelled Belenos*, here his name is embedded with *lor*, which means "moon," and *nos*, which means "night."

Boscawen* — (boss-CAW-en) Kernow's most sacred circle of stones. It is the home of the arch brihem, Trothek's friend. Near modern-day Penzance*.

Bosvenna Abbey — (bos-VENN-ah) An abbey of the Celtic church, which was created by the missionary efforts of early Christians in Britain, Ireland, and Scotland — Pádraig (Saint Patrick) being one of the first. *Bosvenna** (or *Bos-menegh)* means "the abiding place of monks." There is another older abbey to the west established by Guron.

Bosvenna Moor — (bos-VENN-ah) The highland area in central Kernow, covered with forests and marshes. Before the monks came, it was known as *Tir Gwygoen*, "land of the woodland moor." Today it is called Bodmin Moor* and is cleared for grazing.

Bosventor — (bos-VEN-tore) The village and fortress built upon the slopes of the mountain called Meneth Gellik, it was established six years after the abbey. South of modern-day Bolventor*, Cornwall, an actual iron-age village and fortress existed at this exact location.

Brihem — (BRIH-hem) The order of judges within the wider order of the druidow. There are five regular brihemow, and one arch brihem, making a total of six who vote. The arch druid and arch fili also vote. In olden times, the chief bard and High King were included in the vote, if present, but these offices have been abandoned by the druidow because they fell into the hands of the Christians. Alternative spellings are Brithem* or Brehon*.

Brinnoc — (BRINN-ock) Trevenna's uncle, who lives in Oswistor.

Brioc — (BREE-ock) A shepherd and farmer who lives in the village of Bosventor.

Britain — (BRIH-ten) The land occupied by the people who speak various forms of the ancient Brythonic* language south of the River Forth*.

Brunyek — (BRUN-yeck) An oat farmer in the village.

Bysall — (BY-sall) A small coin of Kernow, usually a ring of brass or iron. Bysallow is the plural, and it takes eight to equal one silver coynall.

Caygek — (KAY-gek) A fili loyal to Trothek who does not follow Mórganthu. He leads a secret resistence. He is named Cai* in the Arthurian legends.

Colvarth — (COAL-varth) This is the name taken by the Chief Bard of Britain, who serves High King Uther. *Colvarth*, which means "criminal bard," was originally meant as a druid epithet against him after he converted to Christianity. He took the name as his own, however, to remind himself of his culpability before God. His given name is known to only a few.

Connek — (CON-neck) A young thief who hangs around the village. Owain and Merlin recently caught him stealing and sent him to Tregeagle for judgment.

Constans* — (CON-stans) A former High King. He is Uther's grandfather and father to Aurelianus. Murdered by Vitalinus Gloui for the throne of Britain.

Coynall — (COIN-all) A single sided coin of Kernow made from silver. It is worth eight bysallow, and it takes three coyntallow to make one screpall.

Crogen — (CROW-gen) The head scribe at the abbey. He is a bit portly. Becomes the new abbot.

Crom Cruach* — (crom CREW-ack) An ancient Celtic god of sacred mounds. He is represented by the sun.

Culina* — Latin for "kitchen," from which we get the word *culinary*.

Denarius* — A small silver coin of the Roman empire. Equivalent to a Kernow screpall. Denarii is the plural.

Dinas Crag — A rocky hillfort in Rheged, north of Kembry, where

Owain is from. His father was once the chieftain, but now his older brother, Ector, rules there. Modern-day Castle Crag*.

Dinpelder — (din-PELL-dehr) The abode ruled by King Atleuthun when Owain visited there. This is east of Dineidean (Edinburgh*) in modern-day Scotland and is known today as Traprain Law*. *Dinpelder* means "fortress on a steep hill."

Dintaga — (din-TA-guh) The fortress of Gorlas, king of Kernow. *Dintaga* means "the strangled fortress" and is modern-day Tintagel*.

Dosmurtanlin Lake — (doss-mur-TAN-lin) A lake north of Bosventor, on the other side of the Meneth Gellik. Legend says that when a portion of the Dragon Star fell, it gouged out the earth, and the water filled in the crater, forming the lake. *Dosmurtanlin* means "the lake where a great fire came." It is the same as modern-day Dozmary Pool*.

Dragon Star — The comet that Arvel saw in the night sky seventy years before the story's beginning.

Druid* — (DREW-id) The order of priests within the wider order of the druidow. They also carry out the laws as set forth by the brihemow judges.

Druidow — (DREW-i-dow) The plural form of druid, this term can sometimes refer to the wider order of all the druidow, filidow, and brihemow judges combined.

Dubrae Cantii* — (DEW-bray CAN-tie) Dubrae is a city among the Cantii tribe south of Lundnisow. This is the primary area where the Saxenow were invading. Some of Uther's warriors come from this area. It is modern-day Dover*.

Dybris / Dybricius* — (DIE-bris / die-BRIK-ee-oos) A monk who recently joined Bosvenna Abbey. He brought Garth, the orphan, with him from Porthloc, a small village on the northern coast of Difnonia. He is known today as St. Dubricius*.

Dyffresin — (die-FRESS-in) A guard at the Tor who works for Tregeagle. He is loyal to Uther.

Difnonia — (dife-NO-nee-ah) The kingdom to the east of Kernow, today called Devon*. Ruled by the Roman-established town of Isca Dumnoniorum (modern day Exeter*).

Dyslan — (DIE-slan) Natalenya's younger brother.

Eilyne — (EYE-line-uh) The oldest daughter of Uther and Igerna, and sister to Myrgwen and Arthur. She is thirteen years old. In the legends, she is Elaine of Garlot*.

Eirish — (EYE-rish) The people from Erin, which is modern-day Ireland.

Elmekow — (EL-meh-cow) A coastal British kingdom south-east of Rheged.

Elowek — (eh-LOW-ek) The village blacksmith who died and gave his trade to Owain.

Erbin — (ERR-bin) Tregeagle's lictor and servant, he protects the Magister as well as executes his judgments.

Erin — (ERR-in) The island of Ireland west of Britain.

Fili* — (FILL-ee) The order of sages and poets within the wider order of the druidow. Filidow is the plural, and they are led by the arch fili.

Fowaven River — (foe-AY-vehn) The stream that lies east of the village of Bosventor. It generally runs southward through Bosvenna Moor and, fed by many springs, it soon becomes a river, known today as the Fowey*.

Fowavenoc — (foe-WAY-vehn-ock) A major town on the southern coast of Kernow where the Fowaven River spills into the sea. Modern-day Fowey*.

Gana / Ganieda* — (GAH-nuh / gah-NYE-dah) Merlin's half sister, who is nine years old; daughter of Mônda.

Garrinoc — (GARE-in-ock) A village northwest of Bosventor built near the mountain of Meneth Garrow, which is today called Garrow Tor*.

Garth / Garthwys* — (GARTH / GARTH-wiss) An orphan who lives at the abbey with Dybris. His father, Gorgyr, was a fisherman at Porthloc in Difnonia, and so Garth was raised on the sea. Red-haired and slightly chubby, he is always hungry.

Gaul* — (GALL) Modern-day France, which was ruled by Rome for six hundred years.

Gavar — (GAH-var) An old villager who volunteers to dive down and try to find Gwevian's body.

Gilroy — (GIL-roy) One of Mórganthu's Eirish warriors.

Glevum* — (GLEH-vuhm) The Roman fortress of Colonia Nervia Glevensium and the seat of Vitalinus's kingdom. This is where Vortigern and Igerna grew up. Modern-day Gloucester*.

Gorlas* — (GORE-lass) King of Kernow, whose fortress is Dintaga. He and Uther were rival suitors for Igerna's love, and this rivalry colors their relationship to this day.

Gorseth — (GORE-seth) A meeting place of the druidow, typically denoted by a circle of stones. In ancient times it would have been spelled *gorsedd*, the double-d pronounced like our *th* sound. In Merlin's Blade it is spelled, like many other words, phonetically.

Gorseth Cawmen — (GORE-seth CAW-men) The stone circle northeast from the village of Bosventor. Literally means "the meeting place of giant stones." On modern maps, it is shown as the Goodaver Stone Circle*, though *Merlin's Blade* describes it as having larger stones.

Grannos* — (GRAN-nos) The Celtic god of water and healing. Represented by Saturn in the night sky. The Latin form of the name is Grannus*.

Guotodin* — (goo-OH-toe-din) The most northern Brythonic kingdom. It was ruled by Atleuthun when Owain visited, and it lies between the two walls built by the Romans, just south of the land of the Prithager. Its principal cities are Dineidean (modern-day Edinburgh*) and the fortress of Dinpelder.

Guron* — (GOO-ron) Saint Guron, who founded a monastery on the western side of Bosvenna Moor.

Guronstow — (goo-RUHN-stow) The village where the first abbey established on the moor is located. Now known as the city of Bodmin*.

Gwevian — (GWEV-ee-ahn) Merlin's mother, the daughter of King Atleuthun. She drowned in Lake Dosmurtanlin when Merlin was young, and her body was never found. She is a merging of the legends of Vivian* and St. Theneva*.

Gwyneth — A major kingdom in northwest Kembry. It includes the isle of Inis Môn, which is sacred to the druidow. Spelled Gwynedd* in Welsh.

Herrik — (HAIR-ick) One of the monks, he works in the fields to provide food for the abbey.

Igerna* — (ee-GERR-nah) The wife of Uther, she is Vortigern's sister and therefore descended from Vitalinus Gloui, a former High King of Britain. Her children are Eilyne, Myrgwen, and Arthur. Gorlas vied with Uther for her hand in marriage.

Imelys — (ee-MEL-iss) Troslam and Safrowana's daughter.

Inis Avallow — (IN-iss AV-all-ow) The largest island in the marsh. It has an old tower and broken-down fortress surrounded by an ancient apple orchard. Legend says this was built by a pilgrim and tin merchant known only as the Pergiryn. Its name means "Island of Apples," and it is known in legend as Avalon*.

Inis Môn* — (IN-iss MOAN) The sacred island of the druidow. Gaius Suetonius Paulinus* broke the power of the druidow and destroyed the shrines and sacred groves on the isle of Inis Môn in AD 61.

Kallicia* — (kal-ih-SEE-ah) Literally "the forest people," from what is now known as Galicia* in northwest Spain. Many scholars think they are of Celtic origin. You can still hear bagpipes played there today.

Kembry — (KEM-bree) The land stretching from the Kembry Sea in the south to the isle of Inis Môn in the northwest. It is made up of multiple kingdoms. Modern-day Wales*.

Kernow* — (KER-now) The kingdom that lay on the peninsula of land in southwest Britain, between Lyhonesse and Difnonia. Ruled by Gorlas from his fortress, Dintaga, which is on an island on the northern coast. Kernewek is their local dialect of Brythonic. Modern-day Cornwall*.

Kernunnos* — (kare-NOO-nos) A Celtic horned god of hunting.

Kiff / Kifferow — (KIFF / kiff-ER-ow) Owain's best friend in the village. A carpenter who drinks too much.

Kudor — (KOO-door) A man who accuses Pennar of stealing his cattle in a trial before Uther.

Kyallna — (kee-ALL-nah) An elderly widow who lives near Safrowana and Troslam. She is Garth's favorite because she likes to cook soup and share it with him.

Kyldentor — (keel-DEN-tor) A village a few leagues southeast of Bosventor, which hosted Uther before he came to Bosventor.

Loyt — (LOYT) One of the monks who cooks and bakes for the abbey. He is known for his very prominent nose.

Lundnisow — (LUND-nih-sow) A city taken by the Romans in AD 43 and named Londinium. Because of its river and harbor, they made it the capital of their provinces in Britain. Modern-day London*.

Lyhonesse — (ly-OHN-ess) A thin peninsula of land stretching even farther out to sea from the western tip of Kernow. It is sparsely settled by the Eirish. The name literally means "the lesser." Known as Lyonesse* in legend.

McEwan Mor — (mik-YOU-ahn) One of the Eirish warriors in the service of Mórganthu. He is almost seven feet tall and very strong.

McGoss — (mik-GOSS) Another Eirish warrior who serves Mórganthu. He has a voice that rattles, and the other warriors consider him bloodthirsty.

Megek — (MEH-geck) An elderly fishmonger who cleans and smokes fish for sale to the villagers. His shack is near the docks built out into the marsh.

Melor — (MEH-lore) A monk who gives witness before Uther.

Meneth Gellik — (MEN-eth GELL-ick) The mountain upon whose southern side the village of Bosventor is built. Halfway up on a plateau sits a fortress and beacon, which is familiarly known to the villagers as the Tor. The mountain is over 1,100 feet above sea level, its tallest point is 100 feet above the marsh, and it is the third highest in Kernow. The term *Meneth* means "mountain," and *Gellik* means "brown", making its name "the Brown Mountain." Lake Dosmurtanlin is situated just to the north. Today it is known as Brown Gelly*.

Merlin* — (MER-lin) The son of Owain, the village blacksmith/swordsmith. His face was badly scarred by wolves at the age of eleven when he tried to protect his younger sister, Gana. The attack also damaged his eyes, half blinding him. He can see smudges of color and motion, and with the careful use of his staff and his acute hearing, he can generally take care of himself. The Latin form of his name is Merlinus.

Migal — (MIH-gale) A monk who sometimes helps Loyt with the cooking and baking.

Mogruith* — (mog-ROO-ith) Mórganthu's older brother. A druid, he was imprisoned and killed by the Romans.

Mônda / Môndargana — (MOAN-dah / moan-DAR-gone-ah) Owain's wife, she is the daughter of Mórganthu, the arch druid, and mother to Ganieda. She is Merlin's stepmother, but she despises his Christianity. Her full name *Môndargana* means "Prophetess of Inis Môn."

Mórganthu — (more-GAN-thoo) The arch druid and son of Mórfryn. He is father to Môndargana and Anviv and grandfather to Ganieda. His name is a merging of the name *Mórgant* with *huder*, which means "magician."

Muscarvel — (musk-AR-vel) Arvel from the prologue. Seventy years later, he lives deep in the marsh to the west of Bosventor. The inhabitants think he is crazy and give him the epithet "Musca."

Myrgwen — (MEER-gwen) The youngest daughter of Uther and Igerna, and sister to Eilyne and Arthur. She is nine years old. In legend, she is called Morgause*.

Natalenya — (nah-tah-LEAN-yah) Tregeagle and Trevenna's

daughter, who plays the harp and sings. Merlin likes her but is very shy in her presence.

Neot — (NEH-ot) A monk in charge of the farming; he doesn't like Dybris.

Nivet — (NEE-vet) One of the monks.

O'Rewry — (o-REH-ree) An Eirish warrior in service to Mórganthu.

O'Sloan — (o-SLOWN) The leader of the Eirish warriors in service to Mórganthu.

Offyd — (O-fid) One of the monks who works in the fields to help feed the abbey.

Olva — (OL-vah) Married to a pig farmer; her little son is very sick.

Oswistor — (os-WEE-store) A strong hillfort in Pengwern*, Kembry, and a minor kingdom of the greater kingdom of Powys. Natalenya's mother,Trevenna, has relatives here. Modern-day Oswestry*.

Owain* — (O-wayne) Merlin's father. He grew up in Rheged, north of Kembry, as the son of a chieftain. Owain's first wife, Gwevian, drowned while they were boating on Lake Dosmurtanlin. His second wife, Mônda, is the mother of Ganieda, Merlin's half sister. Owain is the blacksmith in the village of Bosventor and so is given the title of *An Gof*, which means "the smith."

Pádraig* — (PAH-dreeg) Saint Patrick, a Briton who first brought Christianity to the Eirish and then sent missionaries back to Briton.

Pennar — (PEN-arr) A man accused in a trial before Uther of stealing Kudor's cattle.

Pergiryn's Tower — (per-GIH-rin) All that is left of the fortress built by the Pergiryn on the island of Inis Avallow. Some say a light can sometimes be seen from its top-most window. The Pergiryn was an unknown tin merchant who, legend says, built the fortress and planted the apple orchard. *Pergiryn* means "pilgrim."

Picti* — (PIC-tie) The Latin name for the people who live in the wild lands of the north. They often raid the southern realms for slaves and plunder now that Hadrian's wall has been abandoned by the Romans. Also known as the Prithager.

Plewin — (PLEH-win) Allun's mule, which he uses to turn his millstone.

Podrith — (POD-rith) A novice druid who traveled to Bosventor ·with Trothek.

Porthloc — (PORTH-lock) The seaside village in Difnonia where Garth grew up and met Dybris. Modern-day Porlock*.

Powys* — A major kingdom in east-central Kembry (Wales).

Prithager — (prih-THAY-girr) This is the Brythonic name for the Picti*.

Priwith — (PRY-with) The village potter.

Prontwon — (PRON-twon) The abbot of Bosvenna Abbey who taught Merlin about the Christian faith.

Regnum — (REG-num) A Roman city on the southern coast of Britain. Modern-day Chichester*.

Rewan — (REH-wan) A chieftain under Vortigern.

Rheged* — (HREE-ged) A Brythonic kingdom in the north, it is situated northeast of Kembry and south of Guotodin. This is the land Owain is from.

Rondroc — (RON-drock) Natalenya's older brother.

Safrowana — (saf-ROW-ah-nah) Mother to Imelys and wife of Troslam. They are weavers.

Screpall — (SCREH-pall) A double-sided silver coin of Kernow worth three coyntallow. Equivalent to a Roman silver denarius.

Sethek — (SETH-eck) One of Uther's warriors.

Stenno — (STEN-no) One of the many tin and copper miners in the village. His father recently died in a mining accident.

Sydnius — (sid-NEE-oos) A chieftain under Vortigern.

Tellyk — (TELL-ick) A wolf that has befriended Ganieda.

The Stone — A strange stone that was found by Mórganthu at the edge of Lake Dosmurtanlin.

The Tor — The fortress situated partway up the side of the Meneth Gellik. It has a timber-built tower with a beacon on top. Its formal name is Dinas Bosventor.

Tregeagle* — (treh-GAY-gull) Magister of Bosventor and the surrounding tin-mining region. He is the village judge and collects taxes. He is also responsible for maintaining the fortress (the "Tor") built on the Meneth Gellik, which includes a timber-built tower and beacon. His wife is Trevenna, and his children are Natalenya, Rondroc, and Dyslan. He takes pride in his Roman descent.

Trevenna — (treh-VENN-nah) Tregeagle's wife, and mother to Natalenya, Rondroc, and Dyslan.

Troslam — (TROS-lum) The village weaver. Safrowana is his wife, and Imelys is his daughter.

Trothek — (TROH-theck) The old and infirm arch fili who wants the druidow to stick to their present laws and not regress to the ancient ways, which include human sacrifice.

Uther* — (UTH-er) The High King of the Britons, he is descended from a long line of Roman governors and kings. His father was Aurelianus, his wife is Igerna. He has two daughters, Eilyne and Myrgwen, as well as his son, Arthur. His name in Latin is Uthrelius.

Vitalinus Gloui* — (vi-TAL-ee-noos GLEW-eye) Usurper High King who slew Uther's grandfather Constans. His grandson is Vortigern, and his granddaughter is Igerna, Uther's wife. He was slain in battle by Aurelianus.

Vortigern* — (vor-TUH-gern) The grandson of Vitalinus Gloui, who entered Uther's service as his battle chief following the marriage of his sister, Igerna, and Uther.

Vortipor* — (vor-TUH-poor) Vortigern's son.